ONE NIGHT OF LOVE

"There's something I want to tell you," Annie said, praying for courage.

But his hand drifted to the back of her neck, touching her softly. "There are many things I want to tell you," he whispered. Now his hands were removing her shawl, drifting along her arms, his lips were kissing her throat.

"Grant, there's something you don't know about me," she said. "You have to listen to me."

"I know that I want you, Grace." His voice was a feathered whisper as he kissed her ears, making her shiver.

Annie tried again. "Grant, I have to tell you . . . my name . . . isn't Grace."

His eyes were enflamed with passion as he stared into hers, then kissed her more deeply. "You're so beautiful," he murmured.

"Don't you care who I am?" she asked desperately as he sought the fastenings of her gown. Then, without answering her question, he took her mouth in his again as he pushed aside the filmy straps of her bodice.

All thoughts and words were gone now. There was nothing except being here with Grant, in utter ecstasy. An ecstasy she might never experience again.

Enjoy the dream was all she could think. For in tomorrow's light of day, the truth would be revealed. But she would have this night to hold onto, forever.

Mountain Dreamer

Patricia Werner

Zebra Books
Kensington Publishing Corp.
http://www.zebrabooks.com

ZEBRA BOOKS are published by

Kensington Publishing Corp.
850 Third Avenue
New York, NY 10022

First Printing: June, 1998
10 9 8 7 6 5 4 3 2 1

Printed in the United States of America

For Jim, who has supported my writing interests all these years, and for Tracy Bernstein, who has made it fun. Also for Elizabeth Cavanaugh, who always encouraged me to follow my bliss.

Thank you to Dover Books for permission to quote two lines from the song "She is More to Be Pitied than Censured," by William M. Gray, which appeared in their 1973 edition of *Favorite Songs of the Nineties.*

One

Central City, Colorado, May 1878

Annie Marsh wriggled in the netting and satin of her chorus costume. She felt quite daring in the blue satin dress that came to her calves, in which she was about to prance on stage with the theatrical troupe. The respectably brought up daughter of Denver booster Everett T. Marsh dearly hoped that makeup and costume would disguise her from any Denver socialites who might be in the audience at the Central City Opera House performance of *The Bat.*

Annie's strawberry-blond hair was pulled tight and pinned into a bun in a manner in which she never wore it, and a large lavender plume, lodged behind her ear, covered her face when she turned her head to the side.

Close beside her, the glittering Spanish dancer Lola Bonitez peeked between the edge of the proscenium and the velvet curtain into the audience.

"Third row center," Lola's Spanish-accented whisper hissed into Annie's ear. "Roberto. He came to see me. You see him?"

She held the edge of the curtain still so that Annie could peek out into the darkened theater as well. But Annie didn't care about Roberto. It was the other seven hundred forty-nine people, laughing at the players and tossing comments at the stage that made her eyes widen. In a moment they would be watching her! And the rest of the chorus and leading players, she tried to tell herself. Still, the flutters in her stomach would not abate.

"You see him? The dark one there?" persisted Lola. She slinked forward, and Annie squinted into the narrow gap formed by curtain and wall.

Annie struggled to count three rows back, but when she did her eyes halted on a big, broad-shouldered blond man glaring at the stage as if he hated what he saw.

And what a man. Squarish jaw, pleasing mouth, intense gaze. Broad brow with hair the color of hay. His white shirt contrasted with his tanned face above a black satin brocade vest and string tie. A tan felt cowboy hat rested in his lap.

Then the rustle behind her made her drop the curtain and turn around. Lola was gone, and in her place was the stage manager Marcel Dupres. With quick, efficient movements, he snapped his fingers for last-minute preparations, lining up the dancers for the entrance. He placed Annie in line with the others as if she were no more than a piece of scenery.

Then he paused in his regimenting, gave her a dazzling smile, and whispered, "Ready, my dear?"

She stared at him with rounded eyes. Her mouth felt like cotton. Since she'd never been on stage before, she'd never known what nervousness was like. She'd only dreamed of treading the boards as she warbled at the piano in her father's three-story red sandstone home in Denver. There she had practiced dance-steps in her room. But now her friends in the performing troupe were making her dream come true as a present for her nineteenth birthday.

"Go," commanded Marcel in his stage-whisper, and she was carried along in the wave of singers and dancers rushing to their places in front of a painted backdrop depicting a ballroom. They flooded the stage for the party scene in the comedy being performed for the crowd of culture-hungry citizens and hotel guests alike. The more rowdy miners occupied the balcony, from which their drunken cat-calls and jeers showered over the heads of those who could afford the better seats below.

Thank goodness her brother James was occupied with his card game at the nearby Silver Spur Saloon. James thought she had a seat in the orchestra, but she'd never bought a ticket, so there would be no empty seat. And the unsuspecting Denver matrons would never be looking for her on stage—she hoped.

The stage erupted with the laughter and movement of the party scene as the actor who played Prince Orlofsky declared that he was bored and his guests must match him drink for drink. He strutted about in a long tuxedo, complaining in a heavy Russian accent.

"Smile," whispered Lola, who brushed by Annie on the arm of her partner just as the orchestra, located in the pit below the stage, swung into a waltz.

Annie pasted a smile on her face and turned to grip her partner's shoulder. He was a graceful, blond young man about her age, with bright blue eyes, and he deftly moved her feathered plume out of his face.

"Sorry," she whispered.

After the first few breathless seconds, she began to relax and move to the music.

"More champagne," ordered the bored prince from the lip of the stage. "Everyone must do as they please."

The performers renewed their efforts at gaiety, and Annie stretched her smile. Except for the hot kerosene lamps lighting the stage, the setting was not unlike a real party. Her heart beat to the waltz, and her nimble feet followed her partner's. She tried to pretend that she was at a real party and having fun.

The golden voices of the singers all around her burst into the song she'd rehearsed at home. Her heart soared as she lifted her voice to join them, punctuated by the laughter of the supposed party guests on stage. The music and the movement were intoxicating, and her nervousness was replaced by a thrill. She was performing on stage at last! Ah, but that would forever be a secret.

Then the chorus was finished, and she and her partner found a place near the back of the stage to allow the leading players at the costume ball to carry out their dialogue. Annie glanced out into the audience, which she could see fairly well, since the chandeliers kept the house partially lit during the performance. The glowering blond man in the third row was staring directly at her. His left elbow was on the narrow chair arm, his thumb and forefinger rubbing his square, firm jaw. Her heart banged against her chest as she met the displeasure on his face and quickly lowered her head. Something about him made her feel that he could see through her, but she struggled to quiet her fears. She didn't know him, and he couldn't know who she was.

She ducked so the feather covered her face and prayed that she wouldn't be recognized. The ball gown costume, netted shawl and thick greasepaint must surely make her unrecognizable. Her partner slid his arm around her waist and gave her a nudge, making her sway to the music.

She hummed with the rest of the chorus. At home in her room she'd secretly rehearsed this number, but it was different to actually perform it with an orchestra. She turned to the right on cue, but was pivoted back to the left by her patient partner.

"This way, dearie."

"Sorry," she whispered again.

A burst of laughter at the antics of the prince, a resounding chord from the orchestra, and the number was done. Applause; the audience cheered.

"Off we go," said her smiling partner, and he guided her in quick steps to make their exit.

Lola was offstage ahead of them and turned to laugh, covering her mouth with her hands since they daren't make any noise. Drawing Annie further backstage, Lola delivered her words in excited whispers. "How was it?"

"Marvelous," said Annie. Then she too covered her mouth with her hand at the look from Marcel indicating quiet. The show was still going on.

Lola gave Annie's shoulder a little squeeze. "You see? You are, as they say, a natural. Now come, we must get ready for the jail scene."

Colorado cattle rancher Grant Worth sat in his stout hickory theater seat, third row center, with Roberto Martinez and other businessmen from Denver. Their conversation about Grant's favorite subject had continued during the intermission until the curtain rose, but now the men beside him were more interested in ogling the women onstage.

Grant had been just about to bring them around to his way of thinking. Breeding llamas in the 11,000-foot mountain valley of South Park made sense. The country resembled the animal's native Bolivia, where they bred high in the mountains at 13,000 feet. Determined to persuade miners, ranchers, and settlers that these animals were superior to mules and packhorses for carrying loads, Grant was prospecting for backers.

Roberto Martinez nudged his arm. In a not very subdued whisper, Roberto said, "That's my girl in red. Which one do you like?"

Grant blinked. His mind was still picturing the funny-looking doe-eyed creatures he wanted to breed in the high country. The orchestra and singing assaulting his ears served only as background to his thoughts. Now he was forced to focus on the scene just beyond the orchestra pit.

The leading baritone, dressed in tail-coat and white tie, paced at the edge of the stage, while a pudgy, bejeweled Hungarian countess, whose face was masked, confided to the audience that she recognized her husband in the crowd.

But Roberto called Grant's attention to the younger, more alluring performers.

"My Lola, she is beautiful, hmmm? She has many friends. Maybe one for you, eh?" He gave a laugh that left no doubt as to what he was interested in and it wasn't the music.

The players on stage were dressed for a costume ball. The dancers' skirts just covered their well-turned calves, affording the audience a generous view of shapely legs when the dancers turned about.

"Very nice," said Grant.

Pretty ankles were not going to distract him from business. He'd invited these men to Central City to discuss business in the Teller House next door. That meant entertainment as well, so they'd adjourned to the operetta because a troupe was in town. But now the atmosphere of the opera house had taken over, and he feared he'd lost them. The two men on Roberto's other side laughed heartily and applauded. Their slurred cat-calls in response to the comedy on stage was an indication of how much liquor Grant had poured down their throats while he presented his latest plan to them. Now his generosity irritated him.

It looked like business was done for the day, thought Grant, ill-humoredly. Roberto's red-clad, dark-skinned, gazelle-like creature strutted across the stage. He grunted and poked Grant, whose elbow slid off the arm of the seat.

"I'll introduce you after the show."

Grant grunted. "On intimate terms with the troupe, are you?"

"Of course," muttered Roberto behind folded fist. "I always take Lola to dinner. Pick yourself a dinner-date, my friend."

Grant glowered. If he wanted to court backers for his llama herd, he knew it would take more than one meeting before they saw the sense in his plan. And now women were all Roberto and the others were going to be interested in for the rest of the afternoon.

The singers and dancers cavorted about the jail where one of their number was supposed to do time. The Spanish-looking Lola blew Roberto a kiss and gave a seductive wink.

"Hmmmmmm?" Roberto muttered again. "How about it, my friend? Which one do you want to meet? Lola knows them all."

Grant shrugged. It didn't really matter. But being forced to stare at the bared shoulders and arms of the slender, graceful girls made him painfully aware that he'd been without feminine affection for a long time. He gave a long sigh and began to ogle the girls.

There was one that caught his attention. Instead of flaunting her limbs and upstaging the other girls, this one kept her face half-covered by a big feather, her eyes mysteriously hidden. She was pretty, what he could see of her, and her strawberry-blond hair was all done up in a tight bun. A few curls had escaped at the back of her neck and over one ear. A stiff, black, net shawl draped her shoulders. A blue dress hugged her waist. When the shawl fell off her shoulder, it revealed fine skin and a hint of bosom pressed against a low-cut neckline.

The girl he watched looked at the first few rows, but quickly glanced past them as if she were looking for someone. The music soared again and she was swept away. Her smile sparkled mischievously for a moment. The leading players made up with each other, the bored prince gave a toast, and the curtain fell. Grant was on his feet like the rest of them, even if his cheers and bravos were not as drunken as those of his colleagues.

Roberto, who was the same height as Grant, but who had thick glistening black hair and swarthy Texacano skin, gave a loud chuckle and clasped Grant on the shoulder.

"So, which one did you like, eh?"

Without thinking Grant answered, "Blue dress, the one with the big feather."

Roberto gave a pleased grunt. "Good, good. Come then, my Lola will introduce you to the woman of your dreams."

Annie laughed in relief after the curtain call.

"I think," said Lola, "that our trick of sneaking you on the stage was a great success."

Annie flushed with the excitement of her daring. "I hope I didn't ruin anything," she said, her amber eyes sparkling. "It was a great lark."

"Now you know what it feels like, dear," said Marcel, who joined them backstage. He mopped his forehead with a large red handkerchief and then stuffed it into the pocket of the smock he always wore backstage.

"I assure you I could train you, if only you would let me. I am the very best teacher."

He puffed out his chest and flourished his hand in a self-assured gesture. His long brown hair swished just above his shoulders.

"He's bragging," teased Lola in her Spanish lilt. "However, you did do marvelously. Did I not tell you?"

Several members of the audience pushed their way through the melee backstage, and Annie noticed the dark-haired black-suited man in white shirt and string tie, hat in hand, who dropped kisses on all the women's wrists. He was tall, dark, and prepossessing. He approached, and patted the chattering Marcel on the back.

Lola glanced his way and shrieked, "Roberto, you come to see me."

She broke into a string of Spanish, which the man answered, laughing and kissing both sides of her face.

Annie turned to make her way to the dressing room. Time to regain her normal appearance. She felt suddenly nervous that her brother James might be looking for her now that the performance was over. But Lola's hand clasped her arm, forcing her to turn back.

It wasn't the black-haired man with pearls for teeth she saw this time. The blond man she'd spotted in the audience, about the same height as Lola's friend, and with very broad shoulders, seemed to fill the tiny, crowded backstage space. He glanced curiously about him, making Annie swallow hard. She tried to pull her arm out of Lola's grasp, but the big man with warm gray eyes suddenly pinned her with his look, causing a weakness between her shoulder blades and a flutter in her chest. Her silly nerves must be still on edge.

"And who is your lovely friend?" asked the dark-haired Roberto.

Annie's eyes widened as she realized Lola was about to introduce her.

"This is my good friend who just made her debut. Her name is—"

"Grace," sputtered Annie, with a forced smile. She willed Lola not to give her real name. She couldn't risk her stage exploit getting back to her family. Her cheeks felt like stone, and she stared stiffly at the two men before them. "Grace Albergetti." She cast Lola a swift glance.

Understanding dawned in Lola's dark eyes and she grinned. "As I was saying, Grace is new with us. She is my dear friend from . . . ," this time she hesitated, letting Annie fill in the story.

Annie looked at Lola and winced. "Ohio," she lied.

She was about to make her excuses when Roberto reached for her hand and placed it in the blond man's large one, which extended to grasp hers.

"Allow me to present Mr. Grant Worth," said Roberto. "Don't you agree, my friend, that this new flower in the company brings the scent of fresh rain?"

For answer, Gray Eyes seemed to relax. The well-formed

lips settled into a more reposed expression. The planes beneath his well-placed cheek-bones moved to crease tiny lines in the tanned face. She thought he shrugged slightly as if giving in to Roberto's wishes. Annie glanced at his other hand, holding his tan felt hat against his vest. Dark trousers led to black and olive snakeskin boots. He bowed the blond head, which made her chest go weak again.

"A pleasure ma'am," he said in a deep, quiet voice.

She found her own voice. "Likewise." She had to get out of here.

He raised her hand near his lips and bowed his head over it, bringing his lips near, but not touching her. Her heart slid to her knees.

Roberto, who now held Lola around the waist, grinned. "Perhaps the two of you would like to join us for some supper?"

Annie gasped, but her feet refused to move, and her half-parted lips froze. Then she swallowed. For a mad moment she considered continuing the fantasy. What would it be like to be taken to dinner by a man who thought he was entertaining an actress? It was a deliciously wicked thought, but, of course, she could not do it.

"I—I'm sorry," she croaked in a choked voice. "I can't. I'm, um, expected elsewhere." She quickly dropped her eyes, fearing he would read the truth.

"A pity," he said softly.

She glanced up and then away, trying to look anywhere but at him. "I'm sorry, I must change. Someone is waiting for me."

Oh, formed itself on the gentleman's lips. Then he smiled in understanding. Perhaps another time, he'd been too late, the look seemed to say.

She tried to move her weakened knees and finally made her way to the dressing room. The long mirrored room was filled now with the rest of the chorus girls, changing to go to just such suppers as Grant Worth and Lola's Romeo were proposing. A few of the girls left, giving her room to sit down and start removing the pins and feathers, evidence that she'd been on the stage. It would take a pound of cold cream to get the greasepaint off.

Grant watched her disappear into the dressing room, finding himself disappointed that the lovely Grace had other plans. His mind had been so much on business, he only now realized that a little pleasure might not do any harm. But the chance was gone.

"Never mind, my friend," said Roberto, laying a hand on his arm. "Lola has other friends, don't you my dear?"

"Of course."

Grant raised his hand and smiled. "Thank you, no. Don't worry on my account. I'll just try my hand at a little faro."

Roberto gave his pearly grin. "Suit yourself, my friend. But if you change your mind, we'll be next door." He gave a knowing wink. The Teller House had a fine dining room and even finer bedrooms upstairs.

Grant nodded, issued a few more compliments and then followed them outside to the courtyard leading to the narrow street. He let Roberto and Lola go on ahead, then stepped onto the boardwalk himself. Billboards flanked the two arched, paneled doors at the front of the granite-bricked opera house.

Grant walked down the steep boardwalk past the assay office next door. The crowd that had spilled out of the opera house either headed for the saloons or the train station. Some of them climbed up the stair-step heights to their frame houses perched like bird-cages on the hillsides above the gulch where Central City lay. Wagons and riders on horseback cluttered the intersection of Eureka and Main streets, and beyond the stretch of buildings, mining operations clung to the steep hillsides.

Boom towns like this one held little attraction for a man of the wide-open spaces like Grant. What made him a cowboy at heart would never leave him. And he never drank unless it was accompanied by some good conversation. So he might as well take the train back to Denver where his comfortable hotel room waited for him. There were some bankers he planned to see tomorrow and a charity ball he'd take the opportunity to attend.

Roberto Martinez had made money in California and could afford to invest. But Grant would have to wait for another day to find out if breeding llamas in Colorado appealed to the man's pocket book.

"You did marvelously, my dear," said Marcel, escorting Annie through the crowd at the corner of Eureka and Main streets. He had traded the smock for a slouching brown coat and wore a large black silk ascot at his throat. Annie was now dressed in a blue-and-white striped two-piece walking suit with short-waisted jacket, ruffled blouse and matching parasol.

"Don't you want to join the troupe?" he teased.

"Oh, Marcel, you know this was only a lark for my nineteenth birthday. It can hardly be repeated without causing a scene at home."

"Horrify your wicked stepmother?" Marcel gripped her elbow to pull her aside from a buckboard turning the corner.

She made a face. "My name would be blackened in society news, and Hattie would kill me. But I will try to come back to see you."

Her father's second wife, Hattie, tried to make sure her husband's only son and daughter were models of propriety in society. If Hattie knew the real truth, she would have to call for the smelling salts.

Marcel and Lola had become close, secret friends ever

since Annie had met the theater troupe at the Golden Peacock, where she'd gotten James to take her last year to watch the cancan. The music, costumes and the flashy cancan had made Annie tap her foot. Afterward, she'd chatted with the performers, while her brother played cards. The theatrical troupe played all the mining towns and Denver as well, traveling by stagecoach from place to place.

What she would give to dance the cancan herself, she'd thought at the time. She had tried, afterward in her own bedroom, wearing only her camisole and petticoats. It had felt marvelous.

Marcel elbowed his way into the Silver Spur. Annie stood just inside the swinging saloon doors and peered into the smoky crowd. There was the gangly, black-suited James at the blackjack table. She turned to Marcel.

"Thank you, Marcel. There's my brother. I'll be all right now."

Marcel eyed the boisterous crowd warily. "Are you sure you don't want me to stay to make sure he'll leave with you?"

"You'd better go. He's not supposed to know I'm even acquainted with you." She took a moment to squeeze his arm. "And thank you."

He smiled and leaned down to peck her on the cheek. "Any time, my sweet. Let us hear from you from time to time."

"I promise."

Marcel glided up to the polished mahogany bar. She could see he was determined to stay in the noisy saloon until she got her brother safely away.

She took a deep breath, plunged into the crowd and squeezed in beside her brother. She lifted his pocket-watch out of his pocket, the gold chain attached to his buttonhole.

"James," she said into his ear. "It's time to go. We'll miss the train."

He kept his eyes on the cards, but his tone held annoyance. He didn't like being interrupted.

"Already?"

"The performance is over, and everyone is going to the train."

James frowned at his cards and a dwindling stack of bills spread on the table before him.

Annie could see that he'd been more than winning. While the occupation of gambling prevented him from keeping too close a watch on her, she didn't want to miss the train and get left in Central City when they were expected at home. She tugged at his sleeve.

"Come on. If we miss the train, we'll never hear the end of it."

His pale lips turned down at the corners and he finished the hand. He lost. "Very well."

He crushed his derby onto his side-parted brown hair, scraped back his chair and followed Annie as she elbowed through the crowd.

Out of the corner of her eye she saw Marcel talking to the burly bartender at the shiny, crowded bar. She kept her head up, flicked her eyes in his direction, but didn't risk a word.

Outside on Main Street, she tucked her hand into the crook of James's arm, more to pull him along the boardwalk than to be escorted.

The train station was just past the tailings pond that spilled down from the mines on the slope above. The acrid smell from the coal box filled the crisp air as smoke mixed with steam wafted over the train. The cars filled with passengers who'd come up for a day's outing and were now bound for Denver.

The grizzled, uniformed conductor, with pocket-watch in hand, confirmed Annie's fears.

"You and your brother will have better luck with seats

in the parlor car, Miss. Front cars are packed thick as cattle cars."

"Very well," she said. Then to James, "It's the lounge car or nothing at all."

"Hmmm. Might get in a hand of cards there." He rubbed his skinny chin.

It hardly mattered to Annie if he played cards or not, as long as she had a seat. But so thick was the cigar smoke when they entered the parlor car that she had to dig a hankie out of her drawstring reticule in order to cover her nose and mouth. Through the crush of ranchers, businessmen, ladies and dandies, they found two seats upholstered with crimson velvet, at the back of the walnut-paneled car.

She glanced out the window at the crowded platform and the street beyond, but she saw no more sign of her friends.

"All aboard," called the conductor shortly after they got settled.

Above their heads, a curved panel joined a carved and gilded cornice to the raised roof that ran lengthwise down the aisle. The roof panels were covered with brocaded rose silk patterned with cream-colored flowers. At the other end of the car, men pressed around a paneled bar with a brass foot rail.

Gentlemen offered newly arrived ladies their seats, then consoled themselves by moving toward the bar. Annie fanned herself with the theater program she'd thought to snatch on her way out, in order to make it look like she'd been in the audience instead of cavorting on the stage.

After two more cries of "All aboard" rang up and down the platform, the train shrieked its whistle and then slowly chugged along. Those who could, sat down. Annie gazed at the crowd in the car and at the town's hustle-bustle outside the windows. Then her eyes drifted to the plush velvet swivel chairs at the middle of the car.

To her horror, she saw that the handsome, domineering

Grant Worth was seated facing her on the aisle, engaging several other men in conversation. She ducked behind her program, the print blurring before her eyes. She heard his low-pitched laugh, felt his charm even from this distance, and then words drifted to her over the clack and chuff of the train and the rattle of glasses from the bar. From what her burning ears caught, he seemed to be extolling the virtues of some animal.

"Good company for the lonely miner," his words drifted to her through the din. "Smarter than mules. They'll follow you anywhere. And their manure's the best fertilizer in the world."

Two

Annie stared at the houses and mines in the gulch slipping past. She prayed he wouldn't recognize her. After all, she was cleansed of the grease paint, ringlets now coiled about her ears, and her ruffled collar came up to her chin, tight sleeves to her wrists. Her veiled bonnet was some help if she turned away from him, which meant turning away from her brother as well. She slid one gloved hand along her striped skirt, smoothing it flat over her knees and so that it fell evenly to her feet. Only the tips of her gray kid boots peeked out beneath. She'd had so much bare skin exposed backstage when the men had been there that she wanted to hide in her clothes now.

Her worst fear was that the man who'd introduced himself as Grant Worth would approach and say something to ruin her ruse. If James found out what she'd been up to, he'd laugh himself sick. And he wouldn't keep it to himself for one minute. Not only would Hattie try to discipline her, but the whole of Denver would know by tomorrow afternoon. She closed her eyes, envisioning a stern lecture from their father and enforced charity duties under Hattie's watchful eye.

The train hugged the brown mountainside among the gold mines at rooftop level of the small frame houses. The track zigzagged along the grade in order to make the three thousand foot descent in altitude between here and the plains where Denver sprawled. But Annie was oblivious to the mine workings clinging to the mountainside. There was too much to worry about inside the car.

"How was the show?" asked James. He slouched down into his seat and crossed one ankle over his other knee. His eyes wandered across the aisle, watching as one of the men brought out a deck of cards and unfolded a little table that was affixed beneath the window.

"Very good," answered Annie. She only briefly lifted her head to answer James and, as she did so, caught another glimpse of Grant Worth.

She allowed herself a breath. He wasn't looking at her. Instead, his head was turned in conversation with the other gentlemen in the chairs facing each other. His profile, she couldn't help but notice, was appealing. His tanned face was animated when he spoke. His hair was wavy, curling on the nape of his neck in a very nice way. There were a few lines of experience in the planes of his face. She guessed him to be about thirty years old.

The cut of his clothes accentuated his masculine, proportioned, strong-looking body, and the black and olive snakeskin boots visible from beneath his trouser-legs were the kind that cowboys liked for fancy dress.

Was he a rancher then? The only jewelry he wore were pearl shirt-studs, visible above the silk brocade vest. His left hand was visible, and long, masculine fingers lifted when he made a point. Oh, stop it, she reprimanded herself, keeping her head averted. She braced herself on the upholstered chair arm as the train lurched into a turn.

They left the town behind. Below the trestle, Clear Creek foamed along the gorge. She tried to relax. If Mr. Grant Worth did glance this way, she mustn't look like a scared rabbit. She must try to blend in with the other passengers.

She attempted conversation with her brother. "Did you win anything?" she asked, still studying the program she was using as a blind.

James grunted, stuck his hands into his pockets and looked glum. "I might've if we'd stayed."

She forgot and lowered the program.

"Oh James, how could we stay? We're expected for dinner. Don't forget it's my birthday. And besides, you generally always lose."

"Well, *you* had a good time, didn't you?"

"Yes, thank you. Otto Chapman is a fine baritone. And Judith Quittmeyer was in very good voice."

She chirped on artificially about the performance, her eyes straying to Grant, who tipped his head back to laugh at some remark made by one of his companions. Laugh lines formed about the corners of his gray eyes, where humor lurked. A little tingle ran along her spine, and she looked at her hands. She mustn't draw attention to herself by staring at the man.

"Hmmmm," said James, uninterested in performances in general. "I wonder what they'll have for supper at home." He interrupted his study of the card game across the aisle long enough to glance at his sister. "A big cake, I hope. I heard Hattie giving instructions to Maria."

"Oh, that's nice."

Her features froze into a pleasant expression because on her last glance upward Grant's gaze fell on her. His mirthful expression and the direct, appraising eyes stopped to take in the sight of her trapped in the upholstered chair beside her brother.

She acted as if she didn't notice, in spite of the color rising in her cheeks. He was just another man in their car. But her pulse rattled nervously, and she tried to tilt her head so as to listen to James's words, fanning herself very quickly with the long, folded program. Minutes seemed to pass, and then she reached a tentative hand up to tuck a stray wisp of hair back under her bonnet. As she did so, she sneaked a look. He was still pondering her.

He leaned one elbow on the chair arm and rubbed his

chin thoughtfully, making no attempt to hide the fact that he was looking her way. Oh drat, she thought and craned her neck to look out the window, pretending interest at the perfectly ordinary sandstone rocks and pine forest she'd seen a hundred times before.

Grant gazed at the familiar-looking girl. It took a moment to recognize the chorus girl he'd so recently met, but no wonder, for she looked different dressed in street clothes. He paused in his conversation with the gentlemen from Denver with whom he had happened to seat himself. What was the girl's name? Grace. Grace Albergetti.

He stared at the prim, well-dressed, wide-eyed, clean-faced young lady sitting next to a dark-haired man about her age who slouched beside her. She must have turned down supper because she had an appointment with this fellow. And the young gentleman she was with looked surly enough not to want to be bothered. For the moment, Grant contented himself with watching them out of the corner of his eye.

At the same time he half listened to the conversation beside him about the price of gold, the growth of Denver now that it was the capital of the two-year-old state, and the spread of the railroads.

"Midland's building east from Salt Lake City now," said the middle-aged merchant sitting beside him. With gray hair smoothed back and neat waxed moustache, he wore his modest success with conservatism.

"Hmmmm," grunted the stocky cowman opposite the merchant. He was a big man, even for the wide, plush seats. "Good thing, too. When it joins up with the Kansas Pacific in Denver for points east, the high plains'll finally have a direct shipping line to the Missouri River instead of having to go up to Cheyenne first."

Railroads vying for the business of building across Colorado was a sore point with Grant just now.

"What about you, Worth? You've got cattle in South Park. You got an interest in the railroads?" asked the other cattle rancher.

"Damn right," Grant said, dragging his attention away from the young lady several rows down the car. "Everett T. Marsh thinks he can buy my best land and lay track right through the middle of my range."

"And?"

"I refused." His hand came down on the chair arm to emphasize the point.

"Yessir," put in the young law clerk sitting directly opposite Grant. His voice was high with excitement, possibly from the good time he'd just had in Central City. "I heard about Marsh's plan to build all the way to Mexico."

Grant shifted back over from the aisle and sat up straighter. "Not only do I not want to sell my prime grazing land, but I believe there's not enough passenger business on the western slope to keep a north-south railroad in business."

"That's right," grumbled the big, stocky rancher. "We can drive our cattle down to Denver, but they have to have grass to eat in the valleys first or they won't get fat enough."

Grant warmed up to the deep concern he felt about this argument. "The east-west route from Salt Lake City will serve our area well enough now that we have a branch line to Cheyenne. Everett Marsh will stay out of South Park, if I have anything to say about it."

The merchant sitting next to Grant echoed this thought. "From my point of view these railroads racing to beat each other across the country are going to meet disaster. You'll see. There's not enough traffic for all of them yet, so it stands to reason that some'll end up bankrupt. I'd wager on it."

No one commented on that, so Grant glanced again at

the young actress. The longer he stared, the more curious he became. She sat there stiffly in proper street clothes. And she wasn't even being polite to the young man beside her.

How could that young sprig, who could hardly be but a few years older than the girl herself, afford such an expensive mistress? Grant recognized expensive clothes and pearls when he saw them. Most ladies of the theater were supposed to be generous with their favors for the right gentleman in exchange for certain gifts. That would explain the clothes and pearls, but the young man beside this girl certainly wasn't acting the dandy.

Maybe the sprig wasn't an admirer, merely an escort or acquaintance. Maybe Grant would like to find out.

The girl's face swept this end of the car, but there was no sign of recognition in her eyes, not even a warning signal not to approach. The reddish hair was the same brilliant color, but the lack of greasepaint gave her face a scrubbed look. Grant dropped his hand from where it had been scratching his chin. But before he turned away, he saw her glance again in his direction. His eye caught hers for a moment, and then she looked down at the theater program in her lap.

It was the same gesture she'd used backstage when they'd been introduced. The blend of aloofness with the vivaciousness he'd seen evidenced on stage was indeed intriguing—enough to make him decide to inquire.

The gray-haired gentleman merchant beside him pulled out a deck of cards and lowered the hinged table from the wall. "Game?" he said.

"Don't mind if I do," the law clerk chimed in.

"You in, Worth?" said the merchant.

He hesitated, then shook his head. "You gents go ahead, I believe I'll pay my respects to a lady."

* * *

Annie's heart sank as the man she'd been trying to avoid got up and came her way. He grasped the rack beneath the curved paneling as the train took a curve, his feet widespread. His jacket came half open, and her gaze was riveted to the solid torso and muscular thighs.

In a moment, the train straightened out again and chugged along the canyon. Onward came her nemesis until he stood, broad shoulders towering above her, in the center of the aisle before them.

"Excuse me, miss," he said, removing his hat. But his tone held something of a demand.

Her eyes flicked up at him in mock surprise. "Are you speaking to me?" she asked.

Now would be an opportune time for James to get up and join a card game, she thought, but he didn't budge. She was forced to meet the gaze of the pewter-colored eyes that appraised her, making her heart thump. She didn't know which was louder, the chugging and clacking of the train over the rails down the canyon or the roaring of her pulse in her ears.

Grant spoke again, ignoring James. "If I'm not mistaken, we met at the opera house."

She swallowed. At least he hadn't said backstage. She tried a noncommittal smile. "You must be mistaken. I'm afraid we haven't been introduced, though I *was* in the audience."

She smiled a little more brightly and held up the program she clutched in her hand.

For a moment doubt flickered in his warm gray eyes, and his broad brow creased. He looked at the program and then quickly over her dress and back to her face. His smile held enough charm to skim the cream off milk, and he gave a deep chuckle.

"You must have a twin."

Her expression remained frozen to her face and she tried to nod at his joke. He was *flirting* with her.

"Yes, that's it," she answered.

She cast a quick glance at her brother, who still remained fixed in the upholstered chair, his chin raised a little resentfully at the gentleman before them. But the blond man didn't seem inclined to go.

"In that case," Grant persisted, surveying them both, "allow me to introduce myself. Name's Grant Worth, just down from South Park."

He nodded in James's direction and extended a hand that James couldn't avoid taking.

"James Marsh."

Grant's handshake stilled at the mention of the name, and he creased his brows. "Don't suppose you're related to Everett T. Marsh."

"He's our father," answered James as if he wondered why that mattered. Then he looked sideways at Annie, forced to introduce her. "This is Annie Marsh, my sister."

"Oh really?"

Annie fanned herself anew with the program, hoping it would help cool her face. Why was Grant Worth's stare so intent? Could he see right through her little guise?

"Well, well," said Grant. "Pleased to meet you."

She distinctly heard the mockery in his voice, but she tried to maintain her outward composure as she gave him the back of her wrist to bow over.

"Likewise," she replied, giving him a weak little smile. Why didn't he go away?

When Grant finally released her hand, he remained for a moment. Finally, he lifted his hat.

"I can see I was previously mistaken," he said, a guarded look in his glinting gray eyes. "I hope you both enjoyed the performance."

"I did," said Annie too quickly. "I mean, we did."

Grant glanced from one to the other with amused incomprehension, then replaced his hat on his head. "Sorry to have troubled you."

She nodded. James stared at him belligerently and recrossed his legs. Grant gave a nod and made his way back to his seat, where a card game was in progress.

Annie dared to breathe. She made sure not to look that way again for a long time, fearing that he might read her thoughts. She uncrumpled the program in her hand and read it over five or six times, then engaged herself in conversation with James by discussing what Maria might have made for her birthday dinner.

When the train pulled into the station in Denver, Annie followed James onto the platform. From the brick terminal with its imposing arched entrance, they pushed their way along Wynkoop Street looking for their driver, Lin Chu. On the street, a melting-pot of citizens passed. Hunters and trappers dressed in buckskin suits, stockmen in slouched hats, plainsmen in blue greatcoats left over from the war between the states, also rigs with wealthy English tourists, dandies in light kid gloves, and many Indians on their ponies, the men wearing buckskins sewn with beads, lank black hair hanging straight to their shoulders. Wagons rumbled through with goods purchased at one of the many places of business.

"There he is," said James.

Lin Chu had migrated here after the last spike had been driven at Promontory Point, Utah, joining the Central Pacific and the Union Pacific railroads.

And even if the white population in Denver held considerable and sometimes violent prejudice against Chinese emigrants, Lin Chu knew how to ingratiate himself with the family that had given him the chance. He did his best to stay out of the way when trouble was brewing. Self-preservation was the small, lithe Chinaman's mark. And life as Everett T. Marsh's driver and errand boy for the last five years was considerably better than following the railroad crews.

As Annie and James approached, they saw that Lin Chu was engaged in three-card monte beside their buggy on an upturned barrel.

"Oh, dear," exclaimed Annie. "He's at it again. He knows Hattie's forbidden him to engage in games of chance."

James shrugged. "You can't blame him for picking up a few extra dollars in his spare time, Sis."

"James, you know he does nothing but fleece innocent bystanders."

"That's a matter of opinion," said James.

Lin Chu selected three cards from his well worn deck and showed their faces to his audience. He smiled brightly.

"Here you are, ladies," he said to the three women with four grubby-kneed children of various sizes watching him. "Queen of hearts is winning card. Watch closely. Follow with your eye."

He was dressed in short baggy trousers, wide sleeved linen jacket, with brown leather slippers on his feet. His sleek black hair was pulled into a braid at the back of his neck. And like most Chinese, words ending in L's came out softened into something more like a W. He laid the cards face down.

"Here it is, now here, now where?"

His hands swiftly moved the cards about so that there was little chance of keeping one's eye on the winning card.

"You choose correct, you win." He smiled broadly from under the round-brimmed felt hat that shaded his oval face from the sun. "You miss, you lose, ha, ha, ha."

He picked up the three cards again, showing their faces. "Here, you see? Now watch again. I take no bets from paupers, cripples or orphans."

He bobbed his head and put the cards face down on the table again.

"Lin Chu," said James, stepping around the fascinated ladies who were about to lose their money.

The Chinese card shark glanced up. "Uh oh," he said to his audience, "Show over now."

Annie shook her head as the women pulled their children away. "Lin Chu, you know Hattie will apply the hickory rod to your backside if she hears of your tricks." She climbed into the waiting buggy followed by James.

"That so," said the Chinaman, smiling as he folded up the cards and moved the barrel aside. "But she not know."

"You're very trusting of us," said Annie.

Lin Chu assumed a poker expression. "That so, too. You no tell, will you?"

Annie gave him a dry look. She, James, and Lin Chu shared many a secret from Hattie, whose self-imposed, often ineffective duty was to ensure her family's respectability in the city and to help her husband maintain social dominance. In such a mixed community as Denver, a wife was supposed to make sure the citizens knew who was to be looked up to, and Hattie strained to make her stepchildren and servants behave decorously. That they often baffled her was not her fault. She had only come to the family as Everett's second wife six years ago, when Annie was thirteen and James fourteen. That was, perhaps, too late.

"You're right, Lin Chu," said Annie, answering his question. "We've no need to tell her. But others might see you and mention it."

"Ohhhhh." He looked momentarily contrite. "You right."

He sprang up to the driver's seat, took up the reins, clicked his tongue and shouted a string of Chinese, which their black trotter seemed to understand. The horse bobbed its head and moved off, Lin Chu directing it away from the train station into the wide, unpaved street.

They made their way among other buggies, carts, and delivery wagons rumbling by. Denver was a sprawling city of 15,000 souls with stout brick buildings, rising two and three stories in the business district. From Fifteenth Street, where businesses stretched from the terminus of several railroads, the city sprawled south as far as First Street. On most days, the clear, blue sky was unmarred until a few thunderheads grew over the jagged line of mountains to the west.

Trotting up a hill, they came to the tree-lined avenues of the residential district, laid out north and south, with brick, frame and stone homes on spacious town lots. Lin Chu pulled into the drive before their sandstone carriage house, and Annie and James climbed down.

In the large kitchen, their stepmother was attempting to supervise their cook, Maria. An enticing aroma came from the big iron stove, and Maria was waving a wooden spoon.

"Cannot make soup without green chilies. Someone steals my chilies. He will go to the devil. I will take him there myself."

"I'm sorry, Maria," replied Hattie. "We can get more chilies. I can't imagine someone stole them. More likely a cow or goat got into the shed and ate them."

Hattie placed a dishtowel over a pan of cherry cobbler she'd just removed from the oven. She was a fair woman in her thirties with a perpetual expression of uncertainty on her otherwise attractive face. She was dressed in a plain blue house dress and white apron, light brown hair scooped up in back and lodged in a snood. Her blue eyes flicked up from the cobbler, brows raised in doubtful query.

"We harvested chilies last week, I thought," said James. He stopped to pinch off a bit of crust from the cobbler and put it in his mouth.

"James, please," reprimanded Hattie.

Annie removed her bonnet and stopped to sniff the pot Maria was stirring.

"I think it smells all right without the chilies," said Annie.

The Mexican woman offered Annie a taste of the soup in the big wooden spoon.

"Hmmmm," said Annie, nodding her approval.

"How was the operetta?" asked Hattie, deciding not to cover the cobbler after all. She removed the dishtowel.

"Splendid," said Annie, composing herself to smile broadly. "I—" she glanced at James. "We enjoyed it greatly. It was a lovely birthday present."

"That's nice."

Hattie's mousebrown brows dropped and she hastened to inspect the cut up green beans. "Both of you wash up now, dinner will be ready soon."

"Is Father home?"

"In the parlor and hungry, no doubt."

Annie was only too glad to escape up the carpeted staircase to her room on the second floor, where she could shut the door on the world. Alone, she took off her jacket, undid the buttons of her blouse and then wriggled out of it. She smiled secretly at her reflection in the oval mirror on the frame above the dresser. She tossed the dress onto the four-poster bed and then turned to rummage in the wardrobe for something suitable for dinner.

When she'd chosen a yellow-ribbed silk dress with satin black draperies, she sat down at the dressing table and took out the pins that held what was, by now, disheveled hair. Her natural curls sprang back from the brush. Repairing her coif gave her time to reflect on having gotten away with her scheme. She hummed the melodies she'd sung at the theater, tapping her foot as the brush pulled at her thick hair. Then she brushed it upward from the base of her neck.

She stared in the mirror for a moment and imagined Grant Worth. Then she shook herself. She was just lucky he hadn't ruined her story.

Half an hour later, coiffed and dressed in a proper dinner gown, she descended the narrow stairs to the landing. There, she paused beneath the circular window and placed her hand on the large, round newel post. The last flight of stairs was wide, with a low, polished railing, perfect for a grand entrance to the foyer with a view of the front parlor beyond.

This time there was no party to greet, so she hurried down, her skirt and draperies floating above the carpeted stairs. The front parlor was also silent. She opened the sliding pocket doors to the rear parlor, where her father was seated in his large high-backed Turkish armchair.

"Hello, Father," she said, coming into the room.

He glanced up from his newspaper. "Hello, my dear. How was your trip?"

Guiltily, she sparkled a smile at him. "Fine, thank you. It was a lovely present."

Everett T. Marsh was a forty-seven-year-old man of fair height and straight shoulders. Early on in life he'd decided to become a man of means, and so, always held himself proudly. His broad, round, moustached face reflected an attitude of superiority and certainty beneath a slightly receding hairline of springy black, slightly graying hair with thick sideburns.

His stern expression let other men know he was their match, if not their better. But at home, he tried to be a concerned husband and father. He had hidden his own grief when James's and Annie's mother, Susan, had died.

After an interval of two years, he had chosen a second wife who, he hoped, would finish raising his two hoydens. He believed it was a man's duty to provide well for his family, and he harnessed his ambition to the belief that transportation was the key to economic opportunities in a state that was rich in natural resources.

Annie sat on the fringed hassock next to his chair, her skirts rustling around her.

Everett laid the newspaper aside on the circular rosewood table.

"You look so like your mother sometimes, my dear."

"Thank you, Father. I doubt I'm as pretty as she was."

He reached across and gave her hand a squeeze. "You are, when you're not being a ruffian."

She had to press her lips together. Composing her expression, she smiled brightly at him again. "Dinner must be ready. Hattie said not to let things get cold."

"Very well, Pumpkin. I've an appetite myself." He arose, stretching out his robust frame as he did so.

"I'm starved," said Annie, getting up beside him and starting for the door.

She'd been too excited before the performance to eat much at luncheon, and so her mouth watered when they entered the paneled dining room and sat down to a laden table. She ate generous portions of everything. Over lemon birthday cake and after-dinner coffee, the conversation turned as usual to Everett's business.

"How are the railroad plans?" asked James, blotting crumbs from his mouth and leaning back with a manly air. At twenty years old, James was installed as a clerk at the bank, but he knew that his father had a place for him in the new railroad once things got underway.

"I believe the western slope is the way to go," answered Everett, between mouthfuls of cake. He eyed his family to make sure they were all paying attention. "We need a railroad to carry north-south traffic from Denver all the way to El Paso and into Mexico.

"More and more cattle are being raised in the high valleys. Herds of ten thousand are common. The bigger ranches have as many as 35,000 head. As the ranches grow, so will the need for freight. Trains coming north from Cañon City can bring livestock to Denver and points eastward."

Denver had seen dark days when the Union Pacific

chose to go through Cheyenne instead. Now their fair city was finally connected to the east by the Kansas Pacific, which had been built to Denver in 1870. But points west were still served only by a spur connection to the transcontinental line through Cheyenne.

"Denver should rightfully take her place as the Queen City of the Plains," said Everett. "Only a few stubborn ranchers stand in my way."

"Who stands in your way, Father?" James asked, taking another helping of the lemon cake and lifting the coffee pot to pour himself another cup.

Everett leaned back, resting the fork beside his plate. "Rancher by the name of Grant Worth runs his herd right along the best route to build a railroad into South Park. The flat valley floor connects to the Arkansas Valley to the South and the San Luis Valley beyond. Prime railroad country."

Annie coughed, slamming her cup on the china saucer. She quickly touched her linen napkin to her mouth. The rest of the diners looked at her.

"Are you all right, my dear?" asked Hattie.

"Sorry," said Annie, feeling her face warm. She cleared her throat. "I must have swallowed too quickly."

"Try to eat more slowly, dear," said Hattie. "It's more ladylike."

She nodded, and took a sip of coffee, her face glued to the half-eaten cake on her plate. Grant Worth was the man she'd met on the train, and worse, backstage at the theater. Well, she'd just have to make sure she wasn't present when her father tried to do business with him.

"Won't he sell you a strip?" continued James after they'd ascertained that Annie wasn't going to choke on the cake.

"No," said Everett. "At least he hasn't yet seen the sense in my plan. Those ranchers don't want to fence their range-lands. They let their cattle roam free with brands to identify them when it's roundup time for shipping them east. I've heard Worth's raising money for a new investment, some crazy notion about raising South American animals in the mountains. Sounds a little touched to me. Doesn't sound like the type to accept a reasonable offer from the railroad and stop whatever foolishness he's about."

"What kind of South American animals?" asked James.

"Llamas, they tell me. Something like camels, only for packing, not for riding. He wants to sell them to the miners and trappers. Hare-brained scheme if I ever heard of one."

Three

Grant sat with a group of businessmen in Hortense Morgan's back parlor. From upstairs came the thump of dancing feet in the rooms that had been opened up for her charity ball. A chamber orchestra grated away at music that floated down the staircase and hovered in the background where a few of the gentlemen had retired to smoke their cigars.

Grant stretched his tall frame across a leather love seat, while the other gentlemen rested in overstuffed chairs. Thick cigar smoke curled toward the heavy velvet drapes, pulled back to reveal lace curtains. The smokers sipped from cut crystal sherry glasses and listened with varying degrees of interest or skepticism to Grant's pitch for his latest enterprise. He studied each of his listeners as he spoke, gauging their reactions.

"I tell you," insisted Grant. "There's a fine future for South American llamas in the high mountain valleys on Colorado's western slope. Packing comes naturally to these beasts. They've been trained to the lead rope in the Andes for centuries with packs tied to their backs that are a quarter to a third of their own weight, a higher percentage than a horse carries."

"Now, the Andes aren't the Rockies," argued Judge Bentworth, a tall, lanky gentleman with a fringe of gray hair around his bald pate. Silky mutton chops flowed from his cheeks. He eyed Grant over a pair of spectacles balanced on the bridge of his nose.

Grant smiled at his audience and waved the Judge's objection away. "Even though at ten thousand feet, our mountain valleys are not as high, the Andes are closer to the equator. So the winters here are about what the animals are used to in South America. And they are surefooted when being led through snow and ice."

"But miners are used to mules," protested a young man who'd introduced himself as Jacob Morley, a skinny clerk seated at Grant's right. "The beast in that picture doesn't look like anything a respectable miner or a mountain man would want to come near. It'd scare the horses."

"No sir," added the short, jovial dentist with white teeth and brocade vest stretching over a plump paunch. "You won't get miners to give up their mules."

The skepticism only challenged Grant to rise to the occasion with his most persuasive arguments.

"Once they see how much cheaper it is to maintain one of my animals, they'll become convinced," said Grant. "A llama only requires a bale of hay a week. And they don't bite or kick. You only have to show them what to do and they never forget. Lot less stubborn than a mule. I tell you, gentlemen, once you've got the halter on, they'll follow you anywhere. Superior beasts for this kind of work. I've seen it myself."

The judge chuckled. "You may have, Worth, but you'll have to prove it. It didn't work when the Army tried to use camels in the southwest. Too belligerent. Bite and spit is the way I heard it. The Army gave up the idea."

Grant leaned back and stretched an arm along the carved back of the loveseat. "Camels worked well enough for transport, but llamas are far superior. And llamas are for packing, not riding. They're docile on the lead rope. I've led one myself."

Some of the men chuckled, but Grant was undaunted.

He swept his hand upward as he painted a picture for them.

"Thousands of claims in the high country aren't reached by the railroad. Trails are too rough for all the supplies a miner needs packed in to live out a winter. Llama's the perfect beast of burden for a lonely outpost. And their wool can be sold for weaving."

"Miners turning into weavers too?" laughed the clerk. "Where on earth did you come by this scheme, Worth?"

Grant grinned and lifted his glass of sherry. "First laid eyes on the long-necked, furry beasts at a stock fair in Chicago. Love at first sight, you might say. Then I made the trip to Peru to look into importing them. Gone three months. My grasslands in South Park'll make the perfect place to raise 'em, I saw that. With the economy booming now, this could be a wide-open enterprise."

Grant never stopped promoting his new business. He'd gladly paid his donation to Hortense Morgan's charity ball for orphans in order to rub shoulders with the men who ran Denver's politics and finances—men he needed to become investors.

"Well," said the stout dentist. "Time to refill." He held up his empty sherry glass. "And we mustn't keep the ladies waiting."

The other gentlemen unbent their legs and stood up as one. Grant did the same. Judge Bentworth clapped him on the shoulder as they crossed the room into the front parlor and then walked in pairs to the wide staircase.

"Not too bad an idea," said the judge. "I like a man with vision."

Grant still had llamas on his mind when they reached the third floor of the mansion. His ears were assailed with the not quite blended strains of the orchestra. The blur of ladies in evening dresses on the arms of dark-suited gents passed in front of his eyes. Garlands of roses, gold ribbons, and small white flowers were strung from the moldings, blending into wallpaper of the same pattern. The tables had been removed, and straight-backed chairs lined the sides of the rooms.

Then the crowd before him parted and he caught sight of Everett Marsh chuckling at something a fellow beside him had said. And on his arm, frowning and looking around as if for a means of escape, was the young lady he'd met on the train from Central City.

"Well, well," Grant said to himself under his breath. He hadn't meant to be distracted from business tonight, but there was that girl again, all decked out in blue and silver shiny stuff this time.

Her lacey square-cut neckline revealed a pretty neck and shoulders, and the strawberry-colored hair coiled atop her head, with a few tight curls hanging in front of her ears and generous curls cascading down the back of her neck, brought to mind the young actress he'd so briefly met backstage at the operetta. The one Annie Marsh claimed to know nothing about.

He took a step in her direction. Her golden amber eyes, sweeping the crowd, eventually landed on his. They glimmered into recognition, widened, then filled with something like fear.

Grant smiled to himself. There was a story here that needed telling. He prepared himself for a clash with the young lady's escort, the man who wanted to buy his land. Straightening his shoulders, he elbowed his way through the crowd for the showdown.

Annie saw Grant squeezing between the women mingling at the entry to the party rooms and wished she could disappear into the crowd. She increased the pressure on her father's arm.

"Do let's dance, Father. We've been standing about long enough."

Everett patted the hand that rested on his arm and started to pry it loose. "You go on, my dear. I'm sure you'll have no dearth of partners. Here comes a man I need to speak to."

And then Grant was headed toward them. She would have liked to take her father's suggestion of a timely exit, but as Grant bore down on them, his expression changed from dark clouds to one of wary charm, and his silver-gray eyes danced in her direction, preventing her from leaving.

The tall, broad-shouldered rancher was now in full evening dress, as were all the other gentlemen. His waistcoat was white brocade with pearl studs. The white bow-tie and stand-up collar made his handsome features more prominent. Thick blond hair fell to the bottom of his ears. When he looked at her, his eyes seemed to dance with diamond-like reflection. There was enough of the cowboy about him to remind her of a starry night on an open range.

"Evening, Marsh," Grant said, even though he continued to look at Annie. "I saw you standing here with your lovely companion and decided we'd better get our conversation over with. But first, perhaps you'll introduce me."

Her father cleared his throat. "Annie, dear, this is Mr. Grant Worth, a rancher from South Park. May I present my daughter, Annie Marsh. My daughter was just excusing herself to find another dance partner."

Grant's eyes filled with amusement. "Actually, I happened to meet your daughter the other day in Central City at the opera."

She clenched her jaw, readying herself for an appropriate expression and a reply. She held her breath as Grant bent forward with ease and dignity in a slight bow, his face a mask of politeness, even if mockery glinted in his eyes. "A pleasure to see you again."

"Likewise," she managed to utter and then lifted her fan to cough gently behind it.

Grant continued to explain to Everett. "Circumstance

threw us together on the train when we found ourselves in the parlor car."

She gripped her father's arm, but still, Grant's eyes had not released her.

"What a coincidence that we attended the same performance."

Was he trying to share a joke with her? She struggled to speak through dry lips.

"Yes," she managed, fanning very rapidly. "We were seated in the parlor car when the passenger cars filled up."

"Well, then," said Everett. "If you'd care to step into a sitting room, Worth, perhaps I can make you see my way of thinking. My offer still stands."

Grant's devastating smile drifted from Annie's face back to her father.

"I'd be happy to repeat my reasons for not selling any of my land, but why ruin the evening? If you would allow me to dance with your daughter, I could take her off your hands. I know you'll be wanting to speak to some of the other guests."

"I'm a patient man," said Everett, after a pause during which he scrutinized the man before him. "Do you mind dancing with Mr. Marsh, my dear?"

Yes! She wanted to shout. But to refuse would be an insult, and she couldn't risk a scene. There was no way out. It was blackmail. She had to dance.

"Of course I don't mind," she finally said. The man who knew her greatest secret took her reluctant fingers.

Annie felt her heart thump, but nodded weakly and allowed him to lead her into the room transformed for the evening into a ballroom. A din of voices surrounded them as they stepped onto the smooth parqueted floor. Couples parted and reformed. Gentlemen bowed. Gaslit chandeliers cast a warm glow over the colorful silks and satins of evening dress, caught the sparkle of jewels at ladies' throats and ears, and reflected off gold cufflinks.

The orchestra leader announced a country dance Annie knew well, and they joined a square that included the tall, imposing Judge Bentworth and his short, plump wife. Annie barely had time to greet the other two couples in the square when the orchestra began "Nancy Dawson," a lively tune in six-eight time.

Grant smiled at Annie, touched his forehead in a mock salute. The gesture sent a tingle through her, and then they both turned away from each other to move around the other couples. They met again, took hands and he whisked her back to her place as if she belonged to him, giving her a wink as he did. His hands firmly guided her, his grip warm and dangerously inviting. She almost forgot to watch out for the train of her skirt to make sure she didn't step on it.

Since they were the first couple, they had to repeat the pattern, circling around the other three couples. The next time they met, she risked a look at his face, which was studying hers. It made her knees feel weak, and she leaned on his grip to chassé back to their places.

"A practiced dancer, I see," he said when they reached their place.

"Of course," she managed to reply, a little out of breath, before they circled back through the square, between the Judge and his wife. Annie and Grant parted to move around the rest and back to their places.

Now they were allowed a respite as the second couple began circling about.

Annie clapped, contributing to the racket of music and merry-making, but her heart beat harder, her breath came faster. She'd almost forgotten to worry about her secret, except for Grant's comments. His easy smiles, big hands clapping, the occasional stomp of his boot and shout, indicated his merriment.

"Yahoo!" he called.

Then he put his hand on her waist and took her other

hand in his to guide her around the square. His chin came just to her temple. She stole a glance at the striking features of his face and long, lean frame. The rest of the room blurred.

Grant bowed politely to her. "Well now, that was a lively dance," he said. "I thank you, miss."

"My pleasure, sir," she said in shaky tones.

As his eyes lit on hers, something happened deep inside her like a bullet ricocheting across the room. Since she didn't move, his hand touched her waist. It seemed to pull her toward him more than guide her away from the center of the dance floor.

"Would you like some refreshment?" he asked, gesturing with his head that they might leave the room together.

"Yes, thank you," she said, still breathless from the exertion of the dance and needing something to cool her parched throat.

But then she realized her mistake. Now she would have to talk to him. Somehow words of excuse did not come to mind. Consequently, she accompanied him to a room where tables were laden with platters of food. A round-faced black waiter dressed in white evening clothes ladled punch into crystal cups.

"Punch, lady?" the waiter asked as they approached.

"Yes, thank you."

She took the cup and gulped half the fruity liquid before remembering that Hattie would say she should slow down and be proper about her manners. But she was so thirsty.

Grant tossed back the first cup of punch and held out his cup for more. "Tasty stuff," he said to the waiter.

"Yessir, it is." The waiter grinned, handed Grant his cup, and after a moment poured him a third.

This cup Grant was content to sip, but not without Annie, as she learned when he took her empty cup from her and had the man refill it.

"Don't know about you, Miss Marsh, but I need some

air to cool off. Through there," he gestured with his chin, and after handing her the cup, guided her toward some open French doors letting in the evening air.

The square balcony looked out to the wide unpaved street and the other lots on which stood equally large mansions. The cattle barons and mining kings were beginning to show off their wealth now that Colorado's population was growing and Denver, as Colorado's social, economic, and political hub, was taking her place as the state capitol.

"That's better," said Grant. "I don't feel comfortable unless I'm where I can raise my eyes and see the mountains."

Annie grinned. "You can't see them now, it's dark."

"I can see them, over there." He nodded. "The moonlight's left us the line of peaks if you know where to look."

She lifted her head and strained her eyes to the west. Here and there gas lights dotted the neighborhood, but she squinted to look over the trees to see what Grant was talking about.

"Oh, I see what you mean." Sure enough the peaks and passes were faintly outlined in a darker blue than the night sky that twinkled with stars.

Grant lifted his arm. "Just about there is Central City."

Drat! Her smile froze, but she tried to sound natural. "Of course, but you can't see it from here."

"No. But I remember where it is."

She swallowed, searched wildly in her mind for appropriate responses to whatever he might ask next.

He set his punch cup down on a wrought iron table and then braced himself against the wide stone railing. He folded his arms across his chest. "I wanted to apologize for the mistaken identity on the train yesterday," he began. His voice had just the faintest trace of a drawl.

"Oh, that's quite all right. I understand." She struggled to control the way her voice rose when she was anxious.

"Do you?"

Her heartbeat tripped rapidly over itself. *He knew.* Somehow he knew. She hadn't fooled him.

He turned to gaze at her for a long moment, and she felt his eyes travel over her coif, her face, linger on her shoulders and then return to her face. He took his time, as if there were no hurry to fill the silence, and Annie was too busy grappling with her feelings to make light banter that might catch her up. Her eyes dropped from his satiny brocade vest and bow tie to his high-heeled black boots on the smooth balcony tiles.

"That was you up there on the stage, wasn't it?"

She clamped her mouth shut, not ready to give up yet. A glimmer came into her mind, a fleeting thought inspired by words they'd actually exchanged on the train when he'd first commented on how much she looked like the actress he'd just met.

"No," she was finally able to state, lowering her eyes briefly. When she had herself under control she lifted her eyes again to him. "That was my twin sister."

Grant's shifted his weight on the stone railing and smiled in curiosity. "Ah, a twin sister. Now that is interesting."

Annie quickly spun her tale. "My sister ran away a few years ago to go on the stage."

She risked a glance at Grant, built on the lie, her words gathering speed.

"Naturally she was disowned by the family." Her voice took on a somber quality as she spoke into the night. "It's as if she's dead, or rather, was never born."

She frowned at Grant, feeling a tremor, but courageously continuing her tale. "To speak her name is forbidden in the family. You mustn't mention that I told you about Grace. My father would be very angry."

A slow grin suffused Grant's face. "Well now, a twin sister. That explains it. I assure you that when I speak to your father, it won't be about your sister. We have weightier matters to discuss."

"Oh, that's good. I mean, I'm sorry you have to argue, but at least it won't be about Grace."

She pressed her lips together and pinched her face into a look of bewilderment.

"A strict family, then, is it?"

"Oh, yes."

She gave him the most serious look she could. "Hattie especially—my stepmother—doesn't approve. We try to live up to the standards Father expects of us. He has to maintain his position in city business and politics."

"Hmmmm. No stain on the family name and all."

A quick image of James at the gaming tables, herself skipping about in the theater costume, and Lin Chu rolling his loaded dice flashed through her mind.

But she nodded seriously. "We all try to behave with decorum, for Father's sake."

"How admirable of you. Your stepmother must be very strict."

"She is."

To avoid the challenge of his unsettling eyes, Annie gazed at the trees and the lanterns strung along the drive. The breeze cooled her, and now that she'd made up the tale about Grace, she felt a little better. As long as she didn't look at him for long, she'd be all right. But not looking at him was difficult.

The truth was that the man beside her did something to her that other gentlemen did not. His charm created a natural intimacy between them even though they stood half a foot apart.

And the awkward situation did not help. Drat this lie. She would have to be very careful. No matter what he said, she still had the feeling that he looked through her. It scared her. And it thrilled her.

Grant gazed at the girl before him for a long time. This

girl was not unappealing, but she was nervous and fidgety. He felt bemused. Twins. Well, they did have slight differences, now that he thought about it. He'd met the actress so briefly. He'd have to see them together to reassure himself. He shrugged and watched the crowd through the door for a moment.

The air and the punch had cooled him, and he reminded himself of the reasons he was here.

"I don't want to be keeping you," he said. "I need to have that conversation with your father before I leave." He said it without much enthusiasm.

She still looked outward into the night. A door shut downstairs then laughter rose on the night air. A carriage wheel squeaked. Then a giddap from the driver and the horses' hooves thumped on the drive. The carriage wheels rolled into the street and away.

"Why don't you want to sell your land?" she asked.

"Because I have plans for it," he said. "And herds can't roam open range where railroads cut through."

"And the llamas?"

She pressed her lips together. She'd heard him speak of the llamas on the train. It would be all right to mention it. But she'd have to be careful not to mention anything she'd heard him say backstage. She'd have to watch herself.

"So you know about the llamas?" he asked.

"You mentioned them on the train," she said hastily. "That is, I overheard you talking to the other gentlemen."

"Well, now. I didn't realize we were seated that close together."

She ignored his comment and went on. She couldn't tell him the real reason she'd been listening so closely.

"I've read about llamas. Funny-looking, aren't they? I thought they sounded very interesting. No one's thought of breeding them here, have they?"

He chuckled. "Well-informed as well as socially accomplished."

The teasing in his voice challenged her, but she tried not to show it.

"I'm not sure where I read about them, but I know what they look like. They're related to camels."

He nodded. "Trouble is, your father wants a strip of land down the middle of my ranch to lay a railroad through it."

"I've heard him speak of it."

She read the stubborn resistance on his profile.

"There are other routes he could take. I don't care how he runs his business, as long as he stays out of my way."

She shrugged, fanning herself, even though the evening air was pleasant. "I guess I don't know enough about the railroad business to know. But he must have a reason for wanting to build there."

Ambition, power, Grant started to say, then stopped himself. No need to drag this proper young lady into his hatred of railroad magnates. "Well, never you mind. I'll handle it with Mr. Marsh myself."

"Yes, well, I hope you come to terms."

He grunted in reply. He still wanted to know more about this sister, Grace.

He spoke thoughtfully. "Do you ever see your sister?"

"It's forbidden," she said quickly.

There was a breath of silence, and then he asked, "But you saw her in the play. Didn't you go backstage? On the sly maybe?"

"Well . . . , yes, actually I did."

She flicked a glance behind them to make sure no one was listening.

"I did see Grace—during the intermission. We do see each other from time to time, even if it's forbidden."

He turned his head to examine her, and she imagined he was comparing how much she resembled her "twin."

"Ah . . . well, I'm glad," he said.

"You are?"

That you get to see your sister, yes."

Annie frowned at her fan so as not to have to look at his silvery gray eyes that seemed a mite too intelligent and alert to be taken by her story. Nevertheless, she persisted.

"Yes, it is a problem. I do love her." She sighed, the story taking on a life of its own. "Hattie doesn't allow us to correspond. I'd get in trouble if I tried. But when I know the troupe is out here, I do make the effort."

"And your brother? Is he close to Grace as well?"

"Uh, no. That is, he knew I was going to see her. But he won't tell."

"How conspiratorial of you."

Was he mocking her? She fiddled with her punch cup. "Yes, well, we do look out for each other."

"Hmmmm. Close-knit siblings. Good, I suppose." He seemed to reflect for a moment, turned sideways facing her and glanced out over the railing toward the trees. "I had a brother. Lost him in the war."

"Oh, I'm sorry."

"Sisters are married back in Ohio."

"Then you've no other family out here?"

He thought of dear, deceased Kate, who died of a snake bite three years ago. He felt the jab of pain that lingered still. He'd built the ranch for her, and now she was gone. But he didn't let his expression give any of that away. "No family now, except for the boys on the ranch."

"Your ranch hands, you mean?"

"Yeah. Silly Joe's a good foreman. Every man's completely loyal to my brand. If they say something is so, I can take it to the bank. A man can't ask for more."

"No . . . I suppose not." She paused, glanced at the French doors leading back into the ballroom. "You won't say anything, will you—about Grace, I mean."

He shook his head. "No, not if you don't want me to."

"That'd be safer."

He thought about the pretty actress and his missed opportunity to talk with her. And while he hadn't given female company much thought lately, it was odd that he should notice the daughters of his sworn opponent. He shook his head. Life was sometimes like that. You had to pay attention to what it dealt you, because there was sometimes a reason for it.

He supposed Annie was telling the truth, now that he'd heard the explanation. It would be like Everett Marsh to be that strict.

He gazed thoughtfully at the moonlight. "Any chance I might get to see your sister again?"

She blinked. "Who? Grace?"

He turned his head to her. "Is there another one?"

"No, no," she said quickly, then swallowed. "You might see her in one of her other performances, I suppose."

"Hmmmm. Does the troupe come to Denver very often?"

"Uh, well, they have. But I don't know when they'll be here again. They're going up to Cheyenne." Did Cheyenne have a theater? She couldn't remember. "And then to some of the mountain towns."

He brought his eyes back to her and a smile spread slowly over his face, making her tremble.

"Well now, that's mighty interesting. I just might have to catch a show if I hear of one. What did you say the name of the troupe is?"

Her heart rate sped up as she tried to keep up with his questions. If she made up a name, he might find out she was lying and wonder why. After all, the troupe's name was printed on the program. She'd have to go with the real one and then warn Marcel and Lola.

"It's the Gaslight Players acting troupe. They also put on melodramas." Now why had she said that? Her inclination to spin the tale was running away with her.

"I like a good melodrama."

Let's hope you never see one of Marcel's, Annie thought.

He shifted away from the stone railing. "Well, let's move out," he said. "I need to see that father of yours."

This time Annie had the presence of mind to pay attention to the train of her dress. It'd be just her luck to get it caught on the wrought iron table. She had to turn around once just to make sure she got ahold of her skirt in the right place to lift it slightly off the balcony tiles. Then she raised her head, ready to march.

Grant stifled a grin. The other twin was sensuous and mysterious. This one seemed a mite uncomfortable in her sophisticated gear.

They walked back across the balcony, and Annie became aware of the party sounds inside. After the pleasant moonlight talk, the noise and lights assaulted her. She blinked and accustomed herself to the illumination from the gas flames in wall sconces and chandeliers. A crowd milled around the refreshment tables.

She started to turn her head and speak to Grant, but he was hailed by another man cutting toward them.

"Hello, Worth," said a merchant Annie knew from shopping downtown.

Grant extended his hand to the other man. The two struck up a conversation, and some of the light went out of Annie's polite smile. She ought to feel relief that she'd handled an awkward conversation and kept her secret, but as she slipped back toward the ballroom, she felt a little let down. It had been dangerously exciting to stand in the moonlight with a man as strong, handsome and sure of himself as Grant Worth. But if she knew what was good for her, she'd better not do it again.

Four

Back inside, Grant's mind returned to business. He'd worked his way through the crowd, saying hello to old acquaintances and shaking hands with new ones. Some of the party were saying good night and leaving.

Now was his chance to tell Everett T. Marsh to his face that on no terms was his land for sale. If Marsh wanted to run a railroad through the mountains, he'd have to choose a different route.

Downstairs in the front parlor, Everett was bidding some friends goodnight, and turned to face Grant as he approached. He surveyed the rancher with an open, friendly smile that didn't fool Grant.

"Ah, there you are, Worth. Ready to have a chat? I have some fine cigars we might try. And I'm sure there's some brandy around here somewhere."

Grant nodded. He instinctively resented the railroad man, but there was no point in being uncivil. The differences were inbred. Grant was used to the wide open spaces, long days in the saddle; a hard day's work with only a saddle for a pillow when he'd been on the trail. He felt only distaste for men like Everett Marsh, racing to squeeze big profits from near slave labor because the silver mines needed railroads, and politicians wanted Denver to prosper.

It made his blood boil to recall the lives it had cost to

build the Central Pacific east to beat the Union Pacific to Provo, Utah. And no matter what some people said, Grant knew in his gut that the race had been about greed. The railroad who laid the most track got the most money and land in grants from the government. But Chinese laborers died under snowdrifts to get the rails over the Sierra Nevadas. It wouldn't surprise him if Everett Marsh employed just such tactics to build into the mountains and down to Santa Fe, and maybe into Mexico.

As they strode through to the center parlor, Grant focused on these differences. It made him even more determined to keep his land free from the likes of Everett Marsh.

Everett slid the pocket doors shut, so they could have some privacy, and then held out a Cuban cigar.

"No thank you," said Grant.

"Brandy?"

Grant accepted a glass and tipped it back, downing most of the contents. The warmth suffused him, but did nothing to lessen the thundercloud forming in his mind. He considered his opponent. A substantial, proud man with well-trimmed sideburns, high forehead and gray streaks through dark hair. Only the nose and cheekbones resembled Annie's features. He wondered fleetingly what Annie's mother must have looked like. The thought made him frown. Here was a hard man indeed, a man so opposed to the theater that he had disowned his daughter for doing what she pleased. No kind, loving father, this.

How Everett Marsh treated his children was none of Grant's business, but it added to his irritation with the man, nonetheless.

Both men remained standing, taking the other's measure. Each was aware that to sit would give the other the advantage. Everett puffed on his cigar for a few minutes as Grant stared into the fire in the tiled fireplace. Finally Everett held his cigar aside and spoke.

"I understand your determination, Worth. Can't say as I blame you. You cattle drivers are used to letting your cattle roam free, but the country's filling up fast. You're an intelligent man. Surely you can see that. Free range land is going to be carved up into individual homesteads. You'll have to string fence anyway. Then you'll need a railroad to carry your beef."

Grant drew a deep breath and let it out before he spoke. Blind emotion wouldn't help him express his thoughts clearly.

"That day hasn't come yet. And if I do string a fence along my boundaries, I don't want a railroad cutting it in half. You might not understand because it took sweat and suffering to build my herd and acquire that land. I built that ranch from the ground up. My wife and I put up every stick of the house unassisted when we came here. When she died, I traded ranch hands room and board and a percentage of my profit to help me finish the rest. My boys and I have worked hard to grow that herd. It's all been by the sweat of my brow, Marsh, and I'm just not willing to sell you one piece of dirt."

Everett slowly sat down in a leather-tufted chair, crossed one leg over the other and gazed up at Grant, who slung one arm along the marble mantel and tossed back the rest of his brandy.

"I don't begrudge you your hard work," said Everett slowly. "But your views are old-fashioned. Or outlandish, depending on how you look at it." Everett studied the end of his glowing cigar.

So he'd heard about the llamas, mused Grant. Well, let them laugh. He still believed he knew a good thing in a pack animal when he saw it. And he didn't want a bellowing steam engine running over stock that might jump a fence either. Or a railway line to keep a herd from moving to another part of the valley when the grazing was better there. He tried to explain some of this in terms Everett Marsh could grasp.

"I rotate my pastures in the valley," he said. "When I pull my herd out of one pasture, there's still plenty of tall grass standing. If a dry year hits, there's still tall grass left shading the bottom areas so they don't shrink and dry up. If I fence my herds in, I can't do that. You have to have enough range land to leave feed on the ground during a wet year so there's something still there during a dry year. With a railroad cutting through, I can't do that.

"You may think my plans are outlandish, but I don't happen to think so," Grant replied to Everett's implied insult. "Admit it, Marsh. Profit is your motive. I've known your kind. Life and property mean nothing if it stands in the way of the almighty dollar."

His voice had an edge to it, but he didn't care if anyone on the other side of the doors heard it. He had a short temper and deep convictions and he wasn't about to let some slick business tycoon get the better of him. In fact, he was beginning to feel hemmed in by these stifling surroundings. He'd been in the required evening dress long enough and just about decided that this was the last of such affairs he would attend. If no one else shared his dream of a new breed of pack animals in Colorado, then so be it. These men had no vision. They were interested in nothing unless it was a sure, quick profit. Give him the plains and the high mountain valleys. Animals were better company than these city folks.

He set his glass on a small round table then turned to jut his chin at Everett Marsh again.

"You have my final answer, sir. You'd best start surveying a different route. I think you'll find the other cattlemen in South Park agree with my way of thinking. You'll get nowhere with your damn railroad up there."

Everett drew on his cigar then let the smoke circle about

his head. Then his dark, narrowed gaze nailed Grant to where he stood.

"We'll see about that," he said. "You are a man of conviction, Worth. But I'm afraid you may see the day when you are proved wrong."

Grant decided not to waste any more words on the argument.

"Good evening," he said.

He gave a quick nod and then strode to the double doors, which he slid open. As he suspected, a group of women at the far side of the next room broke off from their conversation. All stared at him with rounded eyes.

He paused long enough to bow. "Ladies," he said. Then he straightened and found the front door.

The dry, Colorado night air was just what he needed. As he declined a lift from one of the carriages leaving, he stretched out his legs and walked along the unpaved road. Lights dotted the fledgling city below the slope on which the newer houses were situated. His hotel was located clear over on Holladay Street close to the nearly dry Cherry Creek riverbed. But the walk would do him good and clear his head.

He passed other substantial homes, newly risen on this hill, and a large, sloping park set aside to build a state capitol. Denver was a sprawling western city, full of the carousing of cowboys spending their pay and of miners who hadn't seen women or much of a civilizing influence for months on end.

It was a place of opportunity, and Grant didn't begrudge the hardworking souls who'd come here looking for that opportunity: men like him from the benighted south, or easterners with bleeding lungs, come to the mountains for the cure. All had hope. Some found their salvation. Others died trying. It was only the unscrupulous industrial barons he resented. Men who built railroads on other men's backs. Men who hired near slave labor, negro or Chinese, to dig out their gold and silver, who cared little for the sufferings of the workers but who built show places for rich and idle wives and pampered children. Such men made him sick to his stomach.

When he reached the boisterous throngs going in and out of saloons along Larimer Street, he passed them by. Tomorrow was Sunday, and he was meeting Billy Joe and two of his ranch hands who were riding down from the ranch. They would put up in Denver in the evening so as to be on hand Monday morning to help him unload the first of what he hoped would grow into a small herd of llamas in his mountain valley. Let them laugh at his doe-eyed creatures. He was of the firm belief that he would have the last laugh.

Wash day! Even though the Marsh family had live-in help, it was Hattie's job to supervise the Monday wash and Annie was expected to provide a good example. Hadn't it been drilled into her head that it was up to every good homemaker to set the standard? And of course the housewife usually cleaned the delicates and lace herself, or in this case assigned that task to Annie.

Dressed in a serviceable moss-green cotton day dress that allowed freedom of movement, and with her flaming hair tied back by a scarf to keep it out of her face, Annie plunged the long wooden spoon into the tub of hot water into which she had sliced some soap. She stirred it until it made a fine lather and then immersed the lace.

"Swish it gently, dear," said Hattie from her own tub. She was dressed in similar attire, including head scarf, and was engaged in washing some of her husband's white shirts. "If we are too rambunctious, the lace will tear."

"Yes, I know."

Maria emerged from the back door of the house, hauling a wicker basket full of freshly boiled clothes to the waiting rinse tub. The housemaid Dorthea, also hard at work, stopped to wipe her long, bony hands on her white apron.

"Not too much blueing," Hattie cautioned Dorthea. "Last time there was so much blueing in Mr. Marsh's collars that they looked slightly blue. Oh, dear."

Hattie grasped the plunger with the large metal cup on the end of the long wooden pole and plunged it up and down, agitating the clothing.

Annie swished her laces and then used a wooden spoon to draw them out and rinse them in a small pail of warm water. As she spread them out on a Turkish towel to blot them dry, she began to hum a tune from the operetta. The two servants and her stepmother chose that moment to fall silent, and Annie paused mid-phrase. Embarrassed, she hastily pressed a second towel over the laces to dry them.

"Do continue, Miss," said Dorthea, from where she knelt before her tub. "That was a lively tune. I'm sure I've never heard it."

"Oh, hmmmm," said Annie, leaning on the towel that pressed the laces flat between them. "Just something from the operetta I went to see at the Wednesday matinee last week. Nothing special."

"Must have been very grand to go to the opera," chattered Dorthea. "Do tell us what it was like."

Dorthea might have been a pretty girl, but years of service had chafed her bony hands, and her narrow face was not flattered by the frilly white cap on her head.

Now why did Hattie seem to be staring at Annie so as she patted her laces dry? Annie coughed, trying to act normal. "Oh it was grand, all right. The costumes were very pretty, only with shorter skirts for ease of dancing."

"You mean the women showed their shin bones?"

"Well, of course. That is, from the audience, one could see above the ladies' ankles."

"I imagine the gentlemen enjoyed that," said the maid.

"Dorthea," said Hattie. "That is enough."

Annie concentrated again on the laces, only now remembering that she had forgotten to stretch them to their proper shape before the blotting and drying. She peeked under the towel and grimaced to herself. Trying to correct her mistake before it was noticed, she carefully grasped the lace collars and ruffles and pulled. Being almost dry, they hardly budged. A pulse of horror shot through her as she envisioned Hattie trying to re-attach a lace collar to one of her walking suits—for it had shrunk.

Fearing she could do little about it, she kept quiet and dipped into the warm water to fish out the next set of laces that had been soaking for two hours. She slid them into the tub of soapy water to swish them around, worrying about the shrunken lace.

She slid her eyes upward without moving her head. The other three ladies were occupied by their tasks, and the garden gate scraped open. Lin Chu sauntered in, pushing a wheelbarrow, momentarily distracting the others. Annie snatched up the ill-dried lace collar and plunged it back into the warm soapy water, praying that in the warm water, she could stretch it out again.

When all the laces were finally drying, Annie sat back on the grass and stretched her arms and legs. Hattie stood up while Dorthea emptied her tub on the gravel drive and then went for a pail of hot water to fill it up again.

"Annie," said Hattie, making her stepdaughter jump.

"Yes?"

Her stepmother wiped perspiration from her forehead with the back of her hand. Her face looked a little blotchy from the sun.

"There's something I'd like you to do this afternoon that simply cannot wait until marketing day."

"Oh, what is that?"

"I ordered some fresh trout from Mr. Schold, telling

him to let me know when some had been caught in one of the mountain streams and brought down on ice. He sent word that he has such a shipment in today. I simply must stay and oversee the rest of the laundry, but I believe he'll give you the fair price if I send you. Would you mind, dear?"

"No, no, not at all, Hattie. I'll be happy to go."

Anything to get out of spending the rest of her day on her knees out here, trying to keep her hands out of the damaging water filled with lye and fat. So saying, and still rocked back on her heels, she spread her hands out before her. Her long fingers stretched out, her translucent nails buffed just past the fingertips. A performer's hands must remain beautiful. She limped her wrists at the thought and raised her arms, draping her fingers dramatically.

Then she hastily drew her arms down, afraid to attract the stares of the two servants and her stepmother. Time was when her antics had amused them and she hadn't minded the reproving glances from the woman striving so hard to maintain a wholesome home. But now any mention of the theater, or of the tuneful melodies she played and sang on the pianoforte in the family parlor, gave Annie a stab of guilt. More than that, she was now plagued by fear that she would be found out.

There was another small niggling thought. The lie about her made-up twin had been an expedient to get Grant Worth off her trail and to keep her exploits from her brother, who had been with her in Central City and who would seize any opportunity to ruin his sister's image in the family so that he could have a good laugh.

But she realized that her father had disappeared into a sitting room to talk with the handsome Grant Worth. Surely he had not repeated anything Annie had said, for Father had said nothing. And that was not the sort of story he would let go.

She cleared her throat, wiped her hands and got to her feet. A trip to the market would be just the thing.

Upstairs, Annie quickly changed into her brown, gored walking skirt and tailored, fitted jacket. The severe suit was softened by the creamy blouse with lace jabot at the high neck.

Up went the reddish-gold hair into a practical chignon. Waved bangs covered her forehead. No time to fuss with the curling iron. The strands of her hair draped before her ears were limp waves, not the tight curls she wore for evening affairs. To keep the intense Colorado sun off her face, she donned her walking hat with the white ostrich plume and velvet bow.

Annie was a good driver and so took the trap by herself. The frisky gelding strutted along the unpaved road as if he, too, enjoyed getting out of his stall. She shared the wide, tree-lined street with a few other carriages and couples on horseback, some of whom lifted their hands or nodded as she passed.

In the business district, she slowed to a walking pace to negotiate wagons, carriages, riders and pedestrians. The odors of smoke suffused the crisp, dry air with the industry of the growing city. Canvas awnings shaded merchants, markets and an assortment of stores. Here and there a swinging saloon door slammed against brick or stone. She smelled the acrid fire from a blacksmith and the pungent smell of cattle cars being loaded on the railway sidings. The address for which she steered was located at Nineteenth and Wazee streets diagonally across from the Denver and Rio Grand freight depot.

As she found a spot to tie her horse, the fish odors from the market assailed her nostrils. After giving the horse some sugar, she plucked her handkerchief out of her reticule. Holding it to her nose masked some of the more earthy odors.

She was about to step onto the board sidewalk and enter

the Flint Mercantile when sharp cries came from the other side of Wazee Street. A gathering watched freight being unloaded from a train in the freight yard, half-hidden by the depot building. She was distracted by startled gasps and children pointing. Gentlemen removed their hats, scratching their heads as they stared. Shouts and cries from behind the depot seemed to escalate, though she could not see the action.

Leaving the fish purchase aside for the moment, she hastened across the street when there was a break in the traffic flow, drawn by whatever excitement was taking place behind the depot. She joined some matrons struggling to keep their children from raucous destruction.

"What is it, Mama?" cried one little girl, a smaller version of the mother, dressed in matching cherry suit trimmed with gold braid and embroidery.

Annie's eyes opened wide and her own gloved hand went to her mouth as she glimpsed the strange animal being led from the freight car. It looked like something out of a fairy tale. It might have been led by the rope tied to the halter around its head except that the huge, noisy crowd pressing forward to see it had spooked it, causing its huge, doe eyes to fill with fear. Its tall, pointed ears spread wide over the inquisitive face and then lay back as it jerked back its head.

The black cowboy strained at the lead to keep the animal from backing into the freight car, and the crowd shouted with laughter. But in the next instant Annie's surprise and amazement took another leap as Grant Worth joined the black cowboy and attempted to soothe the animal.

Grant was dressed in chaps fastened over his pants above sturdy boots. His canvas jacket fit tight over his muscular shoulders. The red bandanna around his neck drew attention to the handsome face under the brim of his tan felt hat. Seeing him again gave Annie a warm glow, and she had to suppress a grin as she watched him take control of the animal, calming it with some secret language so that it would walk out on the wooden ramp.

This was the llama he'd spoken of, and indeed it was a strange-looking beast. It could only be about thirteen hands high at the withers, but its long, shaggy neck led to a graceful head with long nose, rather like the camel to which it was related. Its thick, shaggy fur was mostly white with brown patches on rump and neck. Long, graceful, thin legs supported the thick body. With Grant taking the lead and coaxing it, it followed him down the ramp to the ground, a superior expression on its haughty face.

"Keep back, folks," Grant said to the crowd, lifting one hand to make a path for himself and the proud, round-eyed animal. It slowly blinked its long, dark eyelashes.

The amused crowd made way, and Annie moved closer. The animal's gait was elegant, too, the way it picked up its long legs and carefully planted the hooved feet down.

Annie caught Grant's eye as he came her way. A smile lit up his face and he touched his hat brim. He stopped with the llama's shapely head just behind his shoulder.

"Miss Marsh," said Grant. "It seems we meet again. I didn't know you'd be on hand to see me unload the first of my new prize animals."

"I didn't know I would be either. I chanced to come downtown and heard the ruckus. That is, I noticed something going on and came across the street."

She began to feel self-conscious and turned her attention to the llama.

"It's beautiful. Is it a she?"

"Yes, indeed. Due to drop a baby in a month. After that I'll be breeding them at the ranch."

He glanced behind him. "Billy Joe will take this one while I bring along the male." He patted the shaggy neck, encouraging Annie to reach up and touch the rather coarse fur.

"Pat her on the neck," said Grant. "Llamas don't like to be petted on the face or head."

"I see."

Mothers and children began to stare and point, though keeping their distance. Grant touched his hat again.

"Excuse me, Miss Marsh, I've got to keep this crowd at a distance or else they'll be in for a nasty surprise. Llamas have one bad habit I'd not like to introduce Denver citizens to just yet."

"What's that?" Annie said, recovered enough to glance again at his wideset eyes and solid cheekbones.

"Llamas spit," said Grant in answer to her question.

She jerked her hand back, the sensual moment interrupted by the fear of ruining her dress.

"Oh my!" She stepped back, and Grant turned his attention to the crowd.

"That's right, folks. Don't try to touch her right now. She needs some time to get used to things. Llamas are a curious beast and they'll get along with humans if you give them some room. Don't frighten her, now."

Annie watched as he talked in a confident, kind voice to the children who reached out from where their mothers clamped hands on little shoulders to keep them near their skirts. Grant led the llama on down the yard, but that was the last of the quiet as a new confrontation began.

The black ranch hand, who Annie surmised to be Grant's foreman, Billy Joe, rode forward on his brown mare with a long lead rope coiled over his pommel. The horse whickered at the sight of the llama and bobbed its head.

"Easy now," said Grant to the exotic beast beside him.

But the llama's front legs went rigid and its huge eyes widened. Its nostrils flared and the ears lay back. It lifted its regal head to emit a guttural screech that made Annie jump.

"I was afraid of this," muttered Grant, still trying to calm the animal.

He took the end of the longer lead rope Billy Joe tossed through the air and managed to secure it to the halter of the agitated llama. The animal began turning its hindquarters in a circle around where Grant stood working with the halter as the llama bared its teeth.

Annie winced, afraid he would get bitten. But he let go of the halter just as the lead rope went taut.

"Come on, you shaggy old camel," called the black ranch hand from his saddle, tugging on the rope.

But the llama only flattened its ears and danced sideways, making the children scream and the mothers pull them back out of the way of the worried beast.

Grant tried to clear a path. "Out of the way, please. Llama coming through."

Suddenly the llama must have decided it had had enough of these surroundings. It rocked back on its hind feet and lifted the front part of its body off the ground, towering above those within hoof-strike distance. Then it came down with a whack of hooves on hard-packed dirt and bolted forward.

"Whoa," shouted Billy Joe.

But the llama galloped past the horse. The rope only took seconds to play out and then he kicked his heels into his own shying horse as the horse charged forth after the llama.

The crowd burst out laughing. When Annie saw Grant's glare cast her way, she tried to suck in breath to stop laughing, but the tears ran from her eyes.

"Oh my," she said, trying to take in breath and stop laughing. The thunder on his face made her think he did not appreciate being laughed at.

His expression mellowed to grim determination. He leaned over to pick up the hat that had fallen off in the scuffle and replaced it on his head, pulling down front and back brim. He walked over to a wagon where his other ranch hands were loading up sacks of flour and feed. They knew better than to look at him.

Annie half-supposed he'd forgotten about her and thought it might be best to slip away. Chagrin now replaced her laughter, and as she blotted her eyelids with her handkerchief. Her chances of gaining a better acquaintance were worsening at every turn.

What good were further conversations anyway? As Grace Albergetti she could be something of a flirt, but as Annie Marsh, Grant Worth's attentions would never get past the fact that her father was a business opponent. So she turned away to march back across the street to purchase fish for the dinner table. The handsome rancher had no reason to cross her path again.

"Miss Marsh?"

She stopped dead in her tracks, then turned with a gesture as if to inquire whether he was speaking to her. He left the ranch hands to finish their unloading. The dust had barely settled where Billy Joe had galloped after the frightened llama.

Grant took a few steps toward her then squinted along the street. She followed his gaze, but crowds had closed the path horse, llama, and rider had taken out of town.

"I hope everything will be all right," she said.

He gave a grunt. "Llamas don't cotton to horses all that much. I suppose I was ready for a stir. I'll be more careful when I lead the other one out."

She dipped her head, hiding shyly under the brim of her bonnet. "I'm . . . I'm sorry they . . . that is, everyone laughed."

He moved his shoulders in a shrug, his glance forcing her to look up again.

"Don't blame 'em. Besides, that's not the point. When I show mountaineers how well they pack, that's when the business folk'll change their tune."

"That sounds like an interesting venture."

"Well, I'm sure it will be." He paused and she thought she heard the trace of a tease in his voice. "Guess I'll wait 'til the excitement dies down before I bring the other beast out. Nice of you to say hello."

She found it hard to look at his gray, inquiring eyes. "It was nothing. I was going to the mercantile anyway."

He seemed to be in no hurry to get away, and she fooled herself into thinking it was because he was enjoying the conversation. In another moment, all such thoughts were dashed.

"By the way, if you ever . . . write to that sister of yours, you tell her I enjoyed her show."

Annie's mouth paused half open, for she could think of no reply.

He reseated his hat. "Just a thought."

She watched his face closely and suspected that now he was feeling sheepish. She arched her eyebrows, but her wits failed her.

"I . . . shall. Mention it, that is."

He nodded. "Good day to you now."

He paused, looking more serious. "And you might tell your father that I haven't changed my mind."

The lines of his wide, rugged cheekbones hardened, and his eyes glinted to a darker hue of gray. "I hope he's surveying a different roadbed to Santa Fe. He won't get near South Park."

Annie swallowed with a now considerably dry throat. She gave a polite bob of the head and picked up the train of her skirt, squeezing the material in her hands nervously.

"I'll tell him you said so."

Another nod from Grant, then he touched his hat, took a step back and turned back to business.

She darted through an opening between wagons rolling by, one hand holding her bonnet firm. She made it to the other side before three buckskin-clad Ute Indians came down the street on their ponies.

Her mind spun as she stepped into Flint Mercantile and faced Mr. Schold with a blank stare.

"Afternoon, Miss Marsh," he said. "What can I do for you?"

It took several seconds before she collected her thoughts enough to reply.

Five

The next afternoon, after the women had ironed everything that they had washed the day before, Annie stopped by the mail tray in the entry foyer before Hattie could sift through the letters that had come.

Lola's scrawl and the postmark from Cheyenne were instantly recognizable. Annie snatched the letter from the tray and ran up to her room.

Tossing aside the scarf that had held her thick, tousled hair out of her face as she'd slaved over the irons in the kitchen, Annie threw herself on the bed, making the cords that held the mattresses within the sturdy bed frames squeak. She stretched out on her aching back and read the letter in her hands.

The Spanish dancer first gave a colorful description of Cheyenne and then remarked on how the acting troupe missed Annie.

"Would that you could be with us more often, my dear," the actress's words ran.

Annie's eyes sped over the scrawl and then slowed down when Lola listed the plans for engagements in more of the mountain towns. After a week in Cheyenne, they would again travel south. They would play two nights in Golden City and then go on into the mountains. Their destination was Fairplay, where they would perform their repertoire in the small theater there.

"Fairplay," Annie murmured, sitting up again. Near Grant Worth's ranch!

Of course she didn't know just where his ranch lay, but Fairplay was the chief mining town in the vast, rolling prairie that spread some seventy-five or so miles and nestled in the mountains at an altitude of ten-thousand feet.

Annie knew much of this because her aunt Letitia had married a homesteader there years ago. When Letitia's husband was killed in an accident, Letitia decided to stay on and run the ranch. She had some reliable help, and by then the herd was several thousand. The family used to visit Letty's small ranch in the summer.

Annie stretched out on her side, unfolding her legs and dangling the letter off the bed. She'd spent some time in Letty's fine log house and had ridden about the beautiful prairie on fine summer days. South Park was mostly treeless and rich in sun-cured hay for the herds that pastured there.

But they hadn't spent much time in Fairplay, "it being a might rough for a young lady," Annie remembered her aunt saying.

Probably Letty hadn't wanted to expose James to the evils of a wild and rowdy mining town either, but maybe the place was more civilized now. Just look at how refined Central City was getting, what with the opera house and the fine hotel. Maybe Fairplay had some solid citizens, churches and even schools. It might not be such a bad place anymore. A devilish plan took flight in Annie's active imagination.

"Oh, my," Annie sighed.

She rolled over and stretched out again on the fresh-smelling quilt, her hair splaying over the cotton-lace pillow shams.

A tune came to her lips and she tapped out the rhythm with her fingers on the mattress, her feet moving in time at the foot of the bed. Thoughts of the little theater high in the mountains in a mining town filled her mind with adventure. Closing her eyes she could almost smell the pine-scented air, feel the evening breezes in her hair.

There was a knock on the door. "Miss Annie," a voice interrupted her runaway thoughts.

"Yes, coming," she answered, pulling herself into a sitting position and shaking out her linen scarf.

It was the housemaid, Dorthea. "Excuse me, Miss," she said. "Miss Hattie said to fetch you for the icing. The cakes are ready to come out of the oven."

"I'm coming, Dorthea. Tell Hattie I'll be right down."

Hattie took advantage of the cook stove being kept at a constant temperature to heat the irons on ironing day so that baking could be done at the same time. Maria had slid her cakes into the oven over an hour ago. Now they would come out and cool. It was Annie's job to make the frosting.

She dragged herself from the bed, but before going down, she slipped Lola's letter into a cloth-covered box tied with a satin ribbon in which she kept a few mementos. In this household, there seemed to be no end to housework. There was housework from sunup to sundown, except on Sunday.

She shook her head and clucked her tongue as she retied the scarf about her head and then walked along the hallway runner to the stairs. Even if one had servants, a husband—she had read in a ladies' journal—always thought his food tasted better if the dishes were washed by the hands of the one he loved.

As she spun on the landing, her hand on the shiny newelpost, she paused. Grant Worth? What would he expect of a wife?

"Pshaw," she uttered, and dashed on down the stairs. He wasn't looking for a wife. He was smitten by an actress that didn't exist.

Annie stopped in her dash down the hallway toward the

kitchen at the back of the house. Her fingers rested for a moment on the chair rail above the hallway paneling.

"An actress who doesn't exist," she whispered to herself.

She walked more slowly to the kitchen, passing framed sepia prints of her God-fearing relatives. The last one happened to be a photograph of Aunt Letitia in a bridal gown and her husband, taken in a photographer's studio upon the occasion of their wedding.

Even in the stiff poses held so they would not move for the duration of the photographic exposure, there was a certain spark in their frozen eyes. Annie moved closer, looking hard at the photograph in its oval frame.

"Aunt Letty," she mused. It would be good to see her again.

Then all thoughts of the theater, of Fairplay and of daring mining towns were banished as Annie entered the kitchen and took up her position over the mixing bowl. Maria lugged the canister of sugar to the tall kitchen worktable and dropped it with a thump. And soon Annie was pushing butter, sugar, cocoa powder, and grated orange peel around a mixing bowl with a wooden spoon.

That evening after dinner the family drifted to the parlor to enjoy some relaxation after the day of labor. James and Everett had been at their respective offices, and Annie and Hattie had ironed and baked all day. Annie had barely had two hours time to recuperate in her room, re-reading Lola's letter.

She'd managed to freshen up for dinner, piling her hair atop her head and weaving jet beads into it. Her green silk rustled softly as she got up from the tapestried settee and strolled over to the pianoforte. The upright instrument gave a ringing tone, and was often the center of family entertainments with Annie at the keyboard.

Her hands ran idly over the keys, picking out a little of

the melody, "The Rose of Tralee," then she took down one of the songbooks that lay scattered on top of the piano. Flipping open the pages, she came to some of her favorite tunes of the day and played them straight through, singing at first to herself and then more loudly, just to hear the sound of her voice. She gave particular gusto to "Oh! Susannah."

As her hands thumped down on the final chords of "The Sun Will Shine Again," Hattie laid down her sewing.

Annie wound up her recital with a lively Mazurka, fairly rocking off the piano stool with it. James leapt to his feet and pulled Hattie out of her wing chair.

"Play it again, Sis. Hattie and I will practice the steps."

Annie pounded out the Mazurka, while behind her, the thumps of the dancers and the near brush when they came her way were witness to James throwing his stepmother around the room. At last this produced a growl from Everett, who'd been trying to read.

"While the rest of you tear up the rugs down here, I believe I'll just go to my study for a while before I go up."

Hattie fanned herself with a cardboard-backed picture from the viewfinder, looking guiltily around the room to see if they'd broken anything. "I won't be long, dear."

Everett shut his book, pulled himself to his feet and kissed his wife on the cheek.

"Good night, Father." Annie jumped to her feet herself, so that the three of them could practice one of the latest dance steps to the tune of a Scottish reel. After that, even Annie was breathless.

"I'd better go up, children," said Hattie, whose normally pale, but fine-boned, cheeks were tinged with pink.

She gathered up her sewing, the thread trailing behind.

"Wait." Annie picked up the unraveling thread and handed it to her stepmother.

"Oh, dear," remarked Hattie, examining the work that

had come undone. Then she glanced guiltily toward the stairs. Her husband had gone up a good half hour ago.

"Good night, dears," she said to the young people and then hurried into the hallway and took to the stairs, hair half undone by the dancing.

Annie collapsed onto the upholstered horsehair sofa. Her veins sang with exhilaration, even if her limbs longed for a rest.

James tossed himself into a upholstered, walnut armchair.

"I want to dance, James," she said, throwing her arm across the carved back of the sofa in a dramatic gesture.

"You just did."

She drew herself around straight again. "Oh, you know what I mean. I want to do real dancing, with real musicians, fancy dress and . . ."

"Oh, you mean you want to go to a ball. Well, wasn't Hortense Morgan's soiree the other evening enough for you? I daresay there'll be more parties in the weeks to come. You've nothing to worry about if it's dancing you want."

She leaned back, exhaling her breath. She daren't tell James what she really meant. It might spoil her plan.

Plan? Well, her devilish thoughts were taking that sort of turn. She couldn't help it. She walked her fingers along the narrow, polished walnut arm of the sofa.

"I'm going up," she said. "I have some letters to write."

"Oh, really?" James gave a yawn. "I guess I'll get some fresh air before I turn in. Tomorrow is a work day, you know."

Annie sighed and grumbled. "At least it's marketing day for Hattie and me. Better than washing and ironing."

But this last remark was lost on James, who had wandered down the hall toward the kitchen and the back door.

Upstairs, Annie replaced her dress in the wardrobe, then unlaced her corset with a sigh of relief. Once in her nightdress, she let her hair down and brushed furiously. As she gazed at her image in the gilt-framed mirror suspended above her dressing table, she daydreamed.

A picture of Grant Worth tipping his hat to her as she left the freight yard lingered, giving her a warm feeling. She sighed and put down the brush. She must get over thoughts of him. He was not the sort of man her father would want to come courting. Not when they were engaged in a deadlocked battle over a strip of land. She pressed her lips closed grimly. Her father always got what he wanted, and she imagined this was no exception. The problem was that she sensed in Grant the same stubbornness as that in the Marsh family.

What if she were to help Father? If she visited Aunt Letty for a couple of weeks in South Park, she might get to see Grant again. Letty probably knew him. They might get to talking about the land.

"Oh, pshaw," she said to herself, tossing her hair over her shoulder and getting up to walk to the canopied bed.

"He hasn't expressed any interest in calling on *you,*" she said to herself. "Only *her.*"

She turned down the gas lamp mounted on the wall beside her bed and then lay in the darkness.

"Grant Worth," she sighed as she let her mind ponder all pleasant things, gradually letting sleep take over.

When a letter came from Aunt Letitia the following week welcoming any of the family who might like to sojourn up to her place for the hot summer months, Annie took it as an omen. It wasn't that hard to persuade her family that she should go. Everett was too tied up with business in town to think of going. James didn't get a holiday from the bank for another month. Hattie didn't want to leave James and Everett alone, so Annie was spared any company at all on her journey into the mountains.

The stagecoach started before dawn in the cool of a June morning and rumbled fifteen miles from the stage office in Denver across the undulating plain to the foothills. With the earliest light, they entered the foothills, where the valley was studded with sandstone rocks, until they swung into Turkey Creek Canyon. Here the road ran along a shelf cut from the mountainside among thick underbrush and pine.

As the road climbed and the sun rose at their backs lighting the world before them, the travelers were met with grassy mountain meadows and wooded slopes. The white-barked aspen sparkled in all their glory, the green leaves rustling in the morning breeze. They stopped for lunch at a way station at the north fork of the Platte River, forty-four miles from Denver.

From there on, the valley was dotted with small farms, the grassy parks and thick groves of trees lush on the mountainsides. At long last, they came to the highest elevation before the park was reached at Kenosha Pass. Where the road came out at the rim of the park, there was a grand view. Far-stretching country lay several hundred feet below, bathed in the pink glow cast from the western sunset, painted in all its most brilliant colors.

Annie leaned her head out the window to see the breathtaking view. The air was intensely clear, and the distant mountains brought near. To the west, the deep blue mountains surrounded the edge of the golden valley. Further south, serrated peaks rose loftily with veins of snow in granite crevices where the sun never reached.

Then the stage jolted down and across the rolling valley until it reached the chief town of the park, and the driver brought his team to a halt. Stiff-muscled from the long trip, but exhilarated to be here, Annie stepped down from the stage.

There had been a slight discrepancy between the date she had told Letty to expect her and the day she actually arrived in Fairplay. She said she would come Tuesday a week hence and decided to trust to her luck that Letty would have no reason to write to her family in the meantime. She explained to Letty that she would be visiting friends in Fairplay first so that there would be no alarm if someone did mention that she had left Denver.

It was a small enough chance to take for an adventure she couldn't resist. Thinking all of this over as she stepped onto the boardwalk in front of the hotel, she gave a small sigh. It was a weakness to follow these impulses, she knew that. Her own mother, her father, and her stepmother had done their best to give her a proper upbringing and good schooling. She knew that virtue was its own reward.

But there was something, a streak of wildness she got from somewhere, that made her want to taste everything that came her way. The west was a place full of life and opportunity. Nothing ventured, nothing gained.

"There you are," came a cry.

And in the next minute Lola was sashaying toward her, clad in a cherry velvet walking suit arrayed with lace jabot cascading down the front.

"Ma cherie," called Marcel, only a step behind her.

And then they were exchanging kisses on the cheek. Lola took her arm while Marcel saw to her small trunk and carpet bag.

"We were so excited that you were coming," crooned Lola. Her dark eyes glimmered in her lovely, angular face. "It is all arranged. You will have the room next to mine at the hotel. The theater is small, but Marcel has done wonders with the scenery. You can rest tonight and then we start rehearsal tomorrow morning."

"Are you sure you really want me to perform?" asked Annie, halting to face her friend for reassurance. Now that she was this far, she had a few small doubts.

"Why not?" said Lola. "You will learn the cancan with great ease. You can kick your legs, can't you?"

"I suppose so."

"And you will support me in my leading role. I have a most exciting part in the olios where I appear in a body stocking tied to a horse that carries me across the stage, if only there is room for the horse."

"Isn't that dangerous?"

Lola shrugged it off. "Perhaps. But if there is no risk, there is no excitement for the audience. What do you think?"

"I suppose you're right."

"We have already listed your name in the program."

This brought Annie to a stop. "My name?"

Lola gave a sly wink. "Your stage name. Grace Albergetti."

Annie's heart started beating again. "Oh, well, then I suppose that's all right." She winced slightly, hoping it would be all right.

Marcel brought the baggage to the hotel, and in no time the two girls were tossing clothes about the brass bedstead that supported a decent feather mattress. All through supper in the hotel dining room, Marcel described the various acts they would present here before and at the intermission of the melodrama that was the main feature. Annie's head was awhirl with what they expected her to do, slightly guilty that she wasn't supposed to be doing it at all, and secretly anxious that she should do it well.

Her guilt won out after supper and by the kerosene lamp in her room, she hastily penned a letter to Hattie so that she wouldn't worry. She told her stepmother that upon arriving, she encountered old friends of her mother's who had invited her to stay a few days before going on to Letty's and that she had sent her aunt word.

Guilt assuaged, she folded and sealed the letter and gave it to the clerk downstairs at the desk to put in tomorrow's post. Then she determined to get a good night's sleep, which should be no trouble after the thin, brisk mountain air.

The next day sped by. She concentrated hard on the few lines she had to learn to appear as a minor character in the drama about two starcrossed lovers and a greedy villain who wanted the heroine of the piece (Lola) dead so that he could possess her father's mine.

Then there was the altering to be done on the costumes she was to wear. Marcel's older sister, Miss Vivian, was the company's wardrobe mistress, and her nimble fingers measured and stitched throughout the day so that everything would be ready by evening. While she worked, they gossiped gaily, making the time go by quickly and putting Annie at ease.

The dancing was the easiest part. After Lola walked her through the routines a few times, she felt confident of being able to prance around the stage and make no mistakes. And the other girls put her at her ease as well.

Even so, Annie's stage nerves built up by the night of the performance, so that while she looked forward to treading the boards, she had to concentrate on what she was to do to prevent making a mistake.

Her first entrance was in the middle of the first scene. Standing in the wings, she struggled with nervousness. When Marcel touched her shoulder and nodded to her, she took a deep breath to try to calm the butterflies in her stomach and stepped out onto the stage.

She played the part of Lola's landlady's daughter and had only to comfort Lola and listen as the poor heroine told that she was to be evicted because she couldn't meet her rent. Lola had most of the dialogue, and Annie remembered useful expressions gleaned from elocution classes at school.

Her teacher's words came to her, "Gesture is magnetic

and reveals inner emotion in a way that speech is powerless to express."

And so as she struck poses of sympathy, pity and uttered her promises that she would do what she could to change her mother's mind, she began to feel more confident.

In between her speeches, she had time to glance across kerosene footlights at the lip of the stage to the audience, partly in shadows owing to the lowered house lights. Straight-back chairs held mostly gentlemen, and a few ladies, dressed in all manner of suits and evening dress. The faces were but pale ovals, and she only saw the bodies stir and heard their whispers as the dramatic scene was carried out.

"Do not fret, my dear," she uttered just before her exit. "I will speak to Mama. Surely she will not toss you on the street."

"Oh, thank you, kind miss," Lola responded with soulful eyes from where she was draped across a hassock. "You are a sister of my heart, and if ever I can repay this kindness, be sure I will do so."

Annie turned to march off the stage. This time she could see more of the people filling the chairs from the first few rows to the back of the small house. A particularly long pair of masculine legs stretched out into the side aisle. And Annie's stray glance along the torso saw a familiar brocade vest and white shirt. She sucked in a breath, not daring to look at the face, but her heart skipped a beat as she exited into the wings.

Marcel squeezed her arm and smiled, and then she retreated into the darkness behind the scenery to go over her next lines. But the image of who she imagined she might have seen, stretched in his chair along the aisle, proved too much of a distraction. She had to know. Had Grant Worth come to see Grace Albergetti again?

Her mortification was second only to the thrill that raced through her at the thought of him. But the wings of this stage were tiny, and the other performers were huddled there, ready for their entrances. As the villain took to the stage, his voice boomed out over the house, eliciting the hisses of an audience that was thoroughly enjoying it all. Annie would not get a glimpse of the house until her next entrance.

For twenty minutes, she fidgeted. Finally, Marcel turned to look for her and she scooted up to get ready. He gave her a nod and she returned his smile. Then as the voices of the actors portraying the landlady and the villain rose in an argument with poor Lola, a blank was fired from the gun in Lola's hands.

Annie's scream was real, so loud was the gun's report. Then she ran onto the stage, grasping her friend's hand and throwing it upward.

"No, you'll be hanged if you murder them," she said with emotion. "I will be your witness. They have treated you unfairly. My own mother has been blinded by this man."

Lola surrendered the gun, the actors brought the scene to a close and then the curtain lowered for the intermission. But as it did, Annie stole a glance and felt her heart jump up into her throat.

Obviously enjoying himself, Grant Worth leaned back in his aisle chair and applauded, shouting bravos. He looked even more distinguished than she remembered him, dressed in dark suit and string tie dangling over the brocade vest. His high, snowy collar stood in relief to his sun-tanned face.

Annie gulped, then watched the rim of the curtain drop to the stage.

She hardly heard Lola's words as they went back stage. Marcel fussed over everyone's makeup and costumes, and somehow the intermission flew by. Annie tried to discipline herself for the second act so as not to make any mistakes. She didn't look at the aisle this time. Then they were hustled off again to dress for the olios. She hadn't time to think as she slipped into the red satin and black ruffles for the cancan, her net stockings secured by scandalous red garters.

In the daring costume, her exhilaration flowed. She tried to concentrate on the dance she had learned only yesterday. And Lola came by to give her a squeeze on the shoulder, cooing her encouragement.

But as the girls lined up in their scanty costumes with full swishing skirts over ruffled petticoats and black net stockings, Annie had an attack of fright. Never had she worn such a costume, a fitted, strapless bodice with tight corset pushing her bosom high and flaunting it. Her hair was high on top of her head, displaying her long neck, and the daring skirts only came to her knees, in a shocking display that was all part of the dance.

But she could only swallow as the upright piano and banjo struck their chords and the velvet curtains scraped upward.

"Ladies and gentlemen," Marcel called from stage right. "What you've all been waiting for. The famous cancan!"

For a second, Annie thought she would not be able to move, her feet frozen to the wooden stage as the mass of cowboys, miners, dandies and citizens alike in the audience stood and howled. The noise and catcalls went on long enough that the musicians paused before playing the introductory chords again.

One, two, three, move, Annie mentally counted and then her feet did the steps she had learned. Her mind went blank, only her body moved, swayed, kicked. Now the girls reached for each other's shoulders, and in a rhythm that thundered through her bones and thundered through the house, the line of girls kicked in unison, skirts flying, legs exposed, to the delight of the audience.

They turned, they pranced, they regrouped. And each time the chorus seemed louder, more exuberant. Annie executed the circling of her leg with lifted knee and finished the dance in the whoop as the girls turned and tossed their skirts up behind them.

Then she fled for dear life with the rest of them off the stage. By the time she reached the tiny wings her temples were throbbing, perspiration dripping between her breasts. Then she was shoved back on the stage once again, taking her place in line.

"Encore, encore," the voices shouted from the audience.

Annie's face was scarlet. She only flicked an eye in Grant's direction, but there he was, standing and hollering with the rest of them, swinging his hat over his head and whooping with his cowboy friends.

The calls for encore went on and on until finally the musicians once again began the introduction. Annie was breathing hard. She had practiced the dance in her room, but Fairplay was four thousand feet higher in altitude. Still, she kicked high, threw her head back proudly. She was one with the chorus line and felt every bit as talented and limber as the rest.

She realized she was smiling when they reached the end of the dance. Up went the skirts, though Annie let her generous petticoats cover most of her derriere, and then they were running off the stage.

"Wonderful, girls," Marcel was saying as they filed passed him. "*Mes chéries,* you are all wonderful. We give them no more now. They will pay to come back tomorrow."

Panting for breath, and dying of thirst, Annie found herself in the crush of giggling girls, headed back to the dressing room. But she followed Lola into the dressing room the star had insisted they share.

"Come, you can change in here."

Lola chattered about the performance as she unfastened her friend's costume from the back. But all Annie could do was stare into the ornately framed mirror at her flushed face, the wide amber eyes, reddened lips and the undone hair.

Then she shook herself awake to undo Lola's costume. She stepped out of her skirts and hung them on one of the wooden pegs on a stout plank affixed to the wall for just that purpose. Then she pulled one of Lola's wrappers firmly around her, pulled a wooden chair to the dressing table and reached for the cold cream to cleanse her face.

She heard the din of voices on the other side of the door, and then came a tap. Lola called out a merry, "come in," which shocked Annie, since they were not properly dressed yet.

Lola swiveled in her chair to see who was there, while Annie stared into the mirror. She felt her heart lurch to see that Grant Worth stood there, his tan felt hat held by the brim in his hands. Marcel stood behind him to the left and cleared his throat.

"Miss Albergetti," said Marcel, his voice pitched a little high. "This gentleman remembers you from Central City and wished to pay his compliments."

She met Grant's eyes in the mirror for a moment and saw the flicker of interest there. The planes of his face were expressionless, but then a smile touched the corners of his lips. She swallowed, tightened the wrapper around her and turned slowly to extend her hand.

He took a step into the dressing room, filling it with his self-possessed manliness. He gave her a slow, easy smile and bowed over her hand in a gesture that made her glad she was sitting down. She took a breath to speak and then snapped her lips shut again. She was Grace Albergetti now. She mustn't trap herself by making reference to anything he'd said to her as Annie Marsh.

She relaxed her lips and gave a closed-mouth smile as he straightened himself.

"My compliments," he said. "The performance was most enjoyable."

"Thank you, Mr. Worth," she managed, fluttering her eyelids as she felt her face warm.

He turned to praise Lola as well and bow over her hand. "A most agreeable performance, Miss Bonitez. I would not have missed it for the world. My compliments."

Annie thought that Lola did a better job of accepting the flattery, but of course, she was used to it. As the rancher and the star exchanged pleasantries about the performance, Annie sat stiffly in her chair, staring at Grant's profile, the long, hard-muscled, length of him in the tailored frock coat and trousers. Even though he was dressed in town clothes, they did nothing to hide the outdoors man inside them. His broad shoulders and the way he spread his feet slightly, elbows bent, fingertips grasping the hat brim, conveyed his life on the high plains.

After talking with Lola for a few minutes, he turned back to where Annie had not moved a muscle. He dipped his head.

"Do me the honor, Miss Albergetti, of having supper with me. The hotel dining room does a fair steak. You must be ravenous after your exertions."

Her eyes widened at the reference to the dancing, and she felt embarrassed all over again. But the way his glance fell from her face to her shoulders and swept over her figure before returning in obvious pleasure to her eyes again, made her tingle with daring.

"I would be honored," she said. "If you will give me a few minutes to change."

Then she whirled around and busied herself at the dressing table as she watched him replace his hat on his head and settle it by holding the front and back brims in true cowboy fashion.

"I'll be outside," he said, smiling at her in the mirror.

He bowed again to Lola. "Ma'am."

Then he exited, closing the dressing room door behind him.

Annie exhaled a shaky breath and Lola gave a suggestive murmur, her eyelids lowered seductively. "Hmmmm, an admirer. There, you see? You have impressed a fine gentleman. This time you will dine with him, and all will be well."

"What do you mean, all will be well?"

Lola gave a sly grin. "That is for you to say. I just meant that he likes you. It is good to have a gentleman admire you, no? Hmmmm. A handsome gentleman with strong arms and soft lips can bring pleasure. I think you will enjoy yourself." She reached across and gave Annie's arm a squeeze. "You have earned it."

Annie nodded, took a deep breath, fought off any forebodings and concentrated on becoming Grace. As she put on an evening gown in which to dine, she wondered if she ought to tell Grant the truth. But the sensual looks he had given her, and which aroused new feelings in her, were too exciting to mar. If he were told the truth, he would be made a fool and word would get back to her family. For she'd no doubt that Grant would use this as further ammunition in his refusal to deal with her father over the railroad.

Ignoring the complications, Annie tied a velvet ribbon and cameo around her throat. Her blue satin gown exposed her creamy flesh, so she draped a black lace cape around her shoulders to protect herself against the evening chill and tied the ribbon at her throat. Her hair was ornamented with an ivory egret and twin garnet earrings dangled from her ears.

She gave herself a secret smile in the mirror. This was better than one of Lin Chu's tricks. Her misgivings fled as she imagined Grant's face once more. Already rapture sang in her veins. So what if this were a prank. She determined to enjoy it, if only for one daring evening.

She and Lola touched cheeks and gave each other a

small, delighted squeeze, then Lola held her friend at arm's length.

"I think being Grace Albergetti suits you, my dear," said the actress in a purring, conspiratorial tone. "By the end of your time with us, you may consider changing your identity completely."

Lola laughed and Annie smiled. It would never come to that, but she was feeling deliciously wicked at her little ruse. She picked up her trained skirt and approached the door. As she opened it to peer out, she saw that Grant leaned against a post, several paces away. His hat was pulled low over his brow, and his arms were crossed as he idly watched the crowd mingle backstage. The sight of him thrilled something deep inside her.

Then he saw her, tipped up his hat, lifted his chin and waited for her to cross to him so he could offer his arm. She saw the smile of pleasure on his face as he turned to escort her out into the night, and wicked pleasure stole along her veins. In the next moment they stood together on the board sidewalk. Kerosene lanterns cast a soft glow, and tinkling piano revelry issued from swinging saloon doors down the street.

Grant inhaled a breath of pine-scented, mountain air then leaned his head toward her, sending her heart spinning inside her and making her feel light-headed.

"I hope you have an appetite, Miss Albergetti. I surely do."

He tightened his grasp on her arm, and she melted in his direction, giving him a flirtatious smile.

"Please, call me Grace."

Six

"I met your sister," Grant said to the lovely vision in blue satin and black lace beside him. "She told me of your circumstances."

Fleetingly in his mind's eye, he saw the other sister, looking much like this one with a winsome smile, but fettered by her own circumstances. He hadn't believed the story about the twins at first, but here was the living proof.

Fortune had favored him to run into this Grace Albergetti again. Having seen the playbill that was circulating in town, he made a point of being at the show. Perhaps he was treading on dangerous territory, considering who their father was. Maybe morbid curiosity made him want to see Grace again. He found that the more he had watched her prancing about on the stage, the more he wanted to know about her and about the rest of the Marsh family.

And he felt as if he knew her already, having learned of her from Marsh's other daughter. The rip-roaring cancan had sent him backstage to investigate. Blood flowed in his veins in a way he hadn't allowed it to since his courting days. It was a powerful desire. Everett Marsh be damned, he couldn't stay away from this lovely creature.

He liked the feel of her hand in his arm, with just a slight, tentative pressure. He loved the coppery color of her hair, flaming under the lamplight. The perfection of her figure was not lost on him either. He cleared his throat, glad they were headed for a quiet supper at the hotel dining room to get to know each other. He didn't like to rush things.

As soon as she pulled the strings that tied her cape together, he happily reached to take the garment and drape it over the back of her chair. The smooth, graceful shoulders and the tempting decolletage sent a surge of desire through him.

When they were seated at the linen-covered table and had selected from the menu, Grant took his time studying the enticing young woman across from him. She enhanced her lovely features with a trace of artifice, but that would be expected from a woman of the stage. And when she looked at him seductively from her lowered lids, he took that, too, as being a practiced gesture. Orneriness had tempted him to get to know his opponent's daughter. That it would lead to no good was probably true. But now Grant couldn't rein in the reckless desire to talk to this young lady.

"How long have you been with the troupe?" he asked after the waiter had uncorked their champagne and filled each crystal goblet.

Her reddish-brown brows went up, but her cherry red lips curved upwards. "Oh, two years or so. I sometimes play with other troupes as well. And I do concerts."

"Oh, I see. Then your star must be on the rise."

"Mmmm, perhaps."

"To your success," he said, raising his glass to clink with hers.

He liked the way she tilted her head coquettishly. It sent the champagne gliding through his limbs in a pleasant way. He let more bubbly wine slide down his throat. She let her eyes close and open slowly as she savored the taste. He wondered suddenly, a little possessively, if she drank champagne often and with whom.

Then she settled her gorgeous, glittering eyes on him. Eyes the color of cream sherry. "Is your ranch nearby?" she asked.

"Not far. I have frontage on Taryall Creek where I run eight thousand head of cattle, and I hope to raise llamas."

"Oh?" she remembered to look surprised. "Why llamas?"

He launched into his favorite topic, avoiding describing the episode in which his first animal bolted out of town.

"Provided they have water, a bale of hay and enough shade, they can be left alone for several days. The stud is conscientious of his duties, and the female delivers her young in ten minutes to an hour or so, usually in the morning."

"Do they, now?"

He cleared his throat, remembering he was talking to a lady.

There was a spark of humor in her eyes as she listened to him talk. "I've never seen a real llama, only engravings of them on posters. Tell me more about them."

He could tell she was imagining everything he told her. Her interest encouraged him to talk about himself, and about his spread.

He glossed over his experiences in the War Between the States at age 17, not wanting to dwell on them. But he told how he'd come north on the cattle drives from Texas. He spun for her the life of the cattle drive.

"That's how I discovered this valley. I was on the Dawson Trail that came right into the Arkansas Valley. I rode up here by myself once, scouting for the herd boss. When I saw this part I knew I'd settle here someday. It was several years later I had money enough to buy some land and build my own herd. When the railroads reached Denver, fattening cattle here became more profitable since we could ship them to the eastern markets."

"But you don't want a railroad coming clear up here."

His look darkened. "No."

"I'm sorry, I shouldn't have mentioned it."

"That's all right."

She tried to restore the mood and gave him a slow smile. "Your spread sounds fascinating. I'd like to see it sometime."

He leaned forward, his arm on the table. "Perhaps you will, if you're in the area long enough."

Then the platters of food came, and they concentrated on their meals. Grant refilled their glasses, and they ate with intermittent trivial comments. But he knew he was enjoying himself in a way he had not in a very long time. Perhaps it was the devil in him that made him want to keep company with her. He talked more about how he'd brought his wife out here and how they'd built up the ranch.

"She was a good woman, I still miss her. She died three years ago."

"I'm sorry."

Her voice sounded truly compassionate, and he could tell she wasn't acting. She returned her eyes to her plate out of respect for his feelings. It was a nice touch.

When he asked his next question, his voice softened, mellowed by his enjoyment of the woman across from him.

"Tell me about yourself. About your family, and why you left home. If you want to, that is."

Her mouth formed a round, silent, "oh." Then she set her fork down carefully on the edge of the glazed china plate and raised her head, chin slightly forward.

"I always wanted to sing and dance," she began. "When I lived at home, that is several years ago, I learned every piece of music I could get my hands on."

An impish expression came over her face. "Father hired a teacher to give us music lessons at a very early age. My teachers grew upset with me when I insisted on playing the lively tunes. I would hear them in the streets, or as I walked by a saloon. And soon I was playing them at home."

"What did your father think?"

"I don't know that he minded so much. My mother was alive then and she didn't know what to do. She couldn't stop me from playing what I wanted, but she would come into the parlor in a panic whenever Father came home so that I could change what I was playing to one of the masters. I guess she thought Father would be angry if he thought all the good money he put out on my lessons had led to my playing bar songs."

Grant grinned at her, warming to the way her conversation amused him. "And then?"

She shrugged her right shoulder. "You mean how did I come to leave home?"

He twiddled with the stem of his champagne glass. "I admit I'm curious. Your father thinks he's going to run a railroad down the middle of my ranch. He's wrong about that."

She creased her brows for a moment, and her words had a worried tone. "Well, that does sound like him. He does usually get what he wants, as I remember."

"At whose expense?" Grant reached for his champagne glass to take another swallow. He hadn't meant for his ire to show. His argument with Everett Marsh was not her fault.

She fluttered her eyelids. "I'm sure I don't know."

Grant decided not to comment. Still, he knew he was steering the conversation for his own satisfaction. If there were something to learn about his opponent in the railroad issue, he wanted to learn it, no matter what the source. He prodded her gently.

"Did you tell your father you wanted to go on the stage?"

She glanced sideways, looking a little unsure of herself. But soon her winsome smile returned. "No, that happened rather by accident. I made friends with Lola Bonitez and Marcel Dupres. And when they found out I had some talent, well . . . One thing led to another."

"I see."

She gave a sigh. "I left the family a note. A personal one for my sister of course. We've always been close. I said I just had to try going on the stage, even if it meant they disowned me. It was my destiny."

"I see." He gave her a salute with his glass. "And then they disowned you."

She batted her eyelashes slowly.

"Well, Father did. Annie does see me when we get the chance. She doesn't mind."

"Hmmmm. A loyal sister."

"Yes."

"What about your brother?"

"Who, James?" She blotted her lips with her linen napkin, then took another sip.

"Is there another?"

"No. Well, he doesn't speak to me either. Pretends I don't exist. I think Father would be angry with him if he did otherwise, so James must behave as Father wishes. I don't hold it against him."

"I see. What about your stepmother?"

Grace's eyebrows lifted. "Oh, she pretends I am dead to them as well. She must obey her husband."

He twisted the stem of his glass. The liquor was having its effects on him, and he was enjoying the sight of her more and more. Warm desire was creeping through his limbs and he pondered where this might lead.

"Interesting family. Sorry if I pried."

"Oh, no, that's quite all right."

After coffee and dessert he escorted her slowly from the dining room and up the carpeted stairs to the door of her room. She extracted the key from her beaded handbag then turned to thank him for the dinner.

But he knew he wasn't mistaken about what kindled between them. He tipped her chin upward with the tips of his fingers. Then he removed his hat, shielding their faces with it from any passersby. It was easy to slide one arm around her waist and lower his lips to steal a kiss.

Her lips were sweet and pliant and he let the kiss linger. Then he released her, resettling his hat upon his head. His eyes held hers for a long, speculative moment.

"Will you dine with me again tomorrow night?" he asked her.

He could see the way he had flustered her and it pleased him that he had that effect on her.

"Yes . . . thank you. That is, if you will be coming to the performance again."

He gave her a lazy grin, this time allowing his eyes to take their time as he let them drift down her figure. He brushed the base of her neck, just below the ear with his fingers.

"Wouldn't miss it. I'll have a front row seat."

"Well then," she gave a quick smile and then fumbled for the doorknob behind her. "Good night."

It seemed to him she fled inside and shut the door quickly. Even though she'd taken to the stage, her morals seemed to be intact. She was not an easy woman.

That satisfied him, he decided, as he stared for a moment at the panels of her door before turning to stride down the hallway to the stairs again. He would enjoy taking his time with her. Again it echoed through his head that he was playing with a stick of dynamite, wanting to bed Everett Marsh's daughter.

"Serve him right," Grant muttered to himself as he took the stairs.

He passed through the smoky lobby and went out in search of his horse. He hadn't allowed a woman to affect him like that since he was courting his wife, so very long ago, and those feelings had been buried for a long time.

He found using prostitutes somewhat distasteful. He'd had enough of that kind of wild living when he'd been a trail driver. Now he liked to take things slow and easy, savor getting to know a woman.

As he rode slowly down the street and into the darkness of the road that led to his ranch, he savored the image of Grace Albergetti, remembering her scent and the flavor of her lips. Lips he would kiss again.

Annie hurried to the window and lifted the lace curtains to peer into the street. Still trembling, she longed for just one more glimpse of him as he rode away. In a few moments, she saw him cross the street and unwrap his horse's reins with quiet deliberation. Around him, revelers celebrated. Piano music drifted down the street from the saloons. But Grant seemed oblivious to it all. His hat was drawn down over his forehead. Still, there was no mistaking those relaxed, deliberate movements of his as he checked his cinch and fastened his saddlebags. The horse's ears flicked forward in response to something Grant must have said to him.

Then he placed foot in stirrup and lifted himself up, turning the horse in the street and sitting tall in the saddle as he rode out of town.

Head over heels, Annie clasped a hand to her chest and sighed.

"I'm lost," she whispered to herself and then flung the hand outward and spun around the room until she landed on the colorful quilt that covered the rope-spring bed. Then realizing she was lying in darkness, she sat up and lit the kerosene lamp on the night stand. She was far too excited to sleep. Lola would still be out and there was no one to talk to.

She changed into a dressing gown and sat before a heavy walnut dressing table and applied cold cream to her face, wiping it off with a linen handkerchief to remove the last of the theatrical rouge and color from her eyelids and stroked the tangles out of her hair with long, languorous strokes.

He had kissed her! Perhaps no more than a show of gallantry to thank her for her company after dinner. But she would relive a thousand times in her mind the way he had tipped his hat to shield their faces and leaned down for the gentle kiss that had made her blood boil, leaving her stunned.

She uttered a long sigh. Of such stuff dreams are made. Surely pleasant dreams, she mused as she braided her hair in a long, loose braid to keep the tangles out in her sleep. Finally, she stretched out between the sheets and stretched tired, sore limbs. She had achieved her dreams of performing through an entire show, but she'd found new muscles in the process. Housework in Hattie's respectable home had hardened some of her body, but kicking her legs in the air and holding her arms up in gestures of the dance were new.

She gave several catlike stretches and then hugged the pillow, Grant's face lulling her into a peaceful sleep.

The next day she learned that Marcel was a hard taskmaster. Not satisfied with merely getting through the program on opening night, now he wanted to refine the performance, adapt each actor's delivery to the architecture of the small but noisy theater on performance nights. Annie was coached in pacing, gesture, how to throw her voice; how to look at the other actors on the stage but throw her voice into the house.

After some practice, Marcel instructed all the actors to save their voices for the evening. But of the dancers' legs, he was not so sympathetic. The girls donned their skirts to practice the cancan, and Marcel marched back and forth in front of them, his trousers tucked into high, black boots.

"Lift your hems higher," he commanded them, one after one until he'd achieved a uniform line of near perfection.

Annie struggled to kick as high as the others.

"Shoulders back," Marcel demanded from where he stood, hands on hips on the lip of the stage.

First without music, Marcel counting the steps, then with piano accompaniment. Exhausted from all the hard work, Annie could not believe her ears when Marcel leapt back up on the stage to give his comments.

"Good, good, very good. Now once more and sparkle. Smile mischievously. The audience must think you are a bit naughty. From the top."

The other girls grumbled and Annie wiped the sweat from her temples. She felt a moment of chagrin and the threat of tears. She knew she had the knack for performance, but she'd never experienced the grueling rehearsals. Praise was hard won.

Naughty! What did he mean by that? Nevertheless, she took a gulp of water backstage and slump-shouldered, dragged herself into line again. Lola appeared beside her in a dressing gown and hissed encouragement.

"Do not let him scare you, dearie. Your hard work will pay off."

Annie blinked the tears of frustration from her eyes and looked searchingly at her friend. Only now did she fully appreciate some of the life that Lola must endure. Being a star wasn't all glamour and praise.

"Do you think so?" she half-whispered, her voice cracking.

"I know Marcel," said Lola. "He may appear cruel, but he is an artist. It is the result he wants. Do not worry. Do your best, and the rest will take care of itself."

There wasn't more time for talk as the line of dancers started moving and this time shouting as they pranced onto the stage.

Grace, come to my rescue, Annie whispered to herself. And then a wicked smile did appear, beginning at the curl of her lips and then flashing into her eyes. She envisioned her handsome caller sprawled on his chair in the audience and felt a surge of energy throb through her. Back went her shoulders as she thrust her bosom forward, her head at a coquettish angle. Grace would do it thus.

"Flirt with me," called Marcel from the house as he clapped his hands to the lively beat of the twentieth rendition of the music. He threw them kisses.

The girls laughed and hooted, but for Annie, there was no need to do more than throw Marcel a few smiles from over a lifted shoulder. Thoughts of Grant's kiss gave her all the daring she needed. The chorus girls threw themselves into the final crescendo. With a shout they tossed their skirts over their heads as they exposed their ruffled drawers. Then with a kick behind them they ran off the stage.

"Brava, brava," shouted Marcel as he ran up the steps and followed them off. "Do this tonight and you will have them eating out of your hands."

He reached for the nearest chorus girl and planted a kiss on her cheek. Then he kissed all their sweaty brows in turn, including Annie's.

She was exhausted, but she felt the thrill of satisfaction. They had pleased him.

Lola smiled knowingly before she sailed out to begin rehearsing her number.

"Now go rest, my pets," ordered Marcel. "Don't eat too much. Half-past six for makeup."

In the dressing room, the girls chattered around her, but Annie hadn't the energy to talk. She sponged off with towel and basin, hung up rehearsal clothes and costume, throwing on chemise and street dress to make her way back to the hotel. Deciding her poor body needed some pampering, she stopped at the desk to order a hot bath brought up.

As soon as the steamy water arrived and was poured into the hip bath, she climbed in, soaking up the warmth. She would have fallen asleep in the tub had she not roused herself. But then she did fall asleep in the bed and might have been late had she not asked the maid to knock on her door at six o'clock to get ready to return to the theater. Once aroused, she dressed quickly. At the theater, she felt the smiles bathe her face as she came alive with the excitement. It felt daring to paint her lips so red, even for her supporting role in the melodrama.

"The lights will bleach you out, my dear," said Marcel when he came to inspect her. "You'll need more rouge on those cheeks. That's a good girl."

Then, standing in the wings, she felt a moment of breathlessness before she made her entrance. She didn't even sneak a look to see if Grant were there. Concentration was everything as she stepped onto the stage, wanting with all her heart to do her best for her fellow actors, for Marcel, and for herself.

The drama took over and she moved with ease through the scene, reacting and pleading with the characters in the drama. She was distantly aware of the audience, but allowed the stage lights to blur them. And yet she felt she made some improvement at playing to the house that she knew was there. She thought of it as a huge beast that needed to be appeased. While in the back of her mind she hoped Grant was there, she didn't allow thoughts of him to distract her performance. She couldn't risk making a fool of herself.

The players threw themselves into the climax as the audience's boos and cheers became noisier. With cries and sobs, Annie made her moves in desperate attempts to help save her friend's fate until at the last minute, the leading actor came to the rescue. Then the curtain was down.

She felt the hands of her friend grasp hers to lift her up for the curtain call.

She clasped Lola's hand and they proudly stood in line to take their bows. Only then did she focus through the footlights to the place on the aisle where Grant had sat last night. The chair was empty.

She gave a little gasp and almost forgot to bow, but then bent at the waist and stood up again accepting the applause. Her eyes shifted to the side again and relief swept over her, lighting her face with a grand smile. There he was, standing in the aisle holding a large bouquet of flowers with trailing ribbons. Her heart gave a leap and her knees wobbled as he started toward the stage.

But then she realized these were flowers for the leading lady, as it should be. The audience cheered as Grant strode up the steps at the side of the stage and in two steps was past Annie and bowing low in front of Lola, who graciously acknowledged the tribute. Annie clapped as well, too happy with everything to feel any jealousy. Grant handed Lola the flowers and then dropped a kiss on the cheek she turned to offer him.

But in the next moment, as he surrendered the bouquet to Lola, he turned and was looking at Annie. All the flowers had not gone to the leading actress; a single rose remained in his hand and he gave a slow bow and handed it to her.

She accepted the rose, her lips parted in surprise. She looked up into Grant's handsome face, at the broad smile and the gray eyes only for her.

"Thank you," she murmured, sniffing the rose. Then she held it against her heart.

The curtain came down around them all, and it was general hubbub. Grant shook hands with the others, people kissed and hugged, and Annie was swept offstage. In the wings she felt his hands at her waist, and his chin brushed her hair. She turned and had to steady herself with a hand on his brocade satin vest before her eyes found his.

"I'll wait until you change." His voice was caressing, the smile still lingering on his lips.

She could say nothing, only smell the rose again. Then with a quick nod, she hurried toward the dressing room.

The chorus girls were quick to tease her.

"Who is this admirer?" asked Chantal, one of the dancers.

Annie shrugged. "Oh, someone I met at Central City." The blush in her cheeks was not from rouge now.

"Ahh, and he is here to see you every night. I think you must be in love."

"Nonsense," she quipped back, turning so Vivian could undo her in the back.

"I saw the way he smiled at you. I know what he wants," Chantal said.

"Meeeeoowwww," howled another girl. "Get him for all he's worth."

Annie had to press her lips together, not trusting herself to respond. She knew what the girls meant. Men who admired actresses had one thing in mind. And girls like this probably tried to get as much out of their admirers as they could before they bestowed their charms.

The burning sensation in her cheeks now came from a flood of worried guilt. She was playing a dangerous game, swept off her feet because she was smitten with the big, handsome rancher. But he was chasing a phantom, an actress who didn't exist.

She threw down the powder puff, nearly letting worry spoil her euphoria. But then she swallowed and picked up a damp cloth slowly. *I have four days left. I'm not going to let worries upset me,* she told herself. I'm only going out to dinner. I can handle myself.

The efficient Vivian helped her into her satin gown for dining out and did up her back. She had a momentary flash of concern that Hattie might look in her wardrobe while she was gone and ponder why she had taken so many evening clothes for a stay on Aunt Letitia's ranch. But then, even at the high mountain valley ranch, they might dress for dinner or attend the theater!

"Have a good time, dearie," said Chantal, kissing her cheek.

"Tall, blond, and handsome, ooh, la la," the girls' voices followed her as she shook her head and left them.

Then she took a moment to draw a breath and stand tall, remembering who she was supposed to be.

Grant awaited her in the shadowy wings, his frock coat fitting him as nicely as ever. But she saw his smile as he approached her, and he took her gloved hand to kiss her wrist. Goose bumps ran up and down her spine.

"You look lovely, my dear," he said and tucked her hand under his arm.

Outside, Annie took deep breaths of the fresh, mountain air.

"I do so love the scent of pine up here," she said, as they strolled down the boardwalk.

Grant looked up at the twinkling stars himself and then back at her.

"Gives a man a feeling of a lot of space," he said. "That's why I like it." Then his tone formed an edge. "I just want to keep it that way."

"Your ranch," she said, glancing up at him. "For the cattle and the new llamas."

"That's right." He squeezed her hand. "But let's not spoil our evening by talking about business."

She gave him a flirtatious smile. "Whatever you say."

The host led them to a table at the side of the walnut-paneled hotel dining room. Grant hung his hat on a peg on the wall, and they began to study the menu. A group of men at a big, round table in the center of the dining room had finished their dinners and were calling for brandy. She had only barely noticed them before, but now Grant's attention wandered that way and then a shadow marred his expression.

Peeking above her menu, she saw his jaw tighten and his chin lift, but then the waiter came. He ordered champagne and the most expensive dinners on the menu.

His eyes found hers again and they sat without saying anything for a moment. Then his expression relaxed into one of pleasure, and he sat more comfortably in his oval-backed, brocade-upholstered chair.

"I want to know more about you, Miss Albergetti," he said. "Where will you go from here?"

She reached for the water glass to wet her lips. Then she found words, encouraged by the warm glow of his look.

"I don't know exactly," she said. "South, I think."

"I'd like to know more about your love for the stage. Where do you get your talent?"

"I don't know." She chuckled. "I used to perform at drawing-room entertainments put on by society ladies." Her grin widened. "But I guess they were too tame."

"I can see that."

"Cotillion dancing was too restrained for all the energy I . . . inherited from my . . . grandmother."

"Ahh. Then there was another one like you in the family. I wish I could have met her." His expression told her he was truly interested.

"She settled in the Ohio River basin with . . . Grandpa, years ago."

"Was she an entertainer as well?"

"Well, no. I just heard about her from my mother. Grandma did like to sing though. She'd get a sing-along and a dance going at barn raisings. Sang in church, at weddings, things like that. I always loved to hear about her."

"She must have been well-loved."

"She was. Played the piano after they made enough

money and built their house in town. Piano got swept away in a big flood."

"Too bad."

Annie nodded while they waited for the waiter to uncork the champagne and pour the bubbly liquid into the long-stemmed crystal. Then Grant lifted his glass and clinked hers. He gave her a slow wink.

"To Grandma, then," he said.

"To Grandma."

He swallowed with relish and took another sip. "I wonder," he mused, setting the glass down.

"Yes?"

"How was it that you got all that talent and your twin sister got none?"

Seven

She was saved from having to answer the question by one of the men who hailed Grant from the table full of gentlemen she'd noticed when they'd come in.

"Grant Worth," a voice called.

A chair scraped back and a blond-moustached man approached.

Grant turned his head with something less than enthusiasm and made a reluctant move to get up.

"Don't get up, man," said the gentleman. "Don't let me disturb your dinner. Who's the little lady?"

"Grace Albergetti," said Grant, leaning back in his seat but looking none too pleased, "allow me to introduce you to Harwood Hurley. Harwood, this is Miss Albergetti, presently appearing with the Gaslight Players at the Nesting Swan Theater."

Now that he was standing over their table, she could see that his nose was crimson, and he gave the appearance of having imbibed a great deal of liquor. He smiled broadly and swept his hat in front of him in a bow.

"Pleased to meet you, my dear. If you are any example of the loveliness to be seen at the Nesting Swan, I shall have to take in a performance."

"Thank you," she said with some distaste at the alcohol breath that wafted her way as he bowed.

He turned his attention back to Grant and gave a nod

of his head over his shoulder. "My friends here tell me you're still blocking progress for the valley by refusing to secede any of your land to the railroad."

"That's correct, Hurley. I don't want the iron monster here. All our cattle range freely here. My brand suffices to let the world know what's mine. A railroad means a fence, and a fence means less grazing for the cattle. I've explained it to Everett Marsh in terms I think he can understand. I'm afraid your friends will find the other cattle ranchers of South Park holding firm of that opinion."

Hurley gave a grunt.

Annie wished she were anywhere but here. She hadn't thought to observe the boisterous men at the round table in the center of the dining room. If they were railroad men, it was possible that she'd met some of them. She kept her face averted, terrified that Grant was about to mention the fact that her own father was the leader of the opposition. And that would lead to further curiosity and possible comment from the overbearing man beside their table.

"It's not only Everett Marsh and his Denver cronies. The Midland's coming through from Salt Lake to Denver. I suppose you'll stand in their way as well."

"Well now, I'll stand in the way of any who want to carve up free range here," was all Grant said. "I see no need to disturb a valley that's suited for running cattle. Large settlements are located elsewhere."

"From your point of view, that may be true," conceded Hurley. "But I'm afraid there's more pressure than you are prepared to fight. Take some advice, my friend. Give way while there's still time to negotiate the price you want. You may not have a choice if you wait too long."

At this, Grant unfolded himself and got out of his chair. Annie quailed at his anger. He was taller than Hurley by an inch or so and although he stood quietly gazing at the man and then sending a penetrating gaze over Hurley's shoulder to the men leaning back in their chairs at the center table, his intention was clear. Grant Worth was not a man to push aside.

His words were slow and edged with metal. Before he even spoke, some of the gaiety of the other diners around them quieted. A few turned to stare at the two men facing each other.

"Now, you wouldn't be threatening me?" Grant said with a slight turn of the head to include the gentlemen at Hurley's back.

Annie held her breath, hunching her head down in a protective, embarrassed gesture.

"No threat," said Hurley with his snakey smile. "Just friendly advice. You'll find the state will be on our side."

His words were loud enough for the others in the room to hear, as if he were reassuring them that no fight was about to take place.

"Go back to your dinner, Worth," said Hurley.

Out of the corner of her eye, she saw him wink in her direction. "Don't let me spoil your evening. I just thought I'd take the opportunity to let you know the mood of those in the governor's office. Just in case you decide to change your mind."

She saw the rigid line of Grant's cheekbones, saw the corner of his mouth draw downward, and the simmering thunder in his stormy eyes.

"Tell your friends to mind their own business," he said. "They're not wanted in this valley."

Hurley held his hands up in a gesture of surrender. "I'm sure they will attend to their own business," he said, his words weighted with meaning. "I'm just trying to make you see sense."

He lifted his hat again in Annie's direction and squeezed between the other tables to return to his own.

Grant sat down and threw his back against the chair, one arm sprawled across the table, his mood black. She'd been saved any involvement, but still felt stunned by the angry words exchanged. That her own family was part of the dilemma brought home to her even harder the explosive situation. She pressed lips together wishing she could disappear. She'd half thought to come here to learn more about this business, but now she felt she was in too deep. Oh, why did she always have to rush into things headlong?

After drumming his fingers on the table while the anger still seethed, Grant finally drew the linen napkin across his lap.

"My apologies," he said. "You can see for yourself that my life is not one of ease in this valley. The damned railroad wants to cause trouble, and those ruffians have money invested in it."

His eyes narrowed slightly as he gazed at Hurley's group for another moment. "I don't trust them, that's for sure."

The dinners came, saving them from any more immediate conversation. Annie choked down some water, afraid that more champagne would damage what wits she had left.

As Grant chewed on his beefsteak, his mood seemed to return. The men from the middle table finally threw down their money and took themselves off to the nearest saloon. Grant did not look up as they left the room.

"Did you find out where you go when you leave Fairplay?" he asked, startling her out of her quandary.

She frantically tried to remember what Lola or Marcel had said. "To Cañon City, I believe, and then to Santa Fe."

"Hmmmm. Well, then, here's to a successful tour." He lifted his glass as if trying to restore some pleasure to the evening.

She joined him in the toast, her heart still all asunder. As she drank, she had the sudden notion that she ought to tell him the truth. What good was there in this deceptive lark? He would hate her, but it was no more than she deserved.

The words were forming in her mind when he swallowed his champagne and relaxed the features of his face. His eyes met hers with a knowing look that undid her explanation. Then the back of his fingers met the back of hers, still curled around the stem of her glass and she felt the spark from his touch.

She tried to open her lips to speak, but no words seemed necessary. His eyes blazed into hers, and his lips curved in a warm grin.

"You must be tired after your long day," he said.

"Yes, I . . . am, rather."

His smile made her heart treble its beat. "I've been selfish to keep you out so late." There was a slightly mischievous gleam to his eyes as he added, "If we were in a city I would no doubt keep you out all night dancing. But we don't have such civilized entertainments in Fairplay. I don't think you'd enjoy any of the card games at the saloons."

Her eyebrows shot up. "No, I do not . . . excel at cards." She swallowed. Many an actress enjoyed the gaming tables, but Annie had never learned much beyond whist. She doubted she could carry out her pose in such a situation.

"Of course if you want to play, I could . . . watch," she said.

He smiled even brighter. "And bring me luck?"

She returned a noncommittal look. *Tell him,* she still battled with herself as he extracted some bills from the wallet in his coat pocket and laid them on the table. *End this charade before any more damage is done.*

He moved to get up and then stood behind her chair to help her up. The moment was lost. His hand at her waist guided her through the room and into the lobby. The place being public, she could not speak here.

Then they were climbing the staircase and found their way into her corridor. She turned to him at her door.

"There's something I should tell you," she said.

But his sensuous gaze bathed her face and his fingers came up to touch her ear and drift down to her shoulder. The womanly feelings that flooded her stopped everything except an explosion of desire.

"Hmmmm?" he murmured against her temple. Then his lips were on her cheek, his fingers trailed down the bare skin of her back to her gown, and she was engulfed in his warmth.

Somehow he got the key from her hand and inserted it into the keyhole. Then they were inside the dark room, and Grant had shut the door behind them. He grasped her shoulders and she heard his soft moan as he found her lips with his own. She responded eagerly to his kiss, glad that his arms slid around her to hold her up, for the swimming sensations that assailed her were too overwhelming for her to do anything but swoon.

She'd never been kissed like this before. *Oh my,* she heard a tiny voice utter inside her head. Then they were embracing each other urgently, his kiss more demanding, his hands drifting here, then there, as she explored the strength of his torso, encased as it was in the brocade vest and starched shirt.

She knew she shouldn't. Every moment was leading her farther and farther into danger. But she'd never felt like this about a man before. She was losing her head over him and she could do little about it.

"Oh, Grant," she breathed when he released her mouth. But his lips and tongue kept busy exploring her throat and shoulder, while his hands grazed her breasts and rested again on her shoulders.

He stopped for a moment, giving her the chance to break away and turn. She pressed her hands to her flaming face and turned her back to him. What had she done!

Feeling him take a step toward her, she took another step into the room, her back still to him.

Some semblance of sense forced its way into her whirling emotions. Some vestige of her upbringing reminded her of the wages of sin. She could not do what he would expect a lady of the stage to do. But how to explain?

He must have sensed her reluctance and rather than pulling him to her again, he moved to the side of the room and struck a light to the kerosene lamp, lending a pool of light to the room. Seeing the outlines of the furniture in the hotel room brought her further back to reality and she felt a taste of fear in her mouth. Having rushed headlong into this adventure, she must either pay the consequences or think her way out.

She was smitten with Grant Worth, her mind and body told her that much. But what was she to him? She had captivated him by her game, but what did he plan, to love her and leave her? And why not? Hadn't he just asked her where she was going when she left Fairplay?

"I'm sorry," she managed to say, stepping past the bed and going to the window to lift the lace curtains to look out. She didn't really see the street below, it was simply a way to stall for time until she could frame what she must do.

He didn't seem angry. Instead, after lighting another lamp, but keeping the flickering light low, he approached her softly, reaching an arm around her waist, but holding her gently, his chin cushioned on her head.

"It is I who should apologize," he said. "It was just that I am so taken with you. I hardly know how to conduct myself. I would not force my attentions on a lady where they were not wanted."

How could she think straight when she was leaning against him, drinking him in. Oh, if only she hadn't made such a mess. But he hadn't kissed Annie Marsh that way. It was Grace Albergetti he was after.

She bit her lip, squeezing back tears. She half turned, but that was worse, for then she was forced to tuck her head against his chin.

"It's not that I don't want your attention," she sighed desperately. "It's just too fast. I . . ."

"Don't fret," he whispered. "My lovely little dove." He kissed her cheek soothingly.

She gulped a swallow. "I need to tell you some things first. About myself, that is."

"Well, I want to tell you a lot of things about myself as well."

The moonlight fell across his face when she looked up at him. He fingered the curls in front of her ears.

She tried to find words, but all she could do was gaze his handsome, chiseled face. Desire flamed in his gaze and melancholy, hardened by a life that must have seen much. Eyes that looked into her soul and resonated there.

She shut her eyes. Let this moment last forever. If I can't have him for my own, at least I can have him in my memory. When she opened her eyes, she only dared look at his shoulder. She could not tell him. She could not break the spell.

"What did you want to tell me?" he softly murmured.

"I . . . have an aunt."

"An aunt?"

"Yes, she lives here in South Park on a ranch."

"Do I know her?"

"Yes, probably. Her name is Letitia Strahorn."

"Letty Strahorn. Why, we're neighbors."

Annie paused and looked up cautiously. "You are?"

"Yep. Her property backs onto my southern boundary. Her husband was a good man. Too bad when he died."

There was a moment of silence during which Annie's mind raced. "I see," she finally said.

"Will you be seeing your aunt while you're here?" he asked.

Although she still held to his coat lapel with the fingers of her left hand, she was steadier on her feet. Her roiling emotions saw a way out.

"I hope to see her tomorrow," she said. "That is, if I can get away from rehearsals. She sent word that she'd be in town. Unfortunately, she can't stay for the show."

"That's too bad."

She veiled her eyes when she told him the next part of her story. "There's a chance she'll have my sister with her."

A short pause. "Oh?" Grant replied.

Annie twisted around again, facing the window where they gazed at passersby and the glow from saloons and street lamps. He wrapped his arms around her waist, his fingers resting on the lower curve of her bosom.

"Aunt Letty invited my sister for a stay on the ranch. I, uh, don't know if she could make it."

Grant held her against him temptingly. But she was saved from doing something she might regret later. Her body and mind cried out for the man holding her. But in spite of her impetuous ways, these feelings were new to her and somewhat frightening. The new fabrication bought her time.

Grant turned her so he could look at her face.

"It is late. You should rest."

Her lips trembled as she smiled at him. "Yes, that's true."

He grinned sensuously. "It has been a delightful evening, Miss Albergetti. When will I see you again?"

Panic jumped into her throat. She had not told him the truth. She'd weaseled out of it by mentioning her fictitious sister. Let him meet her again as herself. Give Annie Marsh a chance to see if his affections could be transferred. Lacking the courage to tell him the truth, she was banking on her wits to worm out of this and yet get to see him again in another setting. Make him see the other "twin's" virtues.

Her words stuck in her throat. The show was here for

three more nights. As it turned out, his own plans would not allow him to attend.

"The llama's due to deliver in a day or two. I'll be seeing to it myself."

Her eyes widened. "You're going to deliver a baby llama?"

"Sure enough. I've delivered many a foal. This should be easier."

"My goodness."

He smiled at her reaction and then puckered his brow at the dilemma. "I won't be able to see your performance unless that baby's delivered. I'll just have to tell the mama to hurry up so I can get back here tomorrow night."

"Oh, that's quite all right. I do understand. Such a valuable animal."

She moved across the room, her stomach still in a knot. She had to make him go, and yet she didn't want him to go, ever.

From the way he cleared his throat and followed her to the door, it was apparent that he felt the same way.

She placed her hand on the doorknob and he covered it with his own. With his other hand he tipped her chin upward. She saw the regret in his expression. But he was a man of restraint and she knew instinctively he was waiting for her cue. He wouldn't push her.

"One more kiss, just to hold me 'til next time."

She gave a little nod and then he kissed her. And what a kiss. The bells went off in her head and she embraced his strong shoulders and big, strong body with fervor, never wanting it to end. Never wanting him to leave her. This was the man of her dreams.

Her heart trembled, her limbs turned to jelly. If he'd picked her up and carried her to the bed at that moment, she doubted she'd have resisted. One night in heaven. But then never to be with him again?

He broke off, stood back, twisted the knob and opened

the door. His face was shadowed from the light in the corridor.

"Good night, Grace." His voice was husky. "I'll see you again."

"Good night," she breathed shakily.

Then she closed the door slowly after him and pressed her forehead against it.

Grant left the hotel and took himself off into the night. Leaving the sounds of town behind, he rode out along the river, cutting across the upland valley on a track that led over the rolling hills toward his land. In the distance, campfires dotted the range where cowboys were watching the herds.

He breathed in the fresh mountain air and gazed at the cloudless, starlit sky. Grace's scent and feel were still on his mind, giving him a warm feeling. Damn, if he didn't want to bed her, and he could tell she wanted him. But something was stopping her, and he wouldn't rush her. Not yet. But if the baby came tonight or tomorrow night then he would be with Grace on Saturday. The prospect was delectable. He hadn't wanted a woman so much since Kate, and it had been a decent length of time. He was suddenly, intensely aware of his loneliness.

He needed a woman to fill his life and his bed and to bring smiles and sunshine at the end of a day. A partner to work with, maybe even to raise a family. He'd convinced himself that he hadn't had time for it in recent years. But tonight he let his daydreams wander where they would.

He gave his horse her head, knowing she would find the way, then he let his mind cool from the heat of love and return to ranch business. The veiled threat from Harwood Hurley didn't set well. It niggled at the back of his mind, and he decided to post extra guards around the property. Railroad men were known to go to any lengths to get what they wanted, and if it was going to come to a show of strength, Grant would be ready.

By the time he neared the outlines of his own buildings, he had a mental list of matters to attend to early in the morning. But not before a good night's sleep.

Annie spent the next day going over her numbers, but she had other things in mind as well. The troupe was beginning to beg her to stay with them. She and Lola lunched at the hotel. Lola was dressed in eye-catching cream-colored skirt and basque strewn with poppies and green foliage. The overskirt was edged in lace, draped in pleats about the hips and caught up with bows of faille. The sleeves had a lace puff at the top and cascades of ruffles at the elbow. Her hat of twine straw was lined with black velvet and lace. Roses peeked out from under the brim and pink ostrich tips were piled on top.

Annie wore a less showy linen dress with embroidery on the bodice. Her beige skirt had round pleats and a border of brown velvet. A deep collar, square cuffs of embroidery and long chamois gloves made her appear more like the young lady she really was than the actress she was pretending to be.

Lola was helping herself to a generous portion of venison, but after a few bites, Annie found she had no appetite. Her thoughts were fixed on Grant, on the warm, delicious feeling of being in his arms and of her lies that seemed to have no end.

She hadn't meant to lie. And she certainly hadn't meant for those lies to hurt anyone.

"You must eat," Lola chided her, waving her fork as she chewed another mouthful.

"I'm not very hungry. But I suppose I'll need my energy."

"Your eyes have a hollow look, my dear," commented Lola after swallowing. "Have you been sleeping well?"

"Oh, yes. My arms and legs are so tired after the performance that I fall into a deep slumber."

She didn't feel compelled to tell her friend of the sensuous dreams that filled her slumber and sometimes woke her in the middle of the night.

Lola gave her a wicked look. "I thought perhaps that handsome rancher was keeping you up late."

Annie blushed, unable to hide her feelings. "He is a gentleman, but yes, he is a problem." She puckered her face. "Oh, Lola, I don't know what to do."

"Are you in love with him?"

Embarrassment flooded Annie and she looked at her plate, fiddling with her fork. "I barely know the man."

"Love does not always wait upon a lengthy acquaintance," Lola observed. "I can see your dreamy looks, my dear. It only remains to see if he is in love with you."

To this Annie opened her eyes wider and leaned forward, speaking in a stage whisper. "How can I? He doesn't even know who I am!"

"Well, then, why not enjoy him under your present pretenses? He no doubt has the resources to give you a very nice time."

"Lola, you are as bad as I am. You know very well that in two more days I will go to my aunt's ranch and return to my own life. Grace Albergetti will disappear. She walks out of Grant Worth's life just like that."

"Unless you take Marcel's offer and remain with the troupe. Then you would adopt your stage name. You have talent, dearie. There is much you could do."

"I am flattered, Lola. You and Marcel are very kind." She shook her head. "I have thought of what a life on the stage might be like. But I'm not sure enough of myself. I would be cutting off all my family ties. They would disown me if they knew what I was doing. My father would not put up with a daughter of easy virtue as it is assumed all women of the stage are. I'm sorry, I don't mean it as an insult."

Lola grunted. "No insult taken. But doesn't your father want you to use your natural gifts?"

"I'm afraid not. Father is conscious of his social position. Hattie is supposed to be strict with us. I can't explain it, Lola. I've had a very good time. And I may want to perform again. But make it my whole life? I don't think I'm ready to take that step. I'm used to living in Denver. There are people I know that I wouldn't be able to see. Oh, I don't know. I'm not making any sense."

"Well, if you're not ready, I understand. Nevertheless the offer stands." Lola continued her feast for a few moments. Then she took another tack.

"As to your Grant Worth, perhaps you can see him again as yourself, since you insist on returning to your old life. You told me his land lies next to your aunt's property. You will be neighbors."

"But how can I tell him the truth, Lola? A man doesn't like deceiving."

Lola gave her a knowing look. "Then you will have to use your feminine wiles, my dear. Make him fall in love with you. He will soon enough see the truth. If he loves you he will not care who you really are."

"What about his male pride?" asked Annie, not at all convinced.

"It's true that male pride must be fed. But there are ways. Surely your feminine charms will not be lost on him. If he is stupid enough to let his pride stand in his way once he knows he loves you, then, pshaw." She waved a gloved hand. "It is not worth the trouble. There are other fish in the sea. I would not worry so much. Why not enjoy the moment? It is very romantic, is it not? Let tomorrow take care of itself."

Annie gave an exasperated sigh. There were other arguments, but she knew they would be lost on Lola.

"Perhaps you are right. I should stop thinking about it, for today anyway."

Lola lifted the corner of her mouth, coaxing a grin from Annie. "That's more like it, my friend. Life is too short to agonize over what we cannot change."

"Maybe so. But I am agonizing over a monster I created by myself."

"Well, that is something. Since you admit you created this monster, as you call it, you will find a way to fix it, no?"

"Oh, Lola, you make it all sound so simple."

"Life is simple. You have complicated it for the moment. But I have faith in you. Let your instincts guide you. You will know what to do."

For the rest of the afternoon Annie took Lola's advice and refused to worry about anything except her work on the stage. Marcel was pleased with her performance that night, and she dined afterwards with members of the troupe, trying to keep Grant out of her mind. Nevertheless, she found herself glancing at the arched entryway to the dining room, imagining that he might appear there.

When she felt tired enough to sleep, she took herself to her room and spent a long time brushing her hair. Thoughts of the theater, her family, her aunt and Grant danced in her head. Still, the thrill of his lingering kiss stayed with her. She relived his embrace all over again.

Visiting Aunt Letitia might help put a new spin on things. She'd gotten away with her little ruse so far and crossed her fingers, hoping that nothing would go wrong until Saturday when she would show up at Letty's door. Some time in the open air would be good for her. And she wouldn't be idle. She would help with ranch chores.

She stared at herself in the mirror, just wondering who was talking. She'd never in her life liked chores.

"The ranch is different," she said to the image in the

mirror shaking the brush at herself. "I can milk a cow and rub down a horse. Really, I can."

She arched her eyebrows. Qualities Grant Worth would admire in a woman?

"Oh, stop it," she said, getting up from the dressing table and going to bed.

Eight

For all Annie wanted to see Grant one more time before she left Fairplay, fear outweighed infatuation. When her relief came in the form of a small note by his hand, she sent up a prayer of thanks. She pressed the note to her breast, treasuring his handwriting in a personal message to her.

"What is it?" asked Lola. They were sitting in her dressing room before the performance, taking their time getting ready for the final night of the show.

"A note from Grant. Here, read it."

Lola continued pinning jet combs around the bun on the top of her head.

"No, no. I do not read the correspondence between such lovers. You tell me."

"He says only that he cannot be with us tonight. The llama is in labor."

Lola paused in reaching for the next comb. "You told me about his strange creatures, but not that one of them was with child."

"Female llamas are almost always in the family way. Grant says their gestation period is eleven and one-half months."

Lola made an expression of distaste. "I would not like to be a llama in that case."

A grin lifted Annie's lips. "Nor I. In any case, Grant is detained. He wishes us good luck. And he sent these."

She lifted a full bouquet of colorful mountain wildflowers tied with a wide white ribbon. Brilliant red Indian paintbrush, yellow monkey flower and blue penstemon.

"Ah, you see. His heart is captured. He sends flowers to his lady love," said Lola, returning to her makeup task.

Annie breathed in their scent. Then a long sigh escaped her lips.

"They are lovely aren't they? I wonder if there is a vase to put them in."

"Ask Marcel."

Annie plucked some of the flowers out, trimmed their stems with a pair of shears and tucked them above her ear. She would wear his admiration all night long.

Closing her eyes, she envisioned being in his arms again, the way she had countless times. But she was also grateful that she would not have to spend another night explaining her imaginary life. She gave a sigh and shook her head. She must get over him. Tomorrow she would go to her aunt's and all this nonsense would cease. If she met him again, she would be herself.

She bent to exchange kisses beside Lola's cheek. "One more night of performing," she told her friend. "You have made my dreams come true."

Lola clasped her hands. "I do not think so, my friend. You have made your own dreams come true."

Annie pranced to the door, going to take her place backstage and gave her friend a conspiratorial wink.

"Whichever one of us is responsible," she said. "Let's bring the house down tonight."

Annie threw herself into her part and then danced the cancan with wild abandon. Even though she knew Grant was occupied elsewhere, she found herself looking out into the audience just to see if he somehow might miraculously appear. In her mind's eye she saw him there, tall, broad-shouldered, firm-jawed. But he was busy tending his animals, and she did hope for his sake that the delivery went well. She would ask about it when she reached Letty's. Of course, as Annie Marsh, how would she know that the pregnant animal was due?

Saturday morning, Annie bid her friends of the theater goodbye amidst pleas that she should again join them. Lola promised to send their itinerary. Marcel alternated between fussing over Annie and pulling his hair out over the scenery that was being loaded onto a wagon. Finally, the group got away as townspeople lined the street to wave and shout good-byes.

No sooner had they left than a cowhand dressed in colorful poncho, canvas trousers, tall cowboy boots and wide sombrero climbed down from his wagon in front of the hotel where Annie had said she would wait. She recognized Letty's Mexican ranch hand, Juan Jose.

"Juan Jose," she called out, stepping into the sunlight. "Here I am."

He beamed her a grin and gave a low bow, sweeping his sombrero before him.

"Señorita Marsh," he said. "I am glad to see you have arrived safely. I will put your things into the wagon."

He did so and then helped her climb up to take a seat on the buckboard. She was genuinely glad to be going to the ranch. With her friends gone, the town of Fairplay seemed suddenly bereft and lonely.

A gust of wind rolled tumbleweed across the porch of the hotel, and Annie held onto her bonnet as Juan Jose turned the horses and started down the street. A few passersby stopped and watched. They had not seen Grace Albergetti depart with the acting troupe and Annie had a moment of dread should anyone call out to her now. She wondered if anyone might pass news along to her aunt that Annie Marsh bore a striking resemblance to an actress lately in town. But as usual, she banished such a thought to be dealt with only if such a thing occurred.

The valley floor was gently rolling for the first few miles and Annie took time to inhale the mountain air. The country was wild and broken with the uplands behind them clothed in piñon and cedar. Sentinel peaks of granite rose above that. In the distance, she could see a herd, which Juan Jose identified as elk. The rolling valley floor stretched away for miles, gradually ascending on the far side toward the Mosquito Range. They followed a wagon road along high banks of a tributary to the South Platte, with shale and sandstone in the bottom. The river was at its low.

Over a small rise they came to the ranch buildings. Letty's ranch house was a log building, the chinks filled with mud and lime. The roof was formed of young, barked spruce planks, a layer of hay and an outer coating of mud. A stone chimney rose from the left of the peaked center section. A little distance away, on a slope under some pines, was the bunkhouse. Beside it was a corral with several horses in it. A barn and chicken coop were situated about fifty feet from a small pond.

"It looks lovely," said Annie. "The ranch couldn't have a prettier setting."

"Good pasture and water," Juan Jose replied.

He drew the wagon up before the house and Letty herself appeared on the porch. She was a strong woman with long limbs, sandy blond hair and tanned cheeks. Her beauty still showed in summery blue eyes that missed nothing, prominent cheekbones and well-formed mouth. Her erect posture was still graceful in spite of the years of hard work on the ranch. Her long fingers were toughened, but her gestures could still be refined.

She wore a print day dress with small blue and white checks and a large apron across the front. Strands of her hair had come out of the chignon at the back. Her smile of greeting was full of earthy enthusiasm.

"Well, here's my niece at last."

Annie crossed the yard and embraced her aunt. "Oh, Aunt Letty. I'm so glad to see you."

A flood of relief at being here suddenly washed over her. It had been a strain to pretend she was someone else, and being with family made her feel at home again.

Her aunt pushed her ahead of her into the house and Annie stopped in the front room to adjust her eyes from the bright sun outside. The cozy room had many new touches that made it seem welcoming. The floor was made of pine boards, with a colorful braided rug in the center. Pine logs were laid in the rough stone chimney for an evening fire. A door led through to a bedroom.

A straight-backed oak settee was covered with gaily colored seat and cushions. A cane-seated rocker still rocked next to the fireplace, and two round tables were covered with fringed cloths. A blue vase held fresh daisies and asters, and white muslin curtains covered glass-paned windows.

"It's marvelous," said Annie. "I can see your handiwork here, Aunt Letty. Although I don't know when you'd have the time to sew."

Letty gave a shrug and moved toward the eating area to the left. Four chairs sat at a sturdy kitchen table, which was covered with bright red-checked cloth.

"Come into the kitchen and talk while I pour some tea. Bread's just comin' out of the oven."

"I can smell it. Oh, I'm famished."

"As I remember it, young lady, you have a healthy appetite. I hope that hasn't changed."

"It hasn't. I've never been one of those tight lacers."

Letty gave a gutsy laugh at the mention of the obsession with small waistlines that many wealthy young women in the cities had these days.

"Corsets without stays are the only things I wear around here. You have to be comfortable if you're going to work a ranch."

"I won't mind that."

After getting costumed and made up every night for a week, it would be a pleasant change to wear serviceable print dresses and throw herself into the ranch work.

The eating area opened into a kitchen with large cooking stove on which a kettle steamed. Baking tins, jars, spice boxes, pots and pans filled the built-in shelves. Utensils hung from hooks. Neatly arrayed on cupboard shelves were fine china and dishes. The large pine table in the center had been wiped clean. Only powdery flour on the rolling pin attested to Letty's morning activity.

Annie settled herself in a curved-back Windsor chair in the corner as Letty used thick hot pads to lower the oven doors and pull the delicious smelling bread out of the oven.

"Makes my mouth water," said Annie, truly glad that she was here.

In a few moments Letty had sliced hot bread and placed butter and homemade jellies on the table. Annie brought cups and saucers and they sat down to enjoy the treat. Between mouthfuls, she filled her aunt in on the rest of the family. Letty inquired after Everett's railroad ventures.

"You must have heard that he wants to run a railroad through South Park, down to El Paso."

Letty's reply was sharp and quick. "There are other ways to get to El Paso."

Annie sat back in her chair, the conversation taking a more serious turn. "So you don't support Father's project either."

Letty's high cheekbones took on a more prominent look and her mouth set. Blue eyes shot a hint of animosity into the room.

"I've been in this valley for ten years now, and there's

not enough grass to support the growing herds if they have to be fenced in. We need free range. Up 'til now we've all worked together to make a go of it. Our brands identify our cattle, and we meet at roundup time to cut 'em out and brand the calves. Can't see that way of life changing. Bringing a railroad through here'll do more harm than good. The tourists have already started to decimate the buffalo herds on the plains. We don't need 'em up here causing trouble."

Her aunt's feelings were even stronger than she'd anticipated. "I understand."

She pressed her lips together and looked at the table cloth. When she found the right words, she lifted her gaze to her aunt.

"I met one of your neighbors, and he seems to feel the same way."

"Who would that be?"

"Grant Worth."

For a moment Letty's smile was noncommittal. One eyebrow raised slightly and then her face became speculative. "How did you meet him?"

Annie tried to make it sound casual. "Back home. He came to a charity ball. I had a dance with him."

"I see. And he spoke of the railroad."

Annie made a face. "Actually I was present when he and my father had a rather strained altercation. I'm sorry. I see the ranchers' side of it, though I hate to be disloyal to Father."

Letty reached over and squeezed her hand. "No, of course not. No one would ask you to. The safest course to take in this case is to stay out of it. The argument isn't settled yet, and both sides have strong feelings. I don't like to think it'll come to more than threats and curses, but it could. Men have their land and their livelihood at stake here and they'll put up a fight if they have to. I'd just stay clear if I were you."

Annie's heart filled with concern at the force of her aunt's words. It was the same conviction put forth by Grant. And if the scene at dinner with Grant and that railroad man back in Fairplay was any indication, the ranchers might be up against a powerful force. A nasty powerful force. Harwood Hurley, she remembered the man's name. Funny, she'd never heard her father mention him.

She tried to shake the feelings away and glanced out the window at the wild grasses bending in the strong breeze. The mountains around the edge of the park rose majestically, and the fresh pine scent was stimulating. She took a deep breath and then returned to the tea and bread. After changing clothes she fully intended to make herself useful. In the evening they could sit by the fire, and she might even have the patience to get her aunt to show her how to make one of those hooked rugs.

Grant walked along the split-rail fence of the corral that separated his llamas from the rest of the ranch animals. A gangly-looking baby llama stayed close to its mother, but already the long, black nose, pointed ears and big dark eyes projected out of a graceful face in intense curiosity. The two adult beasts looked up, and the dark-brown male trotted over to examine the baby. The great doe eyes looked him up and down while the nostrils waggled to take in his scent.

Billy Joe stood beside Grant, having just pointed out a loose rail in the corral. The foreman took the opportunity to fill Grant in on the cantankerous llamas as well.

"Hell to catch," said Billy Joe. "I've spent less time rounding up lost steers. But once you've got the harness on them, they come along docile enough."

Grant made no attempt to pet them.

"From what I've heard, llamas are obedient. Good packers and loyal. But they aren't like horses. They can be a bit more nervous and stand-offish when they feel like it. They just like a game to make things interesting, that's all."

Billy Joe leaned on the fence. "Look, but don't touch, they seem to be saying to me."

"Don't worry, we'll train them. I saw folks leadin' 'em around a ring, making them jump over obstacles and stand on their hind legs. Just takes some time to get to know them. And they're better than sheep dogs with a herd of fleece. Too bad they don't take to cattle the same way they do to sheep."

"What? You tryin' to put some of our boys out of work?"

Grant let the llamas inspect his brown work boots and denim pant legs. With their long necks and thick bodies, they did look like something from an exotic land. But he was determined to get packs and halters on the male and take him into the hills soon.

"See if you can rig me a pack that will fit over this one's back," said Grant pointing to the male, who had the darker brown over most of his body; only his neck and head were white. "He ought to be able to carry a hundred pounds."

"Will do, boss."

Grant gave his foreman an understanding grin. "And Billy Joe, when they rib you in the bunkhouse, you just tell the boys to get used to the sight of these beasts. They might become their bread and butter come a few years."

"I dunno, boss. These boys are cowmen. They're suspicious of anything with this much shaggy hair on 'em. Too much like a sheep."

"Well, these llamas aren't any danger to close-cropping our range the way sheep do. No comparison. The llama is an animal of quality. High-class. The royalty in foreign countries keep them as pets. You tell the boys that."

"If you say so, boss."

A wind had picked up, and both men looked away as

puffy gray clouds began to poke across the sky from the western range. A wind came across the high prairie and the gusts made the llamas jittery.

"Looks like a storm brewing," said Grant.

He gazed at the skies and the tumbleweed rolling across the yard and tried to judge the severity of the coming storm. Wind gusted around the corner of the barn and tried to lift his hat off his head.

"Better secure anything loose," he told Billy Joe. "Looks like we're getting some weather."

"Right, boss."

Billy Joe had reached the same conclusion and turned around to get some help battening things down.

Grant continued to watch the sky and wondered if he ought to put the llamas in the barn. The corral he had them in was meant for horses, and while it looked secure enough, he hadn't tried to see how high the llamas could jump if agitated.

With the wind picking up and the scent of rain in the air, the two llamas trotted to the other side of the corral, and the baby followed. Grant climbed up and over and called to the female, clicking his tongue.

"Come on, now, don't give me trouble. Gotta get you two in the barn."

But seeing the harness in his hand, the two llamas divided and circled around as Grant approached. He reached to catch the female, but she eluded him. For several minutes he dove after both beasts with no success. He was beginning to hope no one was watching; he was taking enough ribbing as it was.

The llamas trotted around the corral as if it were a show ring and Grant felt exasperation beginning to boil. The two animals had no intention of being caught. He muttered a few choice curses, but tried to remain calm. A horse could sense a man's emotions and no doubt these animals could too.

He stood still at the side of the corral, the harness held down by his side as if he weren't giving it a thought. He hummed to himself while the male llama ignored him, his head stuck out over the fence, watching the ranch hands pull wagons into the barn. He knelt down to try to get the baby to come to him, knowing the mother would follow. The mama decided to cooperate and came up to Grant, who was clucking and reaching out toward the baby. He caught the female, got the harness over her head and led her off to the barn.

After bedding mama and baby down in fresh straw, he went back to the corral.

Then suddenly he heard the sound of hooves on hard-packed earth and some of the cowboys coming in for lunch galloped around the house and into the yard. The ruckus startled the male llama, still in the corral, and he gave a deep-throated screech. Then he reared back on his hind feet, placing his front feet on the top rail, towering over Grant.

"Get down here, you," commanded Grant.

But when the frightened male lowered his feet, it was to dash around the corral fence in a run. Grant sensed what was about to happen and muttered a stronger oath, looking for a freshly saddled horse. They hadn't had time to fix the loose rail, and in the way animals seem to know what you don't want them to know, the llama turned suddenly, heading right for the loose rail.

The male llama halted in front of the fence. Then he lifted his great long legs and kicked away the top rail, sailed his cumbersome body over the remaining rails and trotted away.

"Dammit," said Grant, heading for the gate.

He let himself through and fastened it securely behind him. As Grant raced for his horse, the llama headed for the prairie, and Grant suddenly wondered if llamas were as smart as they were made out to be.

He was in the saddle in the seconds it took the llama to dash past the ranch house. Grant cursed to himself as he lit out after his investment.

He felt the first spatterings of rain as he galloped through the prairie grass. The llama was headed out into the open, which was to Grant's advantage. He would be able to toss a lasso over its head in a moment, for the horse had the greater speed.

But the llama stretched out its legs and took a sudden turn south. Grant's horse followed, closing more distance. They were coming to a ravine and when the llama disappeared into some cottonwoods, Grant slowed for the descent. He ignored the rain spattering down and got into the trees along the creek seeing, with some frustration, the llama sail easily across the stream and climb up the opposite bank.

"Come back here, you fuzzy beast," he yelled over the growing wind. "I didn't bring you all the way from South America to have to chase you all over the place."

His horse scrambled up the other side and then followed the llama, which had chosen a course that would lead to the neighboring ranch. Letitia Strahorn's property adjoined his at the creek to which they both shared water rights. Now the llama was bounding up the next grassy slope as the rain came down harder.

Readying his lasso, for he was sure to catch the llama now, Grant bent forward, his hat brim keeping some of the rain off his face. Ahead of him the llama was making for Letitia's outbuildings. It skirted her corral, making the horses skitter around. He thought the llama would run right into the barn, but then Letitia herself appeared, pushing the barn door ahead of her. She came out to see the ruckus as the llama veered left and made a beeline toward the chicken coop.

Grant didn't stop for amenities as he dashed passed her,

dismounting just as the llama kicked the door open and entered the chicken coop.

"Hey," shouted Letty running up behind him.

But he had his lasso ready, and as a terrible squawking set up and feathers flew, Grant followed into the noisy tempest. The llama added high-pitched screeches to the frightened chicken's squawks. Feathers were everywhere, but the coop was narrow and the llama could not turn around.

Grant had the lasso around its neck and securely fastened, then got in front of it to push it backward. Once outside he could secure the harness.

"What's going on?" shouted Letitia from the chicken coop door.

"Don't worry," replied Grant. "I got him. I'll have him harnessed as soon as we get out of here."

"Need any help?"

"Not yet, just keep out of the way of his back feet."

But Letitia had squeezed in to make sure the cages were secure. There was so much noise from the flapping chickens that they could hardly hear one another and both of them had to blow feathers away from mouth and eyes.

Grant shoved until his llama decided to move backward, but he kept a secure hold on the rope. Once outside, he turned to lead the animal away.

"Go in the barn," called Letty, emerging half covered with feathers from the chicken coop.

Seeing that the rain was more persistent now and the sky more leaden, Grant decided to accept the hospitality. He led his ornery beast to the barn and thanked his lucky stars for the dry shelter, smelling sweet with fresh hay.

Letty followed with his horse, and after he had tied the llama to a stall, he helped her shove the door shut. Feathers stuck to their wet clothing. Grant gave an eye to the animal that had led him a chase. He took his horse to a stall on the other side and began to unsaddle it.

"Thanks, Letty. Glad your place was here. We might still be chasing around in the wet."

Letty brought him a blanket and implements to rub down the horse.

"What is that? It's got four legs, but I'll be darned if I've ever seen such a long neck. I wouldn't believe it if I hadn't seen you chasing it into my chicken coop."

"Sorry. Chickens all right?"

"Seem to be. Just riled up some."

"I'll see to any damage. My fault."

He continued to dry off his horse as Letty saw to some feed.

"We had a loose rail I meant to fix. Llama got spooked by some of the hands ridin' in and jumped the fence."

Letty went to inspect her new guest and the llama moved its neck and head in her direction, its huge eyes looking just as curiously at her as she was at it. The long, pointed ears swiveled forward.

"Funny looking thing. Where'd you get it?"

Grant came over with the blanket and rubbed off the llama's fur as well. "Had two of them shipped here from Bolivia. I got two and the female just dropped a baby. Going to breed them."

"Whatever for?"

He smiled. "Packing. They're easy to care for and they carry one-quarter of their own weight. Easy to train, they say."

She lifted a skeptical eyebrow, but Grant persisted.

"They've been domesticated for a thousand years in South America."

"Oh, well, I can see that."

He didn't miss the irony in Letty's voice, and indeed the llama seemed to be gazing at her with extremely self-important condescension as Grant saw to its needs.

"Well, they do say they make good domestic animals, once you got 'em trained."

"Oh, I believe you."

He sighed, placed a bale of hay and some water where the llama could feed and dusted his hands off on his pants. He was too worn out to explain about the beasts of burden he'd seen on Bolivian ranches, meek and obedient, even if they did enjoy games and obstacles.

"Come on to the house and dry yourself off," Letty said, now that the animals were cared for. "My niece is here from Denver. Seems you've met."

"Oh, really?"

"Annie Marsh."

Letty had continued toward the barn door, but the name gave Grant pause. He took his hat off and shook his head in small wonder. Then he remembered Grace saying that her sister was making a visit to South Park.

"I'd forgotten," he muttered to himself.

"What's that?"

"Oh, nothing. That father of hers isn't anywhere hereabouts, I hope."

Letty drew her mouth into a line of determination, one hand on the barn door. "No, he isn't."

"Well, that's good then."

"Be easy on Annie. She isn't any part of her father's schemes."

"Maybe she can learn to understand our point of view and relay it to the man."

"That's hardly fair," said Letty. "I wouldn't put a girl like that in the middle of this argument. It's her duty to obey her father."

"You're right," said Grant, grimly settling his hat on and coming to the door. One problem averted, he was now reminded of another. Maybe a cup of hot coffee would put him in a better mood after all.

Nine

"Sorry about the ruckus," Grant said as they pushed against the wind toward the house.

"Chickens didn't get out," she replied. "That's the important thing. Don't think your animal hurt my coop. The llama will be all right in the barn until this storm dies down."

They climbed to the porch and Letty pushed in the door. The house felt quiet after the wind blowing up outside. Grant hung his wet hat on the peg by the door.

"Come on in," Letty said. "My niece is in the kitchen." She lowered her voice a notch. "I'm tryin' to teach her how to cook."

Grant followed his neighbor through the eating area into the spacious kitchen. And sure enough, there standing at the large pine table in the center of the room, her arms covered to her elbows with flour, was Annie Marsh. She was wearing a simple blue house dress and large apron tied around her neck. Her hair had been pulled into a net at the back of her head, but was escaping in flyaway fashion. Her mouth was puckered and her face screwed up as she stuck a fist into a lump of dough. He couldn't help smiling.

"Annie, we have company," said Letty.

She looked up, dropped her jaw in surprise at the sight

of Grant, and looked about the room as if for a means of escape.

"Grant chased his llama over here and we put it in the barn," Letty continued to explain. "I'll just heat up some water to make some hot coffee."

Annie still said nothing, but stepped backwards looking doubtfully at the big iron cook stove while Letty filled the tea kettle with fresh well-water from the pump.

"Oh, I . . . didn't know . . ."

She clawed futilely at her hair and tried to brush some of the flour off her arms, creating a billow of white around her.

Grant inclined his head, smiling at her confusion. He cleared his throat, not wanting to say too much about his thoughts.

"Sorry if I'm barging in on your work. Didn't mean to arrive so suddenly. My llama took fright and knocked out a loose rail. Before I knew it, the critter was dashing across the prairie. I chased him over here."

"Into the chicken coop," Letty finished.

She had the kettle on the hottest part of the stove and fetched down a canister of ground coffee. "But no harm done except feathers flyin'."

Grant grasped the curved back of a wooden kitchen chair and swung himself into it backwards, crossing his arms on the back.

"Now Letty, you just let me know if any eggs broke on account of my animal. You know I'll pay for 'em."

She let her normal business-like expression turn into one of mischief. "I could send you out there right now with my frying pan to see. We can have scrambled eggs for dinner."

He knew he was being teased. "I wasn't planning to stay for dinner."

Letty glanced out of the small kitchen window at the heavy, darkening sky.

"I don't reckon you'll be returning home right now. I'd say we're in for a bad one. Annie, those pies ought to come out of the oven. You serve up some pieces while I go fasten the shutters."

"Need any help?" offered Grant.

"No, you sit right here. Only take me a minute."

She left the room while Annie grasped some hot pads and stared at Grant, her heart in her throat. She had tried to use the moments while Grant was talking to Letty to gather her wits, but they still felt scattered.

She opened the oven door and felt the wave of heat hit her face. The pies were a nice golden brown, and looked mouth-watering. Annie shook her head in amazement. How had Letty known they were ready to come out?

She managed to lift the pie plates onto the top of the stove. Grant reached to close the heavy oven door for her.

She risked a shy look at him. "Thank you."

Did he still believe her lie? Couldn't he see at once that there was no Grace Albergetti? Only Annie Marsh. She bit her lip, expecting for his accusation to pour forth any minute. How would she explain to Letty?

But Grant said nothing, only bent over to examine the pies. "Maybe I'm not so sorry I chased an ornery animal halfway across the valley," he said.

"Aunt Letty made them. She's very good with pies." Now that was a dumb statement, Annie thought. But she still didn't know what to say to Grant.

"Need some help? I know my way around my own cook stove. Had to do for myself for a time before I was married."

She felt her stupefied expression as she looked up at him. "You can cook?"

"Sure can. But not such as you might want to eat."

A sly grin crept over his lips and Annie tried to blink away the rising tide of flush that she was sure must be coloring her face as he moved easily around the big pine table.

Without being told to do so, he took the hot pads and moved one of the pies from the stove to set it on a cutting board on the table so the hot pan wouldn't scorch the table surface. When he stood back, Annie seized the pie-cutter and tried to concentrate on dividing the pie into eight pieces.

When she handed him a plate from the dishrail, he leaned a few inches closer and spoke.

"I saw your sister in Fairplay. She told me you might be here."

Annie didn't dare look up. "You did? I see."

Then she looked nervously at the door. Letty would be back any moment.

"Don't mention it to Aunt Letty," she said in a quick, hushed tone.

She tried to gain control of her features to resume the Annie Marsh appearance and to recall what she'd told Grant about all this in the first place.

"Letty is family, you know. She's my late mother's sister and we don't discuss Grace because Letty might be upset."

Grant scratched his head. "Well, all right."

That Letty shared the family's horror of the stage didn't fit with the Letitia he knew. He didn't think a rancher's wife who'd broken her back to help build a place up here in the mountains would be so concerned with propriety. She wouldn't socialize with dance-hall girls and soiled doves, but Grace was in an acting troupe, and that was a cut above the rest even if some folks didn't think it too respectable. He'd seen for himself that she didn't have loose morals. but there was no telling about family feeling. He let it go.

He leaned over to reassure Annie. "Don't worry," he whispered. "The secret is safe with me."

She gave a quick nod. One hurdle crossed.

The wind was rising outside and Grant peered out the kitchen window as Letty came back. The storm was coming from the west. Her concerned expression confirmed what he was beginning to feel from the gusts pressing the house and the tumbleweeds lifting and sailing past.

He followed Letty into the eating area to look out to the west. The sky was even heavier than before, low clouds swirling menacingly like a pot trying to boil.

"I don't like the looks of that," he warned.

Twisters were not uncommon on the plains east of Denver. And even here where the cold air of the north met the warm air coming up from the south, nasty weather could develop.

He and Letty went out to the porch. As he looked at the other weather signs, she dragged a couple of chairs inside. He helped her bring in some tools and utensils.

"It looks bad," he said when they got inside again. After a pause, "Where's your storm cellar?"

"Around back."

She leveled a look at him that said she saw the signs herself and they were in for it. "You're right, we'll be safer in the cellar. I'll get Annie and we'll turn the horses loose."

"Meet you there," he replied and bolted out the front door for the barn.

He hoped Billy Joe would secure the other llamas in the barn. People might think they were crazy, but these damned animals were too expensive to lose. And he hadn't even got a herd started yet. A double reason to preserve his investment.

Annie and Letty went across to the corral to turn the horses loose. Letty shouted to him above the rising wind.

"Where're you going?"

He pointed to the barn. "To get the llama."

With Annie's help, Letty started to lift the cellar door. But she turned and shouted at Grant. "There's not enough room."

He waved at the women. "You go on then, I'll take my chances out here." He'd paid five hundred dollars for the llama and wasn't about to leave it alone.

He turned and glanced back just before he reached the barn. The cellar door was open, but neither woman had climbed down. Annie was standing with her hands on her hips, shaking her head. Letty was gesturing.

Grant sensed an impasse, but there wasn't time to waste. The angry clouds were starting to dip into an ominous shape that made the hairs on the back of his neck stand on end. He hauled open the barn door.

"Wait," yelled Letty, running toward him. "I'll help you."

He held the door for her and she got herself in, catching her breath. "It seems my niece will not go into the cellar unless you come too. You might get hurt out here. Bring the damned animal."

He gave a quick grin then untied the lead end of the harness on the large-eyed beast, patting the animal's neck to calm him. "Come on now."

The llama was frightened, but must have decided that his safest route was with Grant. He followed docilely on the lead rope while Letty managed the barn door and then followed them to the cellar.

Annie was still standing on the rim, holding her hair with one hand from blowing into her face and trying to keep equal control on her skirt. She hadn't even had time to take off the apron.

Grant guided his prize to the cellar door. He'd seen llamas do obstacle courses including stairs. But would this one go into a dark cellar? At the top step, the llama stopped and balked.

"Get behind him and push," Grant directed the women.

He took his position in front of the llama on the steps.

"Come on, you mangy critter. If you're gonna be this much trouble, I might just give up on the likes of you. If you're gonna be too stubborn to sell to my customers you might as well blow away in this storm."

He pulled on the lead rope, and the llama lowered its head. The two women shoved from the rear. At last the animal decided to go. It trotted easily into the cellar and stopped in the middle of the small space, looking around. Annie and Letty tumbled after it. Annie tripped and was squeezed between the llama and Grant, who caught her in his arms.

He felt her sway in his arms and then find her footing.

"Sorry," she mumbled.

Letty pulled the door to and they were in darkness. But at least the heavy door blocked some of the shrill howling going on above.

Annie's blood hummed when she found herself in the close quarters, pinned between Grant's broad chest and the llama's springy, coarse fur, which being wet, smelled quite pungent. If it weren't for the storm that threatened danger outside, she would enjoy being thrown into Grant's arms. She removed her hand from his warm one and grasped a handful of llama fur for balance until Letty got the lantern lit.

A glow of light illuminated their quarters, which were tight indeed. Hand-built shelves surrounded them and baskets filled the space in front of the llama. Grant shifted himself by Annie, moving her slightly forward beside the animal's neck, which she petted instinctively for comfort. The animal turned its head around to study her and Annie met its inquisitive gaze with a round-eyed look of her own.

"I better make sure the door's secure," said Grant, scrambling up a couple of steps to see that the thick two-by-four that passed through the wooden inside handles was secure.

"Seems all right."

He pressed back between the llama's rump and a shelf of glass canning jars. Letty was on the animal's other side, clearing a space on the hand-built shelf for the lantern. There wasn't room for any of them to sit down with the llama present, and they spent the next few moments trying to adjust to comfortable niches in between bushels of apples and baskets of Letty's garden vegetables.

The roof of the cellar slanted downward ahead to where the potatoes were kept. Annie quickly realized that if the llama were turned around, its long neck and head could stretch over the steps, giving the three of them more room to crouch. But it was too late now. They all gazed at the doors where thin cracks let them know there was little daylight outside. But with every crash and bang, Annie shuddered. It was eerie to stare at the beams that supported the roof and fear what nature was letting loose above.

Annie shivered and instinctively moved closer to Grant. He must have sensed her worry, for a comforting arm came around her shoulders, nestling her against him. Her attention went immediately from the throes of nature above to the warm desire that made her want to cling to him down here.

He doesn't know who you are banged in her mind. The horrible dilemma made her stifle a sob. Grace would have wrapped her arms around his waist and rested her head against his shoulder. He might have lowered his face to kiss her. They would have enjoyed a treasured moment of intimacy in the face of the destruction above their heads. But as Annie, she could only stand there, reveling in being so close to the man she was falling in love with. The revelation hit her with all of the force of the storm raging above. What had begun as a whim had grown into a ruse that had trapped her wayward heart. She loved a man who barely knew she existed.

A sob must have escaped her throat, for Grant, no doubt thinking it was the storm that worried her, squeezed her shoulder and touched his chin to her temple.

"Don't fret now, storm'll most likely pass us by."

She swallowed. "I know."

Across the llama, Letty was grumbling and shoving to get to the end of the cellar where she had to crouch to look under the llama's head at Annie and Grant. She crawled through and stood up, close to Annie on her other side.

"Does this beast lie down?" asked Letty. "Or maybe if we could turn it around."

"That's what I was thinking too," said Annie, trying to take her mind off Grant. "If . . . is it a he or she?" she stopped to ask.

He patted the llama's back. "This one's a male. The mama's safe with her baby at the ranch, I hope."

Grant moved his arm away from Annie's shoulders but still stood close as he scratched the llama's neck, crooning softly to it. Annie and Letty continued to look toward the cellar doors, hoping they would hold.

"How long do you think it will last?" Annie finally voiced.

Grant craned his neck upward as if by looking at the beams just inches above his head he could see through the earth above and give a prediction.

"Hard to say."

He looked over at Letty, who had more practical knowledge about such things as storms. Her aunt nodded solemnly and then uttered an expletive as the llama's cold nose found its way to her face. She pushed it away.

"This beast is wrong way to. We should have brought it in backwards."

Grant chuckled. "Haven't trained him to do that yet, although they will walk backward."

Letty grunted with a huff.

They continued to huddle by the llama, and Annie found herself hugging it around the base of its neck. With Grant so near, she felt the need to clutch something to her. Emotions within her fought for attention, but she finally put her self-interest aside to glance with concern at Letty.

"Do you think there'll be much damage?" she queried her aunt.

Letty pressed her lips in a straight line and shook her head. "Can't say."

Annie's heart went out to her sturdy relative. She admired a woman who could live up here alone except for her hired help. Her own life had been so easy, all she had to worry about were her own pleasures, or lack thereof. She had come here to be useful, and she was determined to prove her mettle.

Her aunt had not had a pampered life, but had helped her husband build a ranch before this valley was settled. The lines in Letty's pretty face, the mix of white strands in her sandy blond hair and the rough skin on her hands showed the kind of life she'd lived. It made Annie ashamed. What had *she* ever done that had required grit and determination? Her escapades on the stage were daring, to be sure. But she was in no danger of having her scalp removed or watching her home go up in flames . . . or a tornado.

She looked toward the cellar doors, and it seemed that the furious roaring outside had begun to die down. It was suddenly so quiet she could hear her heart thump. She grasped Letty's hand, and the two women gave each other a squeeze.

Grant handed the lead rope to Annie. "If you hold him, I'll go check and see if it's safe."

Annie accepted her charge. Momentary irritation flashed through her as she felt resentment for Grant's concern being consumed by the fleecy animal instead of holding her in his arms. Mentally, she chastised him for trying to seduce her in Fairplay and ignoring her now, but she could say nothing. It wasn't his fault.

She frowned at the long-lashed beast, envying the place the animal had in Grant Worth's heart.

Grant scrambled up the steps and removed the two-by-four, then pushed open the door, letting in a flood of what seemed like blinding sunlight after the darkness. He poked his head up, and Annie gripped Letty's hand even harder.

"It's OK," said Grant, pushing the door all the way open. "Storm's passed."

Then he came back to get them. "Some damage, looks like. But the house and barn are still standing."

Letty gave an audible sigh and Annie hugged her saying, "Thank heaven."

The sunlight seemed to cue the llama to turn around and while they could not have made him do so by force, he began to twist about, shoving Annie and her aunt farther into a corner with cries to look out.

"Don't worry," said Grant, reaching for the lead rope. "He won't step on your feet. Come on now."

He clicked his tongue and coaxed the llama around until it followed him up the steps and into the light.

The women followed and Letty stopped to extinguish the lantern. Outside, it took them a moment for their eyes to readjust to the light, but a thrill of thankfulness flooded Annie's heart as she saw that the damage was minor, the most serious being that the roof of the chicken coop had been torn off and rested some hundred yards away. Chickens fluttered about the yard between shingles that had come away from the barn roof.

"Some of your chickens are probably at Fort Garland by now," said Grant. "But I think you can count yourself lucky."

"I think I can, too," said Letty.

Annie could see the relief in her aunt's face and sent up her own prayer of thanks that the tornado had not touched down here. The high winds that had accompanied it had worked some damage, but it could be repaired.

The corral fence was a shambles on one side, but remained standing on the other side. And they were all safe.

Then to their further relief, Juan Jose appeared in the distance, riding his mule.

"He must have found shelter," said Annie.

He waved his big hat and Letty said, "Praise the Lord."

"Tell you what," Grant said. "You ladies see about the house while I do what I can out here."

"Oh, Grant, that's not necessary," protested Letty. "My boys will come straggling in from the range. At least I hope they will."

"I'm sure they will, but I owe you."

The llama's long ears tilted forward as it made its fastidious inspection of the debris that lay around. Grant led the animal off toward the barn, calling over his shoulder.

"I'll have that cup of coffee before I go."

Juan Jose rode up and got down to report excitedly on the storm. His rapid Spanish, peppered with English, was accompanied by many gestures. Annie was able to grasp some of it. Apparently he had been near a ravine and took shelter there when he saw the storm touch down. Fortunately it had headed west, bypassing him by a mile.

"It laid the trees flat in the path," he said. "I see them later, roots on top of the ground, when I ride back." He expressed his agitation at the bad weather and crossed himself.

Annie was distracted by Grant leading his pet, for that is what she'd decided to call it. Her feelings were a confused stew of longing and consternation. She barely listened to Letty and Juan Jose exchange observations on the destruction left by the path of the storm. Annie's heart was stirred by her own little storm as Grant's sure, long-legged stride coaxed his llama to the barn once more.

She took two steps in that direction, but then realized she mustn't betray her heart. She tried to follow Juan Jose's Spanish as he and Letty settled on what must be done first.

When Juan Jose went off to care for his horse, her aunt turned to her.

"Lord knows what's happened to the herd," she said. "We can only hope the other men were as lucky as Juan Jose."

"Yes, of course. Oh, Letty, how selfish of me. I wasn't thinking of them."

Her aunt only nodded thoughtfully. Juan Jose hadn't seen the cowhands or the herd. But he was riding in from the north, and the herds were to the south. "There are plenty of gullies where the herd was grazing. If the men had any sense, they would have taken cover."

"Maybe they weren't right in the path," observed Annie, as they took the steps to the house. "And look," she said, as they paused on the porch. "It missed the house entirely."

She and Letty looked into each other's eyes for a moment. The near escape brought a lump to her throat and she hugged her aunt, both women wiping moisture from their eyes.

"Why don't you help Juan Jose pick up what's scattered around out here?" suggested Letty. "I'll make everyone that coffee."

"Of course," said Annie. She cast a glance toward the barn before following Juan Jose to the damaged chicken coop. She couldn't stop her heart from pounding fast, both in the aftermath of danger and because of Grant.

Grant Worth, she said silently to herself as she bent to pick up a pitch fork. Whatever was she going to do about him? More tears sprang to her eyes, this time tears of frustration that he didn't see her for who she really was.

Was that it? she pondered, bending to rescue the iron triangle that had blown loose from its chain on the porch. It had landed near what was left of the corral.

It wasn't that he didn't see her for who she really was,

it was that he didn't *care for* who she really was. He was infatuated with a woman who didn't exist.

She stood up, fighting back her emotions. Infatuated by a pretty actress. She carried the pitchfork and the triangle back to the porch, but her thoughts were elsewhere. Grant was taken by a pretty actress, a young woman who had abandoned her railroad tycoon father. Well, she *was* that pretty actress. What could she do to show him?

Thoughts of what he wanted to do with Grace sent a new rush of passion through her. She recollected their evenings alone. Surely if he saw Grace again . . . But how could that happen? Grace was no more.

She muttered an oath, tossed the triangle onto the porch and trudged on toward the barn. She watched Grant cross some distance ahead of her as he went to assess the damage at the corral. She didn't dare speak to him now, but continued on her way.

Inside the shadowy barn, the llama perked its ears up and stretched its long, straight neck over the stall toward Annie.

"Oh," Annie exclaimed, reaching to touch him. "You are the silliest animal I've ever come upon."

An ache of yearning sprang up in her breast as she petted the llama. Grant loved and cared for it. She knew how badly she wanted his tender caresses for herself.

"You're getting carried away, Annie Marsh," she murmured so that only she and the llama could hear.

The animal blinked its long eyelashes once, the lifted black nose giving it a haughty look.

Grant was at war with her father. Perhaps he saw Annie as an extension of the family's railroad interests. But her "sister" Grace had left the family and had nothing to do with that.

"Oh," she said again, tears coming into her eyes. "This is silly."

She had never been like this before. Her pranks had

never gotten her in this deep. She knew she couldn't be Grace Albergetti forever. She knew that Annie Marsh would never do with Grant what Grace would do. What they both wanted him to do. She just knew it. He was the man for her. He completed her. She wanted to be with him so much she could taste it.

A chicken set loose from the damaged coop entered the barn, flapping and squawking.

Annie sniffed and wiped her eyes on her sleeve. There was work to do. She mustn't let everyone down. She must not let Grant see her crying. It was a sign of weakness. She took a few moments to gather herself together and go back out into the sunlight to help pick up the refuse from the storm.

The llama puckered its lips and looked haughty.

"Oh, you're no help," she told it. "No help at all."

Ten

Annie worked until her limbs ached. Grant was everywhere, advising Juan Jose on the broken corral fence, then up a ladder to inspect Letty's barn roof where the shingles had blown off. He seemed to have endless energy. Annie tried to ignore him as she and Letty turned the water trough upside down to empty out the branches and debris that had landed there. Then she pumped fresh water from the well to fill it again.

The rest of the ranch hands straggled in, each with his own tale to tell. The herd was safe, and they pitched in to help with whatever needed doing. Letty sent some of them on fresh horses to search for any strays that might have gotten trapped by the storm.

Never mind Annie's tangled hair, the sweat that moistened her blue gingham dress, her scratched and dirty hands. Grant wasn't looking at her anyway. His intense gaze, when she could see it, was directed at the work. Finally, he came striding toward the house. Annie self-consciously wiped her hands and tried to smooth back her hair.

Beside her, Letty shielded her eyes with her hand to gaze at the westering sun. "We've worked hard enough for one day," she said. "I reckon Grant will want something to eat before he heads back."

Annie gazed curiously at her aunt. "I wonder how his own ranch fared."

A trace of resentment escaped in her voice. He certainly was showing a lot of concern for his neighbor's ranch when his own might be worse off. For the first time, jealousy of her aunt sprang into Annie's heart. Was Grant doing all this because he was fond of Letty?

As Grant approached, Annie gazed from one to the other. Their expressions revealed nothing. Letty spoke to him with the same reserve she showed everyone. Grant barely glanced at Annie but gave Letty his assessment of what they'd done.

"I appreciate it, Grant. You don't need to spend any more time away from your ranch, but I'll have dinner on the table in fifteen minutes if you'll stay. We didn't get to have a noon meal yet."

His face relaxed into a smile that included Annie this time. "That's right neighborly of you. I have to admit I worked up an appetite."

"You're the one bein' neighborly," said Letty quietly. She turned to go to the house.

Now when had she had time to put a meal on? wondered Annie, frowning into the sunlight where Grant stood. She suddenly noticed he was looking at her.

"What about your own place?" she finally asked.

The pleasant smile had not left his features, and his gray eyes still made her heart sing. He leaned over to take a drink out of the dipper of fresh water and splash his face. After he replaced his hat on his head, he answered her.

"The path of the storm veered west before it broke up. My ranch is north of here."

"Oh, you mean the storm couldn't have touched it?"

He shrugged, and they both started walking toward the house.

"Some weather, no doubt. But not like here. I reckon my ranch hands have everything taken care of."

She made herself walk slowly, hoping he wasn't noticing her disheveled appearance. That was the trouble, she thought. He wasn't noticing anything. Not like he did when she was Grace.

Inside, she freshened up in her bedroom and discarded the soiled gown. Opening her trunk, she fingered one of her white batiste tea gowns trimmed with Battenburg lace for town. But it would look silly to put it on for the afternoon meal here. Instead, she chose her clean moss-green cotton with scattered pink roses. It did have a soft ruffle about the yoke and flattered her hair, which she brushed hard to get the tangles out and then twisted up in a loose chignon.

Grant got up when she entered the front room. He had changed into a fresh shirt, probably one of Letty's late husband's. Again, a spurt of jealously made her wonder about Letty's relationship with him.

She stood awkwardly with him in the front room for a moment, glancing from his face downward. She couldn't look at that serious, handsome face for long without a flush coming into her cheeks.

He cleared his throat. "Guess we ought to see if your aunt needs any help."

"Yes, of course."

Letty had everything ready and they sat down to steaming bowls of stew, hot bread with mouth-watering butter and applesauce for dessert. After the meal, they lingered over coffee.

Grant gazed pensively out the window toward the mountains deepening into indigo. When he turned back to face the women, his words surprised Annie.

"They say I'm standing in the way of progress." He gave Annie a pointed look. "Your father and others, that is."

"You mean the railroad," she said quietly.

He gave Letty a look that conveyed the fact that the two of them had had this discussion before. Letty only returned his look with a knowing one of her own. She poured herself more coffee and explained to Annie.

"Settlement will follow the railroad if it goes through here. The likes of us don't want that. These were federal lands once, free for the big cattle drives of the past. For a long time the herd owners have been lobbying the government to prevent small homesteaders coming into this area. It would break up the range too much for our liking."

Grant tipped his chair backward, nodding. His gray eyes had that stubborn look Annie had seen before.

"I don't know about anyone else, but I like things the way they are."

"You do know about everyone else," Letty huffed. "You've been to the meetings. There's not a one among us in the cattle business wants a railroad through the middle of our range. As it is, we drive the herds down to Denver every fall and spring, and that's fine and dandy. More people up here and there's not enough grass to go around."

Annie's chest tightened. "I didn't know about the repercussions. I'm sorry Father wants to interfere with your plans." She looked at her plate in embarrassment. "I guess there's a lot I don't know."

Letty gave her niece's hand a squeeze. "We're not saying it's your fault. You can't influence what your father does."

"No, I suppose . . . ," she looked up and her words trailed off. Grant was staring at her in a most peculiar way.

"Um," she stammered, "I . . . mean, I don't know . . ."

One dark blond brow was lifted on his broad forehead, and his eyes held a speculative look. His head shifted a little to his left as if a thought had occurred to him.

What thought?

Then his brows furrowed and he dropped his gaze to stick a spoon in his coffee cup and stir. "No, I suppose not."

Her glance flew to her aunt. The crease between her

brows and the firm line of her lips emphasized her decided objection to whatever it was that had occurred to Grant.

"No," Letty said. "I know from experience that no one has influence over Everett Marsh. I don't mean to be disrespectful of your father, Annie dear, but he and I have locked horns over more than one matter."

Letty lifted her chin as if she did not want to speak of it again, and for one terrifying moment, Annie was afraid Grant would interpret that remark to refer to "the wayward Grace."

"I know," said Annie quickly.

Grant broke the moment of tension by easing his chair back into its proper position and getting up.

"I thank you, ladies for a restoring meal. Time I took that llama of mine back home and got back to work."

"You're welcome any time, Grant. And thank you for helping us out."

They followed him to the porch and then watched him make his way to collect his llama and his horse. When he re-emerged from the barn, he had the llama in tow. Its bright eyes and pointed ears gave it a look of cheerful nonchalance, as if not at all concerned that it had led Grant on a chase halfway across the valley.

Grant lifted his hat and waved from the distance, and Annie watched him ride away. She felt Letty's pensive gaze and tried to hide her expression as she glanced at her aunt.

"Hmmmm," grunted Letty. "I think you have eyes for that man."

"Me? Who him?" But she felt that her remonstrance was going to fall on deaf ears.

Letty shrugged in unconcern. "It's natural. He's one to admire. Handsome face, minds his own business. Don't say as I blame you, but I'd be careful if I were you."

"Why? I mean, not that I care." Annie picked imaginary crumbs from her skirt, the tightness still in her chest.

"Grant loved his wife. Not a speck of scandal about him in the valley. But he's cared for nothing but his ranch since the woman died."

Annie wanted to know more, but was afraid to ask. "He doesn't have anyone then," she finally said.

"Not so's I know of. Course he may take to fancy women from time to time if he's as red-blooded as most men like him. I wouldn't know about that."

Annie had to look away. Fancy women! Like Grace Albergetti! She said no more but went into the kitchen to pump water into a copper kettle to heat on the stove to wash up the dishes. So what if her hands got rough and chafed from hot water and hard work. Grant would never notice.

Grant's own ranch had fared much better. The hands had seen the twister out on the plains and felt stiff winds. But the worst of the storm bypassed them to blow over the range far to the west.

After seeing to the llama and making sure the top rail of the corral was repaired, Grant ate dinner prepared by his black cook, Chalmers, who had been with him since the cattle drives. Chalmers had prepared biscuits, sow belly, white gravy and black coffee for every meal of the 1,500 miles from Texas to Abilene, but before that he'd been trained as a cook when he'd worked on a plantation in the south, and now Grant was treated to the best in southern cooking when the ingredients could be had. When they couldn't, Chalmers took recipes he'd learned from Mexican cooks and added some unusual flavors of his own.

Tonight he presented Grant with baked, stuffed bread shell filled with onions and chicken meat. Grant knew better than to ask what it was spiced with. Chalmers would take offense unless praised. Only then would he elaborate on how he made the dish.

The second dish was beefsteak and oysters shipped from Oregon to Cheyenne. This, Grant had learned, was a Chinese dish that Chalmers had picked up. To soak up the juices, there was Irish potato bread.

"How do you like it?" Chalmers asked after he had everything on the table and brought a silver urn of coffee to the ornately-carved sideboard.

The cook was garbed in a long, white apron around his wide middle. Though Grant always invited Chalmers to take his meal here in the dining room, the cook insisted on eating in the kitchen.

"Delicious," said Grant, wiping his mouth after a big mouthful of the beef. "Can't say as I ever get bored with the cooking around here."

Chalmers beamed at the compliment. "Got to please the nose and the taste buds as well as the stomach. A meal is to be enjoyed, not just bolted down. Not like you boys had to do when we was on the trail."

He poured some coffee into a glazed china cup with gold rim. Grant would have dispensed with the finery his wife had brought to their home, but Chalmers enjoyed making meals a dining pleasure. It was a luxury for him after all the years on the cattle drives. So the china plates, the good silver, the coffee urn and the like had remained in place.

Grant washed down another mouthful. He wasn't too sure about the stuffed pumpkin, but he smiled with his mouth full and nodded to assure Chalmers, who watched him with eagle's eyes until he knew his employer was pleased.

"Go and enjoy your own dinner," Grant said when he could speak again. "I'll be fine."

"You call when you're ready for dessert."

Grant lifted his coffee cup in a salute and the cook passed through the door to the kitchen.

Being alone gave Grant a chance to savor the meal, sip

his coffee and reflect on the day. He gazed at the portrait of his late wife that still graced the dining room and wondered what she would say if she were here. He hadn't been able to bear looking at the picture just after she'd died, but she'd been gone three years now and his grief had mellowed to memories.

Sometimes he did feel like she was here, and he could talk to her. It gave him a feeling of companionship, as if she was offering comfort.

He sipped his coffee and gazed about the room without seeing. His mind went back to the evenings spent with Grace Albergetti. Her vivacity was different from his late wife's calm, nurturing love, but Grace Albergetti had done something no one else had done for the last few years. She'd made him feel alive again.

It was time for him to find love again. He couldn't remain dead to everything but work forever. Grace had done the job of starting to bring him out of his self-imposed shell. And she didn't even know it.

He found himself recalling the details of her lovely body. Long limbs, uplifted breasts in those eye-catching costumes of hers. Hair all piled up so he could gaze at her lovely neck. And when he kissed her, delicious lips.

He shook his head, not wanting to get all heated up and not be able to do anything about it. Problem was, what could he do about it?

He scraped the dining room chair back and went to pour himself some whiskey from the sideboard. Then he took it into the sitting room where Chalmers had already lit a fire. He stretched himself out in the big, comfortable armchair.

Still images of Grace Albergetti danced before his eyes in the flames licking the logs in the fireplace. The firelight seemed to reflect her shimmering costumes, her long legs, revealed when she'd kicked her skirts up in the cancan.

He scratched his chin and pondered. What if he had

bedded her? Would that have satisfied him? Or just made him want to see her again? And when *would* he see her again? He knew where the acting troupe was going, but it would be easy to lose track of her. He was giving himself a chance to forget her. But he had not forgotten her.

And how could he, with her twin sister at the next ranch, reminding him so much of Grace. He thought of Annie Marsh and of her jittery nervousness and wide-eyed ineptness. That too made him smile, and he supposed she was not used to ranch life. She was obviously a spoiled and pampered young lady brought up in a proper and very strict home. It was no doubt good for her to get out here and see what real life was like, away from the city.

She had Grace's features, but not Grace's confidence. The two faces melded into one in the fire. He would like to see them together.

Now that was a thought. Annie always seemed to be able to visit her sister; the two kept in touch, but something about the two of them didn't fit. But the whiskey dulled his wits comfortably after the long, hard day and he didn't feel like puzzling.

"Well, that settles it," he said to the fire, taking another swig of the whiskey and letting it warm his throat. He could always find out where Grace was by asking Miss Marsh.

He remembered the warning not to talk about Grace to Letty. Letty was stubborn and determined in her own way. She didn't like her brother-in-law, Everett Marsh, any more than Grant did. But out of respect for her late sister, Annie's and Grace's departed mother, Letty evidently held to the notion that Grace had abandoned her family for the stage and wasn't to be spoken of anymore. But he knew how to reach Annie, so if Grace continued to haunt him, there would be a way.

He drank some more whiskey and then headed for his bed. He'd been up early and it had been a strenuous day. Time for some shut-eye.

He undressed down to his drawers and climbed into the rope-spring bed, pulling the cool sheets and heavy army blankets up to his cold chin. As he let out a groan of exhaustion, blurred by the whiskey, he shut his eyes and tried not to think of soft limbs and inviting thighs. Lust stirred again and he tried to ignore it. He stuffed a pillow next to his stomach. He couldn't let this woman thing get out of hand.

Sunday morning Grant joined the rest of the community for church service in the little white church they had put up in the center of Fairplay. The building and its tall spire nestled on the green slope that rose gradually from the center of town. Wildflowers in glorious colors sprinkled the grassy hill. The town had been laid out with lots drawn up on a grid, but houses were still spread far apart.

From the slope he gazed over the town and out into the valley. The Mosquito Range stretched along the west side of the valley, turning from green to blue in the distance. Across the valley, wooded foothills lifted from the rolling grassy park, topped by the Tarryall Mountains. He inhaled the invigorating mountain air that he loved so much. He was early to church. There was time to walk up the hill to the little cemetery and pay respects at his wife's grave.

He liked this solitude, walking among the graves, many marked with carved wooden tombstones. He'd taken care to order a marble one for Kate. He knelt down to spread the flowers he'd brought. He spread them loosely, a shower of flowers rather than a bouquet.

It was funny. He knew that her bones rested here, but her spirit had gone on. She had gone on to the next life, wherever that was. He knew it somehow with certainty. And yet he also felt that she watched over him. Here, at her grave, he could talk to her, and it helped sort out his thoughts.

* * *

Annie perched beside her aunt on the polished wooden pew. She had dressed in her finest this morning, church being the one opportunity during the week to cast off the serviceable work dress and look one's best.

The corset laced under her blue-and-white-striped foulard made her sit up straight, her white-lace-gloved hands resting on the hymnal in her lap. Her curled, strawberry-blond chignon was anchored cleverly with pearl combs under a small bonnet with peaked crown turned down at the left side and curving up on the right.

The crown was covered with blue and white grosgrain, and bows of white satin ribbon. A spray of pink roses and tiny green leaves were set against the trimming on the upward-turned brim. The blue and white colors with just a sprinkle of pink flattered her bright hair, and long hat pins held the whole thing in place. On the ride into town in the buckboard, she'd taken care to clamp her hands over the bonnet so the gusty winds wouldn't carry it off.

The long, trained skirt fit smoothly over her narrow hips, and the skirts were held close to the knee in front by ties, restricting her movement to small steps on the rocky path from the wagon yard up to the church steps. But sitting here now in the pew, she felt the care she'd taken with her appearance today was worth it all.

Grant sat several pews ahead of them and she'd heard his lusty, tuneful voice during the hymns. He was slouched at the edge of the pew, one arm resting along the top behind a passel of someone else's children. She couldn't tell if he was paying attention to the preacher or not. She wasn't. Beside her Letty sat with chin uplifted, looking pretty in a basque and skirt of soft gray faille with pink ruffled blouse and feathered bonnet. The lines from her hard labor showed about her eyes and along her mouth when she lifted her chin, but Letty had a certain determined beauty in her maturity.

Annie liked to stand up and sing. And she hoped Letty couldn't tell how often she glanced at the back of Grant's head, trying to imagine what he was thinking.

The service was over soon enough, and they got up to greet their neighbors. Annie was presented to the other ranchers, some of whom she'd met before. Too late, she realized that some of these people might have seen her performance in Fairplay, and she found herself glancing down shyly, hoping the ribbons from her bonnet would trail over her face and help hide her identity.

Outside, the men drifted down the hill toward the wagons to talk, while some of the women gathered about the church yard and strolled up toward the little iron-fenced cemetery. Annie excused herself and walked up toward the graveyard, wanting to be alone. She wandered among the graves, finding the setting oddly comforting.

When I die, she thought to herself. *I would want my bones to rest in such a beautiful place.* To distract herself, she read some of the names and dates on the gravestones—wooden ones that had been chiseled and were cracked and weathered, and a few granite ones, ordered and placed here by loved ones.

She saw the strewn wildflowers before she read the name and then felt her heartbeat quicken as she read Kate Worth, 1850-1875. Her ears burned as she stood at the grave. How lovingly the flowers had been placed there, recently too, strewn across the grass like a caress. Her thoughts tumbled and her emotions turned melancholy. It was so personal. She felt like an intruder, and yet she was rooted to the foot of the grave, drawn in.

She'd been so caught up in stumbling onto the grave that she only now heard the crunching of the grass and the gate squeak behind her, giving her a start. She turned and caught her breath as Grant came up the hill. She felt embarrassed and self-conscious, but there was nowhere to hide.

He reached her and took off his hat, holding it in front of him with both hands. His black Sunday suit, string tie and boots only made him seem all the more masculine, and Annie felt the blushes in her face like the tide creeping up to a shell-strewn shore.

She gulped and turned to face in the opposite direction, looking down the hill from where she stood beside him. Neither one said anything for a time. She didn't know quite what to say. She hadn't meant to be caught standing here like a ninny.

Finally he lifted his head and half turned. "My late wife's grave. I brought the flowers this morning."

She dared to peek sideways at him. "They're very pretty. I'm sorry about your wife. Letty told me." She almost felt like saying, *Grace told me.*

"Thank you." His expression was pensive, but not sad. "She was a good woman. It didn't seem fair at the time she died."

"No, I'm sure it didn't. I felt that way about losing my mother. It never seems fair. You . . . must miss her."

He half turned to study her, making her look away to gaze over the little valley where the town sat next to the winding South Platte.

"Sometimes, I do, very much. But I try not to mourn. She always felt that life was for the living."

A little tremor went through Annie, and she had to resist the impulse to slide closer to him.

"That's for the best then," she muttered.

They started walking together back toward the church, and he touched her elbow in gentlemanly fashion to help her negotiate the uneven ground. Little did he know how his touch set off flames of remembrance of the intimacy they had shared and could have shared more of if "Grace" hadn't drawn the line.

Grant must not have thought it proper to bring up Grace inside the perimeter of the little graveyard. But after he'd shut the gate behind them and they resumed their stroll, he cleared his throat as if wanting to change the subject.

"Do you hear from your sister?" he asked.

Her head came up. "No. That is, I don't expect to hear for a while. The troupe's headed south, I believe. Cañon City would be their next run."

He grunted acknowledgment, making Annie's cheeks burn. Then an idea niggled. Perhaps she could get him to tell her something of what he felt for Grace.

"You and Grace," she said when they stopped on the hillside. Neither one of them seemed to want to return to the group below. Up here no one would know what they spoke of.

"You saw a lot of her when she was here?"

Her words were quick and she pressed her lips together, afraid she was saying too much.

"I did that."

He betrayed no emotion, but stood straight as a rod, his hands clasped in front of him, his hat shielding his face from the sun.

She plunged onward, seizing the opportunity. "I think . . . I think she returned your . . . feelings. I mean she did say she saw a lot of you."

When she stole a glance she saw the corners of his mouth rise slightly. His eyes took on a faraway look and his complexion deepened just a shade. Her pulse quickened. Then he gave his head a shake.

"I wouldn't mind seeing her again."

"Would you . . ." Her mouth felt a little dry, and she paused to moisten her throat. "If she were free . . . of the stage, that is. Would you, um, want to keep company with her?"

He gave her a curious look and she lowered her eyes and clasped her gloved hands, her beaded reticule swinging from her wrist. He must think her forward if not mad. If she said any more it would look suspicious.

He regarded her so hard that she was forced to look up into his pensive gray eyes. He seemed to be deciding how much to say. Then finally he gave a slow grin that set her heart a fire.

"I'd like to see Grace again. I told her that. But I didn't have enough to offer her to make her give up her acting."

Annie gulped a shallow breath and took a step closer in spite of herself.

"You mean you would want her to give up her career if she wanted to be with you?"

She had to look away, the conversation was too embarrassing.

He gave a chuckle. "Well, maybe we didn't get to know each other that well. You're asking a big question. I reckon I'd have to think it over."

"Oh, I'm sorry. I didn't mean—,"

"It's all right. Naturally you would be curious about who your sister was seeing."

Lord, what a tangle this was. She sought some way of extricating herself. "I just wondered that's all. I promise I won't breathe a word of what you've said when I write to her."

He smiled lazily. "You can tell her I hope to see another performance. I might even be able to get away in a week or two."

He paused and thought for a moment. Then he bent and yanked up a long, dried stalk to put between his teeth.

"How long did you say they'd be in Canon City?"

She needed to tell him the truth. But they were nearing the rest of the church goers, still mingling socially about the little white building. Now wasn't the time. She needed to be alone with him when she did that. But she had to answer his question.

"A week, I believe."

He murmured an acknowledgment.

His next words were muttered to himself and she barely caught them. "Chasing an illusion, then."

"What?"

"Oh, nothing, just thinking out loud."

"I see." She glanced away, thinking hard. "Shall I let you know if I hear from Grace?"

He nodded thoughtfully. "Yes, you do that."

"Well, I'm sure you'll be hearing from her."

He offered his arm in gentlemanly fashion to escort her back to the crowd.

From her circle of women friends standing by a patch of colorful wildflowers in the buffalo grass, Letty had only half-listened to the ladies' chatter. One eye had been on her niece and her neighbor the whole time. There was something going on between them, she would wager. It was natural enough for Grant to walk up to the cemetery after church. She knew he always scattered flowers there on Sunday.

But he and Annie had stayed conversing for a long time. Even at this distance, Letty had caught the way they glanced at each other and then away as if neither was quite comfortable with a straight out exchange. Something was passing between them.

Grant Worth was a fine man. He would make a fine husband for any woman who was willing to work hard at his side. But Annie hadn't been brought up to work. Letty had argued about that with her dear sister. Her sister had married a man who was striving to be a leader in Denver City, and appearances helped him maintain his position. Annie had a good education, but she'd been brought up to be genteel, to catch a wealthy society son herself. With her personality, she would charm the town.

But on a ranch out here? Letty had her doubts. She

watched the two of them descend the slope, keeping a large gap between them as if to let others know they were not on intimate terms. Well, she would say nothing unless asked. You could never tell how love might play a part in things. For love, a woman might change her ways entirely.

Eleven

Wednesday morning found Grant at his roll-top, going over the bills. His bank account was healthy enough, and with the strength of the herd, he should do well this year. Well enough to spend some time marketing his idea of breeding llamas to pack in the hills. He did some figuring to see if it would be wise to purchase another female. In the meantime he could begin to show the male to prospective buyers, mine owners in Leadville and the like.

He was so deep in his figuring that he didn't look out the window until Chalmers stuck his head into the study.

" 'Scuse me, boss, but a lady's driving toward the house in a buggy."

Grant leaned back and tossed his pencil on the desk. The numbers were a jumble in his head anyway. Now, who was coming calling?

He got up and went to the window to watch the strawberry roan trotting toward the house. The horse belonged to Letty, but he soon saw that the driver was Annie Marsh. In spite of himself his spirits lifted at the thought of a bit of feminine company. He hadn't allowed himself to ponder the situation with Grace any more. There were some meetings coming up in the valley that would be important, and he had a lot of things to attend to.

He watched Annie rein in and let Chalmers go out and help her down. She looked fetching in a burgundy calling costume, her bonnet secured with scarf material tied under her chin. Something stirred in him, and he recognized the new desire that had awakened when he'd met Grace. Must be that Annie Marsh reminded him of her sister, for he suddenly felt like he'd never noticed her attractive qualities before. In the next moment, he quelled his wayward thoughts.

He went out to the porch to greet her.

"Morning, Miss Marsh," he said, lifting his hat.

She gave him a shy smile and lifted her skirts to come up the steps. "Good morning. I hope I'm not disturbing you."

"Not at all. I needed a respite from the infernal paperwork. Do come in."

He stretched over to push the door inward and then followed her through. He watched her eyes glance around at his sitting room and knew she must be looking at it from a woman's point of view. He hadn't changed it much since Kate died, and Chalmers kept it clean.

Annie sat down on the burgundy brocade settee, while he took a seat in the big rocking chair and stretched his feet out on a small, wooden stool.

"What can I do for you?"

She looked into his silvery gray eyes and felt her heart bump. She clutched her handbag tightly in her fists. In a moment she would have to pull the drawstring apart and hand over the letter she had brought him. She tried to arrange her features in a pleasant expression.

"I," she began, then fumbled with the beaded bag. "I brought you a letter . . . from Grace."

His feet came down to the floor as he rocked forward. "Oh?"

She nodded and pulled out the ivory envelope. Holding it only a moment in hesitation, she leaned forward and handed it to him.

"Grace wrote to me asking that I deliver this to you. I suppose she thought it was faster."

He was tearing open the envelope and pulling out the folded note. Then he frowned and set it aside on a small round table beside a beaded-fringe kerosene lamp.

"I'm sorry. I'll read it later. Would you care for some refreshment?"

Annie felt herself shaking as she got up. "No, thank you, I have to get back. Letty could only spare me for an hour or so. I just wanted to bring the letter."

He nodded solemnly. "I thank you for that."

She gave a quick smile and then moved toward the door. On the porch she turned to look up at him again.

"If you decide to go to Colorado City, tell my sister hello for me."

He hesitated, then said, "I'll surely do that."

He saw her to the buggy, helped her in and then lifted his hat as she picked up the reins and clicked to the horse.

"Give my best to your aunt," he said.

She nodded and then jolted away.

Once on the beaten track that led back toward her aunt's place, she closed her eyes a moment against the strong sun, hoping she hadn't done the wrong thing. She needed to tell him the truth, but she'd decided to do it as Grace Albergetti. Grace was the one he loved. He would listen to her. If Annie told him the truth, he would suffer a loss. He would feel grief for a phantom. But as that phantom herself, she could show him that she was the woman he desired but that she was also Annie Marsh.

She had agonized over this decision, but in the end, she decided the intrigue had best be played out in a place like Colorado City. In the letter she said that the troupe had turned north from Canon City instead of continuing south. They were afraid of Indian attacks at Santa Fe, so they'd gotten an engagement in Colorado City, a place where many people went to take the waters at effervescing springs and take excursions among the strange and beautiful upright rocks in nearby gorges. She said she was going to take a few days off to remain alone for a rest at Manitou Springs when the troupe was finished with their engagement.

For Annie's purposes, it was far enough away from family that she would have Grant to herself and have time to explain to him. It was two days' ride from here. She gambled on Grant's wanting to go that far to see his lady love.

Now she gripped the reins and sent up a silent prayer that this would work.

"Grace will not fail me," she said out loud. And then feeling better, she relaxed.

If there were other tempting motives behind her decision to go to Colorado City, she barely admitted them to herself. She wanted him to see Grace one more time. She wanted to feel his arms around her, his lips pressed to hers. Then if he were the man she thought he was, he would come to understand, maybe even to admire, her daring and talent.

"Oh, Grant," she murmured on the wind. "Please don't hate me when you find out."

The stagecoach rattled through the canyon between tall, red, awe-inspiring rocks, then through a forested glen out to the rolling prairie to deposit its passengers in the treeless settlement of scattered houses with the ambitious name of Colorado City. Annie smiled in relief to be able to climb down from the unsprung stage and waited while her baggage was unloaded.

She approached a likely-looking young man at the livery stable to inquire if it were possible to hire a ride to the Manitou Hotel, three miles from here. As there were several passengers going there, baggage and trunks were transferred to an open-sided depot wagon with poles supporting a covered roof, pulled by a strong-looking team of dappled-gray horses that looked like they could pull the load up the hills.

Soon the prairie was left behind again, and they were traveling up into grand scenery. A torrent rushed through the narrow valley, with snow-covered mountains rising fifteen thousand feet above it. Several cabins were situated among the trees.

The hotel where the depot wagon let them off was quite as grand as anything seen in Denver City. And indeed city folks passed in and out of the pillared entrance. The lobby was tastefully decorated with fine furniture and crystal chandeliers. Annie paused on the red carpet leading to the polished oak desk. That she had gotten this far was a triumph. but if any of her family knew she was here to meet a man, they would disown her.

She had told Letty that she was meeting her brother here, so Letty put up no protest that her niece would be traveling on the stagecoach alone. She had written her family that she was continuing her holiday with her friends from Fairplay, and would be well-chaperoned. All lies.

She didn't like the lies and she was here to stop them. But she had to see Grant alone to untangle it all. And so as she slowly crossed the soft, cushiony carpet, she reassured herself that she was doing the right thing. This was a respectable place where many consumptives came, hoping that the dry climate and the medicinal waters would heal them. She would not seem out of place in such genteel surroundings. And yet there was enough privacy to see him.

She stepped up to the desk to register, then was shown to a comfortable room with four-poster bed, sturdy dresser and writing desk, and gauzy curtains over a window that looked out on the picturesque view of pine- and juniper-covered mountainside and a path beside a rushing stream. Misgivings were displaced by the entrancing beauty of the view. She sat down at the dressing table to unpin her hat and unbutton her traveling costume for a rest. Now, she only hoped that Grant would come.

By the time she went downstairs for dinner that evening, she was dressed in an evening dress of coral faille whose fitted bodice ended under scarf drapery of ivory Sicilienne. The chenille train was caught at the waist by red poppies matching those in her hair. She wore a lace shawl across her shoulders, clutching it tightly. Long, white kid gloves were complemented with silver bracelets. Around her neck was a black velvet ribbon from which hung a silver filigree pendant studded with pearls. She had done her curls carefully around her face, pulling up her tresses to coil from her crown down to the nape of her neck with a strand of pearls and garland of cloth poppies wound among her tresses. Then she applied color to her cheeks and lips and darkened her eyelids.

She felt like a queen, and didn't even mind that there was no one to greet her when she stepped into the lobby. She needed some time to get her bearings, to become Grace Albergetti again.

The host in the dining room showed her to a quiet table with all the propriety and gentility she could ask for.

"Will you be expecting anyone?" he asked as he handed her a large menu and lit the candle in its crystal holder.

"Perhaps. I'm not sure," she said in the sultry voice she was practicing. "There may be a gentleman joining me later."

He nodded discreetly and asked her preference for a beverage.

"Mineral water, please," she replied.

This was a common request where the water was famous for its medicinal qualities. And she needed to think clearly if Grant did arrive.

Since there had been no time for Grant to send a reply, she did not know if he would appear. Her ruse was that she had left the troupe for a few days to come here to rest. It was a blatant invitation to see him alone, and she knew it, but she didn't want the added complication of having to perform, even if she could travel to where Lola's troupe was now.

She prayed that Grant would come. She didn't want to spend the entire evening alone. She ordered several courses anyway, sipping the mineral water and trying to keep from chewing the rouge off her lips.

She was halfway through her soup when he appeared in the dining room entrance, his profile to her. Her heart sang out uncontrollably at the sight of him. Her fingers bumped against the white china, and she grabbed her napkin to blot her lips and bodice. Then she took two breaths as she watched Grant exchange a few words with the host.

The host smiled, gestured toward where Annie sat and led the way. Her face flushed and she was glad she was sitting down. He looked more handsome than ever, took off his hat and nodded to the host, who pulled back the chair and then left them alone.

His smile was disarming as he reached for her hand and lifted it to his lips. Her heart sailed into her throat. He hung his hat on a peg and took his seat, his eyes feasting on her. His lips curled upward with pleasure, and she thought with a wince, that he never looked at her like that while she was being herself. But there was some humor there, too, and it flashed through her mind that maybe he had figured out her ploy on his own. Maybe he knew and had come anyway. How easy it would be then. . . .

"Your sister gave me your note," he said. He leaned forward intimately. "How fortunate that you were traveling north again. Are you well? I hope you aren't here to take the waters because you've taken ill."

She found her voice and smiled, lowering her eyelids seductively. "I just needed a rest."

She gave a sigh, giving herself time to breathe and hope that her pulse would behave normally for long enough to carry out her plan.

He looked up as the waiter approached and ordered two glasses of champagne. He only glanced at the menu and chose something as if it really didn't matter what he ate. He unfastened the single button that held his coat across a satin vest and stiff-collared shirt and made himself comfortable.

He cleared his throat and let a frown mar his features. "I'm sorry to have unpleasant news, but I have to go to Denver next week," he said. "A number of us from the valley have to make a showing in protest of the bonds your father's trying to raise for his railroad."

She puckered a brow. "A protest?"

He nodded solemnly. "He plans to make a speech at the Inter Ocean Hotel. We need to be represented so people can hear our side of things."

She grimaced. "Father won't like that. I mean, it's been a long time since I've seen him, but I remember . . ."

Grant sat back, resting one elbow on the table. He had that stubborn look again. "I'm afraid you're right. Let's just hope things don't get nasty."

"There won't be any danger, will there?"

"I hope it doesn't come to that, but railroad men have strong feelings. So do ranchers."

His grim expression almost made her forget her own concerns. But what he said made her shiver. She'd never seen anything stand in Father's way. It gave her pause to think about his business methods, something she'd never been bothered about before. Now she wondered.

"I see," was all she said.

The main courses arrived, and they ate for a while. After

several bites of his smothered steak, Grant laid his knife across his plate.

"I didn't mean to ruin our evening. I wanted to see you again."

"Likewise," she said, giving a feeble smile.

She decided to put off her confession until they were alone. He smiled at her and refilled his champagne glass.

"Tell me about the shows. Are the Gaslight Players meeting with favorable audiences?"

She lowered her lashes. "Um, yes."

Watch it, she cautioned herself. Annie was the one who stammered, not Grace. She gave a sweet smile.

"We've done very well. After the engagement at Colorado City, I pleaded for a rest. The others have gone on. I'll join them later."

They finished their dinner and ordered fresh peach cobbler for dessert, but Annie was too nervous to eat much of it.

When they were finished, Grant helped her from her chair and draped her shawl around her shoulders, his face hovering near her ear. "You look very lovely," he said. "I hope you took pains just for me."

She smiled, but said nothing. When they reached the lobby, she paused. Now was the moment of truth.

"There's something I wanted to tell you," she began.

But his hand had drifted to the back of her neck, touching her softly. "There are many things I want to tell you," he whispered.

His words made her quiver. *Not this way,* she thought. She needed to face him squarely, but not in public.

"I . . . ," she swallowed, already drinking in his sturdy strength, the way his gaze was fixed on her. "We need to be alone," she said. Then added hurriedly, "So I can talk to you."

She heard the sensual suggestion in his smiling reply. "Just what I had hoped."

She floated up the stairs in front of him and had the key out of her handbag before they reached the door. Her hand shook as she unlocked it. He closed it behind them and then took her in his arms. The suddenness of his move caught her off guard, and all she could do was tremble being so near to him. All she wanted to do was drink him in.

"Grace, I've wanted to see you again ever since we parted. I admit I resisted this at first. No time for a woman, I said to myself. But it's too late. You've won my heart."

She opened her mouth to reply but they embraced instead. Oh, the thrill of being in his arms once more.

"Oh, Grant," she said, as he released her mouth and crushed her against him. "I needed to see you, to explain what you don't know."

He looked at her face, making the blood pound in her veins. But his hands were removing her shawl, drifting along her arms, his lips were kissing her throat. This was what she had really wanted, but she hadn't let herself admit it until now.

"Grant, there's something you don't know about me," she said huskily.

"I don't care. Whatever it is can wait. We have time to get to know each other. I've waited long enough."

Her skin tingled to his touch. "You have to listen to me."

He did pause for a moment and grasped her shoulders. His face studied hers. She had to fight to resist lifting a finger to touch his cheek.

"You mean about the stage," he said in all seriousness. "You want me, but you want to remain on the stage. I think I know that. But I want you, Grace Albergetti."

He smiled, looking over her shoulder at the four-poster bed behind them. "You wouldn't have invited me here if you didn't want me."

His finger found her chin and he lowered his lids to

look at her mouth. His voice was a hoarse whisper. "Maybe for once we can let tomorrow take care of itself. I want something to remember you by."

"I . . ." But he kissed her again and she succumbed to the rush of passion that kindled between them.

His voice was a feathered whisper as he kissed her ears, making her shiver.

"Grant, I have to tell you . . ."

"What do you have to tell me?"

But he'd thrown his coat aside and was unbuttoning his vest. She stepped back, trembling against the bed post as she watched his handsome form.

"My name . . . ," she swallowed. "It isn't Grace Albergetti."

He unhitched his belt and sat to pull off his boots. Deep within her a throbbing heat pulsed. Then he strode across to her and slid an arm around her waist, eyes inflamed with passion as he gazed appreciatively at every feature in her face and then her evening costume.

"You're beautiful," he murmured.

"Don't you care who I am?" she asked desperately as he sought the fastenings of her gown, gray eyes glinting with happiness and desire.

"Your real name instead of your stage name, you mean."

Then without waiting for an answer, he took her mouth in his again. Her traitorous arms found their way around him and her heart hammered in her chest. She wanted nothing more than to hold onto him forever. That she would not be able to made a huge sob of grief rise in her throat and tears spring to her eyes. She kissed him harder so he wouldn't see.

His clever fingers began to undo the buttons of her bodice, while hers undid his shirt. Somehow his shirt came out of his trousers and she felt his warm skin.

"Oh, my," she whispered to herself as he pushed the straps of her bodice aside. It fell backward to the waist, and he gazed on the rising flesh pushed upward from the corseted camisole. She could actually feel the flesh burn from his gaze.

She was breathless as he kissed her throat and chest. Then he reached down with one long arm to lift her skirts and touch her thighs. She gave a gasp.

All thought and words were gone now. There was nothing except being here with Grant in utter ecstasy. An ecstasy she might never experience again. She wanted to hold onto it with all her might.

Her skirt fell away. Then he gathered her up and they pressed hard together so that she could feel every inch of his body. The only light came from the street lamp outside. The tinkling of piano drifted in from the saloon across the street.

Grant's fingers untied the corset strings and let it loose, then he reached behind her to untie the petticoat, kissing her deeply at the same time. She drank in the pleasure of his mouth, parting her lips to seek his tongue with the tip of her own.

The petticoat fell away and then the corset dropped. Now there was nothing between them but her thin, lacy camisole. Her heart raced as his hands glided over her.

"I want you, woman," he murmured deeply into her ear.

No less than she wanted what he was doing to her. Then he stepped back to unfasten his belt-buckle and lower his trousers. His shirt remained, and her hands found their way under it to his bare skin, sending a flame through her.

Then he scooped her up and laid her across the bed. It squeaked slightly when he added his weight, but she heard nothing but the pounding in her ears as he touched her shoulder by the camisole strap and then followed it with a kiss. Her hand caressed his hard chest, and he deftly undid the laces of her camisole until it parted and her breasts were bared to him. He paused, and in the faint evening light from the window, she saw his look of passion as he gazed at her breasts. Then he covered one of them with his hand and lowered his mouth to tease the other one.

Sharp new throbbing sensations leapt from her loins through her body. The feeling of his mouth sucking gently on her nipple was like nothing else on earth. Nothing on earth.

"Oh, Grant," she moaned as he nudged and tantalized her.

She could feel his hard maleness pressing against her thigh and looked down to gaze. Heady sensations made her dizzy and she was thankful to be lying down.

He lifted his mouth to take hers again in a breathless kiss while each explored, fondled. It was too wonderful, more than she had dreamed. Her cries of ecstasy mingled with his murmurs of pleasure. Still, he seemed not to rush her but to enjoy every moment of newfound sensation. His mouth moved down her throat to cross her torso and kiss every inch of her skin. His fingers drifted across her inner thighs until the want of him was so great, she thought she would die.

She reacted to him, firmly, the way the experienced Grace would do.

Finally his excitement became too great.

"I want you now, Grace, do you want me?"

"Yes," she breathed. "Yes, yes."

He turned on his back and scooped her up with his arm so that she was on top of him. Her mouth was open in feverish breathlessness as she felt his erection against her. Giving a wicked smile she bent down to kiss him before lifting herself to her knees.

She felt the pain, but masked it by letting her hair fall over both their faces. He waited until she was settled before he began his movements again. Even though the tight new ache was there, she could forget it as he held her against him, murmuring love talk into her ear.

Cupping her buttocks in his hand, he rolled them over and then braced himself on his elbows. He kissed her deeply, his tongue penetrating and shooting in and out with hers as his lower body began slow movements that soon quickened. His pelvis began to move of its own accord and he lifted his head to groan aloud in pleasure. The bed rocked with their passion and Annie held on to his shoulders, gripping hard against him. She uttered a muffled shriek as he halted, plunged deeply once more and then collapsed his perspiring head against her damp one.

They clung to each other, catching their breath. The dull throb of ecstasy and pain mingled in her loins, but her heart cried out. *I love you, Grant,* she so desperately wanted to say. There was nothing else for her on earth. Nothing.

He held her for a long time, and she was thankful for the darkness. Surely he could tell it was her first time, but he was too much of a gentleman to say anything. She snuggled against him until she began to drift off in a peaceful slumber, aware that his breathing was even as well.

Enjoy the dream, was all she could think. For in tomorrow's light of day, the truth would be revealed. But she had this night to hold onto forever.

Twelve

Annie opened her eyes, still feeling the warm glow of being in Grant's arms. Then alarm set in. He wasn't in the bed, nor anywhere in the room.

She sat up and reached for the dressing gown laid out on the chair beside the bed. The soreness between her legs was equal to the chill of sudden loneliness. Guilt, too, crept along her spine and she stumbled to the dressing table to look at her disheveled state.

The realization of what she'd done last night hit her solidly as she stared at her reflection in the mirror. She had given herself to a man with no promises exchanged between them. Her hands flew to her face as she closed her eyes and rubbed them. She'd gone too far. At last the impetuous, impulsive Annie Marsh had gone too far.

She peeked at herself above her hands and looked in the mirror. She was no longer a virgin. Conflicting emotions roiled inside her, and she felt the tug of inexplicable grief. She'd lost her maidenhood, but oh, what a beautiful thing it had been.

But where was Grant now? Surely he would not leave without saying goodbye. The thought that he might have done so left her feeling utterly cold and bereft. She turned from the dressing stool and looked carefully around the room. All of his clothing was gone. There wasn't even a note.

Tears started to threaten when she heard the doorknob squeak and the door moved inward. Grant appeared, fully dressed, his hat pulled securely down on his brow. She gasped and clasped both hands to her mouth.

He came across the room and reached down to gather her up in his arms. Her chest tightened as he pressed her gently against him. But his body felt tense, and she sensed that something was wrong.

"What . . . ?" she asked, pulling away to study his face.

He kissed her cheek and then let her go, somewhat reluctantly, so that she sank to the stool.

"I'm sorry I wasn't here when you woke up," he said tenderly.

His finger traced a pattern along her face, but his face looked surprisingly grim.

"Where did you go?" she asked, hearing the husky sleepiness in her voice.

"I was called downstairs. The clerk had a message for me."

This information was not what she expected, and combined with all the other thoughts and feelings of the morning, she blinked at him dazedly. He held out a piece of paper with a hand-scrawled message, which she didn't try to decipher.

"Why? What's happened?"

His wide cheekbones took on a harder look and he stepped away, his hands pushing back his unbuttoned coat to rest on his hips as he gazed toward the window.

"Trouble at the ranch. Billy Joe sent the message on the mail coach."

His words boded ill. "What kind of trouble?" she breathed.

"Vandalism. The corral gate's broken this time, but purposely, Billy Joe seems to think." His jaw tightened. "One of the llamas was found in a ravine. Fortunately, it wasn't injured."

She felt stunned. "Maybe it broke the gate and got out?"

But she could tell from the anger in his eyes that he didn't believe it was the llama's doing this time.

"I'm sorry," she murmured. "Of course you'll have to go."

His chin came up and he swung around, but he didn't look at her.

"I'm sorry to leave this way. I'd hope to settle some things between us."

She became aware of how awful she must look. Grant was used to seeing her at her best. She seized the hair brush and began brushing out the tangles as a way to release her pent-up energy.

She watched him in the mirror.

"What things?" She didn't want it to sound demanding, but she was desperate to know what was in his mind.

He came to stand behind her and planted his hands on her shoulders, gazing at her face in the mirror. She tried not to sway against him.

"Odd turn of affairs, now, wouldn't you say?"

"What do you mean?"

"I lose my heart to a pretty woman who happens to be the daughter of my worst enemy. Fate couldn't have dealt me a meaner hand. But then fate sometimes behaves that way."

"You surely don't believe this vandalism has anything to do with Father?"

But his steely stare when his eyes came back to her face left no doubt. "I may not be able to prove it, but I have my suspicions. I'm sorry. Even if you are estranged from your father, you may not want to hear that."

He removed his hands from her shoulders and she felt a coldness come over him. She blinked her eyes open wider and swiveled around to face him.

"How can you believe it's his fault?"

"I know his type. Maybe you've been away from home

for too long. He's an ambitious man, your father. He's a ruthless businessman."

She had to be careful what she said. She lowered her eyelids and moistened her lips, giving herself a chance to think.

"You're right, I've been away from home for several years. I would be sorry, though, to learn that he's caused you harm."

Grant leaned against the bedpost studying her. His own eyes were narrowed slightly and his words came out slower.

"I hope I haven't been the fool. I come down here on your invitation. As soon as I turn my back on the ranch, someone does a little damage, sending a message if I'm not mistaken."

The silence grew heavier between them. She trembled at his words. Not only was she still stunned at having made love to him, something a girl like Annie Marsh would never do before marriage, but now here he was, standing before her other persona, implying that Grace might have been in league with her father. And she was no nearer the truth than she had been when she came here.

A great sob built up within her. Tears glazed her eyes. Truly she was lost forever. She would roast in hell now. She'd given in to Grant's caresses and had failed herself in her purpose in coming here. Grant was at war with her Father. It didn't matter anymore who he thought she was.

"No," she said, her shoulders shaking. "It's I who have been the fool."

She shook her head and her hands flew to her face. She cried uncontrollably, no longer caring what Grant thought. It was all a debacle from which she'd never get extricated now. What did it matter anymore?

For a moment Grant did not stir. But then she felt a hand on her shoulder and he lifted her up and sat with her on the end of the bed, pulling her head against his shoulder.

She sobbed on and on. At least he didn't hate her yet.

"Sorry," he finally said. "I didn't mean to accuse you of anything, my dear Grace." He gave a long sigh. "If you have no part in this then I owe you an apology."

He tipped her face up to his and she blinked at him through her tears, still sobbing at her own dilemma. He brushed tears away and kissed her cheeks, not knowing why she really cried. She could see his face through the deluge pouring from her eyes, but her features were so contorted she could not speak.

She cried harder and he pulled her against him again, rocking her gently.

"Poor Grace, shhhh, now. Don't worry."

After consoling her for some time he began to wipe her face with his white handkerchief, and she kissed his fingers. Why did he have to go? Couldn't they just forget everything and spend the day as lovers?

But already the harsh sunlight was creeping across the floor from the window, telling her that there were matters out there affecting their lives that couldn't be ignored. She struggled with her planned speech about who she really was, but Grant didn't give her time to explain.

When her crying had subsided and she blew her nose into the handkerchief, he got up to pour her a glass of water from a pitcher on the night stand. She gulped it down, only briefly glancing at his eyes.

"I don't want to leave you like this, but I must. My livestock are in danger. If some nastiness is going to occur in the valley, I have to be there. Do you understand?"

She nodded helplessly. "I could go with you," she said.

His expression regained some compassion, but she felt relief as she saw the slight shake of the head. If she went with him, she would either have to let Letty in on her secret or become two people at once. The thought of either made her blanch.

"Thanks for your concern, but I need to handle this on my own."

He walked toward the window, rubbing the back of his neck. She felt terrible about the weight of his responsibility.

"I wish there was something I could do," she whispered.

She slid off the bed and returned to the dressing table. Her reflection showed her she looked worse than before, and she got up again to pour water from a porcelain ewer into a basin and dip a towel in it. She sponged off her face and then sat down to brush out her hair. Still, her cheeks were blotchy and her eyes were red.

Being Grace instead of Annie, she carried with her some of the cosmetics Lola had pressed on her when she'd left the troupe. She dabbed some cream on her cheeks and rubbed it in, hoping to restore a smoother more creamy look.

She began braiding her hair loosely and coiled it up, stabbing it with combs to anchor it on her head.

Grant crossed the room and stood on her left side. "I have to return to the ranch before something else happens."

"I know."

"Will you be all right here?"

She nodded.

"When this is settled, I'll come back to you, I promise."

"All right." She dared not look into his eyes.

"Where can I find you?"

She thought quickly. "You'll be so busy." She avoided his eyes. "We might be in Cripple Creek, . . . or Denver."

"Very well."

He bent down and kissed her again. She turned and snaked a hand around his neck, but she didn't hold him. The kiss was warm and delicious. But she knew he had to leave.

He looked into her eyes deeply, his look of concern melting her. "You've no family anymore. I hope to rectify that when we have time to talk it over."

She watched him cross the room. At the door, he turned for a last look. She saw his eyes sweep her figure and she blushed anew. The corners of his mouth lifted in remembrance, and he held her gaze for a long, long time. Then he touched his hat and was out the door. She heard the latch click behind him.

Grant didn't want to think about the complications he'd involved himself in just now. But as he rode hard up the valley beside the red rocks reaching out of the ground and claiming the hills, he still had her taste and her smell about him. This wasn't how he'd wanted their meeting to end. And the anger in his heart toward her own father had colored their farewell.

He felt a deep regret about that and wanted to put it right. But there were weighty matters at hand and he didn't like the dread that accompanied his ride back through the green, pine-covered mountains. Above him, the imposing gray summit of Pike's Peak towered far above timber line.

He loped quickly through the higher meadows past stands of quaking aspen with their tall, slim white trunks like sentinels. He rested and watered his horse in a shady spot by a creek. The wind in the leaves sounded hollow on its way through further valleys, to whirl up dust on the lower plains further south. As he crossed Ute Pass, he watched carefully for any sign of Indians.

The Utes that previously hunted in the San Luis Valley to the south had been removed to a reservation on the western slope some years ago, but the more warlike Arapahoe still raided settlers from time to time if they took offense to their treaties or if their hunting wasn't good that year. Grant knew little of Indian affairs and had always treated fairly those he'd traded with. But he was a wary traveler, wanting to be prepared, should he meet any unfriendly warriors.

He followed uplands clothed in pine, cedar and dwarf oak until he came to the creek that would lead him to the South Platte. The creek turned westward, passing two red buttes that cut into the mountain like solid tables. He let his horse pick its way along, following a sandstone ledge to the right that formed the wall of the valley.

Coming out of the ravine, the prairie opened wider. To the west, the rugged mountains undulated blue and majestic. The stream widened, and they came to the river bottom, lined with cottonwood, oak, ash and box elder.

The day was exceedingly quiet. Birds twittered in the branches. After seeing to his horse, Grant drank from the cold, mountain water tumbling across the rocks where the stream joined the South Platte. He stretched his legs and went to stand on the high banks, listening to the screeches and caws of magpies, crows, and steller's Jays, the coos and hoots of meadowlark and redwing blackbirds. His every sense read the messages in nature all around him. Being a cattleman meant knowing how to read the signs and knowing when there was a danger to your cattle.

Then it came, faint at first, but with his second breath he knew he was not mistaken. The smell of smoke was being carried on the strong winds. His spine prickled and he wasted no time whistling to his horse and mounting up again.

It was too far to make it home by nightfall and if the situation weren't so dire, he would spend the night at a camp that he knew some hunters favored on the western side of the long valley. He considered passing that way to find out if they had news of a fire to the north. He'd like to think this was just someone's campfire, even that of the Arapahoe. But a sixth sense told him it was not.

He pressed forward and bypassed the turn-off to Trout

Creek Pass that would take him to the hunters' camp. He would have to ride after dark, but a sense of urgency made him press forward now.

It could be his ranch, it could be someone else's ranch. It didn't matter. If there were a fire in the valley everyone would pitch in to help stop it from spreading and killing livestock that might be trapped in river bottoms and ravines. He didn't like the nasty possibility that this fire might have been set on purpose to burn out the ranches that had an already tenuous hold on a valley only recently claimed from Indian tribes who'd been moved elsewhere. What could they do? Cut their losses by selling land to the only outfit that had the power of the politicians and government land grants behind them—the railroad men.

When shadows claimed the high mountain valley, and the granite-tops to his left turned a deep purple with dark green carpets at their feet, Grant double-checked his ammunition in the revolvers slung from his hips and in his gold-engraved Winchester rifle. If he ran into trouble, he'd be ready. He rode on in the gathering darkness, trusting his horse not to stumble, but keeping his eyes and ears alert for signs of danger and for the dreaded glow of a fire to the north.

Nearing a gorge just to the south of his lands, he saw almost invisible clouds of smoke rolling down the river bottom. His horse shied, and he got off to lead it. Then the tell-tale flickering of a mass of flame danced along the far hillside and he could see that the side of the mountain was on fire.

He pressed on and in another quarter hour he saw that a belt of dry brush on the stream banks, still half a mile away, caught fire and the flames spread out. When they got nearer, his horse reared and pawed and Grant held tight to the reins, turning the horse away from the crackling brush and the roar of flames traveling fast across the mountain. Clearly they could not go that way.

He mounted again and kicked his horse into a trot away from the advancing fire, but a low hill prevented him from reaching the open prairie. A slight breeze springing from the east carried flames across the river bottom and the flames jumped from bush to bush on his right.

"Let's get out of here," he called to his already frightened horse, as it shied away from every tuft of smoke and flame that ate up dry grass.

Grant cursed at having come this way. It would have been better to stick to the open prairie. Now only one more hill blocked his way and he saw the danger of his position. The night was illuminated now and peaks and ridges were visible in the light. The river bottom roared with the mass of flame, and he pressed his horse to get around the hill to the prairie, which would be bare of cedar bushes, though the grasses might burn faster.

He had to cross the creek, and he raced the flames eating away at the bank. The horse did not want to cross, but finally succeeded in plunging into the water. Then angling downstream, Grant headed for the other side.

He was just climbing up the opposite bank when a puff of smoke came at them. The horse reared, but Grant clung, and when the horse's feet came down, they climbed further downstream. Once safely through the burning line of brush, he raced for open prairie and didn't stop for another mile. Feeling his horse tire, he reined up.

"Whoa, boy, whoa."

The horse had a chance to rest and Grant turned to survey the burning mountainside. Grim anger coursed through him. True, the brush was dry and they had lacked rain. He would like to believe that this was some accident or started by lightning striking a dead tree, but in his heart he didn't think so. The fire was far enough away that it might not have caused damage closer to home, but there was still much to find out.

He clucked to his horse. "Come on, boy. A few more miles then we're home."

He used his neckerchief to wipe off the sweat on his face and neck. His body was tense from the danger and he was angry at whoever had caused it, as his faithful animal carried him onward. With relief he saw that the one side of the mountain had burned alone. The hand of nature had spread it southward, but the slopes to the north and grasslands where his herds grazed had been spared. At least he hoped so.

His horse whinnied just before three riders came out of the darkness. The voices of the men came to him on the wind and he trotted forward, recognizing the shape of Billy Joe. He rode up to his ranch foreman and the two other cowboys.

"Billy Joe," Grant called.

He wanted to be sure they recognized him before they drew their guns at presumed danger.

"It's the boss," he heard Billy Joe say to the others in evident relief.

He joined them where they'd been surveying the fire. "What's happened here?"

"Fire broke out along Antler Ridge. We got there as soon as we saw the flames. The boys are still digging trenches and watering down the buildings just in case."

He ground his teeth. Antler Ridge was on his property.

"Well done. What about Letty's place? The wind's going to put her place in danger as well. The fire's spread pretty far along the creek bottom. I was nearly trapped in it myself."

"I sent Dugan and Jake over there to see if she needed a hand."

"Good. We'll ride by there on the way back. Any losses in the herd?"

He saw the look exchanged between Billy Joe and the others and felt a warning slither up his spine. Billy Joe's shoulders rose and fell an inch as he evidently realized he was elected to tell Grant some bad news.

"One of the llamas was on the far side of Antler Ridge just before the fire broke out. Don't know how it got there. I put both those animals in the barn at sundown, and the baby was with its mother. Slid the bolt on stalls and barn door. I knew it would be my hide if anything happened to them, especially after one of them getting into the ravine."

"And?" Grant demanded.

"Lucky for us the fire didn't spread that way. It was trapped in a gully, but young Caleb got to it on foot and led it out. Just a little singed fur from what I could tell. Didn't have time to do a thorough examination."

"All right, let's go. There's going to be work to be done before this thing burns out."

He glanced at the cloudless sky. Rain would help, but it was unlikely. It had been a dry month. The buffalo grass was like tinder. If someone wanted to burn out the valley, he couldn't have picked a better time.

He felt like the point of a knife dug into his ribs and twisted. Whoever had done this had aimed at him personally. Knowing that the llamas were his prized possession, someone had sneaked onto his property and gotten the animal out before starting the fire. When this was all over, Grant would find out who, and that man would pay.

He felt old responses of self-preservation and quick reactions rising from long years in the war and on the cattle drives fighting rustlers. When it came to killing or being killed, he'd learned to distance himself from the pain of it all and protect himself and his comrades. And this was now a war.

They galloped along in the darkness, a dull glow on the prairie from moonlight and the flickering blaze that garlanded the hills to their right. When they reached Letty's place, he sent Billy Joe and the others ahead to look for shovels or picks or whatever they could find that would rip up grass and make a trench. From the squeaks at the well, he could hear even before he saw that Letty and some neighbors were filling buckets to douse the buildings. Her ranch hands had gathered and were working a bucket brigade.

The fire was some distance on the hillside, but one gust of wind could bring flames rolling in on a tumbleweed or jump it from bush to bush.

He reined in and jumped from his horse, calling out to her. He wondered at the same time if Annie Marsh was here.

"Grant," Letty called waving and pointing.

He strode up to her and walked back with her to the bucket brigade. He was relieved to see that a number of neighbors must have seen the fire and were now doing the backbreaking work of helping her save her property.

"Just rode in. Got caught in the smoke on the creek bottom. How long have you been at it?"

"Just an hour. Juan Jose woke me up. He rode for help while I got the animals out of the barn. So far we're safe. But the wind worries me."

Her grim tone told him how worried she was. "I can lend a hand."

"What about your place?"

"Billy Joe got things under control. One of the llamas was caught near the fireline. Caleb Johnson rescued it."

"Oh, Grant."

The grim fury in her face reflected what he felt. He didn't have to say what he thought. But there wasn't time to stand around talking. His eyes flicked to the house.

"Anyone still in there?"

She shook her head, wiping dirt from her face. "No. Annie took off yesterday to see a friend. Should be back tomorrow."

"Then let me see what I can do."

She laid a restraining hand on his. "You should go on. You might be needed at your place."

He felt torn, anxious to protect his own property, but aware of the duty neighbors showed one another in these parts. "I've got more men than you have, Letty. And that blaze is traveling south. My place isn't threatened unless the wind changes."

"And if it does?"

"The men are digging trenches and watering down the place. I can be spared for the moment."

"All right. You stay and help. But if the wind shifts, you go."

"Agreed."

Grant peeled off his coat and pitched in. They watered down the dry wood of all the buildings and the corral. Then he helped dig a shovel into the hard earth, pitching dirt onto a long embankment. At least if the fire ate away at the grass, it would stop at the gully they had made. They worked through the rest of the night and Grant at first couldn't believe it when he felt a drop of rain on his cheek.

He paused in his digging, thinking it was just dew or someone had splashed him. But there was another drop. He peered at the graying sky and saw a small gathering of clouds, not big thunderheads, but small cumulus that might carry a light shower. He grasped his shovel and strode toward the house.

Letty was so disheveled from the night of work he barely recognized her.

"I took care of your horse," she said. "He's fed and rested and should be ready to ride now."

"Thanks."

"No, I owe you a debt of thanks."

He accepted the tin cup of water and they walked back to the house where his horse was tied to the hitching rail.

"Guess I'd better get along. But I'll see you later. We're

going to find out who's behind all this," he told her. "For my part, I believe it was a threat of the personal kind."

Letty's eyes flashed out of a grimy face and she shoveled straggling hair back behind one ear.

"You're right about that," she said. "And whoever it is is going to be sorry."

Thirteen

Annie stepped onto the heavy-laden stagecoach for Denver. She'd had to rise in the dark to dress, for the stage left just as there was morning light. She would have preferred to be alone instead of among strangers, to consider her newfound elation from the experience of making love, coupled with the guilt that accompanied it and her failure at telling the truth.

In the dewy morning, she had but to close her eyes and relive the thrilling moments with the man she loved. How tender and personal were these newfound emotions. Never mind that the sequence of events was wrong-way to, and that she was more than ever immersed in a secret life from which there seemed no way out. Never mind the scandal, if it were known that she had become a cowboy's mistress. But she was not given time for silent contemplation of these matters.

She squeezed into the stagecoach between a plump lady traveling with her kicking six-year-old and a grizzled miner on his way to Denver, no doubt to raise a stake for his next venture. Across from her sat a pale gentleman in a suit that had seen better days and a top hat that seemed too big for his skull. One of the consumptives, most likely, here to try to cure his symptoms in the mineral waters and dry air.

Next to him were two spinster sisters with baskets of crocheting on their laps, though how they would be able to see their work in the dark stagecoach, much less stitch once the coach was bumping along at a brisk pace, was a mystery to Annie. In the third row, several more gentlemen squeezed in. Once the baggage was all stowed behind and above, the driver gave a shout, cracked his whip, and they were under way.

Not having the blessing of a window seat, there was little Annie could do but try to rest her shoulders against the seat. It didn't take long before everyone knew everyone's business, but she wasn't in the mood to talk. The coach lurched along quickly, with the pine-clothed foothills rising in a long line on their left. Annie sent the hills a fond farewell and a thank you, for in the folds between the hills where the Manitou springs bubbled, she had found heaven in Grant's arms.

She gave a deep sigh, knowing that harsh reality awaited her in Denver, but she wasn't yet ready to face any part of her life there. It was too soon. She could almost be thankful for the long, sweaty, jolting ride to the city on the plains.

The horses strained up the largest hill that protected Colorado City from the rolling prairie and bluffs to the north. About halfway up, the driver halted the team and set the brakes. Hopping down, he threw open the door.

"Everyone out," he barked. "Time for a fine walk to the top."

With some complaining and much chatter, everyone obliged. The break afforded Annie one last look at the undulating line of mountains and the shadowed folds of the hills with the majestic granite top of Pike's Peak far above the line where the timber stopped.

"If only . . . ," she murmured to herself. But she hardly knew if only what, so she picked up the skirt of her traveling suit and trudged up the hill behind the spinster sisters who commented on nature as they went.

Once back in the coach, she had to hang onto her bonnet as the driver whipped the team into a frenzy and they dashed along a fairly straight road. Rocky mounds, half covered with low scrub oak, dotted the landscape to their right as they followed the line of foothills that stretched northward. One would think they were being chased by wild Indians, so fast did the team gallop along. Annie thought her tailbone would break every time she was lifted off her seat and slammed back down. The horses didn't slow until they came to a rest stop at noon, a way station that offered a plate of greasy food, which Annie decided to forgo.

She would have preferred to walk or ride all the way to Denver than get back in the stage, but there seemed no alternative. Besides, she was in enough deep water already without any more adventures. So she took her seat, closed her eyes and hung on to the strap above her head as best she could.

The sight of Denver almost seemed odd after her sojourn in the mountains and in the smaller settlements she'd just visited. Two- and three-story buildings were spaced along a grid on the east side of the South Platte River. The grid plan straddled the smaller Cherry Creek, which fed the Platte. The Denver and Rio Grande was chugging around a bend at the edge of town, heading into the station, a painful reminder of what Annie had decided to come home to do.

Grant might never forgive her when he found out who she really was. But if it were true that her own father was applying pressure to the ranchers of South Park, she could at least find out. She could not believe he would do such a thing, but there might be a way to help Grant. Annie had paid little attention to her father's business up until now. Those were men's affairs. But it wasn't entirely unheard of for a woman to take up a cause. Unusual, but not unheard of. So Annie was determined to learn her father's plans.

The coach merged with other wagon and horseback traffic crowding onto the wooden bridge that spanned the river at Fifteenth Street. The noise and bustle of the workaday world was in stark contrast to the dream she'd been living. Here were the reminders of the hard work that had brought civilization to the plains. Smoke rising from newly built factories near the river and the railroad tracks, two-story businesses and brick warehouses with cast-iron pillared entrances. Telegraph wires and church spires, with homesteads dotting the square city plots. Five thousand souls made a home in this sprouting city at the edge of the sparsely-settled, arid plains.

The stagecoach creaked to a halt and Annie found her legs to get down into the bright sunlight. She had to blink several times as her eyes got accustomed to the light. Carriages rolled by, but she knew she wasn't expected. No one would come to meet her, so she had her trunk stowed at the express company depot until she could hire a buggy. But when she reached the livery stable she remembered that today was Wednesday, marketing day. If Lin Chu or her stepmother were in town, she could ride home with them.

Slowly, the routine of their household came back to mind as she weaved in and out between pedestrians intent on their business along the boardwalks in front of shops and businesses. The pulse of commerce was punctuated by the roll of wheels along hard-packed streets and the jangling bells of horse-drawn streetcars. In spite of the clement weather, and the azure sky marred only by a few milky clouds, the heartbeat of the city seemed foreign to her.

She was beginning to feel thirsty and wished she'd simply hired a buggy instead of hunting along Market Street for members of her household. She was about to turn back when she rounded a corner and spied Lin Chu doing something that made her stop and stare. She thought she was up to all of his tricks, so she could only gawk when she saw the sly Chinese servant beating a large drum that was slung from around his neck. He was nodding his head to a rousing hymn being sung lustily in the open air by three women and one man in the military blue uniforms of the Salvation Army.

Annie was aware of these missionaries to those in need because Hattie had helped raise funds for them when they'd arrived in Denver. The Army, which had begun in England, brought religion to those who might not be welcome in a church, and they had opened a small hospital for the needy.

Annie's mouth dropped open as she gawked. Lin Chu a convert? It couldn't be. She closed her mouth and stepped back against a brick wall out of the way of traffic to watch. A black cast iron pot with a wire handle sat in front of the singers and every so often when a passerby attempted to negotiate the boardwalk in front of them, Lin Chu broke off from his drumming to wave a stick at the hapless pedestrian. The Chinaman stepped forward and tapped the edge of the pot, smiling broadly, his gleaming teeth and snapping black eyes forcing attention to the request for donations. When the businessman searched his pockets for something to give, Lin Chu nodded in satisfaction and retreated to again accompany the hymn singing with the beat of his drum.

This went on for some time until the pot had collected quite a sum. Annie stood through four verses and sent up praise when they reached Amen. Then she stepped out onto the walk and accosted her servant before he could start another hymn.

"Lin Chu," she called out, waving as she approached. "Lin Chu, what are you doing?"

His head came up as he recognized her and he smiled broadly. "Miss Annie, you back to town."

"Yes, I am back, and I would kindly like a ride home. Why are you playing in this little band?"

The other singers were turning their pages and conferring over their next hymn while she talked to him. He smiled and nodded at them when they turned to look curiously at his new companion. He pointed to her with a stick by way of introducion.

"This Miss Annie Marsh. She my employer daughter."

Annie nodded politely, but she took out her impatience on Lin Chu. "Today is marketing day. Did you bring Hattie to shop?"

"Oh, yes, she shop at mercantile and vegetable market. I come help friends at Salvation Army."

Annie turned her back on the little choir and lowered her voice. "What are you up to? Surely you haven't just now been saved?"

He narrowed his eyes to a cat-like cunning, looking very pleased with himself. "I go to their church one night. They give me meal. I make business deal."

"You what!"

"I say I play drum and help get donations for charity work. I get ten percent of money in pot."

"Lin Chu, that's terrible. You're extorting a charity."

"Oh, no, no. They not get as much money without me. I help."

She gave an exasperated sigh. "Well, they'll have to do without you for now. Put down that drum and come collect my trunk. When Hattie is done shopping, I want to go home. You already have employment, in case you forgot."

Lin Chu saw that he could not argue further. He explained that he had to leave and accompany his mistress now. She stood by politely, trying to look pleasant while he transferred the drum to the other gentleman. Some hushed words were exchanged, no doubt about his "take" for the morning, which they would count out and save for him. Then he hurried along to Annie, who turned and marched back to Market Street.

They found Hattie looking up and down the street for

her wandering servant, her relief evident when Annie called out her name. She was also surprised to see her stepdaughter show up so suddenly.

"Oh, my dear Annie. There you are. We didn't know when you were coming back. Was it today? Oh, dear, and no one to meet you."

Lin Chu took the packages from Hattie's arms and then Annie followed her into the mercantile where she addressed a clerk.

"We're here now. That is, I've found Lin Chu. He will see to the supplies I asked for."

Annie helped her stepmother organize her purchases, and Lin Chu shouldered sacks of grain, beans and sugar, which he loaded into the buckboard. Annie carried smaller packages wrapped in brown paper. Hattie extracted a long pencilled list from her reticule and scanned it.

"I hope I've got everything now."

"Did you order anything else at any of the other shops while you were waiting for Lin Chu?" asked Annie.

She mopped her perspiring brow with her handkerchief and wished this were all over. When the western sun went down, it would be cooler. By that time she wanted to be home, sitting in their claw-footed bathtub and looking forward to a change of clothes. But they would never get there unless the typical Marsh inefficiencies were cleared up first.

Finally Hattie had everything she needed and Lin Chu obediently unwrapped the reins from around the hitching rail. He took the driver's seat and yelled in Chinese at anything and anyone on the street to make way.

Annie and Hattie held onto their seats as they rumbled down Seventeenth Street. It seemed like hours, and Annie's mood failed to improve. The glow of her night of love had been replaced by new worries. Looking at the busy life of the crowded little city only reminded her of her true position here. She was no longer a show girl, and soon Grant would discover that the show girl didn't even exist. Would he try to find her? If so, Annie was his only link; he would have to come see her to seek out Grace.

They left the noisier businesses behind. Further south on Broadway were placid homes on comfortable lots with young trees trying to shade them, surrounded by lawns, flower gardens, and vegetable patches. The odor of fresh bread drifted from open doors and smoke rose from chimneys, attesting that for many households, Wednesday was also baking day.

Annie turned to look back toward the river and dreamed for a moment that she didn't have to come back, that she could turn herself into Grace Albergetti permanently and live with Aunt Letty. She wouldn't mind hard work during the day if she could curl up in Grant's arms at night. The thought sent a stab of longing through her. Then she was jolted as they turned up the hill and she had to hang onto her seat.

The thump of high-steppers brought her back to the present as a turned-out pair approached, pulling a fashionable Victoria phaeton. The coachman was dressed in livery and top-hat, and both Annie and Hattie waved at Mrs. John Evans, wife of the former governor of Colorado when it was a territory.

Hattie grumbled. "That was so showy. It's hard to keep up with such ostentation."

Annie didn't comment, but she wondered if her father was putting pressure on his wife to make a similar show of fashion and social position, things that might help him politically with his railroad.

Worries about the railroad remained in the back of her mind as they pulled into the wagon yard behind the house and busied themselves getting things in. Her brother was at his job at the bank, but Maria and Dorthea were glad to see Annie and wanted to hear about life on Letty's ranch. She appeased them by saying that she was too dirty and exhausted to speak, but that after a bath, she might come down for tea in the kitchen before supper. Then she escaped upstairs while Dorthea ran her a hot bath in the claw-footed tub.

With grateful relief she divested herself of her clothes, pinned her hair on top of her head and went along to the bathroom. Dorthea was running the bath water and had laid out the towels on the wooden washstand.

"Is there anything else you need, Miss Annie?" said Dorthea, placing back scrubber and soap within her reach.

"No, thank you. I'll just soak awhile."

"I'll bet you had a lovely time in the country," said Dorthea.

Annie tried to answer patiently. "I'll tell you all about it, but I am tired now."

"You have a nice bath then and we'll have some hot tea waiting in the kitchen."

Left alone to soak in the soothing bath water, Annie rested her head on the back of the porcelain tub and closed her eyes. She tried to rest and let the hot, soapy water soothe her aching limbs, but thoughts of her dilemma made her jump at every sound in the house below. Certain that somehow word of her tricks would reach the household, she speculated in vain as to what to say if the truth came out.

She threw one arm above her head, letting the water drip down her face. Cast out of her household for the lies and humiliation she would have brought on the family, what would she do? Her only friends at the moment seemed to be Marcel and Lola. They would welcome her into their fold.

Her eyes flew open and she stared at the stamped metal patterned ceiling above her head. How ironic if she were to fulfill her fantasy by being kicked out of her house and having to take to the stage to make a living—just like she'd said Grace did?

She slid upward in the tub, sloshing water onto the wainscoting, and seized a sponge. Her heart murmured in fear. A door slammed downstairs and she jumped. Having lost her heart to a man her family considered an enemy, she'd come home to try to find out if her father were the villain Grant said he was. Having given herself to her lover, she had committed a sin in the eyes of propriety. But somehow in the sparsely-settled mountain valleys, propriety had been the last thing on her mind.

But fear of her father's wrath was not lost on her.

"Think," she commanded herself and commenced scrubbing her skin as if she could wash away the dilemma she found herself in.

The water got cold and she let the tub drain, filling it with hot water again. At length, worried that she would shrivel up like a prune from hiding out in the bath too long, she stepped out to dry herself with the fluffy towel. She'd best take care with a modest appearance when she dressed for dinner. The plainer she looked, the more it would help her deny that she'd recently been wearing rouge and jumping around in scanty clothing in a mining town.

She reached her room, closed the door and sat down at the dressing table. Her hands went to her flushed cheeks and she knew it would be impossible to get the color out of them. Surely her family would see she was guilty of something.

She told Dorthea that she needed the tea brought to her room. She wanted to take a nap before dinner. The servants would have to wait until tomorrow to hear the gossip they longed for.

"You rest then, miss," said Dorthea. "I'll bring that tea. It was a long trip up from Colorado City, no doubt."

An hour later, Annie heard James come home. She envisioned the coming dinner scenario and wondered whether her father would stand by her when she was disinherited or whether he would roar with laughter. If she were made to walk the streets tonight, perhaps Lin Chu would sneak provisions and money out of the house. The longer she thought about her coming punishment, the worse it got, until in her mind she was wandering along the Platte River, looking for shelter in some warehouse until morning.

The little clock on her bedstead chimed, startling her.

"Good heavens, seven o'clock," she said out loud. Father must be home.

She flew to the armoire and pulled out a dress then yanked on the bell-pull for Dorthea to help her dress. By the time the housemaid tapped on the door, Annie was in her underclothes.

"Did you rest well?" the maid inquired as she helped Annie on with the corset and started to pull the laces.

"Oh, yes, thank you. Ow, not too tight." She sighed. "On the other hand, maybe the tighter the better. I won't be eating much tonight."

Dorthea's bony countenance scanned her mistress's face. "Are you ill?"

"Hmmmm a little. From the heat of the travel, I suppose."

"Miss Hattie might have a remedy to help. Should I tell her you're feeling ill?"

"No, thank you. Everyone will know soon enough."

Dorthea looked bewildered, but knew better than to pry. There were times when it was best just to take one's orders.

Finally dressed and coiffured, Annie straightened her spine and descended the stairs. No one waited in the entry hall or the front parlor. She heard muffled voices coming from the back parlor and proceeded toward her firing squad. She opened one of the sliding doors to find the rest of the family there, bent over a piece of paper on her father's knees. He looked up and smiled at her.

"Ah, there you are, my dear. Have a good trip?"

"Yes, Father."

She stood there stiffly.

"Well, come here and give your old father a kiss."

She blinked as he got up and came to her instead. She turned her cheek upward and received his kiss. Just then Maria appeared in the doorway.

"Dinner is served, sir."

"Thank you, Maria. Well, shall we all go in?"

She accepted her father's arm and made her feet move to the dining room with him.

"Good news," said Everett. "James was promoted at the bank."

Annie turned to lift eyebrows at her cocky brother. James strutted around the table, cleared his throat and placed one hand inside his jacket in a self-important pose.

"Promoted?" she said.

"My dear sister," he said in an imperious voice. "You sound as if the idea were unthinkable. Of course the institution has recognized my ability and given me a position of more responsibility."

"As they should," said Everett, sitting down and shaking out his napkin.

Annie somehow found her seat and James slid it in for her. Hattie smiled. Annie noticed her stepmother looked poised and refreshed in cream-colored faille with purple satin stripes. Perhaps it relieved her to have the four of them sitting down at table once again.

James went on for a while about his supervisory responsibilities at the bank, and they were treated to a history of that institution.

Maria served fish soup and then, while she was removing the dishes, Annie fanned herself nervously. The main course was pork chops with a new sauce that Hattie was anxious about. Never mind that Annie had been away for two weeks, was burdened with falsehoods that seemed to have trapped her in an inextricable position, was afraid that her reputation had suffered and needed to find a way to make Grant not hate her when he found out the truth. Her chaotic family seemed not to notice!

"Well, no one seems to care about my visit to Aunt Letty," Annie finally blurted out.

The other three looked toward her as if they just now remembered she had been away. She ought to be relieved, but she had been so sure that she would meet with criticism when she returned, that she lowered her eyes to her plate, afraid she'd said too much.

"Oh, yes," said James. "Do tell us how Letty is."

Annie pressed her lips together. How much to say? Surely her father was aware that Letty's range land was on or very near property that might be needed for the railroad. She tested the waters gently.

"We, um, had a storm, a cyclone actually touched down on the . . . range."

"Oh, my," said Hattie. "Was anyone hurt?"

"Well, no one was hurt. We took refuge in Letty's root cellar in time. But there was a little damage."

"Too bad for Letty," said James, wiping his lips with a napkin. "Will she be able to repair it?"

Annie shrugged one shoulder. "She had some help . . . from some neighbors."

She flicked a glance at her father, who was looking in her direction now. He chewed slowly and thoughtfully and she looked down again, stabbing some cabbage with her fork.

No one spoke and Annie's nerves jangled. Only the sound of silverware on china and of water glasses being lifted and replaced on the table. Finally Everett sat back and put his napkin on the table.

"Letty's ranch is near the north end of South Park, if I remember rightly," said Everett.

Annie nodded. "That's right. At the foot of the Tarryalls."

That seemed to be the end of the conversation as Maria brought in the coffee urn and placed it on the sideboard.

"I'll have coffee, Maria, if you please," said Everett.

Maria handed round the coffee and Annie stirred cream and sugar into hers.

"Does it make a difference?" Annie said before they had a chance to go on to another subject.

"Does what make a difference?" asked James.

"Aunt Letty's property. She runs a small herd, um, east of the Tarryalls."

James shrugged, but Everett narrowed his gaze slightly. "So, she must have spoken to you of the cattlemen's attempt to block my railroad."

Annie's heart hammered into her chest. She had his attention at last. But she set her spoon down carefully before she looked up again.

"I overheard her speaking of a railroad with her neighbor. I don't know. Is there another one, besides the one you're planning?"

His mouth tightened slightly and skepticism crept across his formidable cheekbones and into his brown eyes. "Annie dear, I don't think this is supper table conversation. Hattie has a rule, no politics at table."

"Oh, I'm sorry. I forgot."

Somehow she got through dessert. Then she and Hattie got up to retire to the back parlor and let James and Everett discuss business to their heart's content. Hattie picked up her needlework, and Annie pawed through a stack of music on top of the piano for something to do. But every song reminded her of the theater, and she didn't feel like playing.

James and Everett joined them and everyone picked up reading material. Annie looked at a novel, but she kept peeking over the top at the others. The hands of the mantel clock seemed to crawl by until Hattie finally decided to go up. She kissed her husband on the cheek and said good night. Annie tried to will her brother to leave. She needed to talk to her father alone. With relief, she saw James set down his book and stretch his arms over his head.

"Well, I've an early morning tomorrow. Good night."

Annie jumped up to walk with him to the pocket doors. She smiled at him. "Good night, James. Oh, and congratulations."

He lifted his eyebrows at his sister. "Thank you, Sis."

As soon as he was through the square entryway, she pulled the doors to. They banged together harder than she'd intended.

"Sorry," she said, turning around.

Everett set his catalog and his spectacles aside and appraised his daughter.

"Well, now," he said, indicating that she might take a seat. "It seems you've poked your nose into this business up in South Park. Knowing my daughter, I can just imagine what curiosity you are hatching. Perhaps we can negotiate an agreement."

There was humor in his face, but it didn't mitigate her nervousness. She tried to walk steadily and sit daintily on the high-backed tapestried sofa, folding her hands in her lap.

"Well," she began. "I know it's none of my business, but I was curious. I mean I've never asked about the railroad." She found courage enough to look into his eyes. "But I am . . . interested."

His brows arched even farther at her last words. "You are, are you?"

She looked around the room, afraid to get out of her depth, but afraid not to speak.

"Well, one couldn't help being interested. Up there in the valley, with everyone talking of the coming railroad and what to do with their herds." She looked at her father.

"What *are* they to do with their herds? They don't like to fence them in."

"Aha," he said, lowering his arm and rocking back in the chair. "So that's it. You've heard about the cattlemen's objections. In fact I'm going to address their questions at a meeting this Thursday night. If you've a head for such matters, I will give you permission to attend. I've always liked your Aunt Letty, and I assure you, my company is making fair offers for the land we need to lay track down South Park. Settlement will follow. That land is fertile and homesteaders will do well in that valley. The cattlemen simply don't see reason."

She scooted forward on the tapestried seat.

"It's because the cattle need to roam free to get enough grass. The terrain on the mountainsides is too rocky, you see. And if they eat all the grass on the prairie lands they need to roam to find more. The ranchers round them all up in the spring and fall and brand the calves. They've never had trouble separating the herds, but the railroad will change all that."

His eyes were wide open as he listened to this speech, and he took his time with a reply.

"Yes, I know their arguments. The ranchers even want the government to pass laws forbidding homesteading on these open lands. But that is impractical. More and more settlers are moving to Colorado. We had to struggle to get the railroads to come here. It took a great deal of effort for the Denver Pacific to complete the branch line to Cheyenne to join up with the transcontinental line. You wouldn't remember the dark days before we raised financing for that venture. With the Union Pacific miles to the north, going to Cheyenne, and the Kansas Pacific bogged down in western Kansas, it looked like Denver would be left behind."

He turned to face her to make sure his words were sinking in. "Property values spiraled downward. We were considered a sinking ship. Only determined resistance salvaged our future."

He stopped rocking, looking backward at the years he had worked so hard for the city.

"We got citizens to contribute what they could. Fortunately, both the Union Pacific and the Kansas Pacific wanted to tap the mining resources of the territory and both gave some aid. But it still took a great deal of lobbying in Congress to get them to give us a 900,000-acre land grant. When the Denver Pacific's silver spike was driven eight years ago and we finally had that branch to Cheyenne, it meant Denver finally had an outlet to the rest of the country. That helped the Kansas Pacific market additional securities and resume construction. In August of that year, the first locomotive moved across Kansas tracks into our fair city."

He looked at Annie again. "You wouldn't know how much that took to accomplish. Now we're in an enviable position, tied both to the transcontinental and to Kansas City to the east. We're a state now, and we need transportation to our southern parts, a north-south spine with feeder roads west to the mining camps and east to the newly-settled agricultural communities in the valleys. If we don't do it now, the Midland will come through from Utah and do it for us."

Annie stood up and paced to the mantel. "That's what it is then, a race for development."

He frowned, impatience glittering in his brown eyes. "For profit yes, if that's what you mean. We want a future for Denver, homes like this one. Do you have any objection to that?"

She widened her eyes. "No, I . . . mean, I appreciate what you've done, Father. It's just that . . ." Her mouth went dry. "I wondered about the ranchers, that's all."

She immediately felt guilt flood through her again. She

had made herself a rancher's woman, although no one knew the truth of it but herself.

"The ranchers," said Everett. "Well, now. I see that a few weeks among them has made you a loyal friend of theirs." He shook his head. "They need to see reason. They aren't the only ones who want to make a living in the mountains. There's enough range land with water on it for them to fence in their herds. They just have to get used to the idea."

"And if they don't?"

He looked at her sharply, but she maintained her gaze, looking for signs that he would take stronger measures if his path was blocked.

"What do you mean, if they don't?"

She swallowed. "What would you do then?"

He grunted. "That's what the meeting on Thursday is about. Present our side and make them see the other issues. They'll get their money, if that's what they want."

She didn't know how to ask about the fire, without sounding disloyal to her own father. She wanted to mention it, but she couldn't outright accuse him.

"That's all, then, just negotiations," she tried.

"Yes, what else?"

"You wouldn't . . . I mean, I guess I overheard, in Letty's kitchen, that is. That some of the ranchers . . . feel threatened."

"Threatened?"

She gave a little shrug. "Well, accidents, and such. Some of them are blaming the railroad."

His face darkened and he asked gruffly, "What accidents?"

"Mr. Worth has some valuable animals. He thinks they were let out deliberately so they could get hurt. I knew you couldn't have had anything to do with it, and I told them so."

Everett got up and strode toward the tall, narrow bookcase and replaced the big, heavy catalog he'd been paging through before their conversation. Then he turned slowly and folded his hands in front of him, standing up straight.

"I do not believe in such underhanded measures. Politics is sometimes a nasty business, but I would not allow any such cheap tricks for my part. My railroad will purchase the land it needs, fair and square. Everyone has a price, even the ranchers. If they don't want customers for their beef and they plan to block a railroad that will only develop communities the state needs, then I feel sorry for their ignorance. But they have little to gain by such fraudulent accusations, or by assuming that I would condone underhanded threats."

The discussion was over.

Fourteen

Annie warily followed her father into the lobby of the Inter Ocean Hotel. A large room in the four-story brick hotel was the meeting place for this evening's gathering of railroad promoters and the leading ranchers of South Park. The meeting was open to any citizen of Denver interested in the issues at hand, and notice to that effect had appeared in the *Rocky Mountain News.*

Everett and his fellow-promoters were to inform the citizens and ranchers of the financial status of the Denver Central and its proposed branch lines. Annie knew it was important to keep informed of these issues if she were to help Grant's cause.

She was all too aware that appearing here beside her father would confirm in Grant's eyes on which side her loyalty lay, but there was little else to do. How ironic that her real purpose was to "spy" for the man she loved and see what she could do to help.

With her usual habit of acting on the notions that occurred to her, she had come here to step into the middle of the debate. After all, she reasoned, things could not be any worse.

"Evening, Everett," greeted the tall, distinguished Judge Bentworth. "Ah, I see you have your lovely daughter with you tonight."

The judge nodded over her gloved hand and she smiled

nervously as he inquired, "Joining into politics, hmmmm? Not a usual feminine occupation, but perhaps the presence of a few ladies in the audience will keep things civilized."

She gave a demure smile. "I hope to learn about the issues. My father was liberal enough to permit me to come."

She stood by, feeling like her face was cast in marble as she tried to smile pleasantly to other businessmen of her father's acquaintance.

Where was Grant? She peered unobtrusively over the shoulders of the politicians. Her heart gave a lurch when she spied a knot of men dressed in felt cowboy hats, flared coats and leather boots. She reacted by turning the dipping part of her hat brim that way, hoping to prevent Grant from seeing her before she spied him. It might just be possible to prevent his knowing that she was here at all. Her father would have to sit on the platform at the front of the room, while he would leave her in a seat near some of the other ladies at the back.

"Good evening." She smiled and gave her hand to another well-wisher, then scanned the crowded room for a seat in which she might hide.

She tugged on her father's sleeve. "I'll be over there in a seat by the door, Father."

She gave him a cheery smile and squeezed around him before he could object.

"Very well." He nodded, and was soon led forward.

She fled to a position on the other side of some potted palms creating a wide entrance beside the pocket doors of that side of the room. From there she could see the swelling knot of ranchers beginning to fill seats on the other side of the room. If this had been a wedding between the offspring of town promoters and mountain ranchers, it would have been clear which side of the room one's friends were on. But the din of voices coming from each group was already full of barely contained, heated opinions. She began to feel nervous that the meeting might not go well and was glad for her position near the door.

Still, she could not remain standing. Already gentlemen were beginning to look at her as if wondering why she was cowering alone behind a palm. She gave one such group a smile and nod and scampered to a seat by the far-left aisle. Finally, she dared another glance.

There he was! Standing tall and determined with some of his acquaintances. And there was Letty! She hadn't given much thought to the fact that her aunt might be present, but of course she had a vested interest in this issue. Drat. If either of them saw her, they would either glower at her or come over and speak.

Her heart turned over at the sight of Grant. His fierce demeanor made her worry about what he might do.

"Oh, my," she whispered to herself, closing her eyes and hunting in her reticule for her fan. The room was warm, and while she wasn't the fainting type, she didn't want to embarrass herself.

Letty disappeared into a seat, but Grant remained standing against the wall. Some of the other ranchers did the same, so that when the chairman banged a gavel on a block to quiet everyone, the sight of the bulwark of cowboys and ranchers lining the other side of the room and spreading to the back made her shiver. She ducked her head again, remembering to try to keep Grant from seeing her. The advantage was on her side, of course, for he wouldn't be looking for her.

Denver's mayor, a rotund man with thick mutton chops, stood up from his seat on the platform and raised his hands.

"My friends, I now call this meeting to order. I'm glad to see so many of you here tonight, for we have many things to talk about. Our fair city, indeed our young state has seen great growth in the last years, and many of you here know how hard won that has been. It is my hope now to see that growth continue to serve the best interests of all the residents in this glorious state. And to that end, this special meeting has been called."

Voices in the audience rumbled, but there were no outbursts. The mayor lifted his hands again as he continued.

"I believe Mr. Everett Marsh will tell you all about the financial soundness of the Denver Central and the work in Congress for land grants for laying track. It will not be long before Denver realizes her dream of a north-south road linking the transcontinental to the north with Mexico in the south."

Applause burst out from those of the town contingent, but the cowboys and ranchers around the room remained with arms folded. Like any good politician, the mayor knew there was a contingent here to protest the road going through South Park, and he addressed the other side.

"I am well aware that there is an issue of debate about the proposed route of the north-south road. We are here tonight to discuss that matter and to hear reports from Congress about the progress of land grants. There will be a chance for all views to be aired."

Annie's father stood up with a smile on his face that communicated his excitement for his project. With broad gestures and a carrying voice, he reported on their progress in Congress and handed out printed copies of the Denver Central's financial statement. While the papers were being handed around, Annie stole another look at Grant. She recognized that rigid jaw line and tightened skin across broad cheekbones. He didn't betray any outward signs of anger, but when his eyes swept the room, she saw the fierce determination there.

Once she thought he must have seen her, but she turned her head quickly away. When she glanced back a few moments later, he was propped against the wall, his hat low on his brow, studying the crowd and the men on the platform. She was right, he hadn't been looking for her, so he wouldn't see her unless she drew attention to herself.

Everett took questions from the floor, but Annie didn't pay any attention to the financial discussion. She fanned herself industriously, feeling fidgety and anxious.

A sound that had been in the background for some time coming from outside began to register: A Salvation Army hymn was being sung down the street. She could only just hear the militant voices raised by the soldiers of God, but the boom, boom accompaniment of the drum punctuated her thoughts. It was far enough away to blend with the sounds of rolling traffic and the music from the bar downstairs, but there it was. Boom, boom, boom.

She tried to ignore the distraction and listen again to the discussion. Finally it began. Everett was droning on about laying track along the stage road through Kenosha Pass when one of the ranchers shouted out an attack.

"You're going to cut the spine of the meat business if you go that way, Marsh. Don't you want us to feed the miners in the hills with our beef? Starving miners won't support your railroad."

Immediately the grumble swelled. "Here, here . . . ," a penetrating voice shouted.

The quiet business meeting got out of order as both sides began to argue. A few fists were shaken, but no real scuffles broke out.

Annie clung to her seat but pinned her eyes to Grant. He had moved away from the wall now and was facing the businessmen with a scowl on his face. Her heart pounded. She didn't want either Grant or her father to get hurt.

Everett was shouting to be heard, and the mayor stood up again, pounding the gavel, ordering everyone to be quiet. After a while the pandemonium settled down and Annie breathed again.

"We'll hear everyone's side if you'll all be patient," exclaimed the mayor. "Just settle down. Nothing's going to be done without reasonable debate. One at a time or you'll never all be heard. Now please allow Mr. Marsh the courtesy of finishing his report. Then we'll hear from the ranchers. All in due time."

He placated the crowd enough that those who'd risen took their seats. The ranchers still looked angry, but held their tongues. Annie forgot to be retiring and realized she was on the edge of her seat, hanging on with one hand to the curved back of the chair, her lips parted expectantly. At that moment Grant turned his head and looked straight at her. He almost looked away, but his head jerked back as recognition filled his eyes. He even started forward, toward her and she gasped, trembling as she slid back into the seat.

Her face burned as she felt him cross the room behind the seated audience. Out of the corner of her eye she saw him coming and sucked in a deep breath. When she looked up again, his look had cooled. Then she turned to face him as he came around her chair. He towered beside her.

"Evening, Miss Marsh," he said.

She looked up shyly at the gray eyes, now looking cynical again. Her heart missed a beat as she realized that his first look of surprise had not been for her; it had been for Grace. For the space of a breath, he had thought his beloved Grace Albergetti was here. As he crossed the room, logic had reclaimed his mind. It would make more sense for his opponent's other daughter to show up in this place.

She stood up to move to the back of the room with him so that they could speak without interrupting the meeting.

"Good evening," she managed in a hushed whisper. Her eyes slid sideways toward the rest of the audience only to avoid looking into his. "I thought you might be here."

"Of course," he replied in a lowered voice. She felt the

warmth of his breath on her cheek as he spoke near her ear.

"It's in my interests to be here. I see that you left your aunt's ranch in South Park in time to attend this meeting with your father."

She didn't miss the bitter accusation in his voice.

She ducked her head, trying to hide her eyes beneath the brim of her bonnet. He took a step back so as not to get punctured by the flowers and ferns atop it. She looked up again.

"I thought I'd best learn about the issues."

"Taking part in politics now?"

She gave a stiff shrug. "When . . . members of my family hold interests on opposite sides, it is my responsibility to be informed."

"Hmmmm," he grunted an acknowledgement. "Not the stay-at-home type, I see."

These last words were said under a breath, but her heart hammered with hope as she thought she'd scored a point in her favor.

Oddly, at that moment, she also became aware of the increased beating of the Salvation Army drum outside the windows. Had the missionaries opened fire on guests coming and going from the hotel? Her own pulse throbbed at standing so near to Grant, but their conversation was forced. She couldn't think of what to say.

How could a man be so stupid? She'd been so worried about getting caught in her ruse, she was certain that he would see through her plain as day. Was it the other weighty matters on his mind that blinded him to seeing that the woman he loved was standing right here beside him? She resisted the urge to tug on his sleeve and draw him out into the corridor to tell him so. But there was enough going on both in this room and outside to keep her from setting that explosion.

A South Park rancher was on his feet making a point in

a loud voice. His colleagues were murmuring in his support. Everett waited until he was finished, then spoke loudly, answering his question. But it was all lost on Annie now.

Finally, Grant seemed to determine that he could not easily exchange words with Annie and touched her elbow, nodding to the door. Her heart leapt into her throat. He wanted to speak to her alone.

They ducked around the potted palm and opened the doors just enough to squeeze through. Then they were in the carpeted corridor, illuminated by the yellowish light from the gas chandeliers.

She trembled as he guided her a little way along the corridor. Now the singing of the hymns in the street provided a distinct background to their conversation. Grant stopped and took her measure. Her mouth went dry. *It's me,* she wanted to say. But she said nothing.

The deep creases of concentration on his face relaxed a trace. "I'm glad to see you," he began.

Her startled look must have shown in her expression, the *why?* she did not voice.

He lifted his chin. "I didn't suppose you'd know anything about this, but since you're interesting yourself in your father's business . . ."

"Yes?"

"A fire broke out behind my ranch."

She lifted her hand to grasp his arm and only prevented herself from doing so at the last moment.

"A fire? I didn't know. But," she thought frantically for what she could say to him that she was supposed to actually know. "I . . . did speak to my father about what he would do if the ranchers refused to sell any land."

He frowned. "And?"

Her voice became stronger. "He denied having anything to do with threats. He said that he would not stoop so low as to use underhanded tricks to persuade the ranchers to sell . . . or something to that effect."

"He wouldn't, would he?"

"No, you must believe me. My father is not an evil man."

Grant only favored her with a disbelieving raised eyebrow. "Then someone near him or someone who wishes to gain his approval did it."

Her lips trembled. "I wouldn't like to think so."

"Nor would I."

His eyes roamed her face for a moment and then dropped to her lips. She wanted to lift her face to his, but forced her head away. Not before she saw a light in his eye. Then he gave his head a shake.

"Sorry. You reminded me of Grace for a moment."

His chest swelled with the intake of breath and she thought her knees would give way, so she sat down on a convenient love seat.

She gasped for a breath. "How is Grace?"

He slowly joined her on the love seat. He didn't speak for a moment, and all manner of frightening thoughts dashed in and out of her head.

When he did speak, his voice had a reminiscent quality about it. "I saw her in Manitou Springs a few days ago. She is well."

Then he couldn't resist a grin. "She is a beautiful woman. I hope to make her a part of my life. When I first saw you tonight, I thought you were she."

Annie opened her fan and let it move the air across her face. "Oh, really?"

"Since she bears such a strong resemblance to you."

She blushed, trying not to look at him. "I don't know. Some twins do not look alike."

"Ah, but you do." She thought his voice took on some teasing warmth. "There are gestures common to you both. Although you behave as a proper daughter of respectability, sometimes, I . . ." His voice drifted off into thought.

"You what?"

He gave a soft chuckle. "She's won my heart, I don't mind telling you."

"She has?"

He frowned. "You won't speak of it to your father, now will you? I'll have to do that myself."

She fanned harder. "Oh, no. Grace's secrets are kept from him. I mean, I'll keep whatever you say close to my breast."

"Your father and I don't see eye to eye on many matters. But seeing as how he's disowned his daughter, he can't mind my stepping in, now can he?"

Her face heated even more. A sudden fear filled her that he might spread it around that he was dallying with Everett Marsh's daughter. He wouldn't dare think of using that as ammunition to blackmail him regarding his railroad, would he? Or worse, what if he came to the house to sue for Grace's hand in marriage?

"You wouldn't, um, ruin Grace's reputation, would you? I mean, I know she's left hearth and home, but she still has her pride. I mean, I'm sure she has pride in such matters."

She saw the sensual grin and the desire that filled his eyes. "It's no one else's business. Of course I don't mind speaking of it to you, since you seem to know everything your sister is doing."

"Yes, it's true, I do."

He leaned back against the love seat and cleared his throat. "I'm afraid I might have hurt her feelings some. I'd just heard about the trouble on the ranch. Half accused her of being in league with your father on the matter. I don't like to think so, though. Maybe you'd know."

"Know what?"

She saw the twinge in his face as if he didn't want to

think it was true. "Grace wouldn't be trying to help your father for any reason? Maybe this story of her being disowned is all a hoax. Maybe you two girls are just concocting a story to keep a man on his toes."

She felt as if she would go through the velvet seat beneath her. "Why would we do a thing like that?"

His broad shoulders lifted and dropped. "Can't say. All I know is I wanted to get to know her better." He allowed a smile to play over his features, then his dark, guarded look of concern returned. "Women can be coy sometimes. I don't want to start some trouble I can't handle."

"Oh now, I'm sure you wouldn't."

They sat in awkward silence for a little longer. Annie's voice became husky. "When will you see her again? Grace, I mean."

"I'd like to see her soon."

She could almost feel the lust emanating from his strong, masculine body. She'd never been with a man who made her blood heat like this. He continued, his very words a caress.

"I'd like to make her mine, but I've got business to attend to first. Then I don't know how she'd take to ranch life after being on the stage."

"She'd like it. I mean, I think she would. Why wouldn't she?"

"Because she's used to the excitement and glamour of being an actress. Just look at the likes of me. She's got me wining and dining her. She's used to what luxury the western territories offer. Hard to settle down after that kind of life."

"Well, I do see your point. But, you see, actresses do get tired of all that travel after awhile. She's talked to me about it now and then. I know how it is with her. The acting troupe are good people, but everyone wants a . . . a good man." She swallowed. "The theater life is lonely after a while. I'd think that Grace would want a different kind of fulfillment. If you . . . love her, I would not give up on your dream."

He rested an arm along the back of the love seat. "You seem to know your sister very well. You even know what she thinks."

Afraid that he was teasing her, she straightened her shoulders.

"I think I know her." She risked a glance. "I know what I would want if I were she."

He narrowed his gaze curiously at her, and she only held it for a long, heart-throbbing second. As if in accompaniment, the Salvation Army drum pounded below the window at the end of the corridor. His attention was drawn that way.

"What is that infernal noise?" he asked.

They both stood up. "The army of salvation. Missionaries looking for converts and seeking our money to help the indigent."

"You seem to know a lot about them. Is there anything you don't know?"

She gave an exasperated sigh and walked to the window to look down. But the overhang covering the boardwalk below prevented her from seeing whether Lin Chu had chosen this opportune time to "help" the missionaries.

The voices from inside the meeting had risen again. Grant looked toward the closed doors.

"If you'll excuse me, I'd better see to my interests inside. Will you need an escort?"

"No, that's all right. Father will take me home." She glanced at the window and then at Grant.

He gave her a disarming smile. "I hope to settle things with your sister then, next time I see her."

Her hand went to her chest. "When will that be?"

"As soon as she wants it. She knows where to find me."

"Oh, well, I'm sure her travels will bring her back this way."

"That'd be real nice, real nice indeed," he said, and reached for the doors to reenter the meeting room.

When the doors opened, she saw over his shoulder that the meeting had disintegrated to arguments. The mayor was banging his gavel to no avail. She glimpsed her father waving his arms and trying to address a rancher who was booming objections to the railroad's plans. Others got up and voices were raised as arguments erupted. Annie instinctively moved back toward the window. If trouble were to erupt, it might be safer downstairs. Some of the cowboys were armed. And in this young city, many a man made his point using the serious end of his revolver.

She winced as Grant disappeared into the fray, pushing opponents apart as he strode down to the front. She was torn between fleeing downstairs and rushing in to drag him out from behind the podium.

Never being one to shy away from danger, she made her decision: She needed to help prevent bloodshed. If someone were hurt, the argument could turn into a nasty battle. There was already the unexplained fire in the mountains. Until that issue was settled satisfactorily, the two squabbling sides would be at each other's throats. A distraction was needed.

Quick as a flash she raced down the stairs and out through the lobby. As she had surmised, Lin Chu was engaged in his fundraising efforts. She ran into the midst of the little band, shouting his name.

When at first he only smiled, she grabbed his drumstick and forced him to stop playing.

"Quick, come upstairs. There's a fight brewing. You've got to help me stop it."

She gestured intently, her desperation communicating to the singers, who looked at each other and nodded. They squared their shoulders as if marching off to war and followed her through the lobby, Lin Chu with his drum in the lead.

"Up here," said Annie, regaining the front of the line.

And the odd little parade squeezed up the main staircase and onto the corridor into which attendees were already spilling out from the meeting.

Annie turned and nodded, and taking this as a signal to begin singing, the Salvation Army started up their throaty rendition of "When the Saints Go Marching In."

"Follow me," said Annie as Lin Chu pounded on his drum.

And she led the group into the midst of the meeting room where all semblance of order had been lost. Heated voices shouted, citizens stood on chairs. There was no sight of her father. Letty was holding her own, one long finger pounding out her point at three red-faced citizens.

The booming drum and the blue-uniformed salvationists drew some attention as some of the boisterous citizens were silenced by the sudden interruption. Annie herself clapped her hands, marching through the hot-bed of exploding tempers.

They pushed their way down the center aisle where she hoped to rescue her father, but just as they reached the platform, someone yelled, "Quit that racket."

A gun exploded, and a light fixture shattered. Women in the back of the room screamed and the madness only accelerated. Annie was crushed between shoving individuals, and fists began flying. She saw Lin Chu lift the drum out of harm's way, and her only thought became how to avoid being trampled. Her bonnet slipped to the side of her head, blocking her view.

Suddenly a pair of strong arms slid around her waist and she heard Grant's words in her ear. "This way."

She flung a grateful arm around his waist and he extricated her from the crowd. Even so, shelter at the side of the room was impossible, and he pulled her aside just as two men wrestled toward the window.

He led her toward the platform and through a small door at the back of the room.

"My father . . ."

"Your father can take care of himself."

She didn't miss the gruffness of his tone, indicating that Grant held Everett responsible for the uproar in the first place. Grant's hand was clasped over hers, pulling her along the corridor until they found a set of back stairs. They stood aside as a maid came up carrying a tray.

"Come on," Grant said. "There must be a way out."

Annie was torn. Her father wouldn't know what had happened to her. Lin Chu would probably never let her hear the end of it. And the Salvation Army band might be trampled in the confusion. But her feet took her down the narrow, dimly lit staircase until they reached the bottom.

They came out in the hotel kitchen. Workers paused from their tasks at large pine worktables to watch them.

"Excuse us," Grant said politely. Clasping her hand firmly, he pulled her along until they found an exit.

Then they stood in the alley behind the hotel, the noise from above and the noise from the streets muted by the solid brick buildings that backed onto the hotel.

"Oh, dear," said Annie, collapsing against the wooden railing of the fire escape. Her bonnet was still askew, her chignon loosened, her skirt torn. She pawed at the bonnet, looking up apologetically at Grant as she tried to extract the hat pins and wrestle it free.

There was no gas lantern to light the alley, and his face was partly in shadow cast from moonlight overhead. But when he shifted his face slightly as she struggled to adjust her hair, she saw his eyes.

A puzzled look resided there and something else that made her heart beat even harder. The old guilt flooded her at the same time she was aware of his raw, masculine nearness, something she was more familiar with than he knew.

He reached to take the bonnet from her so that she could continue to withdraw the pins and combs that hung amidst her tangles. Still he stared at her in a most disturbing way. She tried to smile and take normal breaths.

"Sorry. I guess what happened was my fault."

He moved his chin only slightly. "Why would that be?"

"The band. I thought it would break up the meeting. Tempers were getting too hot."

Suddenly she felt like crying and sobbed, "But it only made it worse."

Grant moved closer to her, sliding an arm around her back. "It wasn't your fault."

His voice sounded consoling, smooth, emotional as he gently held her against his chest. She clenched a fist and rested it on him. What a mess she'd made of everything.

"I just wanted to help you," she sniffled.

A man's white handkerchief appeared in front of her nose and she accepted it. As she dabbed at her eyes and blew her nose, Grant patted her softly on her back.

"I know you did," he murmured quietly into her hair.

She didn't know whether she leaned into him or he laid his lips against her temple, but she felt his comforting kiss. She shook her head. She wanted him to hold her the way he had done in Manitou Springs. She wanted him to make love to her. But he would never do that again, especially if he knew the truth.

Fifteen

Grant breathed in the scent of the girl in his arms, a scent he could swear he'd breathed before. Confusion clanged inside him as he dropped a kiss on her temple. He felt the same sudden arousal that he knew with Grace, but this was her sister.

He'd meant only to come to Annie's rescue, to do the gentlemanly thing to comfort her. It must be that he missed Grace so and here was a nearly identical image of the woman he'd so recently had in his arms and in his bed.

"Annie dear," he whispered, as much to comfort himself as her.

What was happening to him? His body was responding with a newfound lust that he had quelled for a long while after his wife had died. It must be that having tasted the delicious rewards of love, his blood simmered for more.

But this wasn't seemly. His mind and body were playing tricks on him. He disciplined his limbs to offer comfort not caresses, felt his own longing ache inside him. A lesser man might take advantage of the situation and satisfy himself in soft limbs that needed someone to lean on. In the darkness of the alley, it would be easy to steal a kiss.

But he clenched his jaws shut and planted his heels into the dirt. In a moment Annie would regain her senses, be over her spell and want to go home. Any further advances would be deemed an insult. He'd already confessed to being in love with her sister.

He pushed his coat back and planted clenched fists on his hips, leaning his weight on one leg while Annie mopped her face with his handkerchief.

"You all right now?" he asked.

She nodded, inhaled several breaths, and appeared more calm. "Thank you, I'm sorry for the outburst."

"Natural under the circumstances. A lady shouldn't be in the middle of a meeting where both sides are going to get hot under the collar. Come on, I'll take you home."

"But Father . . ." she gestured helplessly.

"Your father knows his way home, and that Chinese servant of yours saw you leave with me."

"He did? How do you know?"

"He was standing on a chair and looked right at us as I opened the door behind the podium. He'll know you're with me."

Not arguing further, she let him lead her to the street where the various parties from the meeting were now spilling into the street. She worried suddenly about Letty.

"My aunt Letty," said Annie. "Did she come down with you?"

"She was among those of us who rode down here together. She'll escape to her room at the hotel."

Still Annie wouldn't move until she was certain her aunt was all right. She could have been trampled to death, for all they knew.

She saw in Grant's eyes that he read her look correctly and exhaled a long sigh. He leaned against a hitching post.

"Very well. We'll wait right here until everyone comes out. Then we'll go ask after Letty. I'm sure she's in her room by now."

Annie braced herself against the hitching rail as the hotel continued to disgorge excited attendees of the meeting. One of the last to leave was her father, surrounded by his cronies. He was too engaged in discussion to see Annie and Grant, and although she felt relieved that he was safe, she didn't really want to be discovered. Every moment she was with Grant was one more moment she could hang onto.

Her father shook hands with several others who departed, then he hailed Lin Chu.

"Lin Chu, have you seen my daughter?"

"Yessir. She all right. Nice gentleman took her out when the trouble started. I wait here to find her. Then I take her to her auntie."

"All right," said Everett. "I'll trust that you see her safely home or into my sister-in-law Lettie's hands. I saw Letty to her room just now, myself."

"You no worry," said Lin Chu.

And Everett stepped into the mayor's waiting buggy, followed by the mayor himself.

"Probably going to talk some more," Annie murmured.

She and Grant were about to step into the lobby when the rest of the disheveled members of the Salvation Army band emerged.

"Oh, no," said Annie. The little band looked like it had gone into battle, and she felt responsible. She hurried along to Lin Chu.

"Lin Chu, is everyone all right?"

"Oh, there is mistress. Hello. Everyone all right. People inside room there very angry. What they fighting about?"

She looked apologetically at the women and the gentleman member of the band.

"I'm so sorry. I thought your distraction would help break up the meeting. It was about a railroad my . . . father wants to build. Oh, never mind. Please let me give you a contribution for your work. I didn't mean to place you in danger."

One of the women, a slim, stern-looking person stepped forward to take her hand. She was not unattractive, but with her hair pulled straight back and rolled into an ordinary chignon and with only the severe looking costume, her delicate bones were not enhanced.

"We are not afraid of danger," she said, squeezing Annie's hand. "We go where sin is. If there was danger in that room, then that is where God called us to go."

"Oh," replied Annie. "Well, nevertheless, I'll see that you get a contribution." She glanced with irony at her family's servant. "Lin Chu can bring it to you tomorrow."

The woman nodded and the rest of them dusted themselves off.

"None the worse for wear," said the man with them. He gave her a good-humored, somewhat proud smile, and she speculated that perhaps they were glad to have been called into the line of duty.

She did catch a glint of amusement in Grant's otherwise carved and determined expression.

"If everything is settled here, I'll escort Miss Marsh home."

"It's all right," she said, embarrassed by the mess. "Lin Chu can drive me home. I'm sure he has a conveyance of some sort here."

Lin Chu bobbed his head. "I drive Mr. Marsh here."

"Yes," replied Annie. "And Father has gone off with the Mayor. You may drive me home, Lin Chu."

The Chinese fundraiser surrendered his drum to the missionaries and bowed. "I drive now. Buggy this way."

Grant cleared his throat. "I insist on escorting both of you to your door so that no more mishaps occur. I feel it is my duty."

Annie's cheeks warmed. His duty to whom? Was he already being so loyal to the family because of Grace, even though he did not see eye to eye with Everett Marsh?

They followed Lin Chu to the buggy and Grant helped her in. Then he fetched his horse and followed them through the busy evening traffic until they reached lower

Broadway where the tinkle of piano music and the evening revelry was left behind. Annie sank into the buggy, grateful for the respite. She closed her eyes and rested her head against the back of the seat, breathing deeply and trying to get ahold of her feelings.

When she felt the incline of the hill up Seventeenth Street, she felt new anxieties. She hoped Father would not be home, so that she could escape to her room. And what would Grant do? Surely he would not come in. Or did he want to wait for Father to get home so that he could give him a piece of his mind personally?

And what then? She knew now that she simply didn't have the courage to end the charade. It was a revelation to finally know her limits. It came as a bolt from the heavens to her to realize that her daring and impulsiveness had nothing at all to do with courage. What had seemed fearlessness to her in the past was nothing but impetuous action with lack of forethought. How could one be afraid when one didn't foresee consequences?

Real courage, on the other hand, was something she knew now she sorely lacked. Courage of conviction, truth, a steel spine in the face of adversity.

"Oh, dear," she said to herself and felt tears threaten again. She had no backbone when it came to truth. She had just proved that. She was a terrible disappointment to herself, and all because of a man.

She couldn't tell Grant. She couldn't, couldn't, couldn't.

Not that she believed he would think any better of her if he found out on his own. It was just that she didn't want to be there when he did.

She didn't even look out of the buggy to see if Grant was following. He'd said he'd see them home, so she knew he was there.

They turned into the drive beside the house and pulled up before the carriage house. She heard Grant's leather saddle creak and then he came to help her down. She took his arm and let him lead her to the door, but she dared not look at him to bid him good night. He stood there, a firm bulwark against the night. Neither of them spoke. What was there to say? Finally, Grant broke the silence.

"Perhaps I should wait for your father."

"Whatever for?"

She heard the air hiss between his teeth. "To tell him the truth. That I'm seeing his daughter, the one he has forgotten about."

"Oh, no!"

"Why not?"

It was nearly impossible to hide her alarm now.

"He's not in the right temper now, you can understand that."

"Well, maybe I'm not in the right temper to wait. Maybe Everett Marsh and I had just better have things out once and for all. The line's been drawn, I'm sorry to say."

Her look of pleading must have communicated her desperate position to him. His anger softened and he looked away. Still, he did not take any of his words back. Her hand pressed against his chest.

"Please," she breathed. "Not now. Wait at least until tomorrow. I'll think of something. I mean I'll talk to him myself. Now that he knows I have an interest in what's going on in South Park, he'll listen to me. Let me find out what happened that you want to place at his door. Maybe he's telling the truth. Maybe he had nothing to do with it."

"Maybe." He looked at her suspiciously. "And maybe not."

"Oh, please. If you come in now it would ruin everything. Everything."

He lifted his hat brim just enough for her to see his eyes in the shadowy flicker from the lamps on the covered porch where they stood.

"Please," she whispered again.

She sensed his impatience and realized with the piercing of her heart that part of it stemmed from his desire to resolve things with Grace. In some distorted way, Grant wanted to reach Grace through her father. Annie's hands went to her cheeks. What could she do now?

"It's Grace, isn't it?" she whispered.

His look came back to her, and though he didn't move a muscle of his face, she saw the truth register in his eyes.

"Grace," she whispered softly, then dropped her hands.

"For her sake," she said with a more firm tone, "wait a while. Wait until I've talked to him. I'll send you a message. Grace will be in Denver in a . . . month or so. I think she mentioned it."

She flicked her glance at him and saw the look of interest there.

"You'll see her then. If I haven't found out the truth from Father by then, you can do what you want. It would be better for us, for Grace and me, that is, if you and Father weren't enemies."

His brow puckered, but after what seemed like a long moment, his chin came down and he spoke thoughtfully.

"I don't know why you're doing this for me, but I agree. I don't see how your father and I can reach any agreement, but I'll not be accuser, judge and hangman without a fair trial. If I can catch whoever is threatening me and the valley, then he'll come to justice. If your father's hands are clean then we'll settle our business differences in a different fashion. One that everyone can live with. But you'll have to do some pretty hard talking to get him to change his plans. He wants a railroad to reach those gold and silver mines, and the cattle be damned."

She swallowed. "I'll try to explain it to him. I'll try to get him to find another route."

"All right. You do that."

He took a step back and then offered his hand to shake on the deal. Annie took it, his hard grasp sending waves of hopeless yearning through her. But she had prevented a ruinous confrontation tonight. Surely with a little time, she could make a plan. Surely she would come up with a way out.

He took another step back and she put her hand on the door.

"Good night, then," she said.

He went down the steps and turned to face her, feet spread a little apart. He touched his hat, sending her heart swirling the way it always did when he looked like that.

"Good night."

She heard his steps on the flagstone walk, but didn't wait to listen for the sounds of his mounting his horse. He was part of the night now, and she pushed the paneled door inward, stepping into the familiar halls of home.

Grant would have waited in the street for his opponent to return home and confronted him then and there. Everett Marsh owed him some answers. But for his feelings for Grace he would have acted on his instincts.

But now other confusing feelings dwelled in his heart! It had been Annie he had protected tonight. The dim glimmer of an impossible thought occurred to him, but he rejected it as being too fantastic to believe. Both Grace and Annie had an air of independence that belied the man Grant believed Everett Marsh to be. And he'd now seen for himself the wayward Lin Chu who evidently was servant and driver. But in places like Denver, servants reflected their employers. What kind of household allowed a servant to play a drum in the streets for a Salvation Army band?

Grant drew in the reins of his horse and sat beneath a spreading elm, looking at the lights from the windows in Everett Marsh's house. The mansion itself spoke of success and money, the kind of money he resented for he still believed it was built on the backs of laborers who tasted none of the rewards for the work they did for such men. He could understand why a girl like Grace would run away from such a home. But now Annie bothered him.

He reached out to pet his horse's neck and talk to him. On the long cattle drives he had talked to his horses a lot and found nothing unusual in the habit.

"She's a strange girl," he told the bay gelding. "Sometimes I think . . ." He shook his head in the darkness. "No, that couldn't be. Just couldn't be."

He turned and walked the horse on. He was conscious of a growing affection for Annie Marsh. At first he'd thought it was because of her relation to the woman who had bedazzled him in the mountains. The woman he had held in his arms and taken to his bed. He furrowed his brow, still denying his growing suspicion. There had been unexplained things about Grace as well. Damnit!

He needed a drink. Things were getting too tangled. He was sorry the meeting downtown had gotten out of hand. A small delegation to meet with Everett Marsh and a few others might work better.

"The railroad barons think we're nothing but a bunch of wild, shoot 'em up cowboys," he told his horse. "We have to show them we mean business but try to offer them an alternative." Yep, that's what they needed, an alternative.

He frowned. That's what Annie had said! Was he just parroting her own ideas and trying to make them his own? He shook his head, feeling that he was getting in too deep. That was sometimes the way it was with women.

Annie was composed when she came down to breakfast in the big, empty dining room. Sausage, fried potatoes and fresh eggs steamed in covered platters on the sideboard and she picked out some food. When Maria came in, she inquired after her father.

"Came in late last night," the cook said. "Though I never known him to sleep late in the morning."

Annie pour herself some apple juice from a crystal pitcher. "He'll probably be down soon then."

Indeed, Everett Marsh appeared soon after. He looked tired from his late night and somewhat worried. Annie saw the creases at the corner of his eyes and between his eyebrows as he dropped a kiss on her cheek.

"Good morning dear, I was worried about you last night. But Lin Chu told me he would wait and bring you home in the buggy or take you to Letty. I hope you were all right."

"Is Aunt Letty all right?"

"She stayed over last night. I invited her to the house of course, but she wouldn't hear of it. She's returning to her ranch today."

"I see."

Everett selected his breakfast and Annie laid her silverware across her plate and sat up straight.

"Father, I want to speak to you about the railroad."

"After last night's debacle, I'm surprised you'd still want to have anything to do with it."

"Oh, yes, very much. In fact, I want you to give me a job."

"A what?"

"I want to work for the railroad."

He screwed up his eyebrows. "Have you lost your mind? Whatever for? You should be thinking about other things I would think. Beaux and dances and a marriage to the right man, I would hope someday."

Father and daughter took each other's measure, and then Everett shrugged. His words held a tinge of resigned humor. "Of course it should not surprise me that you're not interested in beaux and dances. None of my family has ever been interested in what I expect them to be interested in."

"There's plenty of time for dances later. I want to work

on the railroad right now. I want to learn about it. And I think I might have something to offer."

He leaned forward, looking at her curiously. "What would that be?"

"Well, um, ideas."

"Oh."

Everett was used to indulging his daughter, a weakness that stemmed from his love for his late wife. That Annie was willful and had independent ideas, he was well-aware. He had hoped his marriage to the refined, self-effacing Hattie would help temper Annie, but he realized too late that the opposite had happened. His children were beyond their stepmother's capabilities. It wasn't Hattie's fault, she was simply unprepared for them.

Mostly, he lost himself in his work. The household held together enough to keep him satisfied and able to hold his head up in society. All of them were pioneer stock after all, the kind of people who would stick it out for a better life here in the west. So he was able to ignore some of his family's slight eccentricities.

But he would be a laughingstock if he brought his daughter to work with him. James, perhaps, after some training at the bank, could be brought into the railroad, but Annie should be thinking about getting married and raising babies of her own. He drummed his fingers on the table and delayed an answer while he sipped his coffee. Then an idea occurred to him.

"All right," he finally said. "You may attend some board meetings to see if you are really serious. After all, you and James are both my heirs. In case you do not marry, for whatever reason, you might as well gain an appreciation for building a railroad if that is to be your sole income in later years. But you may not speak at any of the meetings until I give you leave to do so. Will you agree to that?"

She only hesitated for a moment. "For how long must I not speak?"

"Until I have determined that you know enough about the subject to sound intelligent. There is much to learn and the only way for you to learn it is to be silent and listen."

"But what if I have questions?"

"You may ask them of me privately in my office or here at home after supper of an evening. And I will give you my partner's son, Vernon, to work with."

Annie had met Vernon and wrinkled her nose at the thought of working with him. But if she must, it was better than nothing. Her father looked satisfied with himself and Annie knew she would have to go along with the plan. Well, all right. She could be fair to both sides. She would resign herself to a lengthy apprenticeship.

"Very well. I agree. I will go every day and when we are not in meetings, you must give me maps and charts to study. If I am to be of help to you, I must know all about the territory and about the narrow gauge."

"I will make no judgment until I see how quickly you learn. My surveyors could certainly use some good help."

She smiled. "Good. I would like to start in a matter of weeks, after I do some work for charity first."

"Charity now, is it?" He scratched his head, but decided not to ask. "Assuming Hattie and I can divide your time so that you don't shirk your household duties, you may start whenever you wish in the afternoons. You can do your household chores in the mornings, if Hattie agrees."

She made sure her smile remained on her lips even if her mind quickly schemed to figure out a way to reduce those household duties.

"Thank you, Father. I will let you know when I'm ready to begin."

Fortunately it was Thursday, the best day for calling. Annie had little trouble persuading Hattie that they should pay a call to Hortense Morgan, that wealthy and generous patron of many of Denver's fledgling charities. Hortense and Charles Morgan owned one of the most prestigious mansions in the city's finest residential district. Charles Morgan had been one of the city's movers and shakers, and the couple had turned their wealth into charities that the thriving city needed.

They got down from the buggy and sent Lin Chu home. Hattie had more sense than to risk having her unpredictable driver wait in front of the brick mansion. They had but to stand in the portico for a few seconds before a liveried butler answered the door. Hattie handed him her card and they were invited in.

Hortense Morgan had that easy grace that came from the certainty that one was at the center of society and had no need to impress anyone. She drifted down the curved staircase even before the butler handed over their card and came to greet them with outstretched hands.

"My dear Mrs. Marsh, how kind of you to come." She pecked the air beside Hattie's cheek.

"And Miss Marsh. I don't believe I've seen you since our ball."

Then they all rustled into the formal parlor, accented with sunlight coming from the west. The room was long, with an elaborately-carved marble mantel opposite the large-paned French doors. Hortense led them to a grouping of brocade chairs and nodded to a crisply uniformed maid at the other end of the room. The girl disappeared through a small door, presumably to the kitchen.

After the trivialities of catching up on family news, Hortense turned her good-humored gaze upon Annie.

"And what have your been doing with yourself, my dear?"

Annie gave a formal smile and replied, "I have lately taken an interest in my father's railroad."

"Oh?"

"Yes, he allowed me to accompany him to a meeting

the other night when some issues were discussed. I decided to learn more about the business side of the railroad."

Hortense's eyes were now wide with amusement, but Hattie intervened.

"You must forgive our unconventionality, Hortense. I believe it is my husband's intention to disabuse Annie of the glamour of business. And of course Annie's involvement with the railroad does not preclude her domestic and community responsibilities, does it, dear?"

Annie shook her head. "No, in fact that is why we came. I wanted to offer my talents for your next fundraiser."

"Oh, indeed. How would you like to help?"

"Well, I have in mind some entertainment."

Hattie tried to smooth the way. "You've heard Annie sing, have you not?"

Hortense seemed to search her memory while at the same time remaining polite. "I believe I have."

"I had in mind," continued Annie, "performing several different kinds of numbers, from quiet ballads to something, um, more lively."

"Well, I'm sure we can find a way to incorporate your gifts."

"I would need an accompanist, someone to rehearse with.

Hortense put a finger to her chin as she studied Annie. "Yes, I think that can be arranged. Martha Evans' nephew, Trevor is talented at the piano. Perhaps we could persuade him to accompany."

"Good," Annie replied. "Then we may be able to solicit others to entertain as well. I wouldn't want to dominate the evening. I'm sure Denver's finest would contribute generously at such a performance, don't you agree?"

The tea tray came in time for them all to digest the idea. When everyone was served, Hortense picked up the idea again. She hadn't earned her reputation as planner and organizer for nothing.

"The hospital could use some funds for their laboratory. Perhaps an outdoor party on the lawn. The piano could be moved out to the patio. And in August my late summer plants will still be in bloom. How does that sound?"

"Very generous," said Hattie, sipping her tea.

"Excellent," agreed Annie. She swallowed a bite of sandwich and then set her plate down. "There is something else."

"Yes?" asked Hortense.

"Perhaps this fundraiser could be used to help mediate some of the disagreements between the parties on both sides of the railroad issue."

"I'm afraid you'll have to explain how that would be done," said Hortense.

"Well, at the moment, the ranchers in South Park don't want the railroad coming through their valley. They are rather piqued at Father because he wants to route his road that way. One reason I'm helping him in business is to try to help find a different route for him to use."

Hortense sighed and set her tea and saucer on the inlaid teakwood table beside her chair.

"Charles has spoken of those difficulties. There was an article about the disruption of last Monday's meeting. Something about a Salvation Army band getting into the fray. But go on with your idea."

"Well, if some of the members from both factions are invited to the fundraiser, maybe it would help pull the community together as a whole. I mean if everyone is here to help raise money for the hospital, it will remind them that we're all on the same side. That is, we all want what is best for the community at large."

"That is a noble idea, but I hardly think the ranchers of South Park will come all the way down here for a hospital fundraiser. Won't they be getting ready for their roundups?"

"I think that some of them might attend. After the disaster of the open meeting the other night, some of them probably want to meet privately with Father to discuss the issues. Perhaps the meeting could be arranged on the day following the fundraiser."

"Ah, I see. So that the ranchers would be in town."

"Yes."

Hortense looked at Annie with new interest. "Well, we need some new blood injected into the charity set." She smiled at Hattie. "I had no idea your stepdaughter was so innovative."

Hattie smiled weakly. "Oh, indeed, you could call her that."

Annie could see from Hortense's expression that she was pleased. The older woman set aside her teacup.

"I'll invite my committee here to discuss the plans. I do hope you'll attend, Annie."

"Oh, yes, of course. That is, if I have Father's and Hattie's permission to be away from my other duties."

Hortense got up. "I think Thursday next in the afternoon would be best. The other women are finished with their morning gardening by then and can come here to work. Would that suit?"

Annie deferred to Hattie, who looked from her stepdaughter to Hortense. "Of course," she said, finally realizing that she was being asked permission. "We can get along without Annie then."

"Good," said Hortense. "Then it's all settled. Now come and see my garden."

Sixteen

Hortense had no trouble arranging the charity musicale. Others with some talent, and some with no talent, offered to perform. Whereas no society damsel or gent would deign to set foot on a theater stage, it was deemed part of a young lady's training to be able to sing and play the piano to entertain at home after dinner parties.

And many of the men were fond of harmonizing popular songs, so several barbershop quartets had been formed.

Annie threw herself into the production, helping to produce the over-all scheme as well as to rehearse and perform her own numbers. It kept her from thinking about what she was about to do. She even involved Hattie in a frenzy of sewing, for she insisted that the different styles of songs she was going to perform demanded different costumes.

"But isn't this short red satin skirt with black ruffles and black net stockings rather daring, dear?" asked Hattie when Annie sketched out the pattern.

"That one is for the end of the evening, Hattie," she replied. "It fits the song I'll be singing. If I lead up to it, I don't think the audience will be put off by it."

"No, I'm sure they'll enjoy it, dear. I just don't want you to be unseemly."

"After the sedate numbers before this one, I doubt they'll think that. Rather that I am versatile. It is, after all, a charity benefit. We can get away with the lighter songs as well as the others."

Hattie mumbled some misgivings, but continued measuring and fitting.

The sewing went quickly, as did the rehearsals, and Annie spent many an hour at Hortense Morgan's mansion working out details.

"You are a most skilled organizer, Annie, dear," said Hortense one afternoon as they took tea in the formal parlor.

They had been working since noon, drawing out the arrangement of the tables and going over the list of refreshments that had been ordered. Annie even helped approve the plans the decoration committee had brought.

"Thank you," she replied. "I do hope you'll mention it to my father. It is important to me that he appreciate my ability to organize."

Hortense smiled. "Is that because you persist in this unusual notion to learn about the railroad business?"

"I want him to take me seriously."

"And, if I may ask, just why do you want to involve yourself in such business?" asked Hortense, selecting a small sandwich.

"I want to prove my mettle," said Annie, though she didn't add that the person to whom she wanted to prove that mettle was not her father. "It is rather complicated."

But Hortense had the sense not to ask just how complicated the subject had become.

Most especially did Annie insist on helping Hortense write out the announcements about the charity extravaganza, inviting leading citizens of Denver and leading ranchers up and down the front range of the Rockies from the settlements of Golden City at the base of the mountains to Pueblo City in the south.

Nothing, of course, was mentioned about the railroad squabble. This was simply offered as a chance for those who wished to socialize and contribute to the hospital. In Grant's invitation, Annie added a personal note that she wished he would come, that she had a special surprise for him. She desperately hoped the mystery would make him accept the invitation.

As the replies came in, Annie held her breath. For two weeks, they heard nothing. Then, as Annie was digging through the scrawled notes in a silver tray at Hortense's home, she felt her heart leap when she saw his scrawled signature. Hastily scanning his reply, she began to breathe again.

"Will plan to attend, if business matters allow," he wrote.

Annie had not mentioned anything about Grace in the note. That was to be the surprise.

Some weeks after the debacle in Denver, Grant stopped by Letty's for a neighborly cup of coffee. There had never been anything romantic between the two, he had respected her husband's memory too much for that. He felt only the camaraderie natural to the ranchers who shared grazing lands in the valley, and who banded together on issues that affected them all. Letty had also received an invitation to the charity extravaganza, but had declined to attend.

"No time for charities," she said, as they sat at her table. "Too much work to do here. I'm surprised you can get away."

Through the four-paned windows they watched the long fingers of pink hues, gold and blue in a glorious sunset stretched along the mountain barrier that protected their valley.

Grant sipped his coffee, satisfied after the piece of hot apple pie she'd just served him.

He shook his head. "The only reason I'm taking it in is that Everett Marsh has agreed to see just a few of us to discuss this damn railroad matter. I'm sorry you're not joining us."

She made a wry face. "I don't think I would help matters. Being as how I'm related might only make me lose my temper. I'd best stay put."

"Whatever you say." Grant looked into the distance at the sky above the mountains. "I admit I didn't think of the idea myself. Never wanted to talk to the bastard after what happened in Denver. Ranchers and railroad men don't see eye to eye. Never will."

"I suppose it was his way of trying to worm a deal out of us. If he offers a price that tempts you and those with you, the rest of us will fall in line. I know how he works."

He turned back to look at her, a corner of his mouth lifted. "You might be surprised to hear it was Annie's idea."

Hattie blinked. "Well, well. Taking an interest, is she?"

He shrugged. "It seems natural. She's close to you, and she seemed to like being up here."

Letty set her cup down. "There's more to it than that."

"What do you mean?"

She shook her head. "Men. Blind as bats."

He waited. She scowled.

"She's smitten by you. Course I suppose that's natural too, bein' up here and meetin' you. Then she saw the danger our property was in and couldn't believe her father had anything to do with it. High-tailed it back to Denver to find out. That girl carries a torch for this valley now, and I don't think it's because of her dear-old auntie."

Grant smiled. Letty had it wrong, but how to tell her? He'd promised Annie never to mention Grace in front of family, and Letty was family. And Grant abided by his own moral code. Once you gave your word, you didn't go back on it. Of course if Letty told him, that would be all right.

"Annie is mysterious, all right," he said. "Spirited and mysterious. Guess that runs in the family, from what I can see."

Letty grunted. "Pig-headed is what you're trying to say, and yes, that does run in the family."

They were interrupted by Juan Jose who reported that the cowboys who had moved the herds from the burned out ranges had found all the cattle trapped in ravines. They were all safe, on good grazing slopes. Realizing that he'd spent more time here than he'd intended, Grant took his leave. The time didn't seem right to try to draw Letty into conversation about her family. But if things got resolved in these parts and he saw Grace again, he knew what he was going to ask her. And then the world would know.

Once again Annie prepared to go on stage, but this time, the dressing room was a bedroom on the second floor of Hortense Morgan's three-story mansion. The hostess had lent her personal maid to help with Annie's costume changes. Other performers were housed in other bedrooms of the sprawling household, where all was organized down to the last detail.

What was not organized were Annie's emotions. She had practiced her music assiduously, so that she knew every note by heart, every phrase and how to convey its meaning. She'd practiced in the presence of her family, welcoming distraction as a test to see if she could carry off the songs without fail, no matter what happened. And there had been a run-through at Hortense's with grand piano in place at the back of the patio and tables and chairs set up to give the illusion of an audience. All had gone well, including the timing of the costume changes.

But she could not rehearse in front of the living, breathing audience that would contain Grant, if he lived up to his promise to come. There was no way to rehearse where she would find him sitting, how to direct her performance so that she was aware of his reactions but did not have to look only at him, which would make her too nervous.

And so her nerves nearly took over as she dressed in sumptuous evening gown of blue satin, reminiscent of the ball gown in the first scene of *Die Fledermaus,* in which Grant had first seen her posing as Grace. Of course this ball gown fell gracefully to the floor in flounces with a train behind. But the song she would sing would serve to remind him of the party scene. In this way, she was going to let Grant see for himself that Grace and Annie were one. If only her ploy would work. It was cowardly, she realized, but the result would be many hundreds and possibly thousands of dollars put to good use by the hospital.

She had craned her neck out the window earlier to try to see who was arriving. The carriage drive was at the other side of the house, but this window did give a view of the patio and lawn. The beds of chrysanthemum added color, and Mother Nature had cooperated to provide a perfect, calm, late summer evening. The round wooden tables placed on the lawn were covered with tablecloths of small blue and white checks. Hurricane lamps in the center of each table would be lit when it got dark.

The kitchen had been busy for days as Hortense's chef prepared a menu of pâtè-de-foie-gras with truffles, cold meats, fruit and lemon pastry. But Annie was far too anxious to eat.

Nana, the maid, fussed over her train and worried over the elaborate coif they had styled for her. Her hair was pulled up and back the way she had worn it at Central City, and a long lavender plume was fixed over her ear and curved above her head. She hoped it was enough to send her message to the man she prayed would be here to listen, to think and to reach his own conclusions.

"You look lovely," said Nana. "But you mustn't pace around so. You are apt to tear your gown or loosen your chignon."

"Thank you, Nana," said Annie. "It's just that I am so nervous. Perhaps if you leave me now, I will just go over my numbers alone."

"As you wish. Pull the cord if you need anything. There's a glass and fresh water in the pitcher on the tray. Mrs. Morgan said to be sure you had enough to moisten your throat before you sing."

"I appreciate that. Don't worry. I'll be fine."

Left alone in the large guest room, she went to the window. The drapes were tied back, and she only lifted the gauzy curtains a little, trying not to attract attention from anyone below who might look up. It was still quite light, being only about the hour of seven, and the guests were mingling and visiting. Laughter and chatter floated up to her open window. But of the ranchers there was no sign. She let the curtain fall, disappointed. Perhaps her peacemaking attempt was not to bear fruit this night.

At last the hour arrived. Annie went downstairs to the back parlor where all the entertainers were gathering to wish each other well. Trevor Evans came around to wish her good luck.

He was a tall, slender lad with light brown hair and cheery, youthful looks. His silk cravat tied at the base of high stand-up collar made him look very artistic.

"Well," he said companionably to Annie. "I suppose we're prepared to knock them out of their seats."

She allowed a chuckle. "I only hope we entertain well enough to keep them *in* their seats until the end."

"Yes, indeed. Until Hortense collects all their envelopes full of cash and bank drafts for the charity."

The double-pocket doors opened and Hortense entered the room, pausing to close the doors behind her. She smiled at them regally, looking elegant as usual in a lime-green taffeta gown with a giant corsage on her left shoulder and matching flowers gathering the left side of her skirt.

"Is everyone ready?" she asked them all.

After a pause for their murmurs, she informed them of her plan. "As soon as they are settled, the waiters will light the candles in the hurricane lamps. I'll give my little speech, encouraging them to be generous in their donations. Then we will begin."

Trevor nodded his acknowledgment; he would be the first one to emerge to the little patio stage.

"Very well, then," she said to her flock, "let us begin."

Grant arrived late feeling ill-tempered and wondering why he'd agreed to come. He told the butler at the entry that he would keep his hat and strode on through, as directed. Though he touched his hat to some familiar faces, he didn't see anyone he knew until Everett Marsh spied him and broke off from a conversation.

"Evening, Worth," said Everett, coming up to shake his hand.

"Evening."

Everett seemed relaxed, but Grant was wary to any smooth-talking the man planned to do.

"I'm glad to see you here. My daughter said she had made sure you got an invitation."

"Oh?"

Everett grunted. "My daughter has taken quite an interest in our mutual affairs, it seems."

"Which daughter?"

Everett looked surprised, but then decided he was joking. "Annie, of course. I have no other daughter."

Anger at the way Everett denied his other daughter's existence only further blackened Grant's outlook. He was in a mood to talk turkey tonight. But Everett's next words surprised him.

"Annie has insisted that she wants to learn the railroad business."

"What for?" growled Grant.

He listened to Everett, but scanned the crowd of Denver's elite, decked out in their evening duds.

"Feels she has something to offer hard-headed businessmen like myself. Says there are a few women who have a nose for business. Wants to find out just what it is that keeps a roof over her head."

Grant's gaze came back to Everett, whose face was surprisingly free of the determined lines he'd seen in that face before.

Everett went on conversationally. "She seems to be taking your part in our discussions," he admitted.

That got Grant's attention. "How so?"

Everett cleared his throat. "She's the one who wanted you and I and those with the most vested interest to meet in a small group to try to negotiate what might be beneficial to both sides."

"I fail to see how anything you might suggest could be beneficial to South Park ranching. I already told you that all the money in the world won't oust us from the best grazing land hereabouts. And your underhanded threat tactics don't work either."

"I am not responsible for those threat tactics," Everett said. "And I see that you're standing firm against my offer. I'm not prepared to say anything more. Come to my office tomorrow morning. We'll discuss it further."

"I hope you're not wasting my time, Marsh."

Everett lowered his voice. "Look here, Worth. There's no reason for things to get nasty between us. I have to say I was convinced that the route through South Park was the best one. But," he cleared his throat, "in fact, Annie has made me agree to consider other possibilities. I'm not saying I'm convinced yet. Just that if someone can show me another good route, I'll consider it."

The hatred in Grant's breast quelled slightly. He'd seen Everett as a ruthless, hard-hearted, greedy railroad baron after nothing but money. Could the man be trying another trick? He was sweet-talking him into sitting down at a bargaining table for some reason. He made no reply, and Everett didn't seem to expect one.

"Just come to my office tomorrow. We'll talk it over then."

Grant was irritated that the man was baiting him. He wouldn't admit to himself that the evil deeds he'd attributed to Everett might not be his doing. But he couldn't think with Everett's claim that Annie was influencing business decisions. A son, yes, but a daughter? Had Everett gone mad?

Then Hortense Morgan came over to greet him and encourage him to take a seat. The entertainment was about to begin. Grant found a place on one side by a round table near the front. After shaking hands with the other occupants of the table, he indulged in his own thoughts while waiters lit candles, and the kerosene lanterns around the small stage area on the patio were turned up. It wasn't dark yet, the sky was still light blue, even though the sun had sunk beneath the horizon an hour ago. Now evening was drawing on, but they had timed the musicale so that with the help of the lanterns, they could still see the performers.

Hortense Morgan graciously welcomed her guests and droned on about the charity. Grant had stuffed some large bills into an envelope and would hand it over at the end. He only really started paying attention when Hortense announced the opening song, a piece from the operetta *The Bat.* Annie appeared, looking very pretty. His mind went briefly back to his last sight of her after the disaster at the Inter Ocean Hotel. She had recovered from that scare and now looked composed, her cheeks with an attractive blush.

She nodded to the young man accompanying her on the grand piano and opened her mouth to sing. He gave himself up to the moment, enjoying the sight of her, feeling a tug of familiarity. Impossible not to think of his beloved Grace.

The audience around him clapped politely and smiled.

"Such a talented young lady," said the woman next to him.

"Seems to run in the family," was his reply.

Four little girls were led out next with a woman who was presumably their dance teacher. The little ones dressed in short, satiny costumes with stars pinned to their heads, struck dance poses. To some syrupy music the lady led them through their routine. She herself, clad in ankle-length netting, looked silly prancing around the stage, but it was all in fun and for a good cause.

Grant shifted his position, glancing around the audience in moments of boredom. He had time to ponder Everett Marsh's words and for the first time allowed himself to think that if it could be proven that there was a kernel of truth in what he said, that he might listen.

Finally Annie returned. This time she was clad in a long nightdress that covered her from chin to ankles and wrists. She carried a candle in a holder and after smiling at the audience she cocked her head, resting it on her other hand in a coy pose. The piano struck its notes.

"Oh, we never mention Aunt Clara," she sang. "Her picture is turned to the wall. Though she lives on the French Riviera, Mother says she is dead to us all."

The audience smiled as the song progressed and began to chuckle as the more risqué verses were pronounced. Clearly Annie was doing a good job of warming up this rather staid group of Denver's finest. But a peculiar feeling lurked in his stomach. He'd heard this song before. In the next moment he remembered where. Two other girls had sung it on a stage somewhere. Central City? No, the operetta hadn't been followed with any olios. It had been in Fairplay.

He remembered clearly now, three girls dressed as Annie was now, holding candles and circling around with modest gestures as the song got bawdier and bawdier.

"At church on the organ she practiced and played," came Annie's lilting voice. "And the preacher would pump up and down. But his wife caught him playing with Auntie one day, and that's why the preacher left town."

Annie's eyes rounded in dismay. But Grant's own eyes narrowed suspiciously. What was going on here? He looked closer. He wondered if . . .

But no, that would be impossible. Grace herself would never be admitted to this august society. Annie was imitating her sister. But why?

He paid no attention to the rest of the song, only stared as a slow, feeling of uneasiness crept over him. Was it just coincidence that Annie had chosen to sing something her sister performed regularly? And that operetta number was familiar too. If it had come from the operetta he'd attended in Central City that would be just too much coincidence.

He didn't like being played for a fool, damnit. And he was about to lose patience with these Marshes. He would have gotten up and left the lawn party had his curiosity not been so great. Better sit back and see just what was going on here.

Annie exited breathlessly, congratulated by her fellow entertainers. How reminiscent of her stint as "Grace," except that backstage was a fancy parlor, and the society sons and daughters were having a high old time in the name of charity rather than trying to please a rough and tumble mountain audience.

She'd seen Grant plain as day where he'd been sitting at the side of one of the round tables near the hedges. But she was thankful that it was getting dark now, and the small pools of light cast from lamps and hung lanterns failed to illuminate his face. His outline was plain from his familiar tan felt cowboy hat to the broad shoulders in dark suit with elbow planted on the table, one boot stuck out from under the tablecloth.

She couldn't allow herself to think about anything but her numbers, for a flawless performance was essential to her plan. She knew when he failed to applaud the Aunt Clara number that she had his attention.

She darted upstairs to change into the final and most daring costume, a replica of the one she'd worn in Fairplay for the cancan. Not that she would go as far as to perform that dance here, but she'd found in her collection of music a very French song from the music halls of Paris. It spoke of the night life there.

Downstairs, when he saw her, Trevor puckered his mouth to pretend he was whistling through his teeth. She just smiled nervously.

"Ready?"

He patted his sheet music. "Oui, mam'selle."

Her French wasn't so bad, and she gave the number the nasal affectation of a Parisian entertainer. The audience was on its feet, some of the men whistling through their teeth, even if a few of the matrons looked a little shocked.

Grant had left his seat. By the time she had bowed and hurried off after the number was over, her heart was thundering for a different reason. She started for the stairs to her dressing room and as she'd expected, she saw Grant looking for the stairs. They spied each other from opposite ends of the corridor and she stopped dead in her tracks.

He paused with his hand on the newel post, looking at her. But before she could take a step toward him, Hortense rustled up behind her.

"Come back, dear. They are calling for you. I fear you will need to do that encore."

She gave Grant a fleeting look, saw him gaze up the staircase curiously and then back at her. Even at this distance she felt the murderous suspicion in his heart and as she turned to follow Hortense back through the parlor, he placed a foot on the carpeted staircase.

Then she heard the yells and clapping and went to bow once more. Grant was going upstairs to the dressing room. Well, that's what she'd wanted, wasn't it? She had planned it this way. So why did tears choke off her throat and water her eyes?

While she drank a glass of water and tried to smile at her public, her lover was going to find out the truth.

Seventeen

In that moment he saw her in the corridor, something turned over in his gut and he didn't like the feeling. The impossibility of what he suspected ground in his mind, though he still could not believe it.

With his heart thumping hollowly in his chest, he climbed the stairs. The servant he'd accosted in the entry hall when he'd gone around to the front door had said the dressing rooms were upstairs; she would go up first to see if anyone was dressing. His glower had been enough to send her up, but he wasn't going to wait down here to find out what he wanted to know.

He climbed the wide, carpeted staircase and stopped on the second floor. A long runner stretched down a corridor with high ceiling and molded chair rail. The maid was just closing a door at the far end of the corridor. He met her half-way there.

"Miss Marsh isn't here," said the maid. "She must be downstairs, now."

"Thank you," he said, stepping around the girl. "I'll wait for her here."

"Oh, but . . . ,"

He cut her off. "I'm an old friend."

And he barged into the room where Annie had been dressing. He shut the door behind him so as not to be interrupted by the maid doing guard duty.

Clothing was piled on a four-poster bed and on a daybed under a window. Combs and other hair implements along with jars and powder puffs littered a heavy, carved dressing table. A tall, oval mirror stood in its frame in the corner of the room in front of an over-sized armoire. There were petticoats, shoes and gloves everywhere. It was the scene of hasty costume changes, much like a theater dressing room between numbers.

From below, the hoots and applause had died and the piano began a final melody. The stage must be directly below the window because there was no mistaking the voice that floated upward. *Her voice,* one that was only too familiar by now.

He picked up a trailing petticoat as if holding it in his hand provided the evidence of his betrayal. The mocking voice crooned her little ballad:

"She is more to be pitied than censured. She is more to be helped than despised."

Grant turned away, throwing the petticoat onto the bed and slamming his hand against the bedpost.

Liar! Deceitful, cheating little brat. She would pay for leading him on. His own humiliation made him see red. He'd been tricked, hornswoggled and he'd eaten every bit of it. *The two girls were one.* The words pounded into his head harder than a ten-gallon hangover.

He turned and seized the hand mirror in which she must have admired her artifices. Was she laughing at him every time she saw him? He shook his head slowly. Why hadn't he seen it?

Because he didn't want to believe it, that's why. He couldn't believe that the daughter of such a powerful Denver social tyrant as Everett Marsh would be allowed to prance around on a stage unchaperoned. How had she done it?

He turned on his heel and stomped through the door, leaving it ajar. He passed the maid at the top of the stairs, ignored her questions, and barreled down to the entry hall. He nearly set the butler spinning as he shoved open the front door before him and took the front steps.

"Your carriage, sir?" a liveried groom asked on the circular drive where buggies were lined up waiting for their owners.

He plowed on toward the stables. No lackey was going to wait on him. He'd find his own damned horse and get out of this snobbish, two-faced, gutless, society affair as fast as he could. When he did locate his horse, he kicked open the stable door, turned the animal around, mounted up, and pressed his heels into the horse's flesh.

As they galloped out of the stables and into the drive, servants and bystanders gasped and scurried out of the way. Grant reached the street and turned east. Then he gave the horse its head and galloped eastward until he decided the streetlights weren't bright enough to prevent his horse from stumbling. He continued on east at a walk.

The streetlights and fancy houses were left behind as they came to homesteads at the edge of the city, farms that provided their goods to the residents he'd just left behind.

"Whoa, boy," he finally told the horse and pulled up by a fence.

He let the horse rest as he propped a foot on the bottom rail of the split-rail fence. Above them a quarter moon offered some feeble light. In the distance, lights from some farmhouses glimmered. But Grant was thankful for the darkness.

In his mind the mocking faces of Annie Marsh and Grace Albergetti merged into one. He relived every moment of seeing both of them, seeing it now, seeing how he'd been tricked. Some fine actress she was, he didn't deny her talent. But why she'd elected him to humiliate in this way he didn't know.

He'd made love to Everett Marsh's daughter. That was some ironic consolation. Whether or not he'd ever tell the man he was in no state to decide right now. Right now all he could think of was that he'd been fooled.

But why? He shook his head, removed his foot from the fence and turned around. His horse nuzzled him and he spoke to it.

"Why did she do it, old boy? Why?"

He remembered seeing her on the train that first day. That's when the lie began. She'd finagled her way on stage and obviously her family didn't know. Thus the lies at the dance that night. And the story about her sister. But then she'd done it again. She'd gone to Fairplay and sung and danced again. That's why he hadn't suspected they were the same person. He never would have thought the stay-at-home daughter of Everett Marsh so enterprising and daring.

He inhaled a bracing breath of night air and walked the horse back to the road. He'd walk awhile, though. He was in no hurry to get back to civilization. He certainly wasn't feeling civilized.

"Damn you, Letty, why didn't you tell me?" he grumbled.

He remembered seeing Annie at Letty's, making him swear secrecy. He slapped his reins across his thigh.

"Secrecy, of course," he said to the night. Because Letty didn't know. *Did she?*

He'd never seen the two girls and that had been his downfall. And tonight she'd revealed the truth to him in a way she knew he would understand. The costumes, the songs. The dressing room. There weren't two of them, only one. No disowned sister, a disowned sister wouldn't be performing in Hortense Morgan's house. For Everett Marsh had been there and he would never have allowed such a thing.

No, the joke was on him, Grant Worth, and no one else. No one else had been so taken in. Well, how about that? he mused to himself.

He plodded onward past the homesteads and back to the edge of town. He didn't remount; the walk did him good. And when he reached the hotel, he'd a mind to get dead drunk. He had a meeting with Everett Marsh in the morning that at the moment he didn't mind if he slept through. He had no idea what he would do or say about the ruse just played at his expenses, but by tomorrow he would think of something. By tomorrow she would know that her insult had cut him deep. And Grant Worth was a man with pride.

Everett Marsh had to examine his motives in agreeing to let his daughter learn about the railroad business. It would take some talking to explain it to his partners. So as he buttoned his vest and slid his arms into the morning coat his wife was holding for him, he frowned suspiciously at his reflection. Hattie brought the clothes brush and dashed away a few specks, making sure his appearance would be respectable.

"I suppose I do indulge her," he said, continuing a conversation his second thoughts had prompted with his wife this morning.

She had not finished dressing, but had come into his room to help him get ready for the day, as usual. He allowed her to knot his cravat while he still mumbled at the tall, oval mirror.

"I know the partners will think it odd, a woman taking an interest in business."

"Don't worry, dear," offered Hattie. "It's just a mood she's in. She'll get tired of it soon enough."

He turned to check his final appearance and tugged on his wide lapels. Finally he faced Hattie.

"And then what? She seems to have little interest in marriage. One would think she scares the suitors away."

"Perhaps she does."

Everett took a second look at his wife.

"It might be well, then to make sure she gets out more. We must know some people with eligible sons. Have you taken her calling at all the right houses?"

Hattie's brows pressed downward in bewilderment.

"Well you know that the last few weeks she's been so busy with the charity extravaganza. Spent more hours at Hortense Morgan's than I've spent knowing the woman. You would have to say that's one of the right houses."

"You know what I mean. Hortense doesn't have eligible bachelor sons. I don't suppose Annie met anyone in that crowd that took a fancy to her. I suppose that is too much to hope."

Hattie tried a smile. "You are too hard on her, dear. She has a lively spirit."

A sigh escaped Hattie and she rescued a handkerchief that had leapt out of her pocket and replaced it there. "I do think something happened to her when she went to Letty's, though. But she won't talk about it."

Everett was ready to go down to breakfast. "Do you think so?"

"Yes, well, woman's intuition. She might have met someone there. Someone of Letty's acquaintance."

"I shouldn't have let her go up there. Right into that pack of ranchers causing me so much trouble."

"You couldn't keep her in the city all the time, dear. And Hattie is your sister-in-law."

"Hmmph. Well, perhaps I'd better talk to my daughter."

"That would be good idea. You talk to her." Letty headed for the door adjoining their bedrooms. "I must hurry and finish dressing. I'll try to be down before you leave."

Everett entered the dining room to see Annie, dressed for the street and swallowing a gulp of apple juice. The hope that she'd changed her mind about accompanying him to his office was dashed.

"Good morning dear, you look well."

"Thank you, Father. I haven't forgotten today is the day I start learning about the railroad."

He selected fruit and cheese from the sideboard. "Are you sure you still want to?"

"Yes. I'm afraid I do."

Her tone was so dejected that he peered at her. "You make it sound as if you're going to have a tooth pulled."

"Oh, no, I don't mean to. I, um, just mean that it is a great responsibility." She sighed deeply. "I have so much to learn."

He sat down and shook out his napkin. "I still don't see why you insist on doing this. I know you have concocted some notion of saving South Park from the evils of my railroad."

He watched her closely enough to see her eyes widen and her chest swell.

"I was just speaking to your stepmother about my unwise decision to allow you to visit Letty recently. I'm afraid Letty might not have kept an eye on you properly."

"Father, I am nineteen, you know. Almost an old maid."

"That's what I'm worried about."

"What do you mean?"

"Well, it is a good time to marry, I should think. I married your mother when she was seventeen and I was twenty-one."

Annie avoided his eyes. "I might not marry. That's why I want to learn a trade."

"My dear, learning a railroad isn't a trade for a woman. School teaching or nursing is more along the line of feminine occupations I should think."

She set her jaw. "You're not going to change your mind about letting me come, are you?"

"No, you may come. Just remember our bargain."

She nodded slowly. "Yes, of course."

"You can start by learning about the topography we have

to deal with. The railroad, even the narrow gauge, can only be built over certain types of elevations and terrains. We have surveyed and there are topographical maps that you must learn to read."

"Oh, yes, I'm most anxious to study them."

"Good. Then if you'll pass me some cream so I can finish my breakfast, we will depart in a half hour."

Hattie joined them, bringing with her an envelope that had been left in the mail tray. She handed it to Annie along with the letter opener.

"It's from Hortense Morgan, dear."

Annie stared at the florid handwriting and then used the letter opener. She scanned the contents in which Hortense thanked her profusely for being the inspiration behind the charity party and mentioned how the amount raised would purchase new equipment for the hospital laboratory.

"Well, what does she say?" asked Hattie.

Annie handed the letter over and burst into tears. Hattie read the appreciative letter and tried to ascertain what had upset Annie, to no avail, of course. Annie didn't feel like making sense.

The Marsh business interests were conducted on the second floor of a brick building at the corner of Fifteenth and Blake streets. Annie was ushered past the clerks and into a small room that at first appeared to be mostly storage. However, a large square table filled most of the room and on this, the charts and maps could be laid out and studied. In a few moments, a young man joined them. Everett reacquainted them.

"Annie, you remember Vernon Dewiler. He will teach you how to read the maps. Vernon is fairly new with us, himself, but I think he'll be able to answer all your questions."

The lanky young man with prominent Adam's apple gawked at the girl he was supposed to instruct and then cleared his throat and bowed to her.

"How are you Vernon?"

"Fine thank you, Miss Marsh. It's a pleasure to see you again."

Annie smiled prettily to put the nervous young man at his ease and then took a seat while he pulled a large chart from one of the flat drawers located in an oak cabinet. Her father left them for his meeting with the ranchers. Annie knew in her heart that Grant would not be among them.

"Well," croaked Vernon. "I shall do my best to instruct you. Do stop me if it seems too confusing."

She merely smiled and began to study the curving and undulating lines on the map. It was like nothing she'd ever seen. But remembering that she had a purpose in being here, she drew in a large breath and began to apply herself to the task.

In the outer office Everett greeted his colleagues, Vernon's uncle, John Dewiler and William Abograst.

"Morning, gentlemen. My daughter is with me today. Wants to learn a bit of the business, peculiar as it sounds. I have her closeted with young Vernon in there, going over maps."

John Dewiler leaned back and folded his hands over his stomach. "Well, well. We'll just see how much she learns from my nephew. I don't mind if they get their heads together, if you know what I mean."

"Hmmmm. I thought so, myself. Glad you're in agreement. Well, if your nephew does a thorough job of it, perhaps Annie will decide by the end of the day she's had enough of this business."

Dewiler winked at him. "And decide to pursue other interests, perhaps?"

Abograst paused before sitting down to the financial reports one of the clerks had left him.

"This the daughter that set the citizens on their heads with her songs at the Morgans' the other night?" he asked.

"This one and no other," replied Everett.

Abograst tugged at his moustache. "Quite a handful, that one, I would think. Now you say she's here looking at our survey maps?"

Everett admitted defeat. "Some fool notion she's got in her head since she spent some time with her aunt in South Park."

"Oh, I see."

"Don't know what kind of trouble she stuck her nose into up there. But now she's got it in her head to know the issues, there's nothing for it but to show her the facts."

"Good idea, Marsh. She'll soon tire of it."

Annie, however did not tire of it. The lines and notations of elevations on the giant charts gave her a headache, but she persisted with her usual dogged determination.

In the outer office, Everett and the others conceded that the ranchers were still holding their grudge. Not one of them showed up for a private meeting.

On the second day, Annie studied the proposed routes into the mining communities and then asked to see the proposed budgets and profit and loss statements. She plied Vernon with questions, but kept silent when around anyone else.

Vernon nearly turned handsprings to fetch her the information she needed. They stayed closeted in the map room most of the time, emerging to accompany her father down the street to a restaurant for tea if her father decided to work late. After that first day, she worked in the office only in the afternoons so that she could keep her part of the bargain about doing chores in the morning.

By the end of the week she was exhausted, but it was the kind of exhaustion she needed. When she was alone in her room, her eyes misted over with thoughts of Grant. She tried to forget him but could not. Her ploy of revealing who she was had worked, for the last she'd seen of him was that glimpse with his foot on the stairs at the Morgans' house.

He'd left the party and had not returned. And she'd had no word from him. His anger and hurt must be deep, but she was powerless to do anything about it. She deserved her fate.

When she left the family gathering after dinner in the evenings to go up to her room, they all assumed it was because she was so tired. Little did they know that she spent an hour every night braiding her hair and weeping.

Not one to indulge in self-pity, her grief soon turned to self-recrimination, but she didn't bother to relive all her mistakes. It didn't do any good to tell herself that if she'd done this or that things would be different. Things were what they were. She would turn into an old maid and become an eccentric oddity among Denver's citizenry. For not only would she never marry anyone else, she was sure that with her ill mood, no one would want to marry her in any case.

So she poured her intellect and energy into the confusing figures and material at her father's office. While he waited patiently for her to get over her phase, she delved deeper and deeper into all the issues surrounding the need for a railroad going north and south. She even went to talk to the town developers of nearby communities and spent hours at the newspaper office reading over all the articles that had been written about the Denver Pacific and the Kansas Pacific during the period they were being built.

In a month's time she began to speak of what she'd learned. Only a little at first, but then she began to take up the topic with her father after dinner. Everett found, to his surprise, that she had learned a great deal and had knowledge of the terrain between here and Santa Fe that he never expected to be retained in a woman's head.

The work helped Annie think of something other than her woes. She began to bring reports home to read at night and often fell asleep over them. Hattie took to looking in on her to make sure her reading lamp was extinguished and to tuck her in.

Her brother James began to think she was turning into a strange creature, but he half-listened to her prate on in the parlor after dinner and finally looked over some of the maps she unrolled at night on the dining room table.

Finally, she approached her father one night in the back parlor after such a bout with James, on whom she'd rehearsed her plan. She carried a topographical map rolled up under her arm.

"Father?"

Everett peered over his reading glasses at his daughter. "Yes, Annie."

She sat on the armless upholstered chair next to the round table in the center of the parlor.

"I have something I'd like you to see, Father."

"Oh, and what could that be?"

He knew very well what it could be—some scheme having to do with the railroad. In fact, he had to admit that Annie's persistence in the matter of the railroad had surprised him. That she hadn't lost interest after two weeks had earned his grudging respect. His partners had humored him by allowing her to continue coming into the office. And as promised, she hadn't made any trouble for them. So he could hardly ignore her now.

She moved a few books aside and unrolled the map. Everett joined her at the table and adjusted his reading glasses. He recognized the map as being one of the front range of the Rockies from the northern boundary of Colorado to the southern boundary. A line had been pencilled in following some of the foothills.

"From what Vernon and I can see, Father, there are no obstacles to laying track along this route. We know you want to reach the mines in Leadville and other places, so we also studied possible routes for spurs connecting westerly routes. We've marked where bridges would need to be built to span rivers and have calculated the miles of track needed."

"Whoa, whoa, there. Not so fast. Vernon, now, is it?"

"Well, you gave me leave to work with him. It could not be other than that he helped me find out how to explore an alternate route."

Everett ceased to study the map and was now studying his daughter. "You are still very intent to keep us out of South Park. Can your aunt have indoctrinated you so in the cause of the ranchers while you were there?"

Annie's expression tightened somewhat. "Letty doesn't want the railroad any more than any of her neighbors."

"And you got acquainted with these neighbors, from what you've said."

"I met some of them, you knew that."

"Yes, I did. What I didn't know is just now becoming apparent to me. That you're dedicated to their cause."

He shook his head and leaned back in his chair.

"Something tells me there's more to this than I'm being let in on. There's only one reason for the odd behavior you've been exhibiting this past month that I can think of."

Annie avoided his eyes. "Oh?"

"I am used to your enthusiasms. You are in the habit of going off on wild tangents and always have been. But this spell of yours has lasted some time. I have my suspicions."

"Of what are you suspicious, Father?"

"That you met a man you have taken a fancy to. You're smitten by one of the ranchers in South Park and carry a torch for his cause. If this is so, I would like to know if his feelings are returned and what he intends to do about it.

I've seen no suitors come knocking on our door because you seem to discourage them all."

Annie had a pale stony look, but she answered the question.

"You are partly right, Father. I will not lie. I became involved with the ranchers' cause because of someone I met. However, you need not fear that he will darken our door. His feelings are not returned . . . exactly."

"What do you mean exactly?"

Her heart hammered quickly. How she would love to tell him, to share the burden. And perhaps she should, before he found out in some other manner. He would never be able to understand all of it, but some acceptable truth might help her spill out what was locked in her heart. She swallowed and moistened her lips.

"He does not return my feelings because he believes I am someone else."

Everett's reaction was one of pure surprise and perplexity. "I might have been able to think of several reasons, but not that one."

He narrowed his gaze and watched his daughter carefully. "And why does he believe you are someone else?"

"I told him I was."

"Oh, I see, of course. Makes complete sense."

Everett inhaled a large breath, removed his spectacles and took himself to his favorite armchair.

"Well, go on."

"I'm not sure where to start."

Everett sighed. "From the beginning might be a good idea."

She tried to smile, but it did not reach her eyes. She, too, rose and walked to the tapestried sofa next to his chair. She spread her skirts, giving herself time to think.

"It was just a prank. For my nineteenth birthday. It was when James and I went to the opera at Central City."

"Yes, I remember."

"Well, I didn't actually sit in the audience that day."

"You didn't? Where were you, pray tell?"

She looked away. Would he banish her from the house? Disown her? She looked back at him, pleading for mercy.

"Oh, Father. It was just for fun. No one else knew. No one suspected. You see, my reputation is intact and our family name has not suffered."

What had she done that could be so serious? Everett wondered.

"Yes, I'm listening," he said.

"Please don't punish me when I tell you. I've already suffered enough to wish that day had never come."

His next words were angry ones. "Has someone insulted or abused you? I'll hang the man myself."

"No, no, not that. It was just that I was in the opera itself, in the chorus. I had on a costume and didn't think anyone would recognize me when I went on stage."

Her father was speechless. He had expected many things, but not this.

"You what?"

"I went on stage. My friends, Lola Bonitez and Marcel Dupres, put me in the chorus so I could be on the stage, just for a lark. They thought I did a good job. That's all."

Confused emotions passed across Everett's face. Finally he said, "You were on the stage? And is James a part of this ruse?"

"No, no." She hadn't meant to incriminate James.

"You mean to tell me your own brother was with you and yet didn't know you weren't in the audience beside him?"

"Well . . . he wasn't there either."

Everett folded his hands across his lap. "Oh, I see. And where was he?"

She frowned. "I think it would be best if you asked James that himself."

"Yes, all right. I can understand your reluctance to tattle.

Well, go on. What has all this to do with your heartthrob, who doesn't yet have a name, by the way."

"I know. I didn't think you'd like it if I told you."

"Enough beating around the bush, now. Tell me who has captured your heart."

"Grant Worth."

"Ahhhhh. Yes, that explains it. His property is close to Letty's. Well, I should have foreseen that myself."

"I didn't meet him at the ranch, though, until later."

"And where did you first set eyes on him?"

"That day, at the opera."

The salt and pepper brows raised. Annie continued.

"At the theater. I didn't want him to know who I was. I know what people think of actresses. So I made up a name. Grace Albergetti. That's how we were introduced."

She took a breath and narrated the rest of the story up to the point where she'd told Grant she was a twin. Everett listened intently. When it came to the part where Grant was convinced she was a twin, amusement forced its way into his eyes. She admitted to having seen Grant again in Fairplay, but didn't intimate just how far their relationship had progressed.

"It isn't Letty's fault, Father. She didn't know anything about it."

Everett shook his head in amazement. "You managed to keep all this from Letty as well? Perhaps your acting talent exceeds even what we have recognized as an ability to dissemble. The man thinks I have two daughters and that I turned one of them out of the house."

Then the mirth at the outrageous idea made him burst out in a laugh. He chuckled at the irony of it until he had to dab moisture from the corners of his eyes. Annie was relieved that he found humor in it, but she felt too miserable to share in the laughter.

"No doubt the man thinks I'm some brute, disowning a daughter like that."

"I'm sorry Father. I've only added to your trouble. He didn't like you because of this railroad business. I guess I made him dislike you more."

Everett shook his head. "And so what is to be done about this notion?"

"It's too late to do anything, I'm afraid. He knows the truth now. He found out there is no twin the night of Hortense Morgan's charity affair."

"So you spoke to him then, admitted the truth."

"No, we didn't speak. But he realized the truth because in the songs I sang I appeared both as myself and as Grace. He went up to the dressing room while I was on the patio. He could see for himself that there was only one of me."

Everett could see that his daughter was suffering and so refrained from laughing, though this story would leave him chuckling for a long, long time. He shook his head, feeling tenderness tug at his heart. She was clever, his little girl. Clever and now struck by lost love. Something to which the young were particularly vulnerable. How to comfort her?

He reached over and patted her hand. "That is quite a tale, my dear. And I'm glad you've told me. I don't know what to say."

"You're not going to punish me?"

He cleared his throat. "I would not appreciate having our name dragged through the scandal sheets, but as you've said, you've suffered enough already. You can count on me to keep this little adventure quiet. It seems you've reaped your own punishment. And the fact that you've revealed the truth at last, both to your victim and to me, sits well with me. Honesty is best after all. You've just learned a hard lesson in where lies can lead."

Her chin quivered and the relief at having told the truth flooded through her, bringing with it the need to pour out grief. She got on her knees and threw herself onto her father's lap the way she had done many times as a child when she'd hurt herself. He patted her head as she sobbed, and he offered her his handkerchief.

"He won't ever speak to me again, Father. He's so angry."

"Can't say as I blame him," said Everett softly, to himself.

"You don't hate him, do you Father? He still thinks you or your men are threatening the South Park ranchers."

"He is a business opponent, my sweet, nothing more. I've been looking into those alleged threats and have turned up nothing yet. But rest assured, we'll get to the bottom of that. But I'm glad you've told me everything. It makes it easier to understand. Thank you, my dear."

She cried a little more, clinging to her father's knees, grateful to receive compassion at his hand instead of the anger she'd feared. Then she spent a little longer dabbing her eyes and discussing a few of the details. At the end of the hour she felt a little better. Her plight was still sad, but least she couldn't count her father as an enemy. And she didn't have to keep her secrets all to herself.

She bid him goodnight and left him with the map she'd marked out. As she stood at the pocket doors, she made one last request.

"If you decide to send out a surveying team, I'd like to be with them."

"Surveying now, eh? You do seem as if you want to take over my entire enterprise."

She was able to smile as she shook her head. "Not the entire enterprise. After you build a north-south line from Denver down the front range, over La Veta Pass and then south to Santa Fe, I will retire."

Eighteen

Annie returned from her survey tour full of new knowledge about terrain, elevation, grade, advantages of location for connecting spurs to the mines, the high mountain valleys, and the healing mineral waters. Indeed, she had become a fountain of knowledge.

Vernon had been her willing slave, obtaining supplies and information on their trip. He had completely fallen captive to her charms, but Annie didn't care. She was embarked on a mission now, even though she realized that her hopes were futile. So engrossed was she in her project, that she would have lost sight of her original motivation had not her loneliness and melancholy reminded her whenever she was alone.

And even when she was busy with Vernon and the two surveyors who accompanied them, the perfect climate of a Colorado summer and the majestic beauty of the Rockies, stretched to the north and south of where they worked, failed to sustain any lifted spirits. When she looked at the mountains, all she was reminded of was Grant, of the bliss they had shared. In her mind's eye she saw him striding across his corral, tipping his hat to her at Letty's porch or standing tall and handsome waiting for her after a performance.

And when she closed her eyes, the warm noonday sun reminded her of his caress. The ever-present breezes on the prairie and the waving grasses reminded her of his breath fanning her ear. The touch of a twig on her dress reminded her of his nimble fingers lifting her skirts. Standing alone on the naked prairie, she pulsed with desire for a man she had loved. But then she would turn and drag her heavy heart with her and return to work.

Work must be her consolation. Her heart would remain broken, but she could do the residents of this fair land some good. She even enjoyed her work. She became imbued with that far-reaching visionary zeal that promoters had when they looked around and saw a wealthy resource put to good use by honest labor. She became excited by the possibilities, saw the need for railroads to transport ore, farm products and tourists to spas that would one day be built at the mineral springs. She was perhaps more her father's daughter than either of them realized.

She was devoted to keeping the railroad out of South Park. And at the end of their tour, she believed with all her heart that the alternate route was worth selling to the financiers.

First she laid out her findings to her father. His eyes had been skeptical at first, but by the time he had finished listening to what she had to say, he agreed.

"You've done well, Annie," he had said with evident pride. "I was mistaken to think a daughter could not follow the railroad business. You have eclipsed many a man who might have had a similar idea."

She accepted the kiss he dropped on her forehead and sat down in the chair in the parlor next to where she'd been standing. Sudden exhaustion nearly overcame her. She'd pushed herself so hard both to get the job done and so that she would be too tired at the end of the day to think about Grant. And so Everett let her make the presentation the next afternoon to the partners in the offices.

"Has some merit," said William Abograst.

He and John Dewiler had been forced to sit through

Everett's harebrained scheme of letting his daughter propose to them an alternate route for a railroad south to Santa Fe. Neither one of the leading Denver citizens would have given credence to a twit of a girl's desire to accompany a surveying team. And at first, both of them thought Everett had lost his reason. But over the years Marsh's instincts had been right, and they had not regretted their financial backing to any of his enterprises.

So they had agreed to pay the expenses of a new surveying team, sending Vernon along to oversee matters. Neither of course, was aware that young Vernon was like clay in Annie's hands. Nevertheless, the sprout had done a competent job of managing the trip, and the least they could do was listen to the results they had paid for.

And the results surprised them. They sat over the rolled out map now, taking a second look. Annie had finished her speech and waited quietly in the background, allowing Vernon to answer additional questions.

"Well, well, Marsh," said the stout John Dewiler commented. "Seems our two young people have made a mark for themselves. Knew my nephew had it in him."

"Thank you, uncle," said the lanky lad. "But I must praise Miss Marsh for her perseverance in the matter. It was she who displayed a natural instinct for locating easy grades. And she was right about La Veta Pass. It is most promising for a route."

"Yes, well, of course."

The older Dewiler gave a nod in her direction. Though it was hard for him to concede that the mind behind this plan was that of a woman.

The taller widower, William Abograst, who had no family and who always played fair where credit was due, smiled to himself beneath his moustache. His cheery blue eyes sought out Everett's and then Annie's.

"Well done, whoever is responsible. I'd like to undertake to travel this route myself, now that it's mapped out.

Shouldn't take more than a week there and a week back. If I'm satisfied, then I suggest we hold another town meeting. Perhaps this time we can get the support of everyone whom this route will benefit. It will mean support and an easier time getting the land grants we need."

"Agreed," said Everett. "John, what do you say?"

"Er, of course. I trust my nephew. He's seen this terrain with his own eyes. But if either of you gentlemen wish to set your own eyes on it, by all means."

"William, you go," said Everett. "I'm too busy here. If in two weeks, you agree with these plans, we'll hold a meeting. I see no reason why not."

Letty reined in her horse beside the new fenced-in pasture just west of Grant's ranch house. He'd seen her ride in from where he was busy tending his llamas. Since bolting in the face of the storm, the male had decided to change his ways and cooperate with Grant's training. He was docile on a lead rope and would pull a small cart now. Mother and baby stood nearby watching.

Letty tied her horse and let herself through the gate.

Grant finally led the llama over to say hello.

"Morning there, you two," said Letty.

She stood by while the llama inspected her garb from her cowboy hat, hanging from its strings over her shoulders, to her loose trousers for riding, to her boots. She handed a folded piece of paper to Grant.

"I thought you might be interested in this. Everett Marsh has finally seen things our way and is proposing a new railroad route on his side of the mountains. He's holding town meeting to announce his plans."

Grant took the notice, but glared at it suspiciously. "You saw what happened last time there was one of these town meetings."

"I reckon he learned his lesson from that one. He wants

us to come to an intimate little chat in his offices first, show us a map on the afternoon before the meeting. He doesn't want any surprises."

Grant squinted at her. "Why would he want to do that?"

She shrugged, held out some grain from her pocket to see if the llama would take it from her.

"Don't know. Maybe he just wants to show us his new plan to put our suspicions to rest."

Grant read the words printed on the sheet and then folded it slowly. He gave it back to Letty.

"You go. You and some of the others. I see no need to spend any more time down in Denver than I have to. I've got things to do."

Letty eyed him. His jaw had that stubborn look, and his steely eyes focused on his animal again. The beast stood still while he brushed at the thick fur with his hand. He readjusted the packs the animal was carrying.

"I can see you're making progress," she said by way of compliment to his obsession with his llamas.

"Yup. Follows like a good dog. Teachin' him how to pull a cart. Hell, who knows? I might be able to sell these animals to rich folks in Denver to pull their kids around in carts."

He allowed himself a small grin, but Letty bested him.

"You just said you wouldn't go to Denver, so how could you sell anyone there on these pets?"

He didn't answer. She came around the side of the beast, looking at Grant over its back.

"Matter of fact, neighbor, I've noticed how you've kept to yourself a lot lately. You never did tell me what happened when you went down to that charity do. Did you have another clash with Everett Marsh?"

"Nope. Didn't stay around long enough to engage in lengthy conversation with the man."

"Oh. At the risk of being nosey, you mind if I ask what happened?"

His eyes narrowed and he had the look about him that said he didn't want to talk. She waited, knowing better than to press him. Finally, she gave the llama a pat on its withers and turned back toward her horse.

"Your choice. Guess I'll make plans to go down next week and see what this is all about. You change your mind, you let me know. Oh, and if you decide to stop by when you got any free time, I want you to take a look at my new chicken coop. The old roof never did seem that secure when we stuck it back on after that storm, so I had my boys build me a brand new one. Might see what you think of it."

He squinted at her and gave her a nod. "I'll do that."

She left him to his business, knowing there was something afoot that he wasn't talking about. Well, all in his own good time. Men could be funny about personal things, and she'd just bet this was personal. She knew his feelings for Everett Marsh were strong and he might not be so forgiving even if it were proved that Marsh was innocent of any wrongdoing in this valley.

Then there was the complication of Annie. Letty remembered how she'd watched the two of them talk on the slopes above the church that day. But he'd been silent about that too. Maybe there'd been some sort of falling out. Dammit, Letty was curious. These were two people she liked. If she could do any good for them by sticking her nose into their business she just might do it. But she couldn't do anything unless she lured Grant out.

She climbed on her horse and loped away.

It didn't take Grant too long to take Letty up on her invitation to examine her new chicken coop. He walked around it the next day, inspecting the wooden coop. A nice long bar latched the door against intruding animals.

"Looks sturdy enough to me," said Grant. "I still wish you'd let me pay for the materials."

"Hogwash. Your llama may have stirred up the chickens, but it was the cyclone took the roof off. The old one was set to fall down one day. I needed to replace it anyway."

He chuckled. "Whatever you say."

"I got a fresh apple pie on the table. Thought you might want a piece."

"Well, a man never turns down good food. Chalmers has been feeding me too much spicy Cajun food lately. I'd sure like an ordinary piece of apple pie."

Once she got him installed at her table and shoved pie and coffee at him, she eyed him closely. When he'd eaten enough that he could talk, she plied him with her questions.

"Somethin's eatin' at you, Grant. Want to talk about it?"

He smirked at her and lifted his coffee mug. "Can't say as I'd like to talk about it, but you're lookin' at the biggest fool this side of the Continental Divide."

"Oh?" She grinned. "That's not exactly what I expected."

"Took me for a surprise, that's for sure. Not that I'm lookin' forward to talkin' about it, but I know you, Letty. You'll hound me 'til you find out."

She merely lifted her chin in acknowledgment.

He held up his coffee mug and she poured him some more. Then he scraped back his chair and nodded toward the front room. Letty preceded him in and took a seat on her curved-back armchair, leaving him the settee.

He swallowed his coffee in satisfaction and set it aside. Then he looked at her squarely.

"I'd like to blame you for it, but I had to admit to myself I never asked. If you were keepin' a secret it was my fault for letting things lie. Course I thought I was keeping a promise."

This puzzled her. "About what?"

He smiled the smile of a defeated man, looking up at the ceiling.

"A promise to your niece, Miss Annie Marsh, never to discuss her runaway twin sister. The outcast actress, Grace Albergetti."

This made Letty's jaw drop and her eyes open wide. "What?"

"That's right. Everett Marsh's daughter evidently has some spunk, to say the least. Found her way onto the stage at the opera house in Central City. I happened to be with a gentleman who knew one of the dancers and so was introduced to Miss Albergetti backstage."

Letty just blinked, so Grant continued.

"Later, I saw her on the train in her own duds with her brother. Fine actress, all right. The girl shows real talent. Acted as if she'd never seen me before, though I suspected something was up.

"It wasn't until I was down in Denver at one of those balls that I met her again. I was intrigued." He snorted in self-derision. "Spun a tale to me about this twin sister that'd been disowned by the family and taken to the stage. I believed her, hook, line and sinker. She said no one ever spoke of Grace Albergetti. It was as if she were dead. Then Annie showed up here and repeated her story. Said I had to keep quiet about Grace even around you, that you didn't acknowledge the girl either. Course I thought that was going a little far."

He shook his head. "But a promise is a promise. Shoulda' seen through it though. Shoulda' known better. Guess I was so preoccupied with my own business, I didn't bother to be too suspicious."

Letty's face was filled with amazement and mirth that she could not suppress. She put her hand to her mouth to prevent an outright burst of laughter. Such a prank was not beyond the skills of her niece, though the enormity of this plan impressed her. She cleared her throat.

"So how long did this ruse last?"

Grant inhaled a deep breath and let it out, threw an arm over the back of the settee.

"Oh, this young woman really took me for a ride, I must admit. I saw her again, thinking she was Grace. She seemed taken with me, and I admit I was fooled. I don't mind telling you, Letty, I was taken with her. Guess that's why I didn't want to think she was lyin'."

He glowered at the cold fireplace. "She played her little game and I fell right into it. Guess she had some twisted motive, I don't know. I was a jackass about it. Then every time I saw Miss Marsh, she supported the notion about her sister. They were in communication, she told me, so I never suspected a thing."

Letty's amusement now turned into something more near compassion and she leaned forward.

"Grant, I'm sorry my niece played this trick on you, and I know what it's costing you to tell me. But you must believe me when I say I understand. You lost your heart to the girl, from what I can tell, but you lost your heart to the wrong girl. I don't know what passed between you, but I can only guess that Annie lost her head over you. She thought you were in love with this Grace, this actress, and so she kept up the pretense."

Letty sat back. She knew her niece better than he thought and though she didn't know all the details, this story explained some of Annie's behavior. She'd known the girl was smitten. She just didn't know to what great lengths she'd gone to try to hold Grant's heart.

"You mustn't think so ill of her." But she saw the pain in his eyes.

"I lost my heart to a girl that doesn't exist," he said with disgust. "A phantom."

With woman's intuition, Letty wanted to explain that it was the same girl. It was the talented, quick chameleon that had captured his heart. But he wasn't ready to admit it. In the process, his pride had been wounded, and no man would suffer that. There was nothing she could say to make him see that Annie had done all this because she loved him.

"Perhaps Grace is just another side of Annie," she suggested.

But he gave her a look that brooked no more argument. "I would appreciate it if you would keep this to yourself," he grumbled.

"I've no reason to say things that will damage the reputations of my friends. For your sake and for Annie's sake, your secret is safe. What to you intend to do?"

He got up from the settee and she rose also.

"To stay as far away from that family as I can. If I never see any of them again it would suit me just fine. Livestock are more predictable, for all their trouble."

"So that's why you refuse to attend this meeting."

He nodded.

"Very well, I'll go. I'll take Luke Jackson and Dakota Hanks if they want to come. Somebody needs to find out what is going on."

"I got things to do up here," he said. "If those railroaders are finally going to leave us in peace, I can get on with my business."

It was too soon to argue with him. Letty would go to Denver and have a quiet talk with her niece. She didn't know how far things had gone between "Grace" and her swain, and she didn't need to know. But if the girl would confide in her, perhaps she could do something to help.

She saw Grant out and watched him ride away, back to his llamas. Yes, there was just enough quirk to Grant's own personality to make him a likely match for a girl as clever as Annie. Perhaps all was not lost yet.

* * *

Letty went down to Denver with Luke Jackson and Dakota Hanks. She decided to take her one-seated trap. She could have ridden horseback, but she decided that the buggy would look more appropriate for calling in town after the meeting. And she'd decided that she'd neglected her in-laws for too long. So as Jackson and Hanks accompanied on their mounts, Letty drove along the mostly-graded road over Kenosha Pass with its stunning view, through South Platte Canyon and on into Denver.

Little did her two companions know that instead of pondering what Everett Marsh had come up with and how, her mind was occupied with a bit of matchmaking. She was most anxious to get Annie aside and find out the true story about her leading Grant into such a morass of lies. Annie was a favorite niece, and if there was anything she could do to help, she would. Perhaps it was her long ago memories of her own courtship and loving marriage that had left such a soft spot in her heart. But it was also her love of the valley in which she lived and her respect for the men and women that kept it the way it should be.

Grant had been lacking since his wife had died. It was time for him to love again. Not that she wouldn't consider the match for herself. Grant was a strong and reliable male and would make a good mate. But she and Grant were more like a brother and sister. Maybe because he had been such a close friend to them when they'd first got their start. For whatever reason, Letty did not feel her time to love again had come. And she and Grant had never shared any kind of spark beyond the trusting friendship that the loyal cattle ranchers felt for one another. There was a bond there because they wanted to protect what they had.

So if Annie had lit a light in Grant's sealed heart, Letty wanted to kindle the flame. They were both stubborn, and Annie was certainly impulsive. But Letty always had believed that her niece had her heart in the right place, if not always her notions. In any case, this strange romance of theirs bore looking into. And Letty was just the person to do it.

She showed up at the Marsh door the following evening and let Lin Chu take the reins. She waited in the drive until the Chinese servant led the horse and trap into the stable. Then she presented herself at the door. She was shown into the front parlor and in moments, Hattie rustled in and greeted her and squeezed her hands.

"Oh, Letty, it is good to see you. Everett told me you might be coming to town for the meeting. I do hope you will stay with us."

Letty smiled sweetly. "I don't want to impose. My friends put up at the Inter Ocean. That's good enough for me. But if you do have room . . ."

Her brother-in-law's wife had her usual overwhelmed look, even though she was nicely attired in muslin walking dress for calling. But the bonnet she had evidently just put on her head had slipped a little sideways. Nevertheless, there was an endearing quality to Hattie that must have appealed to Everett when he was looking around for a second wife. She did try so hard to please. Never mind that the people she had to please in this family were all headstrong, independent and likely not to agree on what was pleasing.

"Of course we have room, Letty. You are family. You must stay with us." A hand went to her breast as if she'd just now remembered that they hadn't a guest room ready. "I'll tell Dorthea to see to the room and Maria to lay an extra plate for dinner."

Letty knew she was sending the house into a tizzy by coming unannounced, but it suited her to stay here. It was the only way she was going to get a chance for an intimate talk with Annie.

The room was arranged and after chit chat with Hattie

over some tea, Letty went upstairs. The comfortable little room was indeed cozy with large sash windows offering a view of the garden, lace curtains that hung from the green velvet valence, tall armoire, ruffled canopy over the bed, and inviting brown velvet settee with swooping back. Just the place for a visit with her niece.

Letty had just unpinned her hat and removed it when there came a knock.

"Come in."

Annie entered and reached out for a hug. "Oh, Aunt, I am glad to see you."

Annie threw herself on the bed, and gave her aunt a dazzling smile that shone with pride.

"I did it. You'll see it all at the meeting. Father has finally agreed to withdraw all his offers for land in South Park."

Letty sat down on the velvet settee. The corners of her mouth lifted in conspiratorial congratulations.

"I am impressed. The ranchers will thank you. Though I am sure that it is one rancher in particular that you did all this for."

Annie's glance fell away in embarrassment, but her forthrightness prevented her from trying to skirt the issue. Her brow wrinkled.

"I don't suppose he came with you."

"No, he did not. But we did have a chat before I left with the others."

Annie's eyes same up to meet her aunt's. There was a tentative pause. "Oh?

One of Letty's thick, sandy brows arched. "He told me everything."

Her niece's eyes widened and she leaned backwards, resting her weight on the bed.

"Oh. Everything?"

Letty smiled. "Well, probably not everything. He was discreet. Rest assured, I need tell no one else."

Annie sighed and rolled her eyes upward to the ceiling.

"I've made such a mess of it." She shook her head, sitting up straighter and folding her hands in her lap. "I know what you'll say. I've gone too far. Well, I know I have. Things just got out of hand, you see. I couldn't let any of the family know I'd been cavorting on the stage. I'd be disowned."

"And so you made up a story about a twin sister that was disowned."

"I thought it could work. Only I wasn't counting on . . ."

"On falling in love with him."

Annie's eyes glistened with the truth. "Yes, it's true. I lost my head. Then I was afraid to tell him the truth because he was in love with Grace."

Letty couldn't resist a smile of amusement. "Quite a feat, creating another woman out of your imagination to capture the man of your dreams."

"Foolish, wasn't it?" She gave a dejected sigh, her shoulders slumping. "I gave up hope and so I thought of the idea of working for the railroad. At last some good could be salvaged out of what I knew. I thought maybe he would hate me a little less after that."

"Perhaps he will."

Annie got up and crossed to the settee. She sat down and took Letty's hands. "Oh, Aunt, do you think he'll ever speak to me again?"

Letty shook her head. "I honestly don't know, dear. But I know your heart's in the right place."

She pulled Annie over onto her shoulder and gave her a squeeze. How it touched her to see the young heart all twisted and broken. But there was resilience too. No matter what she'd said, Letty knew that Annie Marsh never truly gave up.

"What can I do?" murmured Annie.

Letty released her and they sat comfortably together. "Well, first of all you must give him time. Men don't take so easily to having their pride wounded, and you've wounded his."

"I'll regret that until my dying day."

"You may not have to regret it quite so long. But for now, you must have patience. If he has any sense, he will realize that even if you've made a fool of him, no one else knows. It helps a man to realize that other men know nothing of his own foolishness. He only told me because he knows I won't tell anyone else."

Annie shook her head and pushed her hair back behind her ear. Her lip trembled a little.

"Do you really think there's any hope that he'll speak to me again? Give me a chance to try to explain? And apologize."

A slow smile claimed Letty's normally skeptical lips. "My dear, where the heart is involved, there is always hope."

Nineteen

Following a successful town meeting, this time with no interruptions, citizens and ranchers alike seemed pleased with the new route. Investors saw the sense in the plan and Everett pursued a bond issue with the county that looked like it would pass. And Everett gave all due credit to his daughter.

Letty pressed Annie to visit her again at the ranch. Annie accepted readily enough. Apart from her misery about Grant, there was another piece of unfinished business that could not rest. If those in Everett's employ hadn't started the fires around Letty's ranch and threatened the safety of the Grant's llamas, who had?

So once again she boarded the stage for Fairplay. As soon as Juan Jose picked her up, she put on her investigator hat and began to concentrate on the job at hand.

"Juan Jose, what do you know about the fires that broke out when I was here? Has anyone noticed anything that might tell us how they started?"

"No, señorita, no one has said nothing. Everyone don't want it to happen again. They guard the herds very close now."

"I'm here to see if I can find out who started that fire," she said, as they bumped along over the wagon road. "I have to prove it wasn't my father's doing."

"You are very brave, señorita, I think."

She shrugged. "Well, I want to help my aunt."

That wasn't the entire reason, but it would do.

"Be careful, señorita. It can be dangerous to look in the wrong direction."

"I may have to look in all directions until I find out which is the wrong one."

Letty greeted her warmly, and expressed pleasure that she had come.

"I know this isn't easy for you, dear," said Letty.

They were enjoying a hearty meal after the long stage ride. Letty looked at her niece's youthful looks. There were some faint lines of maturity that hadn't been there before. A girl could age overnight in the west. Even for a girl of Annie's advantages and upbringing there were challenges to be met and she was facing some of them now. The melancholy in the flashing amber eyes was caused by something else, but that, Letty hoped, time would heal.

"I'll want to go out tomorrow to see where the fire burned," said Annie. "And where the llama was found."

"That naked hillside isn't hard to spot. It'll take years to replace that growth. I understand the llama was found in the ravine just behind it. Lucky for the llama."

Annie was determined to approach this task just as she had surveying for the railroad. And indeed that job had taught her new skills of observation and attention to details. It was also absorbing, something she still needed to occupy her restless mind.

"You can take my mare, Taffey," Letty continued. "She's sure-footed on those slopes."

"Thank you, Letty. I only hope I find something."

In the morning, Annie dressed for the job in sturdy muslin dress with skirt free enough for riding, cotton drawers to protect her legs against the saddle, stockings drawn up to her knees and a pair of Letty's work boots. She tied her hair up with a ribbon and covered her head with a straw sunbonnet tied under her chin.

Then she and the dun-colored horse with dark brown mane and tail made their way from Letty's back pasture up to the top of the ridge that separated her land from Grant's. The denuded trees looked like naked black stakes driven into barren ground. The destruction of nature was sickening, and she got off to walk the rest of the way up the burned hill so that she could have a closer look.

When she reached the top of the ridge, she looked down on the other side to Grant's property. About a half a mile distant were the house and outbuildings of Grant's ranch. Men and horses moved about and she felt a pang as she wondered if he were there. The fire had blown away from his side of the ridge, so they had been spared. His ranch was nestled in golden prairie grasses and hills now touched with the red and gold colors of September.

She led Taffey along the spine of the ridge for a distance and then started down behind the fire line, going carefully among large limestone and granite boulders. She decided to tie Taffey here where she could graze and then continued to pick her way through the short grama grass and lodgepole pines, crossing back and forth as she made her way down into a ravine that had escaped the fire because the wind had blown the other direction. This was where the llama had been found, dangerously close to the line of fire above.

She wasn't sure what she was looking for, but there might be something. If someone had broken into the barn and gotten the llama out, then led it here, there might be some clue. Perhaps the perpetrator had dropped something, left some shred of clothing on a branch. There might be something that would help.

There had been some rain in the two months since the fire, so footprints would not be visible anymore. But when she reached the bottom of the ravine, she focused on examining the surroundings. She wasn't even sure just exactly where the animal had been. Or what would have kept him here once he was led to the spot. If he had smelled the fire above on the ridge, surely he would have tried to get away. And for a llama, it would have been an easy trek out. Unless, he had been tied.

She began to search the branches and trunks of trees to look for any remains of rope. One of the ranch hands had found the animal, and with a fire raging above his head, he probably would not have bothered to untie a rope. He would have cut it.

Narrowing her scope, she began to examine tree trunks and bushes for remains of rope. Futile as it seemed, she was determined to try to find any clue that might then lead to a perpetrator. But how to prove that the perpetrator was connected to someone other than her father? Well, first things first.

She was so engrossed in her work that she failed to listen for the sound of cracking twigs or pebbles rolling down the hillside above. When she heard a footstep behind her and her horse whickered, she gave a start and looked up. Grant was coming around a large upthrust of granite.

He approached on foot and she glanced up to look for a horse.

"I didn't hear you ride up," she said, glad to see him but feeling nervous.

He wore a blue denim shirt and work trousers, scuffed leather boots. A yellow bandanna was tied around his neck, and his hat shaded some of the sun from his face. A face that made her heart stop. It would be their first words since the night she'd revealed the truth to him in such an elaborate manner that she hadn't had to speak to him face to face.

"Left my horse at the top of the ridge," he said after he had scrambled the rest of the way down. "The grazing is good up there."

"Oh."

He rested a hand on the bark of an oak tree near where

she'd been peering at bushes. A few feet away, a trickle from a spring gurgled over rocks, heading for a stream below. The soft breeze whispered through the pines, and a few birds twittered in the warm sun. It would have been a lovely spot for peaceful reflection except that Annie felt anything but peaceful.

He didn't say anything, just slid his narrowed gaze sideways over her and took in the surroundings. He didn't even ask why she was here. But the felt the pulse of warmth between them.

"I'm staying at Letty's," she said to fill the void.

If he wanted to punish her with his flinty gaze, he was doing so. If he wanted to speak to her so badly as to ride up a hill and cross a ridge, he had his chance, and yet he said nothing, just seemed to strip her naked with his gaze. He finally reached for a leaf, snapped it off and twisted it by the stem while he gazed down the slope below them looking toward the stream that rushed downward to fertile valleys beyond.

She straightened, both hands on her hips and half turned toward him. She knew what she had to do.

"I owe you an apology."

He lifted one shoulder in response and took a few steps toward the stream. His profile looked rugged and handsome when she snatched a glance at it. But he made no move toward her. His expression revealed nothing.

She lifted her chin, staring in the same direction at the wealth of nature the little glen offered. Since he wasn't talking, she might as well tell him what she planned to do.

"Letty must have told you that my father isn't going to bother you anymore," she began.

That got a nod out of him and he gave an acknowledgment. "Heard about it. Heard it was your doing."

"Well, it was the least I could do."

"Appreciate it."

The blood pulsed through her limbs as she looked for

the right words. She could almost not trust herself to speak and she felt like she should sit down. How badly she'd wanted these few moments with him over the last two months, a chance to explain, to find out what he was feeling. Now he was here and her mind was just a jumble. Rather than talk too much and make a fool of herself, all she could do was stand there, fighting her own emotions.

Finally, her words poured out on a breath. "Oh, Grant. I am sorry." A sob made her choke.

He turned his head and then his body and rested against the tree trunk. He glowered at her, making her raw emotions feel even more exposed to him.

She drew a huge breath. She was afraid she was going to cry. "You must hate me, and I don't blame you. I don't know how to explain."

Finally he put thought into words. In a low, grumbling voice, he asked, "Why'd you do it?"

She jerked her head around and wiped away some moisture from her eye. "Become Grace, you mean?"

He gave no answer so she assumed that was what he did mean.

"Well, it was who you thought I was. At least after I had made up that story."

He gave a skeptical grunt. "Quite the imagination, I'll hand you that. You ought to be an actress."

"Well, what could I do? You'd been introduced to Grace Albergetti. It had just been a lark to perform that one time. I was afraid you'd tell my father or someone. That would have been the end of me. So I just made up the story about Grace. I didn't reckon on seeing you again."

"Then why did you?"

If he'd had her walk over hot coals, this interrogation could not have been any harder.

She sobbed. "Because I had to."

"All lies." He grunted in disgust.

Her hand went to her breast. "I know, and I'm sorry. I just wanted to see what it would be like."

"What?"

"To . . . to . . . be with you, the way Grace might."

She didn't want to cry in front of him. She didn't want to get his sympathy that way. But she'd been through so much, had worked so hard to make amends, that her ragged emotions raged out of control. She bit her lip and shook her shoulders as the sobs came now. Then Grant took two steps and reached for her.

She didn't know why, but he pulled her gently into his arms, giving her a shoulder to cry on. He must feel sorry for her and she tried hard to control herself. But it felt so good to be in his arms again that she allowed herself to rest her head against his shoulder briefly.

He didn't move except to tuck her head against his cheek. They just stood there and he swayed with her gently as if to comfort her.

"I'm sorry," she said again when she could speak.

He lifted his head and spoke, his words still grated with resentment. "You know what you did to me."

She nodded. "I know."

"I fell in love with a woman that isn't real. I had a phantom in my bed and now she's gone."

She lifted a tearstained face to him. "But she lives, sort of, inside me."

He pulled away so they could look at each other. His eyes searched hers and she saw the pain there, regretting with all her heart making him love and lose again. But why couldn't he see her love for him, Annie Marsh's love?

The corners of his mouth were down-turned with the cynicism that comes from long-borne defeat. His eyes were hard, unforgiving.

"I suppose I always thought there were some things about you that were like your made-up twin. But in my mind there are still two of you. I don't know if I can ever reconcile that to myself."

"I understand. I went too far. I can't expect you do forgive me."

He released her and tried to explain his feelings. He spoke in a low, private voice. "Grace awakened things in me that I hadn't felt in a long time."

She winced. "I didn't mean to hurt you, truly."

He glanced at her briefly, then his eyes slid away. "Why did you let me . . ."

She flushed, knowing what he meant. Why had she done the ultimate, given herself to him under false pretenses knowing that she would have to live with that deed the rest of her life. But she raised her chin.

"There's no shame in what we did," she said. "Not when it was done out of love."

He narrowed his gaze at her and she felt a slow heat beginning to throb between them. Hope fluttered in her chest, and she tried to squash it. Even so his gaze seemed to sear into her. But he didn't touch her again. For even if he felt something that had once been undeniable between them, his pride wouldn't let him acknowledge it. Of that she was certain.

She saw the confusion in his eyes as he gave an ironic chuckle. "What a fool I was."

He jutted his chin forward and she could see the shield around him. Of course he would not betray his emotions for fear of her laughing at him. Her woman's instincts told her some of what was going on inside him.

She bent her knees and sat down on the sloping ground, covered with dried pine needles and dirt. She hugged her knees.

"I didn't do it as a joke," she said. "I never meant to make fun of you. And no one else knew about it except for Lola and Marcel. You must believe that, even Letty didn't know."

"Who are Lola and Marcel?"

"The acting troupe. They were my friends who put me in the operetta in the first place."

"Oh, them."

Seeing that this conversation was getting nowhere, she turned to the matter she'd come to investigate.

"I suppose you're going to tell me I'm wasting my time trying to prove that the fire wasn't started by my father's railroad."

"It's a might late to be looking for clues isn't it?"

She explained her theory. "The llama that was found here, did Billy Joe say it was tied up?"

Grant frowned. "Didn't ask. Why?"

"Well, surely the llama would have picked his way out of danger when the fire threatened. He didn't have any legs broken, so why would he have stayed here? He would have done so only if he were tied. I was looking for traces of a rope."

Grant jerked his chin once in acknowledgment. Then he offered her a hand to pull her up. Together they walked around the area and Annie stifled her heavy disappointment at the emotional barriers between them enough to continue her search for a clue. It was something to have him here speaking to her at all.

He wandered among the scrub oak while she examined the trees. Finally she stopped beside a cottonwood and looked closely.

"Look here," she said.

Grant came over to stand beside her.

She pointed to a faintly visible ring where it looked like the bark had been scraped.

"Your llama must have been frightened when it heard the crackling and smelled the smoke of the fire. He probably strained the lead rope and tried to get away."

"Hmmmm," murmured Grant. He looked for other signs.

The terrain underfoot sloped down toward the stream and pebbles rolled when he took a step. Still, he knelt down and placed his finger in some indentions in the earth that the scant rain had not destroyed.

"This could be the spot, all right. There are enough marks here to make it look like a hoof the size of a llama's tramped around this tree."

She felt a spurt of hope. "So he was tied. We just have to find out who did it."

He exhaled a breath and looked at her as if she'd lost her mind. "And how do you propose to do that?"

His skepticism only made her more determined, so she cocked her head at him in a superior manner.

"We could begin by finding the rope."

She thought she detected a faint glimmer of amusement in his pewter eyes and was struggling to remain hardened to her ploys. But he couldn't very well disagree.

"I'll have a word with Billy Joe about it."

"I don't suppose you'd let me do it."

She could see the way his lips formed a straight line and the skin stretched across his cheekbones that he was trying to keep his armor in place. But she faced him courageously. She loved him. He was too stubborn to see it and he wouldn't let her back into his heart easily. But if she were going to have a chance at all, she had to stay near him. And she wanted to make sure the investigation didn't falter, so she just confronted him until he agreed.

Finally he jerked his chin upward to where the horses were. "Come on."

She followed him as they scrambled back up the hill to the more level grassy slope at the top. There was nowhere to mount so Grant offered her a leg up to the stirrup.

She grasped his shoulder and place her foot in his clasped hands. For a moment their eyes met and held, then he looked down at her boot. But she had seen something, a spark.

She stepped into the stirrup and when he stood up, she swung her other leg over. Again their proximity kindled the old flame. Her pulse still rippled and she felt sure he must feel something. He just wouldn't admit it.

They were in no hurry, and let the horses pick their way slowly down the grassy slope on the ranch side of the ridge. It was a fine, warm day and the cloudless sky stretched overhead for miles. The raw beauty of the beginning of autumn would be all the more enjoyable but for the upsetting circumstances Annie knew she had created for the stubborn man who rode with her.

As they approached the outbuildings, some of the hands looked up from their work and touched their hats. Billy Joe came out to greet them and Grant made introductions. The foreman gave her a friendly smile.

"So this is the little lady helped out at Letty's."

"Well, I'm not sure how much help I was," she said. Evidently Grant had not told his hands about the actress he'd been courting. That made it easier.

"She's got a notion to help us now," Grant explained. "Thinks she can find a way to prove who started that fire."

Billy Joe's face darkened. "If there was any way I could help you find that man I'd see him lynched myself. Damage to property and coulda cost some lives as well. Some kinda evil spirit musta drove him to do it."

"As a matter of fact, there is a way you can help," she said. She glanced at Grant, but he held his peace, allowing her to do the questioning.

She looked back at the tall black foreman. "When you found the llama in the ravine, did it have a halter or a rope around its neck?"

He scratched his head and thought. "Course it did. Chester Seagraves was the one found it. He led it out a' there."

"Do you think you'd know which rope it was?"

He looked surprised but shrugged. "Dunno. But the halters and the ropes for those, er, llamas are all separate from the rest of the tack room. Those animals don't like to be stabled next to the horses, have to keep 'em separate in the barn."

"Good. I mean that's some help. May I see where the lead ropes are kept?"

"Don't see why not."

He led them to the tack room and showed Annie the ropes and halters. Chester Seagraves was found and after some explaining, he located the rope that he'd used to lead the beast out of the ravine. Sure enough, it had been cut at one end.

"Well sure, I cut it," Chester answered to Annie's question. "Wasn't time to mess with untyin' it. The fire was burnin' pretty hard above my head."

"But just now when we located the tree, the rest of the rope around the trunk was gone. You didn't go back later and remove the rest, did you?' "

"Shucks no," replied Chester. "Didn't give that no more thought. Too much work to do around here."

"Thank you." She turned to Grant and Billy Joe. "Someone took pains to go back and cut that rope down. Whoever did that is our perpetrator.

"How we going to find that out?" asked Billy Joe.

"By finding whoever possesses the other end of this rope."

Billy Joe looked discouraged. "Heck that's been more than two months. Coulda' been spliced by now."

That gave Annie an idea. "Are there any new spliced ropes that you know of?"

"Come to think of it," said Chester. "I do remember one of the boys splicing some ropes outside the bunkhouse some little bit after the fire."

"Who?" asked Grant.

Chester had to think a minute. "He ain't with us now, left after that. But we hired him on for the spring roundup—you remember, Billy Joe. He was that greenhorn come up from Denver. Name of Jacob Morley."

Billy Joe puckered his brows, then spoke slowly. "Yes, I remember him. Kinda skinny with dark hair and moustache. More clerk than cowboy, but I gave him a chance. Thought he'd either learn the ropes or quit of his own choosing. Funny, now that you mention it. Couple weeks after that fire, he moved on."

Something about the name sounded familiar to Grant as well, but he couldn't place it at first. He did remember the lad being about the place.

"Kinda kept to himself," said Grant, frowning thoughtfully. "But I think I've seen him before . . ."

Then he stopped, suddenly remembering. He shook his head. "Well, I'll be damned. I met him at Hortense Morgan's charity dance in June. He was in the parlor when I . . ." he paused, cleared his throat, anger beginning to show in his face. "When I was talking about the llamas. He hired on later and I knew I'd seen him somewhere. But he never reminded me where and I forgot until now."

"Maybe he had a reason not to remind you of where you met him," said Annie.

She looked at Billy Joe. "Can we see his quarters?"

"Sure can. But he's been gone over a month now. Bedding'd be all stripped off his bunk. He took everything with him far as I know."

Nevertheless, they all trooped into the bunkhouse and looked over the spot where Jacob Morley had slept. There wasn't any more evidence. If he'd brought a rope down from the ridge, he'd been clever enough to splice it to something else and leave no incriminating evidence. So Annie asked permission to question the rest of the cowboys about what they remembered Jacob Morley doing the night before the fire.

Grant gave her free rein and then he and Billy Joe went about their business.

Annie talked to the cowboys about the place one by one. Most of them remembered Jacob Morley because he'd been such a greenhorn, but none of them remembered exactly what they'd seen the boy do the night before the fire. All of them remembered him doing some splicing, but what he spliced had long ago been put into use and couldn't be identified now. But there was one cowboy who said something that started Annie to thinking.

"I spent a little time with the boy," said Josiah Zachary, one of the most grizzled cowhands who'd worked for Grant since the trail drives. "Felt a might sorry for him. Thought he didn't have any family. Then I saw him writing a letter one night and he said it was to his pa."

"Did you see who it was addressed to?" asked Annie, her heart starting to beat excitedly.

"Did so. Didn't say anything, but thought it was strange. Boy named Morley writing to a pa named Hurley."

"Hurley?"

"Harwood Hurley was the name I seen on the address. The boy didn't know it, I just happened to see him writing it out. The boy was fixin' on ridin' into town to post it himself."

Annie blinked. "Thank you, Josiah. That could be very important to Mr. Worth."

To say nothing of how important it was to her. Harwood Hurley had something to do with railroads. Though he wasn't an associate of her father's, she knew for sure. She raced to find Grant in his study to tell him what she'd learned.

Grant's expression revealed sudden enlightenment as he began to see how it all fit together. He looked out the window and shook his head slowly, hands on hips. Then he turned to Annie.

"Harwood Hurley, you remember him. He was dining at the hotel in Fairplay when you and I . . . that is when "Grace" and I were dining."

She gasped, remembering at once. "The one who came over and threatened you."

He nodded. "The very same."

"Good Lord, Grant. It looks like Harwood put his son up to hiring on here so he could make some trouble. And cover his tracks so you might suspect Father instead of Hurley."

Grant had to admit her reasoning made sense. "Hurley has some interest in the Midland Railroad. They're coming through from Salt Lake to Denver. Haven't heard anything about them coming through South Park, though. We're not on the most direct route."

"No, but don't you see? He wanted you to suspect it was Father's doing. He didn't care what happened to you. He just wanted to slow down Father's plans. The Midland probably resented the Denver Central building through here. After the Midland got to Denver, what would be to stop them from building spurs to the mines? Oh, my, why didn't I see this before? Hurley and his henchmen wanted our railroad to fail."

The two of them were silent for a moment, digesting this new possibility. The soft bong of the tall clock in Grant's little study, marked the time. He studied her, but he would give nothing away.

"Can't prove it," he finally said. "But I admit it fits."

Annie shook her own head in amazement. "Now that Father's going ahead with a different southern route, the Midland may feel like they've bought some time." She looked in concern at Grant. "But they may build spurs near here someday, unless we build ours first."

He gave her a skeptical look and spoke in an unhurried way. "Still a railroad woman, then, are you?"

She flushed. "I tried to settle everything so you and Father wouldn't hate each other. You know railroads are part of progress. You can't stop all of them, Grant."

"No, I don't suppose I can. And as long as they don't bother me in this valley, I won't try to."

"Good."

He looked at her strangely, and she swallowed. Her work here seemed to be done. She lifted her chin.

"I guess I'd better be getting back to Letty's. It'll be dark soon."

"I'll see you back then."

"That won't be necessary."

"Maybe not, but I'd feel better if you didn't go alone."

Since the sun was drawing behind the mountains to the west, leaving an autumn chill behind, Annie didn't argue. When the horses were ready, they saddled up and rode away. The changing colors on the mountain slopes were intoxicating as was the crisp air. It was the kind of evening that made every fiber of her body come alive.

She and Grant loped over the prairie and finally drew to a walk. Near the stream that divided the two properties, they slowed to allow the horses to pick their way to the creek bottom. Grant reined in and dismounted so the horses could drink. Annie got down but didn't say anything as she led her horse to the stream. But Grant's nearness was overpowering. If she were going to break down his defenses, it would be now.

She removed her bonnet and shook out her hair, kneeling to scoop some of the cold water into her hands and touch it to her lips. It refreshed her dry mouth.

She was aware that Grant was squatting close by, also dipping into the stream for a drink. They both stood up at the same time and she trembled, looking away. He broke the silence.

"You were determined to prove your Father had nothing to do with those threats, weren't you?"

She snapped her head around. "Of course, why wouldn't I be?"

He jerked his chin sideways as if thinking to himself, "Kind of loyalty a man can admire."

Irrational hope surged through her. He was giving her a compliment. Why?

He surprised her by stepping up behind her and grasping her waist. Her pulse sizzled as he slid his other arm around her and twisted her around to look into her face. It was a searching look. Then his eyes slid to her lips.

Their mouths were still cool from the delicious mountain spring water and as soon as he kissed her, she drank in the even more delicious sensations of his lips and tongue.

"Grant," she murmured as he broke off and kissed her ears and throat, warming her in his embrace.

He wasted no words, but the passion between them ignited as it always had, giving her hope that he could see the real her, all of her. His hand slid under her skirt and up to her hip. He made sounds of pleasure and took his time. But Annie was ever so willing as he finally began to make love to her.

"I thought you hated me," she said on shallow breaths.

"I did," he murmured.

But he was still kissing her, one hand undoing the buttons of her bodice until the rise of flesh was visible above a lace camisole.

"Then why?" Her own breath was so ragged she thought she would not be able to stand.

"You tempt me, Annie Marsh," he finally paused long enough to say. "No matter who you are."

She gave up speaking then as they embraced and explored. He whisked a blanket out from his saddle roll and lowered her to the grassy slope. When he came to her again, her heart sang in disbelief that he still wanted her. They murmured each other's names over and over again as clothing became loosened and hands and lips sought the familiar intimacy of flesh.

His touch and glance made her skin burn and her blood throb with desire. Once embraced they were not satisfied until he could make love to her again completely. It was glorious and this time new ecstasy filled her as she lay beneath him, giving herself to him, clinging to him with all her heart. She loved him, but she was still afraid that he was only taking what he deemed was his by right. It wasn't until it was over that he cradled her in his arms and gazed down at her passion-filled face.

"Guess I'll never get over you, no matter how you claimed my heart."

She touched his face, too moved by passion and love to say anything. She dared to hope that she might have won at last. It had been the greatest struggle of her life. Finally she was able to croak out a few words.

"You don't hate me then?"

He kissed her temple and squeezed her tighter, "I was furious with you. And I hope you never pull another trick like that. But when you did all that about keeping the railroad out of here I guess you made me believe you did it for me."

"I did." Her heart melted.

"When I saw you today on that ridge, I knew then I wasn't going to let you go again."

She held him tighter. "I hope not. I don't ever want you to let me go. Never."

"I guess you'll have to marry me then."

He pulled her over on top of him and then onto the other side in a playful tussle.

"Get up, now. We'd better go tell your aunt and that father of yours."

"I love you, Grant," she said through tears of happiness.

"I love you, Annie Marsh."

Epilogue

They were married the following month on a fine October day when the aspen was golden. They joined hands and hearts under the whispering pines with the minister leading them through their vows and their friends and family standing among the trees.

There was a big bash at Letty's, of course, and railroad men and cowboys at least talked to each other, even if each group then clustered among themselves for the more casual visiting, and later, much inebriation. Campfires dotted the prairie as the fiddling and carousing went on all night.

But Annie slipped away after she'd seen all the well-wishers and entered the guest room that Letty had taken pains to decorate with very romantic touches. New lace curtains graced the windows, dried flowers were woven into lace stretched over embroidery hoops and hung everywhere. Handmade pillow shams graced the soft coverlet on the bed. Annie opened the trunk and began to change from her lacy wedding gown into something more appropriate for her wedding night.

By the time Grant came to join her, she was lounging on the daybed under the window. She wore a strapless scarlet costume with black ruffles. A crimson plume was in her flaming hair and a feather boa trailed across her bared shoulders and down to the floor.

Grant closed the door behind him and gave her a slow,

sensual smile. He took time to let his eyes travel from her drooping eyelids across her lovely shoulders, passed the revealed cleavage and down to the long, slender legs tucked up on the daybed. He tossed his hat onto the bed and strode across the room toward her.

"Madam," he said, taking her hand and lifting it slowly to his lips for a kiss.

His eyes blazed with desire as he went to his knees, and he lifted one foot in his hand and kissed her calf. His fingers slid along her calf and found their way under her petticoats to her thigh, and he grinned up at her.

She spoke to him with seductively lowered lids. "I didn't want you to forget 'Grace'."

He lifted one eyebrow in speculation. "I won't ever forget her," he said in a lazy drawl. "Guess I'm just lucky I got both women rolled into one. I fell in love with Grace before I came to know Annie's heart."

Then with words of love, he scooped her up and dropped tender kisses on her shoulders, the feather boa tickling his face. Soon clothing was cast aside and they tumbled between the sheets. They were oblivious to the revelry outside as the cozy little room became their heaven. Annie could take her time now, could take pleasure and fulfilling passion with the man beside her. His strength would never wane. His mind would never turn from her. They had gone through too much and had proved the mettle of their hearts. This love would last forever.